A VOICE FROM... THE ETHER

DOUGLAS DRAA, EDITOR

2022. It's strange to realize how far we've penetrated the 21st century. Even though it makes me feel old, I take some consolation in having lived long enough to catch up with at least some of science fiction's predictions for the future. I have a giant viewscreen hanging on my wall, and a communicator in my pocket. And access to all the knowledge in the world at my fingertips. (Thank you, Wikiipedia!) We really *are* living in science-fiction's vision of tomorrow in many ways.

Still, it hurts to see so many of our futures now lie behind us.

2001 and 2010 are more than a decade in the past.

Bladerunner was set two years ago, and Roy Batty was born back in 2016

Back to the Future's "future" was now seven years ago.

It's been 30 years since *Akira*'s Tokyo was destroyed.

Make Room, Make Room was set back before the turn of the century. As was *The Texas-Israeli War of 1999.*

Seeing these "old" futures now gone, clearly the time has come to create some new ones.

This is exactly where *Startling Stories* comes in. The talented folks within these pages are creating new futures to startle and entertain us. Even as we mourn futures past, we can celebrate the amazing futures that lie ahead of us all.

* * * *

As great as last year's issue was, I can honestly say that this year's issue is even better. The latest *Startling* will entertain you from start to finish. Monsters, space opera, music, humor—it has everything. Kudos to Cynthia Ward, John Shirley, Mike Chinn, Darrell Schweitzer, Frances Lu-Pai Ippolito, and Stephen Persing, all the rest of our wonderful authors for rising to the challenge. And this time, we also have an international team of artists on board, including such masters like Bob Eggleton, Vincent Di Fate, and Mark Wheatley.

I want to mention that this year's issue was made possible by a very successful Kickstarter campaign. It financed higher pay rates for the authors, and allowed the publisher to commission artwork from real artists. (John did a fantastic job with the art, considering he had no budget, but having an international team of experienced artists representing half a dozen countries—well, you can't get much better than that.

I wish that I could say something profound, witty, and moving, but I honestly can't come

cont'd on page 4.

STARTLING STORIES™

Volume 34, Number 2

2022 Issue

Contents

FEATURES

SHORT NOVEL

SHORT STORIES

up with anything. Situations like this make me realize I'll never be another John W. Campbell or Fred Pohl. That's okay, though. I still have the greatest job in the world—being able to select all these wonderful stories for you to enjoy.

Welcome to the *new* future.

—Doug Draa
June 11, 2022

PS—Special thanks to John W. Campbell's family for allowing us to run a story set in the universe of Campbell's classic "Who Goes There?" (famously filmed as *The Thing*).

STAFF

Publisher and Executive Editor
John Betancourt

Editor
Doug Draa

Contributing Editor
Darrell Schweitzer

Assistant Editors
Sam Hogan
Karl Wurf

Startling Stories™ is published annually
by Wildside Press LLC
7945 MacArthur Blvd., Suite 215
Cabin John, MD 20818 USA

ARTWORK

OUT ON THE EDGE
by Darrell Schweitzer

So three spacemen walk into a bar on Pluto, and it should be only two. One of them doesn't belong there, like the extra guy on the rope on the mountain-climbing expedition, when they count everybody in the dark and in the howling wind and it's freeze-your-nuts cold and the snow as coming at you sideways and it's sharp as knives on your face and you can hardly see a thing, only somehow you are certain that there is *one extra person* present.

Scary, huh? You were expecting a funny punchline perhaps?

Maybe that sort of a thing can be a joke on Earth, where most people, if they've ever poked their noses beyond the atmosphere for a minute turn tail and go scuttling for the safety of home. But out here, if you've lived all your life in the Asteroid Belt or maybe on the various moons of the big gas planets, you may fail to see the humor in such a situation. Such things happen, or are alleged to happen, or so the spacers will tell you.

They can even happen if you're just visiting, and not a native at all.

Me, I'm an Earther, and if I've traveled to the outer reaches of the System it is more as dead-weight cargo than as a member of the crew of anything. Perhaps it is the occasional sensitive streak I have to continually suppress while writing for what is informally known as the Booze and Snooze section of the *Solarcast Daily* that makes me want to discover what it's like for these people, out here, to stare 24/7 into the yawning gulfs of infinity. (I am sure the editor will take that out.) What do they feel? What are they afraid of? What are their jokes like? More to the point of my ostensible assignment, how does this affect the consumption of alcoholic beverages in cozy settings?

Why I am actually, physically *here* at fantastic expense, rather than just chatting over very attenuated lines of communications, is due to the the whim of the Big Boss, owner of *Solarcast Daily* and most of the Earth besides, the fourteenth generation clone of some narcissistic 21st-century gadzillionaire who managed to leave his steadily-accumulating fortune to himself over and over again. When he says to me, "Frank, old boy, you have been a loyal employee, and as a reward for such you are going on a cosmic pub-crawl the likes of which has never before been chronicled in the entire history of mankind, and you're going to chronicle it, for me," I just have to go. That is my assignment. Believe me, it is not a reward. It is my Herculean labor to visit every drinking establishment in the Solar System, drink there, experience the uniqueness of the place, and report back.

So, yes, there really is a bar on Pluto. It's called the Old Earth Pub, and the level of fakery there actually is impressive, with all the artificial, 3-D printed furnishings and the plastic plants in the corners, and the gigantic moose head mounted over the fireplace that wags its antlers and lights up its eyes every time somebody hits a bull's eye with darts. (Which is harder to do than you might think in microgravity, and dangerous too. I am surprised there haven't been more nasty accidents.) Now you can't for a minute believe that the moose head actually came from an extinct Earth animal, or otherwise was not replicated somewhere on-site. But what should impress you, as the bartender, Mr. X emphasized to me, is that the bar-top itself, the counter along which drinks could be slid (also dangerous in microgravity, but he was really good at it and I never saw him

spill a drop) is *genuine wood*, polished oak, brought all the way from London, England, on Earth, at no doubt a degree of expense even more fantastic than that which has propelled me on my travels and which is no doubt the only piece of actual organic wood many spacemen (such as walk in here, with their phantom companions) will ever see in their lives.

It does give the place a redeeming touch of authenticity.

So, picture if you will, yours truly, sidled up to that bar. You are expecting maybe a rumpled-looking man of fifty something, but still reasonably fit, but with an expression beneath his wrinkled brow that suggests he knows his career is not going where perhaps he once dreamed it would, in a rumpled suit with an antique camera around his neck and a tape recorder hanging on a strap over his shoulder – but my editor or the rewrite man will certainly delete that sort of cliché and of course I have the camera and recorder and everything else implanted in the back of my left hand. As for the suit, and my general appearance, none of your damn business.

So there I was, and the bartender asked the obvious, "Would you like a drink, sir?" and I ordered, and drank, which I did purely in the line of duty, because it is part of my assignment to sample the offerings of every such watering-hole from Mercury to the Oort Cloud – not that there could be, I sincerely hoped, any such places in the Oort Cloud, because by this point I was really looking forward to going home. This was the last stop on my itinerary, and I was determined to have some relief, if only the kind you get from ceasing to hit yourself on the head with a brick after you've been doing it for so long you can't remember when you started.

Besides which, I think I puked up my stomach and my intestines and left them on the floor of a sleazy dive on Ceres, sometime last year.

Maybe that was why the booze actually did settle well into me, with a warming, calming effect, because I didn't have any internal workings left to abuse. I sat there absorbing the atmosphere for a while, which was dark and swirly and a little stale.

The bartender did not seem particularly talkative. But I needed to get the story.

I asked him his name. He replied with something that sounded like *"Tade estin hos eston."* Being the trained professional I was, I got him to spell it.

"That's a very odd name. Is it a name?" I said.

"It's Greek."

(It might be a proverb, or a curse. I'd look it up later. It will be convenient hereafter to refer to the bartender as Mr. X.)

Now I was not drunk, nor was I stupid enough to say something like "It certainly seems Greek to me," which would insult my informant before any interview could get started, so I replied with a simple, "My name's Frank. Frank Weston. Which is not an odd name."

"No, it is not," he said.

I looked around, noting the emptiness of the place.

"Do you get much traffic in here?"

"Most people on the base are involved with the expedition – excuse me."

Just my luck. Three engineering types burst noisily in. I think they'd been celebrating somewhere else before they even got here, and between their drink orders and their ghastly and vulgar attempts at humor and equally ghastly laughter, they kept Mr. X busy for quite some time. So much for atmosphere. So much for anything and everything, so the best I could do was point to my glass for a refill, then sip that slowly. Things proceeded until one of them *did* have a nasty accident with the darts and the moose made a "Whoo-hoo!" sound which was either an alarm or just cheering them on. But the other two assured the third guy that they'd chip in and pay for his new eye, so when they finally left, they were still in a jolly mood, if a little the worse for wear.

But I had not wasted my time during that hour. I took my drink to the other end of the room and settled down by the other notable feature of the Old Earth Pub, which I should have mentioned earlier.

In addition to all the fake Ye Olde Earthe interiors and the moose head and the pink flamingos or whatever, there is also a very large, very good viewing window. We were at the brink of a plateau, and the view was breathtaking, even if you are not drunk: miles and miles of frozen nitrogen plains and gleaming ice mountains in the distance, with Charon hanging in the sky in its half phase, and a couple of the lesser moons (I wasn't sure which) also visible.

I turned a chair around, my back is to the bar, and I seemed to be no longer inside at all, but *out there.*

I continued to nurse my drink slowly, and when it finally ran out I placed the glass on an adjoining table. It was now very late, by whatever time-schedule they're using on Pluto Station – think of it as 4 AM – and the apparently tireless Mr. X came over, refilled my drink, and then joined me.

Now we were making progress.

For a while we both stared out at the ice mountains and the moons and infinity.

"You said there was an expedition," I began.

"Yes. To the Black Planet."

"Do you think they'll find it this time?"

"There's a good chance."

The Black Planet is a semi-myth in these parts. It is supposed to be utterly dark, and huge, big enough to account for all the perturbations in the orbits of the other planets which have been driving astronomers nuts for centuries. The latest theory is that it's made of Dark Matter, which is why we can't see it. I doubt there will ever be a bar there.

"Even if they do find it and land on it, it won't make much difference, will it?"

"How do you mean?" said Mr. X.

Now it felt like something odd was happening. My tongue was the one loosening up, as if he were interviewing me. This might have been unprofessional, but I didn't stop myself.

"Well, think about it," I said. "We might get to the Black Planet. We might even go out to the Oort Cloud and carve our initials on some of the ice and rock out there, but still we're like microbes crawling around on a single grain of sand when there's an infinite beach. This is as far as we will ever go. The stars are too far away. There are no handy wormholes. Yes, with infinite patience and a lot of engineering we don't presently have, we might undertake voyages of centuries, and we might just reach Proxima or a couple of the others if we were sufficiently motivated to do so, and I don't think we are, but that's just the adjoining grain of sand, and we can *see the whole beach,* or enough of it to know that there are billions of stars and billions of planets that we can never reach, ever."

At this point you may begin to suspect that maybe I am in the wrong line of work and should writing something other than the Snooze and Booze column.

I continued my little tirade: "I'd think most people wouldn't want to stare out into that. All it does is remind us how small we are. Why don't you just cover up this window with more fake wood and make the place enclosed and cozy?"

I was not really sure what was happening to me. Maybe so many bars and so many bangs on the head with bricks after so many billions of miles had left me a bit – a bit less than my usual sparkling self.

But Mr. X seemed interested, and strangely attentive, to me, and to the view. His eyes gleamed.

"Of course I could close the shutters if you'd like," he said, "But a lot of people enjoy sitting here and looking out."

"And what do they think while they're doing it? Can you tell me that? What are *you* thinking?"

"I am thinking that we are not alone in the universe."

"What?" That startled me to something close to clear-headedness. After a moment's reflection I said, "Oh it's statistically inevi-

table, I suppose, but you're not talking about flying saucers, are you? Nobody on Earth has believed in flying saucers for a long time."

"People always experience strangeness at the periphery of their world. When the edge of the dark forest was as far as anyone dared go, that is where the mystery and danger were. When the sky was the limit for most people, they saw things in the sky. Here, at the very edge, beyond which, as you rightly say, mankind shall never venture very far, apparitions might appear."

He refilled my glass again. I drank up. But I was not so zonked that I had forgotten to curl the third finger of my left hand *just so*, so that a light beneath my skin blinked to tell me that the recorder was turned on, and I was getting all this. It was not entirely clear who was interviewing whom, but this was good stuff. This weird guy who runs the Moose Ass Pub on Pluto believed in flying saucers. Wow.

Actually, he never said flying saucers. He said apparitions.

I placed my left hand carefully in the armrest between our two chairs, and say, "Do continue."

"Somewhere, out there, some other species may have reached their limit, and they too stared into the darkness at the unreachable stars, and thought the same things that humans have. Or at least the more sensitive humans, such as yourself, Mr. Weston."

He filled my glass again.

"My God, I'd really like to know. Even if we can never meet or talk to them. I'd really like to know."

Now you're probably beginning to suspect that my professional detachment in the sampling of the particular liquid offerings of the Moose Whatever Pub was starting to lose some of its detachment. But I also noted that Mr. X was not tapping my hand with his finger to charge me for these drinks. They were on the house. Generous of him. He must like my company, I had to conclude. I resolved to give him and his establishment a good review.

"Consider, too," he said, "that if you could communicate with these others, you would be talking across *time* as well as space. If you just radio Earth, how many hours does it take before the message gets there?"

At the moment, I didn't really know. I could look it up later. Certainly it would be a much interrupted conversation.

"Let's just suppose that some other species could project their message across space in some manner, and it comes from so very great distance, a hundred light-years."

"It would be like reading somebody else's mail," I said, drinking more.

"Or even further out, a thousand."

"Addressed to the Middle Ages. 'Dear King Arthur, watch out for the dragon –'"

"Or much, much farther."

"'Regards to T-Rex. How's evolution coming?'"

"Billions of galaxies. Billions of years."

"You'd never get an answer," I said. "Why bother? By the time anybody got your message, you'd be long gone, very likely extinct."

"Or else evolved unrecognizably into something else. But there is a reason, Mr. Weston. It is the same reason that kings back on your Earth built pyramids. It is to defy eternity. It is to say, to those who have the sensitivity to understand, *this is who we were*. There is a certain satisfaction in the knowledge or at least the hope that someone will know who you were."

Somehow my tongue had become too large or didn't do what I wanted it to do. I could only think, he's put something in the booze. Or else he's given me the whammy. Hypnosis, telepathy. Like that.

But it was still good stuff. I mean the journalism. I was getting all this, even if I might have been, let us say, not entirely in command of my senses.

I could hear him clearly as he said, "The message doesn't have to be a series of beeps and dashes. It could be a full projection of sounds and images. It might account for apparitions, even materializations. Mr. Weston, let me show you."

He took my left hand, the one with the instruments in it. I felt a vibration and was afraid he'd just erased everything; but I could not resist as we leaned forward and he pressed my hand against the window pane.

I shook my head and blinked. I couldn't be seeing what I was seeing. It wasn't Pluto out there anymore. At first there was only scarlet mist, but then it broke and two suns shone in the sky, a larger red one, and a smaller, more distant white one that glared too brightly to look at. Mountains lined the horizon, but like none I'd ever seen before, formed under I don't know what kind of conditions or out of what materials, brown and green with occasional flashes of blue, very sharp, taller than they were wide, like knives against the pale pink sky. In among the mountain peaks were crystalline structures that might have been natural, or maybe not. As I watched, some of these broke loose and began to fly, like great, gleaming airships. In the foreground, a rolling prairie of what might be plant life of some kind, most of it dark purple or red and gently undulating. Wading through this were various fantastic beasts, but one creature turned and approached, as if it could see me. It was not a human being or even close to a human being, but it did walk on two legs. It had two arms. Its face was blue and spiked, like some kind of lizard. It had a single, dark, wide, oblong eye.

It placed a three-clawed hand against the glass right where I was touching, and I felt a further vibration, and then the words form inside my head, in English, *This is who we were.*

This is who we were.

This is who we were.

I was in an indescribable ecstasy. It was so intensely beautiful. I was sharing that other mind. To know what the other knows, to feel what the other feels, cannot be put into words in any human language, because we lack so many concepts.

Only once did I turn my head and look at

Mr. X beside me, and I noticed that his face was blue and covered with spikes and he had only one, very large dark eye.

"This is who we were. *Tade estin hos eston*," he said.

* * * *

And that was when the lights started flashing and the alarms and sirens went off and two guys burst into the bar, dragged me out, and stuffed me into an ill-fitting, very smelly spacesuit. Emergency! Emergency! It seems an incoming supply shuttle had crashed into one of the domes and depressurized part of the station. I tried to protest that I was a reporter, and needed to cover the story. I raised my left hand to take pictures, but I couldn't because it was inside the spacesuit's glove. Like every other civilian with nothing immediate to offer for the remediation of the catastrophe, I was hustled into a central Safe Area and sealed in. It turned out that our part of the station was never any danger, but it was hours before anybody acknowledged that and let us out.

You don't need to hear about the accident anyway. That sort of thing happens. It is routine.

* * * *

You are probably expecting me to conclude this with an eerie, brain-twisting ending. No, Mr. Editor. That is not what happened.

I don't know what became of Mr. X. He was not with us in the Safe Area.

I've still got the recording of our conversation, all the way to the final, strange phrase, but that is all. It wasn't a name after all. I looked it up. Greek. Ancient Greek. It means what he said it did. He was translating for me, perhaps when he realized that his probing into the collective memory of the human race had gone too deep and he was off by a couple millennia. It means: *This is who we were.*

You are also expecting that I would go back to the bar and find a puddle of strange, foul-smelling goo on the floor and Mr. X's apron floating in it. But that's not what happened.

I didn't I find a spiky-faced skeleton either.

Nor did I go back and be told, to my astonishment, that the place blew up/burned down/depressurized years ago and I couldn't possibly have been there.

Nope. The Old Earth Pub is still there, exactly as I described it. It is operated by an Earther named Chang. He had no idea what I was talking about when I asked about Mr. X. He said he'd been running the place for five years. I interviewed him, just to complete the assignment. See attached.

And this is my report. Use what parts of it you can. I suspect not very much, unless you want to transfer me to the Woo Woo Desk.

* * * *

So, three spacemen walk into a bar on Pluto. Nothing in particular happens. Such folk come and go all the time.

Later, there are two people left in the bar, one of them an Earther reporter, and the other someone who doesn't belong, but took a very, very long time getting there.

ABOUT THE AUTHOR

Darrell Schweitzer is primarily known as a fantasy and horror author, but he has written a small but significant body of science fiction over the years. Recently, PS Publishing issued a two-volume retrospective of his career, *The Mysteries of the Faceless King* and *The Last Heretic*, which reprint his best short fiction.

His novels include *The White Isle*, *The Shattered Goddess*, *The Mask of the Sorcerer*, and *The Dragon House*. His nonfiction and interviews have been coolected in numerous volumes as well. Currently, he lives in Philadelphia, Pennsylvania with his wife, Marilyn "Mattie" Brahen, and their cat, H.P. Lovecraft.

ABOUT THE ARTIST

Allen Koszowski has long been a fixture in the science fiction, fantasy, and horror art fields. He has contributed literally thousands of illustrations to 'zines over his long career. He recently relocated from Philadelphia to the warmer climate of Florida.

A QUICKENING TIDE
by A. J. McIntosh & Andrew J. Wilson

Durante was at peace. He'd drawn his last breath, and his heart had stopped. He was as dead as a proverbial doornail. All that was left was a desire that this dark, silent and timeless non-existence would continue forever.

Then the pain began. At first, it was just pins and needles all over his body, but violent shocks to his chest came next. Then Durante was transfixed by agonizing waves as his lungs and limbs started working again. When the torture was over, he flinched as dull thuds sounded from somewhere outside his aching head. He opened his eyes reluctantly.

Beyond an inspection hatch, a blurry figure was signaling to him with a monkey wrench. He shook his head to clear it and then show he wasn't ready. Maybe whoever was disturbing him would go away. With luck, they'd let him return to rest, to the effortless accumulation of riches.

A viscous eddy swirled around him as sluices opened. The contents of the suspension tank poured away, exposing his naked skin to cool air. Then even colder water flushed the last of the antifreeze out of the tube, and things came painfully into focus. For better or worse, he was back in the land of the living.

Durante scrabbled at the side of the tank as the hazmat-suited figure outside opened the hatch. He focused on his finances, and the possibility that these might have significantly improved during his tax-free period of cryogenic suspension. If nothing bad had happened over the intervening decades or centuries, perhaps he was already loaded at the ripe old physical age of 23.

He shivered as the faceless technician leaned towards him. A gloved hand released the straps that bound him, and then pulled the respirator off his head. A voice crackled out of the speaker on the suit's mask.

"Are you OK?"

Durante nodded.

"Can you feel your toes and fingers? Can you move them?"

Durante wriggled his digits in a half-hearted wave, then nodded again.

"Can you talk?"

"Yes, sir."

"Who are you?"

"Fleet Midshipman Peter Durante, sir, provost's officer in Cryogenics. Frozen aboard the *Spirit of Scutari* on day of departure—September 31, 2315."

"Good."

He staggered out of the suspension tank and into the cryovault itself. The technician circled him, appraising his condition, prodding him here and there with a probe.

"Any questions?"

"I was wondering, sir, how long…"

"Don't worry—often happens—you'll unshrivel in a couple of hours."

"No, I mean, how long have I been out of it, sir?"

"Six seconds," his tormentor said, "17 minutes, 6 hours, 8 days, 2 months and 5 years. Thought you were going to wake up rich? Trust me, you're not."

Durante shook his head, too disappointed to speak. The technician loosened a seal on the neck of the hazmat suit and pulled off the visored helmet. A woman's face emerged from underneath it: older than him, but still young. She was sloe-eyed, expressionless, Mongolian.

"You're on duty, Midshipman," she said. "Report updecks."

Durante staggered forwards, readying

himself for action.

"Wait!" she said.

Confused, he turned, only to find her gauntleted hand gesturing at his crotch.

"Get dressed first, for goodness sake…"

* * * *

"There's nothing to worry about, you see," Serendipidam said. "Officers will read from their mission statement. You'll compare what's said with the neurobrand issued to you, report any disparities, sign the relevant forms afterwards and return everything to the attending provost's officer. Got it?"

Not getting it didn't appear to be an option. That was the Fleet for you, of course. Its unbreakable sinews might hold humanity together across the interstellar diaspora, but bureaucracy clogged its arteries like the worst kind of administrative cholesterol. Heaven help you if you forgot to do the paperwork: they'd string you up with a noose of red tape.

Provost Marshal Mackenzie Serendipidam's eyebrows ruffled, white as snowy owls against the blue-black skin of his face. He peered over his half-moon spectacles and read from a volume of the Fleet's *Manual*:

> In this manner, you will attend five, 3-hour reviews per day for the next month, conducting your private life outwith these hours at all times in solitary with a guard outside your hatch.

"Well, it goes on in that vein for a while—let's see, blah-blah-blah, so on and so forth *ad nauseam…sine ira et studio… eductio ad absurdum*. Ah, yes:

> Upon satisfactory completion of your duty, you will be returned to Cryogenics for refreeze as soon as practicable, with the addition to your cuff of four chevrons and a guarantee of no further interruptions for at least 50 years.

"Does the Reader understand?"

"Sir, yes sir!" Durante snapped.

"Very good. I, of course, shall be dead by then. I'm not one of those with an inexhaustible appetite for postponing the inevitable." Serendipidam smiled at Durante, unnerving the junior officer. "I'll bid you goodbye now. I wish you much pleasure in your future fortune and a splendid career with the Fleet. Be on your guard and try to be decent. For as long as possible, that is. Dismissed!"

* * * *

Durante had warmed to the gruff but affable Serendipidam, and scolded himself for it. Provost marshals were appointed for their cunning not their kindness. This particular example of the species—the most senior political policeman aboard the *Scutari*, his own line commander—should not be trusted by Durante in his current role.

As Reader, it was his duty to check for "the creeps": those gradual, cumulative misunderstandings or collective amnesias that can beset crews on long adventures. He must compare the mission statements in use with those that had been issued and branded in his memory at the voyage's outset. If there were disparities, errors, or indeed, potential frauds or conspiracies, he should flag these up to his superiors.

The knowledge that allowed Fleet vessels to travel faster than light was strictly classified. However, the effects of this apparent violation of causality were well known. The paradoxes involved could corrupt computer systems and drive crewmembers mad. In contrast, the neurobrand stamped in the mind of a freshly revived Reader had been perfectly frozen in time. It represented an incontrovertible record of all the orders that had been assigned.

Of course, the chances of anything significant arising after so soon aspace were vanishingly slim. It ought to be straightforward, and yet he felt as if his premature thawing-out, the sudden jolt from Cryogenics, had left him dazed and disoriented.

Doubt gnawed at Durante all the way down to C Deck, where a hulking marine was already waiting for him at the hatch to his quarters. Durante stepped through, hoping to find a meal prepared, but instead there were four officers seated at the table, studying their files.

"Reader," said the most senior of them, pointing to the braid emblem on a cuff, "we three are *Scutari* Informatics, and over there is the provost's officer supervising. Sit, retrieve, compare."

Durante's brain curdled at the command, and his thoughts were no longer his own. The speaker began reading from a stack of mission folders. Simultaneously, those same words emerged in parallel from a separate, pre-existing text inside Durante's head. For the most part, the sentences unrolled in synch, but when the reader stumbled or mistook, Durante knew at once where the error lay. He would then raise a finger and wait for the necessary correction to come.

The 3 hours passed quickly. Durante came to his senses with the scraping of chairs, and the clipped questions and instructions of the provost's officer. He ticked a box, put his name and retinal stamp to the form presented, and the visiting party trooped out. No one met his eyes or said farewell. He drank a glass of water alone in his galley, then heard the swish of the hatch opening and closing, the raking of chairs, the sound of a new delegation settling itself at the table.

"Reader, we three are *Scutari* Engineering, and this is the provost's officer supervising. Sit, retrieve, compare."

And so it went on—interminable seas of words for 15 hours a day for days on end.

When he was not on duty, Durante slept, waking only to eat, defecate and wash. Devoid of thought and empty of care, he soon lost track of the date. His diet didn't vary and tasted of nothing. He was witless, idle and content to serve, to conform to whatever was demanded of him. This was almost as easy as Cryogenics.

"Reader," said the last of them one evening, "we three are *Scutari* Trade, and after this you'll be free to go. Be seated, retrieve, reconcile…"

* * * *

The final read-through had taken place 4 days previously, time Durante had spent despairing of meeting company or finding anything worth his time on the entertainment feeds. Now he was bored and irritable. His furniture didn't fit, some of it was already broken, and he suspected an Informatics delegate of sticking wads of chewing gum under the dining table.

He drafted a message to the one person aboard he knew—the laconic enigma who'd thawed him out. He worded a brief invitation to chat or eat or exercise together, but realized he had no name or rank or department to which he could address it. Instead, he went for yet another walk alone, watched decorations going up for some forthcoming Captain's Reception and winced over weak coffee at a concourse stall. He reflected that all these strangers who passed him now without a second glance would certainly be older, quite likely dead by the time he next emerged from Cryogenics.

A giant billboard refreshed its screen across the piazza from him. A blonde woman with luxuriant hair beamed down and winked. "So what if I'm 99?"' she flirted. "Inside I'm still 19. I wanna look the way I feel—that's why I choose RECON-STYLE clinics."

RECON-STYLE! What sort of stupid name was that? Durante wondered irritably. What was it getting at? To con people about one's age? Reconnaitre—know again one's former style? Reconcile one's looks with one's perceptions?

Suddenly, he felt his brain lurch the way it had before during read-throughs, and he knew why. *Reconcile*. That word had touched him. It was a trigger that he'd almost forgotten. That word the last of the presenting officers had used to start the last of the dictations. He remembered the figure:

a woman in late middle age, her head large and gaunt, thinning gray hair dragged back from the temples. She must have been lanced once. Her features were rigid down the right-hand side, dimpled like orange peel, the eye pearly and blind.

"Reader," she had growled, saliva foaming in the little recess of her mouth through which she spoke, breathed and smoked, "we three are *Scutari* Trade, and after this you'll be free to go. Be seated, retrieve, reconcile…"

Despite all the distractions, there it was: not *compare* but *reconcile*—to harmonize, make friendly or consistent—the very opposite of *compare*. Surely that was significant, but was it important enough to make a difference? Had someone tampered with his neurobrand or the instruction protocols that accessed it? Or had it been just some knuckleheaded mistake? What should he do with this realization? Report it and come across as petty, or ignore it, not cause problems and take the primrose path to profitable suspension?

* * * *

"I did not expect to see you again," said Serendipidam, "and now that I have, I must say you've got a damn nerve coming here with this drivel… Accusing *Scutari*'s chief trading negotiator of fraud! You, a snotty-nosed midshipman just out of training pants, fast asleep for the past 5 years, strutting into this office and making allegations…"

The Provost Marshal had not raised his voice above a growl, but his face resembled rehydrated plums coming to the boil.

"With respect, sir, I have alleged nothing," Durante replied, choosing his words. "I just thought it was my duty as Reader to raise what could, possibly, be an important difference—"

"Duty be damned! A quite unproven difference. Only you recall any use of the word 'reconcile'."

"What about the provost's officer present?"

"How dare you!" Serendipidam snapped. "Lieutenant Campbell is adamant—the retrieve commands were valid."

"Well, I was the Reader and I'm sure—"

"Stow it, you bilge rat! Any infallibility of recall you may have possessed applied to the mission statements—nothing else! Now, may I remind you that before you were Reader, you were a provost's officer—sworn to uphold the *status quo*, not to run around causing chaos on your first outing. I ask you, does Commander Knott look the kind of person who would for one moment indulge in fraud?"

Durante bit his tongue. With her ravaged, half-immobile face and rigid bearing, Commander Knott looked capable of fraud and plenty else besides.

Throughout this entire interview, she had not seen fit to meet his eye. She had examined the long, curved nail of a little finger instead, as if wondering where best to insert it.

"Of course she doesn't!" Serendipidam growled. "Persons of her rank and experience in Trading appointments are in such positions because they—of all bloody people—are the type whom the Fleet can best trust! Exhaustively vetted, selected only after months and years of training, monitored constantly, beyond reproach in every way and respected accordingly. Except, that is, by one very green officer who has let the entirely temporary office of Reader go to his head, and now stands here demanding an official review."

"Sir, I have insisted on nothing of the sort."

"Enough! I ask you, Midshipman, are you prepared to withdraw these pettifogging objections?"

Despite the disturbing complexion of the Provost Marshal, despite how his eyebrows seemed to be mating, despite the fact that this could deep-six his fledgling career, Durante decided that he couldn't back down.

"I thought not," Serendipidam said before Durante could reply.

The Provost Marshal snorted through the

bristling hairs in his nostrils.

"Felicity," he said, addressing the joyless Knott beside him, "you see, I have tried my best with this…this upstart tadpole, but my hands are tied. I'm afraid we must review the entire mission statement—and on the record. I can do nothing else. The *Manual* is quite clear."

She nodded and regarded her nail from a new angle with her one good eye. As the Provost Marshal spoke into an intercom, issuing orders and summonses, she glanced up and surveyed Durante from top to tail. Durante stared straight ahead, pretending not to notice her basilisk gaze.

* * * *

An hour later, Durante sat listening as Commander Knott read again from the documents that defined her own and her department's role for the duration of the voyage.

This time, there were more witnesses— the Provost Marshal, two top-brass officers from Psychiatry and Speculation, a secretary—and this time, Knott quite definitely, with exaggerated clarity, said "compare". As before, she read slowly, her voice rasping, and as before, she sometimes sped up without warning, as if impatient or annoyed by the sense of the words. From time to time, she would snap down a sheet with unexpected force, ripping the corner, regarding the tattered flag with distaste. Durante couldn't tell whether this was true emotion, an act or some strange effect of her injuries, and he wasn't the only one transfixed by her performance.

At one stage, Speculation jumped so hard that a shirt-button sprang from her belly onto the table. Nobody mentioned it. The long, bulb-ended nose of Psychiatry twitched and flared as he rattled a stylus between his teeth. Serendipidam rested his head in his hands and grumbled to himself from behind a nest of fingers.

Knott read for hours in the Provost Marshal's stuffy office, her monotonous voice growing quieter and slurring with fatigue:

"…and said cargo-compact to be vended either by e-contract or open outcry on Planet Nimbus at the market in Nephelococygia on July 18, the asking price to be paid either by transfer or exchange or…"

For the first time that day, Durante raised a finger and looked up. She seemed not to have noticed and continued without pause. Durante coughed, but there was still no response. He had to rap the tabletop with his knuckles before Serendipidam took notice.

"What is it, Reader? Frog in your throat?"

"Sir, there's an anomaly."

"A what?"

"Between Commander Knott's words and the neurobrand up here." Durante tapped at his forehead, all too aware too late that the superfluous gesture, the little vanity of it, had been noted.

"How so?" asked Speculation.

"Ma'am, Commander Knott has just read 'July 18' as the designated date-to-market. The neurobrand states 'July 15'."

"Do you acknowledge an error, Commander?" asked Psychiatry.

Knott retraced the passage, taking her time. "There is no mistake: July 18 it is— look." The mission statement was passed around. She was right. "Couldn't this be a simple printing error?" she asked no one in particular, dabbing bubbles from the corner of her stricken mouth. "A 5 for an 8—easy enough to do."

"Impossible and insufficient," said the Provost Marshal, crushing that bug before it could crawl any further.

"Well, does it make any difference?" she tried again, this time a hint of impatience creeping through.

Speculation consulted a trade almanac. "As I'm sure you know, Commander, there are indeed markets on both dates. Do we have any reason to believe that one would be more auspicious than the other?"

Knott paused to consider then shook her head.

"I think not," she said. "Each is much like the other, and the price for IVIs is pretty constant throughout the quadrant."

"Ivy eyes?" inquired Speculation.

Psychiatry broke in: "Igneovitreous items, isn't it?"

There followed a pause, an awkward gap in which no words were spoken. Durante watched with satisfaction as a silent imperative to elaborate pressed down upon Knott from around the table, a force she resisted for a good 20 seconds before she broke.

"You know...luxury goods, love-stones, stones of desire...erotic so they say. Just 7 tonnes."

"Fleet is trading in erotic IVIs?" spluttered Serendipidam. "So-called *cocos de mer*? I had no idea. Extraordinary!"

"Yes, Provost Marshal, indeed... That is to say, they are part of my private venture in this voyage, from which, rest assured, Fleet will be pleased to take a substantial cut of the profits. It's all above board, all on the manifest if you wish to check."

The silence fell again. *Was this embarrassment now?* wondered Durante. If so, for what? At the invasion of Knott's business privacy? At the notion of so ugly a creature dealing in love-stones? If so, they were missing the point.

"There is at least one significant difference between the markets," Durante offered. "On July 18, the Captain's Reception will take place here aboard the *Scutari*. I suppose such an important occasion could affect who is and who isn't trading that day on the planet surface, how the market is regulated and how responsive the bidding gradient is. I'm not making accusations of any kind, just suggesting a potential for..."

Now it was Durante's turn to find himself alone in silence. For all his faith in the Fleet, there was not one person here he had good reason to trust. He suspected the Provost Marshal of orchestrating matters, but there was no proof to confirm this intuition. The atmosphere was pregnant, the weight of unsaid things uncomfortable.

Psychiatry put down his pen and smiled. "I believe it falls to me," he said, "to suggest a way forward. I propose we examine Mr. Durante's cryogenic log in detail. It's just possible there may be something in it that might explain the anomaly. Are we agreed?"

From that moment, Durante knew what the result would be. Sure enough, within another hour a temperature flux had been identified in the record, and its source traced to a faulty synapse loop within Durante's suspension tank. A nobody from that department was dragged in to confirm that this could indeed explain whatever the grand panjandrums sitting here might want it to explain.

It wasn't a statement of fact, but of possibility. And yet it was enough to cast doubt on Durante's testimony. His neurobrand was no longer dependable. He could see where this meeting was heading, where his career was bound unless he dug in his heels.

"I must demand that the *existence* of the anomaly be logged," he blurted. "*And* the fact that the Captain's Reception was posited as a relevant market-factor."

"Good grief, Durante, have you been swallowing textbooks?" the Provost Marshal asked. "I've never heard so much Academy gobbledygook in all my life! Still, you're quite within your rights, I suppose. Very well, let it be logged. I don't think we need trouble you any longer, Reader. Dismissed!"

"Fuck you very much, sir," Durante said. As usual, no one seemed to hear a word he said.

Serendipidam levelled a long, even stare at him. And then, without warning, a private wink.

* * * *

Durante returned to his quarters, his mind simmering with suspicions. He could prove nothing. He felt sure he'd been manipulated. He smelled a fix: the familiar scent of his stepmother collapsing under piles of paperwork, the sense of life savings trickling away through the cracks. It smelled like a terminal condition, solicitors' letters and cheap flowers outside a crematorium.

Somebody somewhere wanted an abnormal market for the IVIs, and was angling for it to be on July 18. On that day, every commercial bigwig on the planet would be scraping and bowing at the reception aboard the *Scutari*, fawning for a future audience with the senior trade negotiator or—wonder of wonders—Captain Florian Anderson himself. Somebody somewhere stood to make a nice profit, and Knott's odd date in the mission statement had something to do with it.

Durante turned and stared into his cabin console, hoping for inspiration or at least distraction. There were two messages. The first informed him that the date of his refreeze had been set back 2 weeks while potentially defective parts of his suspension tube were replaced. The second came from the Provost's Office, and concluded with Serendipidam's initials. It was an extract from the ship's public business schedule, a list of corrections and updates and contingent revisions authorized by the Captain. Halfway down the page, an entry caught his eye:

Vending change [Nimbus: Nephelococygia]. Scutari cargo consignment DB5:100101\a to market 7/15 [supersedes 7/18]. Reason given: market distortion by Captain's Reception. Status: official/immediate. MS,PM.

Durante stared and stared, interpreting the message and the Provost Marshal's terse initials, his implicit agreement, the wordless pat on the back, the meaning of that wink. Durante had been listened to: his argument had won. Of course, there was no mention of his neurobrand, but that didn't matter. It was enough for Durante that here, far from home on a huge ship, a young officer could prevail.

He showered, changed and scented himself like an admiral. He settled before the console to reread the evidence of his victory. It was still there, and it still brought a smile

to his lips. He sat daydreaming of a career made up of many more such triumphs, and with quick fingers entered his security clearance and consulted the *Scutari*'s manifest.

"Cascade, take me into the Cargo Atlas. Show me where to find consignment DB5:100101\a."

The datacore displayed a deck plan and outlined one department. Within that, it pinpointed a rectangular space smaller than the cabin Durante was sitting in now.

"Cascade, where is this?"

B Deck: Cryogenics.

Durante was taken aback. "What is the segment indicated?"

Long-stay compartment.

"Is it operational?"

Yes.

"How long has DB5:100101\a been there?"

One month, 6 days, 5 hours, 6 minutes, 75 seconds.

"Where was DB5:100101\a before stowage in its present location, and who authorized the latest transfer?"

High-security cargo hold, highlighted now in red. Transfer authorized by Commander Knott and Zoology.

"Before the transfer to Cryogenics of DB5:100101\a, what occupied the compartment?"

Fleet Provost's officer: Durante, Peter, Midshipman [2315—2320], revived early.

* * * *

Durante left his quarters through a service chute, crawled the 20 meters to a ceiling access point and hauled himself through it. He then followed the route map on his wrist tracker until he reached the for'ard elevator columns. Then he borrowed a luminous jacket from a locker, helped himself to a hard hat and began whistling so as not to attract attention. Boarding an empty elevator, he rose towards B Deck.

Once there, he traced the cables below the floor all the way to the main Cryogenics entrance, shorted the corridor lighting,

eased himself up and through, closed the panel behind him, and ran an anonymized provost's office key through the security swipe. It was 03:00 shipboard time, and nobody was about.

"Right," Durante whispered to himself, "who's been sleeping in *my* bed?"

He located his suspension tube without difficulty, and found no evidence of an upgrade in progress. He peered through the semicircular inspection hatch, switched on the internal lights and peered again. There wasn't much to see: just a stack of love-stones, Knott's hidden stash. Damn it, this was why Durante was being kept from his rightful refreeze and the chance of making money. These were the unsuspected cuckoos in *Scutari*'s nest.

Well, Commander Knott, he thought to himself, *you're not as clever as you think you are.*

From a hook suspended in mid-air, Durante lifted one of the heavy-duty hazmat suits and pulled it on. You couldn't be too careful around extraterrestrial cargo. He flushed the suspension tank and opened the hatch.

Durante took one of the love-stones from the top, and then reached further down for a second from the back of the pile. He replaced the first in its original setting and admired his handiwork. The absence wouldn't be noticed in a cursory inspection, and wouldn't be discovered until the day of the market.

He set the stone down in the middle of the gangway and stood well back. It rocked back and forth like an egg about to hatch. As he turned to close the suspension tube hatch, his boot slid on a streak of clear slime that had somehow dripped out onto the deck. After he closed the hatch, he took off the hazmat suit and used the helmet to scoop up the stone without touching it. A tug on the seal at the neck closed his improvised containment device.

This isn't dishonest, he assured himself as he made his way out of Cryogenics. *This is more like getting even.*

After all, he might be disrupting criminal activity. At the very least, he was stirring the pot in hope that something would bubble to the top, some clue to the identities of those who were behind all this. He allowed himself a smirk: when the love-stones were counted, someone in Zoology would find themselves in a whole heap of trouble.

Durante was attempting to make a graceful exit when something tugged his foot. He looked down at his boot, but there was nothing there. Could he have imagined it? He tried to step forward again, and this time there was no mistaking the yank that pulled him back.

He felt his ankles being clamped together, his whole body dragged backwards. He dropped the helmet and grabbed a handhold on the bulkhead beside him. He looked down again, but there was still nothing to see.

Durante lost his grip and slammed into a pool of slime on the deck. He struggled into a crouch, breaths coming quick and shallow, his head switching from side to side looking for whatever was attacking him. Now his knees and his thighs were being constricted, and he felt something begin to crush him around the stomach. Then, as his head was forced backwards and around, he saw for a moment something only slightly less translucent than the slime pool. Three ink-black eyes stared back at him as a vaguer blob heaved itself onto his back with near-invisible tentacles.

"Get off, you bastard!" Durante yelled, trying to tear the suckers away with his bare hands. A tentacle wrapped around his throat and began to strangle him.

Just as he was about to black out, there was a flash like lightning and his throat was released. Durante sat up, pulling what was left of a slimy tentacle from around his neck, and groggily tried to examine it as the form of the thing dribbled away between his fingers.

"You are a very stupid man, and also very lucky," said a voice he remembered from the first time he'd emerged here.

"What's your name? What are you doing here?" Durante asked the taser-toting figure.

"Later. Now go."

His savior turned without replying and disappeared.

* * * *

When Durante got back to his cabin, he turned his attention to the cause of all this trouble. He'd heard about "stones of desire" before, seen them on screen, but this was the first he'd ever held, the only one he'd examined at close quarters.

Durante propped it on a shelf opposite his bed and was surprised to see how unlike rock its surface was in the angled light of a cabin lamp—more like oiled skin. The shape of it was unmistakable: a curvaceous human female's torso from the navel to the knee. Its incompleteness and the subtlety of its imperfections were fascinating: the way it couldn't be the thing it most resembled, could never redeem the erotic promises it seemed to offer. The love-stone was mineral pure and simple, some odd igneous phenomenon; there was no intent behind it to suggest or comment or provoke. In his mind, Durante knew it had no capacity to satisfy, knew that what looked so inviting, warm and supple was cold, hard and insentient, but it still evoked a response. That, of course, was part of these objects' mystique and value. He grew tired of himself for lusting after it, threw a T-shirt over the stone and forced himself to sleep.

When Durante awoke, sore and stiff, he found a young woman sitting at the end of his bed. She regarded his face without expression, her eyes never leaving his as he belatedly drew a sheet across to cover himself.

"Who are you?" he asked. "What are you doing here? How'd you get in?"

"You feel OK? You can feel your toes and fingers? Move them? What about…other parts? Everything working OK?"

"You!"

"Evidently."

"You were in Cryogenics, the first time, and then…"

"Then I saved you from the squid."

"What were you doing there?"

"My job."

"*Your job?* You keep very odd hours for a Cryogen officer."

"What were *you* doing there?"

"Checking my berth. Why are you here?"

"After I'd cleaned up your mess in Cryogen, I came here to give you a warning. Don't interfere in this business. It's too big for a midshipman to handle alone."

"Too big for Provost's Office as well perhaps? I don't think so."

"Provost's Office already knows."

"So, if Provost's Office knows, who is this warning from?"

"From the good guys."

"Provost's Office good guys?"

"The Provost Marshal is a good guy."

"Why can't Serendipidam give me this warning himself—officially, out in the open?"

"Sometimes, some things are best kept hidden." Her eyes flickered between Durante's face and crotch. Whether in deadpan humor or contempt he couldn't tell.

"Listen—I will not be fobbed off with hints and winks, and I won't be threatened, if that's what you're planning to do next." He reached down beside the bed and brought up the small but vicious-looking pistol he kept hidden there for just such an occasion. "I think you should go now."

His sloe-eyed visitor was unmoved. She uncrossed her legs, crossed them the other way, and seemed on the brink of saying something. But before she could speak, there was a noise like toenails snagging through nylon. She froze, her eyes still boring into Durante's, then followed his gaze towards the love-stone on the shelf behind her. With two, arched fingers she removed the T-shirt and dropped it on the floor.

"Ah," she said, "I see. You stole it. You idiot."

"It's split," said Durante, jumping out of bed to take a closer look. There came another ear-rending rip, a kind of groan or ex-halation, and the black stone shuddered, the tear in its flank widening. Something as pale as lychee flesh was flexing on the inside and then, too fast for Durante to follow, it slithered through the gap and was free, moist and wobbling beside the original.

"Damn it, that's not supposed to happen is it? Has it given birth?"

"It's not alive."

"But Zoology was involved in sending it. I checked the manifest."

"Zoology was involved in sending the squid. Commander Knott has friends and influence in many unexpected places. How many of these love-stones did you steal?"

"I didn't steal anything. I—"

"How many?"

"Just one—that one."

"Wait here. I'll come back. Understand?"

"Yes, but what's your name? What's your authority?"

She looked at him very hard. "Yerzuk. Lieutenant. Provost Marshal's special agent. No more questions."

Durante felt especially naked before the love-stones. He turned for his clothes and heard the horrible splitting sound once again. Now the "baby" had turned black and hard like its "mother", and both had produced more "offspring". Even as he watched, one of the "grandchildren" wobbled from the shelf, fell, bounced across the cabin carpet before coming to rest against his foot. By the time it was still, it had hardened into yet another female torso, and another pallid, pulsating form was pushing from its belly.

Ten minutes later, the floor of Durante's cabin was almost covered. He began scooping stones into a duvet cover, enveloped them all and zipped it shut. It seemed about to burst just as Yerzuk reappeared.

"Good," she said. "Outside."

Together they heaved the load out into the corridor and tipped the groaning mass into a wheelie bin Yerzuk had commandeered from somewhere in the service lockers. They set their shoulders in position and pushed.

"Where are we going?" asked Durante.

"There's an empty chamber dead ahead. Keep pushing."

Over the next 40 meters they picked up speed and momentum. Then they reached the doors of a deserted canteen and rammed the wheelie bin through painters' pots scattered in the dark.

"There's an exit hatch in the galley," yelled Yerzuk. "Run!"

They cannoned on, the stones of desire rattling and rending before them. Yerzuk swung open an old hatch by mainforce and Durante shoved the wheelie bin inside. Then the pair of them swung the hatch back shut and screwed it down. Durante slammed the EJECT button, and as the love-stones floated off into the void outside the *Scutari*, a welcome hush descended.

Sweating side by side, their backs pressed against the cold metal of the bulkhead, they caught their breath for a moment in silence.

"Listen, Lieutenant… I'm sorry about all this, well some of it, maybe. I don't know how much. Look, will you please just tell me what the hell's going on?"

* * * *

Early afternoon on July 15, Durante spending the last day of his shore leave on Nimbus the way he'd spent the previous seven: irritating Yerzuk with questions and never getting a straight answer. He found it hard to understand why he'd followed her here, insisted that she should take him along on whatever mission or madcap heist she was set on. He told himself it was a sense of duty. In his heart, he suspected it was simpler than that. She'd made him squirm, and he wanted to repay the compliment.

The monorail on which they were traveling carried them through miles of boring scenery: a landscape of rounded hillocks—all identical, covered in the same even grass—all squatting dully beneath the gray sky. It was always like this on the northern continent of Nimbus. No grand vistas, no dramatic plunges, no excitement.

"But they were alive," Durante said. "You saw them. They were having babies in front of our eyes."

"No. Not alive. Not intelligent. Not sentient. Not artifacts. Nothing complex—just rocks. Imagine a huge volcano somewhere, very powerful, generating local gravitational forces. What you get is stones of desire."

"Oh, come off it. They're not just rocks. They look like…"

"It's just coincidence. To millions of species, they don't look like…like anything you'd recognize."

"So why were they breaking the law of conservation of mass and having babies?"

Yerzuk's eyes closed to shut him out. "These IVIs are very energetic. In space, where they're cold, the energy can be contained. In warm places, they get volatile, and the energy must escape—it's released in new love-stones."

"Well, *I've* never heard of this! How come all those stones of desire in galleries and museums and private collections aren't multiplying all the time?"

"Because they're dead."

"Dead?"

"Inactive, then," sighed Yerzuk. "Or exhausted or extinct, like volcanoes."

"But our examples were very active, weren't they?"

"Yes," she agreed. "It seems someone has found a way to make the IVIs dormant, to pass as extinct, until it becomes convenient or necessary to kick-start the replication."

"And you, working on the sly for Serendipidam, are trying to find out who they are… Why the secrecy? Surely the Provost's Office is designed for just that kind of mission."

"Where there is potential to create great wealth, there is also an opportunity to generate shifts in political power. And when that happens, the normal channels of authority and justice are not always reliable. That's when the Provost Marshal needs a special agent."

"You."

"Me," nodded Yerzuk. It was the most

communicative she'd been in days.

"Do you think someone needed my berth in Cryogen to keep the love-stones quiet for a bit, until we reached this planet? Knott commandeered my berth there, but did she order my extraction as a Reader?"

Yerzuk shrugged and said nothing as the monorail glided into the terminus.

What had started as 7 tonnes aboard the *Scutari* had, since its removal to the planet surface, increased until the warehouse storing it exploded. It was bought when the market opened at dawn by a company with a credit rating but—according to Cascade—no recent dealings, no known directors, staff, head office or forwarding address. A line of security staff now ringed the creaking mound of IVIs, throwing stones back onto the heap, turning away rubberneckers who'd come to gawp.

It seemed a good time to draw a line under the mystery and quit, but Yerzuk insisted on staying. She wanted to attend the market, she said, to get a feel for the place, to learn. For cover, she'd brought along something to sell, something to get her involved in the whole process, something a bit special to stir up interest: a brand new cybersuit.

Yerzuk had somehow not only accessed Fleet stores and "acquired" this fusion-powered exoskeleton—half spacesuit, half spacecraft—but also spirited it ashore. It didn't escape Durante's notice that she'd named him as the exclusive vendor. He found it hard to understand why he still trusted her.

* * * *

Durante wasn't prejudiced against colonials. His own home world was hardly the center of the universe after all. But here on Nimbus, in this place of cloud-shrouded boredom, there seemed no curiosity or desire, no grit on which to fasten. Wherever Durante went he found the same halfwit inhabitants: people shaped like teapots who stood too close; people with inane grins, asking him to sample their mushrooms, inviting him to supper, offering hugs and con-

fidences. He hated it.

"So why," he asked Yerzuk, as they walked together towards the copper duomo of the marketplace, "do you suppose Commander Knott chose this place to sell the love-stones? It seems one of the least erotic places in the settled universe."

"As you know, the stones are sometimes stimulating."

Durante kept an even pace and did not turn to face her.

"Knott brought down about 7 tonnes to market: that's not enough to stimulate a whole colony. And anyway, how many of these people would want or could afford to buy? Last I heard, a single IVI would cost 20 years' salary down here."

"If sufficient IVIs reproduce enough times, their rarity value would reduce. Perhaps everyone could afford one."

"You're telling me Knott knew how to make the IVIs replicate, and gambled on selling them in bulk?"

"No, I think she sold the 7 tonnes for a small fortune, and the replication method for a large one. Her main investment, or that of her backers, may concern what happens after the love-stones take effect. We're here, look."

The giant duomo combined elements of this grassland's surface hillocks with the numberless legions of mushrooms farmed in barns below. It was, thought Durante, a magnificent attempt to reflect and relieve the tedium of the place. He was the only person studying it. Surrounding him—ignorant or forgetful, or indifferent to any architectural effects—an amphitheater full of traders chattered and gossiped, exchanged mycelial intelligence and crop futures, and cooed at their screens.

The duomo stood 4 kilometers high above them, and was made not of solid metal, as Durante had first assumed, but millions of copper leaves, oxidized green on the outside, brilliantly burnished within. Each leaf was strung upon a thread, and trembled in the constant breeze, producing a sound like whispers, rumors on a global scale. To the eye, it seemed that a concave sky was shimmering in endless shades of green and orange, gray and gold, peach and silver; all the colors of all the coins known to Man.

"We'll sit over there, in the vendors' gallery," said Yerzuk, leading the way.

When they took their places, they surveyed the scene on a giant screen, found their lot on the index and waited for the bidding to start. They looked just like all the others from the *Scutari* there that day, privateers selling off an expensive piece of Fleet kit without the authorities' knowledge or permission.

"You're sweating," said Yerzuk. "Stop it. Relax."

"I *am* relaxed—I'm fine," replied Durante.

"You don't look relaxed. I'm going for coffee—want some?"

"No, it might make me jumpy."

Durante stared at the roof to distract himself. Despite his involvement with the cyber-suit down there, despite consorting with the mysterious and possibly criminal Yerzuk, watching the roof calmed him. Almost mesmerized, he tried to tell if the waves that played across it were indeed wind-powered, or if some subtle program controlled their ebb and flow. Durante was no nearer a conclusion when a hand tapped his shoulder. He turned, and there—emerging from a plume of cigar smoke—was Commander Knott, grinning lopsidedly.

"You hypocritical burgling little bastard," she gurgled.

"Sir?"

"Pompous prating little squab."

"Ma'am?"

"And all the while you were planning to be here, flogging off Fleet stores."

"Ma'am, I—"

"You deserve what's coming to you, Mid-shitman, remember that. When the worst thing you can imagine happens, remember *me*. I'll be laughing."

Another cloud of cigar smoke engulfed

Durante, and by the time it had cleared, she was gone. A moment later, he spotted her limping across a distant jetty, saw her escorted aboard a private vessel trademarked IHIT. It was the same firm that had bought the love-stones.

"Nice chat with Commander Knott?" asked Yerzuk, following his gaze as she returned.

"No. She called you a 'burgling bastard'."

Yerzuk looked unperturbed as she slipped in earbuds to follow the bidding and ignored him.

For the last time, Durante turned to the soothing roof, and as he mellowed, noticed that the sound of it was changing. From a steady shushing, it had grown percussive, more metallic and louder. Now he could see that what was turning the copper leaves was not the wind, but a shower of rain.

"I thought," he said to Yerzuk, pulling out one of her earbuds, "it never rained on Nimbus."

"Right. Only mizzle, in autumn."

"So, what's *that*?" he said, pointing.

Yerzuk cocked her head and listened. "Heavy mizzle—maybe?"

Others around them were staring at the roof too, and listening to the new, unaccustomed rattling of raindrops on the duomo. The leaves had started to spin, producing an odd, stroboscopic shimmer that was difficult to watch and even harder not to. The noise grew deafening.

"What's happening?" asked Yerzuk.

Durante felt a sudden sting on his cheek and picked from his lap the offending hailstone: tiny, opalescent, resembling a marble. As he examined it between two fingers, it turned black and dissolved.

"I'm not sure I like this," he said.

"Follow me—at the double."

Yerzuk pushed past him and bounded down an aisle towards the lowest tier of the amphitheater.

Down in the middle of the market, where all the items up for sale were on display, the noise of the storm was even worse. Silvery nuggets clattered down and pinged from metal struts, ricocheting off internal surfaces. Here and there people were sheltering under tabletops and signal-boards, laughing, enjoying this carnival disruption of business.

"Any ideas, Lieutenant?"

She was standing, grappling with an awkward latch on the cybersuit they'd brought to market.

"Help me open it."

Durante wrenched it free and felt the hail's painful staccato against his legs as they tumbled inside. He peered back the way he'd come, and from the shelter of the suit, saw how the market's floor was liquefying under the pellets. The duomo's folial roof was already disintegrating, and the downpour grew heavier, more intense and deadly with every passing second. In the failing light, Durante watched as those unfortunates caught in the open were shredded, flesh stripped from the bones, bodies collapsing as if in supplication. Agitated pools of blood were lashed into a crimson mist.

"Shut the hatch!" shouted Yerzuk. He obeyed, appalled at what he'd seen and amazed by the ungovernable quickening of events. "When I tell you, hold on to *me*. Don't touch the sides."

For a few seconds, Yerzuk was a blur of knees, kicks and unintended blows, and then she was hanging before and above him, trussed in a webbed harness slung from above. She swung from side to side within the narrow confines of the cybersuit, her breasts swimming before Durante's face as she struggled to interpret the controls.

"Hold onto my legs," Yerzuk ordered as she rattled through a bank of buttons and dials.

Then the whole mechanism shuddered into life and lurched forwards. Durante lurched too, crunching first into a circuit bank and then into Yerzuk's all too suddenly apparent body. There was a blue sizzle, a noise like a whip being cracked and the tang of scorched hair. He looked up, saw Yerzuk covering her eyes, tears streaming down her cheeks.

"Oh shit, I'm sorry! I slipped," he offered.

"Not your fault," she replied, "but I'm flash-dazzled. Can't see a damn thing. Climb onto my back. You'll have to tell me which way to go."

Durante clambered aboard her, sensed her grimace as his legs wrapped round her waist as he maneuvered to see through the machine's dipped windscreen.

"Where's the exit?" demanded Yerzuk.

"Twenty degrees to the right, then it's straight on for 500 meters."

Under Yerzuk's control and Durante's navigation, the man-machine now stumbled forwards, loping like a drunk marine towards the distant freight bay and then the parking lot beyond. Out here, the tarmac was pasted with red smudges. Someone hammered on the outside of the hatch, yelping for admission. Durante battled with himself, trying to concentrate. He was aware of the nightmare defleshing just beyond the armored carapace of the suit, aware too of the taut buttocks pressed beneath his thighs, the scent of her clothes, her skin, her sweat.

She walked them twice round the empty lot, crushing vehicles and shopping trolleys underfoot, until at last Durante got his bearings and came up with a plan.

"This may not work, but let's head back towards the monorail." In clumsy 10-league steps, they smashed towards the deserted platform, lowered the cybersuit atop an empty carriage, buckled on and braced.

"Ready?" said Durante, close against her ear. She nodded, fumbled for and found a button on the launch panel, and tensed in expectation. The main thruster roared, then the afterburner kicked in, and the suit and carriage blasted off down the line, scattering sparks behind them like fiery mares' tails.

There were 15 seconds of breakneck acceleration, then: "Now!" shouted Durante.

"Now!" repeated Yerzuk, releasing the exoskeleton's finger grips and launching them skywards. The battering of the hailstones on the exterior was deafening. One of the outer window-shields cracked into a star. Durante glimpsed the luminescent and yeasty clouds, and then the flare of a familiar ship's tattoo. It was the private vessel they'd seen Knott board, preparing now the final stage before leaving Nimbus' atmosphere. Everything went suddenly quiet as they swooped under its sheltering belly.

"Closer…closer. Take hold!" yelled Durante.

The cybersuit gripped on. Then there was a violent wrench. Yerzuk's head snapped back and Durante felt his face stretching taut across his skull.

A moment's violent shaking, the roar of power, then silence.

* * * *

Two hours later and safe aboard the *Scutari*, Durante and Yerzuk had tumbled free of each other and out onto the *Scutari's* docking bay.

Durante took her arm and she shook him off. Together they examined the damaged suit, running hands over its surfce. There were deep scores all over it, dents and twisted joints, but the window-shield had held, just. They hoped to find "hailstones" jammed into some part of its anatomy, but there were none.

"Where were they coming from?" asked Durante.

"My guess is they were summoned or attracted."

"By whom?"

"The love-stones."

"I thought you said they were IVIs—inanimate."

"True, but even inanimate objects can resonate, stimulate the tendency for balance in the universe…"

"Are you talking about quantum entanglement? For goodness sake, that storm of grapeshot can't have just appeared out of thin air!"

"It could if it came through a wormhole or something similar. Perhaps the existence of too many love-stones summons a 'hail' to destroy them. Some spooky equilibrium, maybe, like Einstein said. This happened before, 40 years ago, on Giselle. Mass self-replication, then 'hail'…"

"…and farewell. So, you're saying all this is just some natural phenomenon, an act of God? I don't buy that at all. You didn't see Knott's face back there on Nimbus. I'm sure she's up to her flash-fried neck in it."

Yerzuk shrugged.

"Well, who do *you* think was responsible?" Durante asked.

"I don't know yet. That's what we're investigating"

"So, what happened on Giselle all those years ago?"

"A consignment of 50 tonnes was landed on Giselle—a short-term measure while the transport carrying them was repaired. Two days later the stones began replicating, and then it hailed. Continuous hail for 6 weeks. Very few survivors. The colony was re-stocked, redeveloped as a resort by a group of venture capitalists who leased it from the Fleet. Called themselves "Interplanetary Habitation and Investment Trading". They made a fast profit, then sold up and disappeared. Now they're back."

Durante shook his head as her meaning became clear. "So, you reckon IHIT and the Fleet collude like this to make money?"

"It's not official Fleet policy, but certain Fleet personnel might like it to be. And maybe you helped them."

"Not on purpose!"

"*You* were the one who insisted the neurobrand was minuted and adhered to. *You* ensured the stones were sent to market on July 15."

"But that was my duty. What of it?"

"On September 18, every commercial and legal brain on Nimbus would have been safe on the *Scutari*, making friends, buying influence, sucking up. Today, they were all at the market. They're dead now. No one's left to stand in IHIT's way."

"You mean I was set up?" Durante yelled.

"It *is* a possibility. A plausible theory."

"You should have told me what was going on from the start, then I wouldn't have played into their hands," he said.

"True," she replied, "but back then we didn't know if you were part of the plot. It was always a high-stakes game. You weren't dealt a good hand from the deck, but you played it better than anyone could have expected. More honestly. Now you have friends as well as enemies in high places."

* * * *

"Nothing too curly," Serendipidam growled.

"Sir?"

"Junior officers favor ridiculous curly signatures, as if they were ruddy Leonardo da Vinci or something."

"Sir."

Durante signed the report without a flourish.

"Well, you've made a fine bloody mess of everything. Proud?"

"Sir?"

"Knott promoted under a cloud. Nimbus in complete ruins. Thousands dead. Fleet cybersuit stolen and reduced to shreds. What have you got to say for yourself?"

"I did my best, sir."

Serendipidam snorted. "Well, you're not getting refrozen after this!"

"But I thought we had a deal, sir…"

"Durante, you're dangerous enough penniless. I shudder to think what damage you could do with any money in your account."

"But that's hardly fair, I—"

"Stow it, laddie! You've ballsed things up wonderfully—just be thankful you're not out on your arse cleaning up the mess ashore. Dismissed!"

"But I don't understand, sir. Can't we arrest someone? Can't we charge them with something?"

"What do you want, Midshipman?" snapped the older man. "Somebody's head on a pikestaff? Is that the only kind of ending that will satisfy you? Is that the kind of posturing, simplistic officer you aspire to be?"

There was a silence. Serendipidam brought his long, blue-black face close to Durante's and resumed: "This is the *real* world not fiction. Sometimes in our line of business there *are* explanations, proofs, truths and resolutions we can believe in with certainty. But very rarely. More often, it's all smoke and shadows and we grope our way through as best we can. Right-thinking folk in this Fleet face many hazards—criminals, politicians, megalomaniacs, incompetents, opportunists, alien idiots, viruses, ruddy great lumps of rock in the wrong place at the wrong time. I don't know which combination of these is to blame for what happened on the planet. I *do* know it wasn't me, or Yerzuk, or you. I know that we—and certain others you'll meet later—are opposed to such horrors. The file on Nimbus remains open. I'll recommend that Nimbus be guarded against salvage bandits, but I make no promises. We move forward. We start again."

"Who is Yerzuk, sir?"

"A good guy. A provost's officer like you, but on special secondment. As you will be from now on. You've acquitted yourself well—not exactly competently, but with decency. I'm assigning you to Lieutenant Yerzuk's tender care for further training. Which should be interesting.

"Now, I have a department of 400 officers to run, 399 of whom are senior to you, so… if you please…get out of my office. Oh, and one last thing before you go, Durante—fuck you very much."

❊

ABOUT THE AUTHORS

A. J. McIntosh is an Edinburgh-based author, editor, and journalist. His fiction has been published by Mercat Press and Tartarus Press among others. He is the contributing editor of the *Broughton Spurtle* (broughtonspurtle.org.uk/backissues/spurtle).

Andrew J. Wilson also lives in Edinburgh. His short stories, non-fiction and poems have appeared all over the world, sometimes in the most unlikely places. With Neil Williamson, he co-edited *Nova Scotia: New Scottish Speculative Fiction*, which was nominated for a World Fantasy Award. Andrew has also been put forward for the Science Fiction Poetry Association's 2022 Dwarf Stars Award.

ABOUT THE ARTIST

Ravden Kolkata is an artist an designer based in India. Raven works as a Senior Graphic Designer at Ravden Technologies, working on Manga and graphic novel illustrations.

PHARMAKON, PHARMAKON
by M. Stern

How the neighborhood kids got their hands on those things, let alone figured out using them, was a mystery to Luis. Awoken by the after-school noise, he made his peace with the interruption of his nap, walked to the window of the small Rygian apartment and watched.

In the center of a circle of teenagers stood a kid with each foot on a separate, thin, black circular platform. The kid crouched, then jumped. A wave bubbled from the left platform, rendering it parabolic and throwing the kid about six feet up in the air. At the apex of the jump, eyes filled with concentration, he bicycle kicked into a backflip. Then hurtling straight downward, he pointed his left index finger in front of him. Before colliding with the ground, his finger touched the platform on the right. The platform somehow flipped him back upright, then shot up above his head and stretched into a floating bar. He caught it, did a series of one-handed pullovers, ended up in a one-handed handstand, then did a full front-flip from that position and landed to cheers.

Luis walked outside and thought of the near-catastrophe that ensued, 30 years earlier, when he handed a curious adult his skateboard. He decided against asking the kids if he could try the Rygian contraption.

A vehicle resembling a floating, wobbling blob of black ink landed and Martin Tesh half-fell out of an opening that liquefied on the passenger side. The Krex driver warped jerkily out with no need for a door.

"I'm on vacation, Marty!" Luis yelled as Tesh stumbled to touch the sand with the hand not gripping a rucksack, righted himself and strode toward him. "You better have beers in that bag!"

The Krex had materialized next to Luis and was looking either at or past him, at where the kids—now absent—had just been. With Krex it was impossible to tell. The Rygian natives were humanoid but uniformly marshmallow white, and lacked features discerning them from one another outside of variations in height. They reminded Luis of mannequins. Luis stepped out of the Krex's way.

"Got a real problem on our hands," said Tesh, stopping and dropping the rucksack. "Grimaldi isn't pleased."

"Grimaldi is a joyless person," Luis said. "Doubly so with this holiday on the horizon. Whatever the Krex are planning to celebrate, he's their Grinch. What's eating him today?"

"Name Skylar Bloomquist ring a bell?"

"Bloomquist," Luis said. "Came up in the last wave of planetary expats, right? Math teacher at the high school. Wife's a diplomat down on Earth, maybe? Though not high up the ladder if she's still waiting to make the trip."

"All correct," Tesh said. "Add that he's currently smashing up PJ's Market."

"Never struck me as the smashing type," Luis said, "Though I've seen life on Rygiat do a number on people's mind before, after the novelty wears off. Still, sounds like a police matter to me. Not sure why Grimaldi wants me—"

"Store security says Bloomquist's shooting beams of light from his eyeballs," Tesh said.

"Math can be tough," Luis said. "So I suppose our friend here will chaperone us to—hey, is he OK?"

Luis jerked his thumb toward the Krex, whose back remained turned to the two men. This was uncharacteristic of the natives of Rygiat, who usually faced any group of humans they were near. Since they could not hear human speech unaided, it was not entirely clear why—the suspicion was that whatever field the Krex emitted to register each other's presence, humans put out something similar that scrambled their radar. That this Krex was still facing away from them was unique enough to issue comment.

Tesh looked flustered. He pulled the human-to-Krex translator rig from his rucksack and stormed over to the alien, saying:

"Oh Jesus, who knows. With this festival coming up they're acting like birds during a damn eclipse."

The H2K translator consisted of a speaker hooked into a long, clear plastic tube which terminated in a thick, hollow needle. Tesh punctured the indifferent Krex's flesh with the needle, pressed a button on the speaker and said:

"Everything alright? We should head out pretty quick."

Luis watched his coworker's words transform into neon pink data fluid which dribbled through the tube and toward the Krex's arm. When it entered the Krex through the needle, the being spun around as if startled.

Luis hoped the Krex was not irritated. Since only Krex could pilot the vehicles that navigated this planet, Luis and Tesh would be hiking for hours if the Krex refused to transport them.

Now facing Luis and Tesh, the Krex pointed its left index finger at the sky. With it's right hand, it pulled a taffy-like strand from its left fingertip and snapped it off. Instinctively commanding the strange magnetism flowing invisibly through the Rygian environment, the Krex made the hovering strand wrap itself into a complicated knot.

Tesh pulled the K2H side of the translator from his rucksack. It consisted of a similar speaker to the first device with the plastic tube terminating in a plastic cone instead of a needle. Tesh held the cone under the floating knot, which dropped into the it.

The knot dissolved into pink fluid in the tube. When the fluid reached the speaker, the device said in a soft voice:

"No impetus for remaining in present surroundings extant. Commute as intended will continue."

That was the closest they were going to get to an explanation. Luis and Tesh began walking toward the vehicle.

The featureless black sphere melted open like a sheet of acetate touched with a lit cigarette and Tesh got in. Luis followed. Looking back, he saw the Krex again warping in that unsettling manner, its body remaining in the same position as it bounced jerkily between invisible chutes of atmospheric magnetism. For a fraction of a second the Krex would stretch into a vertical tube, or seem farther off in the distance or closer, like a cartoon imperfectly animated. For as much as Luis had seen it, he found the display triggered some foundational human uneasiness.

The uneasiness made sense, Luis thought. On Earth, such movement would be unnatural. Here it was tied to nature itself. As natural as the sands below his feet which, as he jumped into the vehicle behind Tesh, shifted and danced in and out of polyhedrons, spikes, and countless other geometric configurations—in response to the magnetic fields which flowed here, invisibly and inexplicably.

The sphere sealed itself around Luis and Tesh. They both sat behind the Krex. Luis felt the sensation of vehicle's departure. The Krex had one hand impaled on a clear spike on the otherwise featureless dash. Blue fluid dripped from the Krex's hand through the spike and into the vehicle, directing it.

Luis sat in silence. Irritation about his disrupted vacation began to set in. But he was Chief Investigator for the Unusual Occurrences Bureau on Rygiat, and while the Bloomquist situation did not sound great, he hoped maybe it was no big deal.

Tesh's earpiece glowed red, then turned green as Tesh answered and said:

"Ah jeez."

Tesh turned off his earpiece.

"Things just got weirder," Tesh said.

"Marvelous," Luis said. "So as I asked before, you got beer in that bag? I'm still technically on vacation."

* * * *

Paradoxes stacked on paradoxes filled Skylar Bloomquist's racing mind.

A few weeks earlier it had started. His mind began poking at half-remembered old chestnuts from Zeno he read in college. Reality as a flip-book of instants, for instance, that somehow moved forward with no force to do the flipping. Things he dismissed as mind puzzles smoothed over by calculus. Until it began.

Within a couple days he was obsessing over those classic problems and devising his own. He imagined having a perfect snapshot of all possible knowledge then being confronted with its opposite. How could the opposite reside outside of everything?

Then the problems revealed their quantum aspect. The Rygian school system was not strict on teacher attendance during the final lame duck week, so he already had a substitute. Rather than unwinding on early vacation, he furiously studied the many worlds theory.

The theory jibed with how he saw things, though he found paradoxes to wrangle with there, too. If each instant in time was the seed of its own universe, leading to an infinite number of disparate universes, then there was logically an infinite number of universes in which the many worlds theory was false.

He began interrogating this paradox by writing a book. He called his wife on Earth multiple times to describe his progress. Just as he wrapped up the writing, he found he was out of food. He needed groceries. As he left his apartment, he was struck with another observation:

That you could reside on both sides of the quantum divide if you just thought hard enough. He wondered how he never saw it before.

* * * *

The unfortunate reality that doing good work is often rewarded not with praise, but with even more work hung heavily in Luis's mind as he flashed his government badge and pushed through the crowd outside of PJ's Market. Granted Luis was, on balance, the best person for this job. Things that everyone else missed were completely obvious to him. He was good at drawing long-shot, far-out, oddball connections between seemingly irrelevant factors. And on Rygiat, oddball connections were the norm.

Back when he arrived on Rygiat, the Earth expat government was still trying to determine why half the time people were suffering from hemochromatosis and the other half passing out from anemia. The whole scientific community was searching for a pathogenic explanation when Luis rolled in, fresh off the spaceship, and pointed out that the chutes of magnetism could be shifting the ambient environmental iron and affecting levels in food. Thus the degaussing grow room was born.

Luis played the role of negotiator, investigator, intuitor, and de-escalator, and if it seemed like someone with such odd intuition was too valuable to send up against an unknown, there were decades of tragic examples demonstrating the folly of sending linear thinkers to tackle alien problems. Luis, had a proven knack for making it out of situations like this alive, intact, and with the information he needed.

Luis flashed his badge at the crowd's front and an officer waved Luis past the police line, toward the door of PJ's Market.

Luis pulled his magnetic field camera from his pocket. It was the most important tool for diagnosing things gone wrong on Rygiat. The smartphone-sized device was like an infrared camera, but with no live read-out. The black-and-white images it captured, when viewed, revealed the tubes of magnetic force, normally invisible to the human eye, that tunneled through the air everywhere on this planet. This incomprehensible characteristic of Rygiat, at odds with how humans understood physical forces to work, was the obvious first place to look when something—or someone—went haywire.

Luis entered the store.

"Bloomquist?" he said.

* * * *

As Bloomquist entered PJ's Market, he felt a tingling in his limbs and a sense of mental ascension. His earlier concerns over paradox seemed to resolve themselves even as a new horizon of them appeared.

Each instant was a universe unto itself. But now he perceived the gaps; empty spaces between the flipped images of reality's endless projection. He threw himself into a shelf. He ran toward a shopping cart. His impact sent it hurtling disproportionately far. He was getting there.

Shouts of confusion and stampeding feet did little to distract him from his research. Someone dove at him, someone else dove away. He was fully focused on this new region he discovered, where the mental bled into the physical.

He felt himself flip photons with a newly discovered reflex. Matter and light were now two sides of the same coin from his perspective.

He was looking, running, scrutinizing the unstable waves of paradox. To live was to unknowingly navigate them. He was successfully surfing between them. Pirouetting and hurling and slamming through PJ's Market, testing to find the correct extra-spatial angle.

Then it worked.

No single language could describe the sensation.

* * * *

The store's interior looked like the aftermath of a hurricane. Torn open packages littered the ground around overturned shelves. Footprints of crushed cereal were tracked on the floor. To the right, smashed eggs, exploded milk containers and sprayed soda soiled the cooler area, and the shattered safety glass of the coolers hung off in sheets dropping tinkling shards. To the left, the registers and checkstands were smashed to splinters. A number of metal grocery carts were bent into abstract junkyard art. The few shelves that remained standing were partially smashed with MREs and canned goods sliding off.

Amid it all, Luis saw Skylar Bloomquist.

Bloomquist was embedded halfway in the potato chip shelf.

The one visible eye of the math teacher blinked and rolled wildly. The half of his mouth that was visible, however, had a madly amused tilt to it; he was in the throes of ecstasy, not pain. The entire right side of his body, from his shoulder to his foot, had somehow disappeared into the shelf. Luis noticed no blood or injury where Bloomquist was conjoined with it. It was more like he was part of a living collage. Were it in two dimensions, it would have looked like someone snipped a photo of the man in half and placed one cut edge against the shelf.

Luis snapped a picture with the magnetic field camera, then said:

"Hey Skylar? Luis Corcuff, Bureau of—"

Bloomquist roared. Then he blinked out of existence. Luis saw the man, for a fraction of a second, as a flickering static disturbance stretched in a thin horizontal line. He reappeared on a mound of dumped toaster pastry boxes a few feet in front of Luis.

"Mr. Bloomquist," Luis said, snapping another magnetic picture without drawing attention to the camera. "I'm here to help. Can you tell me what you remember about today?"

Bloomquist looked at him, opened his mouth, a made a sound Luis had never heard before. The closest thing was the harmonizing ululations of Tuvan throat singing. The man was forming words, or something like them; more like a jumble of phonemes, all off different timbres and tones, all spoken simultaneously. Like he was trying to speak four languages at once. Luis noticed blood running down the man's mouth.

"Skylar! Calm down! We need to get you to the—"

The man blinked out of existence again. He appeared sticking sideways out of a collapsed checkout counter. Then disappeared again and appeared upside-down, embedded in a ceiling light fixture. Then he appeared in front of Luis and rushed him.

Luis stumbled back and pushed a crushed shopping cart in Bloomquist's path. Taking two steps towards the door, he stepped on a can of beans. The can flew at the wall and he fell flat on his back. Bloomquist tossed the cart and loomed over Luis. Luis, anticipating a lunge, hoped his jiu-jitsu was not too rusty, or too terrestrial, for this attack.

Then the look in Bloomquist's eyes changed.

Bloomquist suddenly registered fear, surprise, and confusion, which was quickly replaced by those beams of light Luis was told about. Two spotlights beamed out of Bloomquist's eye sockets as he gaped and growled.

Then Bloomquist went stiff. His eyes went dark. He slumped to the ground.

"Dammit," Luis said, saddened not to have saved him.

Luis got up, took out his smartphone and called Tesh, saying:

"We're going to need forensics. Bloomquist didn't make it. And if this is bigger than just him, we're in trouble."

Then Luis pulled out the magnetic field camera and flipped through the snapshots. There was the room, displayed in its magnetic aspect. Tubes of invisible magnetic force depicted as bright white lines criss-crossing the room wherever they flowed, configured differently in each photo. In the middle of each photo was a huge white spot. That was Bloomquist.

Luis sighed. This was big. Humans did not look like that in the magnetic field camera's pictures.

Just looking at Bloomquist's magnetic signature in that image, you would have thought he was a Krex.

* * * *

"This is what's making me nervous," said Grimaldi.

He pointed at a huge white spot on a blown-up photo on the table. It was taken from a surveillance satellite—one fitted with the original, planet-scale version of the magnetic field camera Luis now had in his pocket.

"Interesting," Luis said. "Send anyone over there to investigate?"

"Those mountains are Krex-only territory," Grimaldi said. "Fat chance they'll fly us up there in a pod, and hiking it gets you a Lenzini Special."

Arlo Lenzini was an Earth diplomat who had visited Rygiat 15 years earlier. Having accidentally wandered into non-Earthling territory, he was able to report numerous unknown features of the daily life of Krex living among themselves. The report came, however, at the expense of his own psychological integrity. When Lenzini was noticed by Krex, he was not accosted, harassed or even addressed. He was, rather, placed outside Krex territory, as if re-starting a level on a video game. The experience left the diplomat with a sense of what he referred to—after being returned to Earth and placed in the care of his family—as "yawning emptiness," "incomprehensible disjointedness," and "a dizzy, waking nothingness." The human government on Rygiat instituted more stringent rules banning off-the-grid travel.

Luis scrutinized the photo closely, then started rubbing a portion of it with his thumb.

"Is there something on the satellite's lens?" Luis said. "Look at that gray spot right there next to the white part."

"Let me see," Grimaldi said with slight irritation. "Gray spot, gray spot—nope no gray spot, just a gigantic bright white security risk."

Luis shrugged. There was definitely a faint gray spot there if you looked hard.

"I don't see how you're sure it's a security risk," Luis said.

"*You?*" Grimaldi said. "You of all people. We've got the Krex planning a hemisphere-sized private party. Your friend Bloomquist starts casually getting himself stuck in the furniture at the grocery store. Now we've got a giant blob of magnetic force appearing out of nowhere. You're not seeing a security concern?"

"Why would the Krex attack us now, after 40 years? They happily line up to fly us places and, at least as far as we can tell, they seem to get a kick out of it. If they wanted to kill humans, why not throw us out of their pods mid-flight?"

"Could be a religious thing, maybe," Grimaldi said. "See, you're not the only one who can form a hypothesis! Bloomquist had the same magnetic signature as a Krex. Maybe that's what their festival is all about. Maybe they're planning conversion by the— whatever happened to that guy."

"If that's their idea of conversion, we can probably convince them they're better off pamphleting," Luis said.

There was a knock and Grimaldi buzzed in Lena Baker, chief medical examiner.

"Either of you two ever come across a brain with 10 trillion neurons?" Baker asked.

"In this office?" Grimaldi said. "I'm lucky to encounter a brain with 50 of them."

"Come on Grimaldi," said Luis. "You've seen me walk and chew gum at the same time in three different languages. Dr. Baker, how many neurons are there in a standard, functioning human brain like the boss's here?"

"Around 100 billion," Baker said. "Which is why I'm asking. Whatever happened to Bloomquist literally smartened him to death. Something induced a type of massive neural cell replication believed to be impossible. The synaptic activity that resulted was so violent that it blew past the thermodynamic limits of the brain."

"At the expense of sounding tasteless," Grimaldi said, "it sounds like he had—"

"Yes, 'mental burnout,'" Baker said. "I've heard that joke down in the lab once for each extra neuron on the unfortunate victim."

"Well we've got everyone who was at PJ's quarantined," Grimaldi said. "Should buy us time while we figure out what the Krex—"

"Doesn't seem necessary," Luis said.

"How's that?"

"Didn't you say that his widow said he was calling her the week before the incident? And he rambled more each call? Whatever happened to him came well before he visited PJ's."

"Better safe than sorry," Grimaldi said.

"I think we're overlooking the obvious," Luis said. "Have we contacted the school? What are they telling the students?"

"Last day of the school year at the high school today," Grimaldi said. "They're ducking the issue and have a statement planned for mid-summer. Want to avoid creating panic."

"Fair enough," said Luis. "How about at the elementary and middle school? Separate building from the high school, but something might be impacting all the buildings clustered in Emswhiller Canyon. Have there been any reports of teachers or students acting strange?"

"Not a one," Grimaldi said. "Believe me, my kids are students at Farmer. One fourth grader, one sixth grader. They tell me everything. If something was up, I'd definitely hear about it."

Luis threw a searching look at Lena Baker, who said:

"I advise on science, I don't give parenting tips."

With that, Lena Baker left. Luis picked the photo back up and rubbed at it again.

"You know what Grimaldi," Luis said. "Tomorrow I'll visit the schools and ask around just in case."

"Knock yourself out," Grimaldi said. "Just don't be late to our meeting with you-know-who tomorrow—it's going to be a doozy."

* * * *

Luis turned the dial on the automated commuter pod which ran from his neighborhood to Emswhiller Canyon. He stepped into the opening, which sealed up seamlessly behind him. On his trip he thought, with some amusement, about how accustomed humans were to trusting Krex transportation technologies. While a driver was necessary to reach a selected destination, these automated pods ran back and forth to and from major transit hubs. Despite Grimaldi's suspicion about the Krex's motives, he still put his children on Krex technology twice a day every weekday.

Luis felt the sphere plop itself on its landing pad in the lot between Farmer High School on the right and Farmer Elementary and Middle on the left.

Beyond the high school, to the far right, was the canyon wall, where the sand spiked and dropped in waves as the invisible tubes of magnetism slammed silently into its surface. To the left, beyond the two schools for younger students, was an empty landscape. Far beyond where Luis could see, he knew there was a heavily restricted industrial zone. That area, which even Luis would have to jump through hoops to access, struck him as a possible source of whatever he was looking for. The repeated assurances from industrial safety authorities notwithstanding, if whatever got into Skylar Bloomquist was environmental in origin, Luis would bet money on that area being the source.

A security guard at the elementary school door looked at Luis's badge and guided him briskly down the hallway toward the office. Luis tried to see what was occurring through each small window on each door they passed. Passing a classroom of fourth graders, he saw a teacher writing out what he could have sworn was a linear algebra equation. The next door was half ajar; fifth graders, and he thought he heard Chaucer being read in Middle English. But by the time he reached the office he was questioning his perceptions. He planned to observe more carefully on the way back.

The guard opened the door marked "main office" for him. Luis approached the administrative assistant behind the desk. She was doing a word puzzle.

"Hello, I'm Luis Corcuff, from the Unusual Occurrences Bureau. I'd like to speak with Principal Malcolm concerning Farmer High."

"Yes, Mr. Corcuff," she said. "You got here just in time—we have our end-of-year assembly in an hour and he's the star."

She pressed a button on her desk and said: "Dennis, a Mr. Corcuff is here to see you."

She returned to her puzzle and said, without looking up:

"Did your paternal grandparents speak French?"

"As a matter of fact, yes. Why would you—"

"That last name is hard to miss!" she said. "It's Breton. The Bretons are descended from The Britons who fled Wales during the Anglo-Saxon invasion of the British Isles in the 6th century A.D. They landed in the former Roman province of Amorica, which was renamed Brittany after its new inhabitants. The province officially became a part of France in the 1500s, so one would assume someone with that last name in the 22nd century would be of francophone extraction."

"All true, I think?" Luis said. "So you're answering the phones and not teaching history?—"

"Mr. Corcuff?" The principal said, emerging from a back office.

"Please, Luis," Luis said. He shook the man's hand.

"Thanks, call me Dennis," the principal replied. "I assume you're here about the—incident? Perhaps we should speak outside."

The two walked out of the office just as, to Luis's dismay, a school bell rang. There was a rush of students into the hall and no chance to eavesdrop on classroom activity.

"We heard about Skylar's circumstances," Principal Malcolm said as the two walked up past the high school. "Off-Earth living can be psychologically difficult."

"It's not so simple as that, Dennis. We suspect something more far-reaching at play. Did you interact with him? Hear about any peculiar habits?"

"He was down here once a day, but passed by fleetingly."

"Fleetingly?"

"Runner," Principal Malcolm said. "Went running every day on lunch, rain or shine. From the high school to the fence on the other side of the canyon and back."

Luis's felt a thrill. If he was on to something here, then nothing he saw inside the school was a coincidence. He dug deeper.

"Impressive staff you've got here, by the way, Dennis," Luis said, "Growing up on Earth, I don't remember teachers *or* administrators being so—cerebral."

"I appreciate the compliment, Luis," Principal Malcolm said. "Not to disparage the educational institutions of our Mother Planet, but overcrowding and the social pathologies born from it has led to what one might politely call variable outcomes there, both in teacher quality and student experience. Here, at Farmer High we have a couple of gifts just by virtue of our unique position. We have room to give drastically more attention to individual students. We have an engaged community of parents. And we have the freedom to experiment with different learning models without a great deal of bureaucracy. We've really managed to put something exceptional together."

The man's elevated tone and cadence made Luis wonder whether if the man had whatever killed Bloomquist. But pulling the principal away from school to find out, with an assembly coming up, would create panic.

Luis's hand brushed against his pocket. There was the solution.

"Dennis, could I get your picture? The Bureau's been working on community outreach."

"Picture? I, sure—"

Luis had to admit, this stunt was hamhanded. But he got what he needed. Holding up the magnetic field camera instead of his smartphone, he snapped an image of the man smiling awkwardly in front of the wall of Emswhiller Canyon, where horizontal spikes of sand rolled across the vertical surface.

Luis noticed the low-battery light on the camera. What concerned him more, though, was the clock next to it. He was late to his meeting with Grimaldi and the Krex diplomats.

Luis resolved to reach out about any upcoming community initiatives and left the mildly confused principal to his impending assembly.

A moment later Luis was back in the commuter pod. He was still just working on theories, but soon he should have some confirmation. If Principal Malcolm's magnetic signature was a white spot on the picture, Grimaldi would order a school closure and they could go from there. Luis took the camera out and swiped his finger to bring up the picture.

The camera, rather than displaying it, ran out of batteries and turned off.

* * * *

Luis tore into the conference room and Grimaldi shook his head and grunted at his arrival. The two Krex diplomats were seated opposite them, both clad in military garb. The conference room had two built-in translators which functioned far better than the portable ones. A bowl sat in front of each Krex's seat and each chair had a tube with a needle on the end built into the armrest. Each Krex disconnected the needle and stabbed it into their hip region. They then turned toward each other and begin rapidly pulling strands from their fingers, psychically knotting the strands, and pressing the knots into one another. This was how they communicated among themselves. After a half a minute of this deliberation, the Krex across from Luis turned to face him, created a knot and tossed it into the bowl, and leaned back.

The screen that took up a large portion of the wall at the far end of the room sprung to life. A cartoon avatar appeared on the left labeled *Kee-1-17-trn-gX* , under which appeared that Krex's chosen Earth appellation *Craig*. Next to it on the right appeared a second avatar labeled a similar unpronounceable real name, and the iffy but adequate human-ish moniker *Corg.*

"Nice to speak with you two again," Grimaldi said into his microphone. "Though I wish it were under happier circumstances."

Grimaldi's sentence liquefied and few drops of pink liquid flowed through the clear tubes and into the Krex. The Krex across from Grimaldi wove a knot and tossed it into the bowl. A moment later, Corg's avatar on the screen said:

"Always a pleasure. However, we are not sure the purpose of this meeting. You are aware that the *Kng-knkKk* Festival is impending on Rygiat. Preparation requires focus. So as to facilitate universal displacement of those Krex not engaged in outside labor."

What, Luis wondered, could "universal displacement" mean? He moved to speak but Grimaldi cut him off.

"We have reason to believe you are testing a weapon that may be unintentionally causing harm to human citizens on Rygiat, a clear violation of interplanetary treaties," said Grimaldi.

The two Krex burst into a rapid flurry of pulling, knotting, and patting each other that any third party could recognize as displeased.

Luis put his hand over his microphone.

"Jack," he hissed, "What the hell are you doing?"

"We're letting them know they can't intimidate us," Grimaldi said.

"We don't know that there's a weapon!" Luis said.

"We're playing 'good cop,' 'bad cop'," Grimaldi said. "You're the good one. Go. Your turn."

"You didn't tell me we're—"

"That's what happens when you're late! Now make with the 'good cop' and get us some information!"

"Hi Craig," Luis said, affecting a polite and conciliatory tone. "Hi, uh— Corg. Thank you for joining us. I know you're all busy with your festival coming up. I think Jack here may have misspoken with his—I

don't want to say 'accusation,' so much as 'claim'—about your posing an accidental threat to humans on Rygiat. We just want to establish more clearly the nature of your upcoming celebration, so that we can avoid causing any unintentional obstructions. Perhaps we could someday find humans celebrating the—uh—*Knrg* Festival alongside Krex, in the spirit of cultural exchange."

Luis felt pretty good watching those words transmogrify into data fluid and spiral down the tube. It seemed he had decently balanced out, or negated, Grimaldi's hawkish blather. He barely even thought through the 'cultural exchange' bit before spontaneously saying it, but it seemed like it could actually have legs. He was excited for the Krex response.

The Krex named Craig wove a knot and dropped it into his bowl. The corresponding avatar on the screen again sprung to life.

"We intended to share with you the details of the impending *Kng-knkKk* Festival, however we are duty bound to respond to your bellicose and honor-impugning accusations punitively."

The two Krex diplomats removed their needles and stood.

"Wait!" Grimaldi said, yelling despite the Krex being disconnected from the machine and unable to hear them. "Craig! Corg! Buddies! No need for punitive anything! We want to learn! Like he said—cultural exchange!"

The Krex were out the door and Grimaldi pounded on the table and then had his head on the table and clutched the back of his head with his hands.

"I guess they don't like 'bad cop' negotiating tactics," said Luis.

"How was I supposed to know they'd get offended? For cryin' out loud, we've been working with them for decades! Punitive! Did you hear that? What does it mean? If they shut down our mining operations, I'll be back on Earth cleaning toilets!"

"Guess we'll see, but in happier news, I think I might be on to something with the—"

Grimaldi groaned melodramatically.

"I'll tell you about it later," Luis said.

"Briefing tomorrow A.M., don't be late!" Grimaldi shouted as Luis was walking out.

In the lobby on an end-table was Luis's magnetic field camera. He had hastily plugged it in when he ran into the meeting. Now it was charged and Luis pulled it excitedly from its charger. He powered it up and flipped to the picture from Emswhiller Canyon. He was certain he would find confirmation there—Principal Malcolm's magnetic signature would undoubtedly be bright white, proving he was afflicted with whatever mind expanding, mind destroying condition killed Skylar Bloomquist.

This was not the case.

The picture showed the canyon wall criss-crossed by magnetic tubes as anticipated. Dennis Malcolm, however, appeared as a dull outline like any human would.

There went Luis's proof that the school was being hit, across the board, by something emanating from that industrial zone.

Luis was out of ideas.

Until he looked closer at the screen. What looked at first like a spot of dirt on the screen was part of the image. It was a dim gray splotch, similar to what had appeared on Grimaldi's big image next to whatever the Krex were hiding in the distant desert.

* * * *

Luis was back down in Emswhiller Canyon. He felt nervous. He knew better than anyone that surprising things happened at night on Rygiat, even in the most familiar areas.

He was also concerned about security robots. He had his badge with him, of course, but no dispensation from Grimaldi to poke around here after hours. He doubted he would be vaporized by a robotic guard, but he might find life difficult when he got back to the office if one busted him, so he moved quickly.

Luis stood thirty feet away from the wall of the canyon with his back to the entrance of Farmer High School. He snapped a magnetic field picture. Reviewing the still image, he saw the characteristic tubes of force lighting up to correspond with where the sand rose on the wall. The gray he hoped to see about five feet up the wall was, however, absent.

He scratched his head. Then he held the camera up and rapidly tapped the button, snapping a series of pictures. He flipped through the resulting images. He saw the movement of the magnetic fields as expected; some tubes leaping around from picture to picture, others remaining static, others disappearing completely. About 20 photos in, there was the gray spot.

"Thought so," Luis said. "Hiding on me, are you?"

Luis walked over to roughly where the gray spot appeared in the one image.

He stood there, threw his arms around, jumped up and down.

Nothing.

"*Gah!*" he shouted. Suddenly, for a fraction of a moment he was surrounded by a swarm of glowing white cubes. He looked down at his forearm.

"*GAH!*" He screamed even louder. "Bastard!"

He slapped his forearm and darted out of the vicinity of the cloud, then peeked under the hand still gripping his forearm.

There was a smashed mosquito-like insect under it.

"Insect-borne," Luis said. "Whatever it is, it's insect-borne."

He walked calmly back to the pod and got in. As it levitated off, he felt suddenly uneasy. There was something bothering him that he could not put his finger on. Until he sat bolt upright and said:

"Dammit! It bit me! I've probably got it! *Dammit!*"

* * * *

Luis tossed and turned and panicked all night until finally, briefly falling asleep around 4 a.m. At 5 a.m. his phone started ringing.

"Grimaldi?" Luis said, answering. "Can't imagine I missed the meeting already—"

"They're gone!" shouted Grimaldi's voice. *"We're screwed!"*

"Who's gone?"

"There's not a Krex anywhere in sight in shared territory," Grimaldi said.

"They're probably all at the same holiday party, no?" Luis said.

"Wherever they are, they made all the pods stop running! No one can get anywhere!"

"I guess that's 'punitive.'," Luis said. "So is the meeting rescheduled or—"

"This ain't the worst of it, Luis."

Luis sat up, figuring that whatever was coming would prevent him from getting back to bed.

"Gimme the worst of it, Jack," Luis said, annoyed.

"Is the name Sheila Brentworth familiar?"

"Yeah, but I can't place it."

"Office admin over at Farmer Elementary School. She's in isolation at the Bureau. Picked her up last night. She's exhibiting similar symptoms as Bloomquist, intermittently. Light-up eyes, fits of rage, then back to—odd behavior."

"I believe I met the woman in question," Luis said. "Odd like how?"

"She's currently explaining the finer points of Xenophon's *Anabasis* to the observation team through the one-way mirror."

"A love for the classics isn't so odd," Luis said.

"She's speaking Ancient Greek," Grimaldi said. "I'm going to be washing dishes in the Earth cafeteria if we don't get this figured out. And Christ—if the kids got it—"

"They exhibiting any symptoms?"

"Mine? Thank God, no. They're so fixated on that Krex toy they jump around on, though, it's hard to pry them away to ask them. I can't even figure out how the thing works!"

"At least they're distracted. Hang tight, Grimaldi. Practice your Ancient Greek and don't worry—I've finally got a lead we might be in good shape with."

"How are you going to check it out with no pods in operation?"

"I'm going for a walk," Luis said.

* * * *

It seemed like a blessing in disguise to Luis. That is, if his assumptions were good ones.

Thinking about the term "universal displacement," it struck him as probable that wherever the Krex usually were, they would not be there today. So it just might be the safest time to stroll through Krex territory. And if "outside laborers" were commuter pod pilots and other Krex working in shared territories, they all had the day off thanks to Grimaldi's big mouth. There would be no surveying from above to worry about without Krex-piloted pods in the air.

And he wondered, with a chill running down his spine, if these long-shot deductions were his own, or resulted from that insect bite.

Luis had been walking for a few hours when the human aspects of the architecture gave way to the spatial oddity of pure Krex territory. The Lenzini Report only partially prepared him for what he saw.

The landscape was dotted with 50 foot high pillars of magnetized sand. Unlike the waves of spiky geometric configurations that blew through the sand on the ground, these pillars bore locked, un-moving clusters of spikes hundreds of times larger. The spike clusters were more intricate, too, and contained an unbelievable range of colors that made them look almost pixelated. They were affixed to the pillars in rings and other configurations, some which seemed at odds with fundamental principles of physics. Though as Luis walked by them, he mentally ran the numbers—Fibonacci, fractals, Fuller, all came together in a way that made sense on a higher perceptual tier than their apparent impossibility.

These were thoughts not quite his own.

He shut them down as if steering his thoughts from an unpleasant hallucination.

He continued to walk.

When he reached a Krex village, one he suspected—from satellite photos—marked the entry to the foothills, he sat down in the swirling, spiking sand and breathed a sigh of relief. The inhabitants of this neighborhood were definitely elsewhere.

The Krex dwellings described by Lenzini, those pure black artifices—some giant bulbs, some massive rectangles—were not there. Or at least, not exactly. It seemed to Luis that they were represented by the black puddles, some circular, some square, that dotted the landscape. When Krex weren't home, their houses apparently melted, fluidly flat. Luis passed other elements he expected from reading Lenzini as well, all currently inert.

His climb up the foothills was difficult but uneventful; the paths were not made for human feet but were not hostile to them. With only a few close calls he made it into the mountains and reached the top of a long flat crag overlooking a valley.

That valley was the source of the giant white magnetic spot on Grimaldi's satellite photo. Yet he saw nothing out of the ordinary.

He walked to the end of the cliff, approximately where the gray spot had been on that photo.

He waved his hands.

A swarm blinked into existence around him.

Thousands of flickering white cubes, each about one cubic inch, each encapsulating a mosquito, surrounded him. He swatted and flailed blindly. His eyes blinked open and, through the swarm, he saw Farmer High School facing him. He blinked again and it was gone. The cloud, though, remained. Scrubbing and slapping at the insects landing on him, he hunched over to try to cover up exposed flesh. He stumbled back and felt his foot half-miss the edge of the cliff. He tried to correct and catch himself, but he was falling.

* * * *

Luis's stomach dropped. He heard the dreamlike echo of his shriek in his own ears. He was tense, braced for an impact he could not survive.

Then he struck something soft. A puff of dust went up around him.

He lay in the fetal position, shivering and moaning.

He opened his eyes and looked around. He was on an outcropping of the cliff hidden from view above, in a nest of some sort. He patted the substance he was sitting on. It felt fibrous. He stood up and found his footing, took a few steps away from the edge, and found that the nest extended into the cliffside.

Then suddenly the nest was collapsing under his weight. He fell and scampered and clawed at the unraveling threads, but the whole thing was sliding in his direction as he pulled on it. He was briefly relieved that his feet touched ground below the nest. It was built over a steep hill inside the hollow cliff. Luis was quickly rolling out of control down the hill.

After a minute, he stopped. Covered in dirt and stone, he got up, brushed himself off and glanced back up to the light emanating from where he came. He waited for signs of an additional collapse. There were only a few residual pebbles continuing after him, then quiet.

Luis was in a huge stone cave, its surfaces all gray, impenetrable, and absent the swirling magnetized sand that characterized Rygiat's outside landscape. He took a breath.

There was a monstrous shrieking sound. He spun to meet it. From a 15-foot-tall opening at opposite end of the cave from where he stood, the source of the sound emerged.

The insect was the size of three or four train cars, with a gelatinous grub-like body. It had thousands or hundreds of thousands of tiny feet running down either ventral edge and could move relatively quickly. It had the two giant black eyes and long black nose of an acorn weevil, though its nose was floppy like a rooster's waddle. A swarm of the white cube-encased mosquitoes, 10 times as large as what Luis had seen so far, swirled around the insect. As it moved closer, Luis observed that a moving blanket of the insects crawled around on the giant thing's body. It was as if it were a home base, or a mother to them.

The thing approached Luis, paused, and stared at him.

Around its face, Luis saw rainbow halos. *Alnalah-nee-nahnahnah*, the thing said into his mind.

Luis stumbled back.

Lemnah-gah-nahnah? It asked.

Its bizarre resonance filled Luis with nausea.

He recognized what he was facing. This was madness. This was intelligence without intelligence.

Something had expanded the neurological capabilities of this creature. But with no native intellect it delivered only psychic gobbledygook, entering his mind with unnerving parodies of language.

Suddenly Luis remembered that he, too, had been bitten. Like this creature and like Skylar Bloomquist. And a moment ago he had been bitten countless more times.

Realizing it made it hit him all at once.

An explosion of words as light. A brilliant dance of information. His senses swam with the satisfaction of a million correct answers per second. All the answers sang to him.

He saw each insect floating in its flashing cube as part of a statistical system. He saw each tiny, microscopic wing fluctuation, each movement of each segmented leg, determined by a cascade of collapsing wave functions in constant interaction with a particle world underpinning reality. He saw each infinitesimal fraction of a second as its own snapshot, and recognized the differences between each. Comparing them, one after another, he realized that there was a deviation from the randomness in the insects' movements as they crawled on and flew around their parent. They were hanging back toward the tunnel where they had emerged from. There was something there.

And they were, for some reason, avoiding a tunnel, slightly closer, on the opposite wall from where they emerged.

Luis deduced the second tunnel was a source of safety.

He moved to the right. The insect mother shuffled to stay in front of him, and a thick tongue emerged from an orifice under its hanging proboscis. The tongue swept towards Luis's foot. He stumbled back, looking desperately for a way around the thing.

Nehgahlanahnuhnah? The insect mother said into his mind. Then it hissed.

Luis picked up a heavy rock with both hands and threw it.

The rock landed a few feet behind the insect mother's head, sunk into the white glob of its body and disappeared. It hissed louder. Its hiss was paralleled by a shriek into Luis's mind which dropped him to one knee. He struggled against it, got up and ran left.

The angered insect mother closed the remaining distance, then began rearing back and striking. The thing babbled in his mind at a fever pitch. He threw himself on the ground and covered his head. He felt the thing hurtle toward him.

Then Luis was on the other side of the room.

He had warped.

Just as those insects somehow found their way between the clifftop and the entrance to Farmer High School.

Just as the Krex vehicles moved.

Just as the Krex themselves did.

The insect mother turned itself around and locked its big weird eyes on him.

Standing there, Luis felt a soft, distant wind blowing into the cave. He perceived its difference from the wind from the cliffside opening he fell from. He looked at the rock faces around him and the infinitesimal marks of Aeolian erosion cut into them, and calculated the hypothetical configurations of other rock faces, farther off in the cave, that the wind would have to reflect off of to hit him, in this chamber, at that angle. It meant there was an exit; a human-sized fissure, a few miles down.

This degree of observation is what he would be leaving behind.

Luis did not want to give it up.

The knowledge coursing through him was pure exhilaration. The superhuman degree of deduction he now experienced dwarfed his cleverest observations by universes of magnitude. A new understanding of physical motion was within his grasp. It would inspire a paradigm shift not just knowledge of Rygiat but in physics on Earth. If only he could somehow preserve it. Survive with it.

The insect mother interrupted his thoughts with the rage it spit into its mind. It charged him. Train-sized, but skittering forward like a millipede across bathroom tile. Flanked by the cloud of impossibly numerous white blocks.

Luis counted. *Three. Two—*

He stepped backwards into the tunnel and jumped to the left.

The rocks of this particular tunnel emitted an incredibly strong, acute magnetic charge. By entering it, Luis degaussed himself. The magnetic force causing data to run rampant in his brain was scrambled and rendered inert.

He hit the ground. It winded him, but the loss of that preternatural knowledge hit him harder.

The insect mother—with too much momentum to correct course—screamed into the tunnel after him. Its mental shrieking dissipated immediately. The swarm of cubes, tied by pheromone and instinct, followed right after. The cubes blinked out of existence and the insect mother flailed, stretching out and writhing and bellowing and flipping. Then it was withering, shrinking, its bellow diminishing to a chirp.

Soon it was the size of a large man's arm. It walked around in a few circles, looked at where Luis was lying and barked, hoarsely:

Sneh!

Then skittered off down the tunnel. The swarm of black Rygian mosquitoes filtered out after it.

Luis passed out.

When he woke up he was slightly nauseated, still reeling from the loss of intellect. He pulled himself together and walked out of the degaussing tunnel into the main chamber. He made his way to the other tunnel, from which the insect mother had come.

He walked down it for a long time, finally reaching a chamber taken up by an abandoned insect nest. It was filled with pillows of maggot silk deposited by the insect mother. Some were soiled with incredibly sticky puddles, the origin of which Luis tried not to speculate about.

He walked around the nest until he reached the far wall. There was a nexus of cracks running down the stone there. Where the cracks met, up near the ceiling, there was a gap where a triangular chunk of rock had broken off.

Luis piled the least disgusting pillows he could find next to the wall, picked up the chunk of rock, and climbed awkwardly up the soft pile. The convergence of the cracks connected to some sort of defect, vein, or tunnel in the stone wall, which went straight through to another, clearly visible chamber of the cave.

Luis looked through. There they were.

Luis was looking into the underground chamber beneath the valley. The highly magnetized blotch on Grimaldi's photo. In the chamber, thousands of Krex milled about, engaging in strange genuflections. Luis imagined countless chambers like this filling the underground space beyond where he could see, with an entire planet's worth of Krex performing identical rituals as these ones. At the center of the room was a pool.

The pool was a blinding bright white, but flickered occasionally with shocks of color like a pressed LCD screen. Every once in a while, a Krex near the pool would perform a ritualistic set of movements and immerse itself. Luis watched the one nearest the edge do it. The Krex appeared to dissipate into the pool. A minute later, something that looked like a white boulder bubbled up on that same side of the pool. It somehow rolled itself up onto the poolside. Luis realized it was a maddeningly complex knot.

The knot then began to untie and unravel itself. It fell into 20 or 30, nine foot-long rope-like structures.

The nearest Krex approached it and did another series of odd movements. The ropes floated up in the air and began disappearing and reappearing, appeared bigger then smaller, horizontal then vertical, all while weaving into one another. Finally a Krex stood there, created or re-created from the ropes.

Luis was unsure whether he just observed Krex birth, Krex rebirth, or a festival rite. He reasoned, though, that the pool contained the Krex's primordial ooze. The ultra data-dense magnetic fluid that constituted them. That their alien physiology locked together and embodied in a way that constituted consciousness.

He reasoned, too, that some common cave mosquitoes had made their way through this hole in the wall. They had sucked up that data fluid and were bringing it back to their mother. The Krex were unbothered by the situation. The mosquitoes, with their invisible transportation pipeline to Emswhiller Canyon, happened to bump into some beings new to the planet, for whom such a thing was more bothersome.

Luis took the fallen chunk of stone and wedged it over the hole. He tore off a piece of the maggot silk he was standing on, dipped it into one of the puddles slopped nearby and smeared the goop in the cracks between the replaced rock and the wall. It solidified quickly. He tossed the soaked silk away and jumped down from the pile.

Luis headed to the main chamber, then followed his quickly fading memory of the path to the exit—and fast. He had no idea when the Krex festival ended. He wanted to be home when it did. He had a long walk ahead of him.

* * * *

Luis, now on vacation, sat at the dinner table at the Grimaldi house.

Not only had Grimaldi not been sent to clean toilets, he got a promotion thanks to the Bureau's role in discovering the source and arresting the spread of a potentially world-ending affliction. On Grimaldi's orders, everyone adjacent to the Farmer School System was brought into the Bureau's offices and photographed with a magnetic field camera. A surprising number of teachers and faculty, some symptomatic and some not, displayed magnetic signatures consistent with getting a dose of primordial Krex data-muck via insect proboscis. Those who had it were shuttled to the Agriculture sector and placed in a degaussing grow room until their magnetic signatures read normal. Surprisingly, not a single child at the school had been impacted—something parents appreciated, though the lab could not make sense of it.

The lab also found that, once the Krex material was deactivated in a patient, there were minimal persistent neurological changes, even to those far along with the condition. Brain cells that reproduced under the influence of the exogenous Krex fluid were instantaneously reabsorbed when the substance was inactivated.

It meant a return to normal. But one Luis sort of lamented. He had felt the intoxication and seen the advantages of extreme intelligence. It would have killed him. But it seemed there could be so much potential for humankind to better understand itself, and the universe, if its neural capabilities could be opened up to that degree—without reducing the brain to a cinder.

Darla and Clarence, Grimaldi's 10-year-old daughter and 8-year-old son, sat two seats down from Luis, across from one another. Darla snapped her gum at her brother obnoxiously. Clarence got halfway up on the table to take a swipe at her.

"Clarence!" yelled Elaina Grimaldi from across the kitchen. "Sit down! We have a guest!"

The two looked at Luis, looked at each

other, and theatrically scooted their seats in and sat up straight.

"I hear you kids got two extra weeks off," Luis said. "You have big plans this summer?"

"Is it true a giant bug almost ate you?" replied Clarence.

"Yes, that's true," Luis said.

"Was it cool?"

"You ever get so scared you crap your pants?" Luis said.

"He craps his pants every day," Darla chimed in.

"Shut *up!*" announced Clarence and was halfway up out of his seat again.

"I told El' there's no need for her to cook when I'm grilling sausages," said Grimaldi, entering the room. "But she went ahead and made burgers in the oven."

Grimaldi placed a plate of inedibly burnt sausages on the table, opened a bag of buns and put a sausage in a bun.

"I think I'm in a burger mood today, actually!" said Luis, as Grimaldi was placing the bunned sausage on Luis's plate.

"Sausage it is," Luis said.

Midway through politely eating the scorched thing, something sprung to mind. Luis said:

"You ever ride a skateboard, Grimaldi?"

"Had one," Grimaldi said. "My sister used to push me down the hill on it. Rolled into a ditch and that was enough for me."

"I was *into* it," Luis said. "Dyed-in-the-wool skater between ages 10 and 20. I'm not particularly athletic, but I got OK. I could ollie a decent four-set, kickflip, heelflip, couple other—"

He recognized Grimaldi checking out of the conversation.

"—Anyway, when I was 16 I was boardsliding a parking block outside the grocery store. A guy in his early-40s comes up and says hey, how do you make that stick to your feet? Is there glue or something?"

The two kids were now listening.

"I explained grip tape and the physics of it, and he asks if he can try. I say sure. I'm

watching him. He slowly, carefully steps onto it, and then the moment he puts his weight on it—"

"—*BOOM!*" Luis shouted, miming an explosion.

The kids both jumped.

"It exploded," Luis said.

"Really?" asked Clarence.

"No," Luis said and snorted. "But the guy came close to a severe injury. He lost his balance and was on one foot and flapping his arms. It was like a cartoon of someone slipping where he has 10 arms and 10 legs all flying around. I grabbed the guy to steady him and he stepped off. Looked halfway between embarrassed and terrified. He said, guess I learned my lesson! His wife comes out from the store and as I skate off, I hear her yelling at him, asking if he's trying to break his neck."

"That's why Jack sticks to cooking," Elaina said, arriving with the burgers.

Grimaldi looked up from the sausage he was now eating, shrugged, and went back to it.

"The point is, there are some things kids are just better at than adults," Luis said. "Maybe that's why none of the kids got sick."

"They're better at avoiding mosquitoes?" Grimaldi said.

"These two might keep them away through annoyance," Elaina said. She rolled her eyes at the game the kids had just lapsed into and said severely:

"No video games if it doesn't stop this second!"

Darla had stuffed her mouth full of more chewing gum and was chomping and snapping it at Clarence, while he threw pieces of bun at her, trying to get one in her gum-filled mouth. They stopped at their mother's warning.

"Maybe they're more malleable," Luis continued. "Maybe kids *did* get infected, but to them it was no big deal. Maybe their minds stretched out to meet the challenge of extra neurons in a way adult brains can't handle."

"That's a little far out," Grimaldi said. "We checked every human, adult or child, who came near those schools during a month-long window. If it affected kids, it would have shown up."

"Fair enough," Luis said.

Grimaldi had gotten up and was taking plates to the sink, and Elaina got up as well, leaving just Luis, Darla, and Clarence at the table. Luis mused quietly, half-to himself:

"Unless the kids somehow figured out how to defraud the magnetic field camera."

He shrugged, stood up, and carried his plate to the sink.

Darla, still chomping on gum, gave her younger brother a funny look.

Clarence raised his eyebrows as if to say, *what*?

Darla looked from side to side to confirm no one was watching. She stretched the gum in her mouth into a long strand.

Then she whipped the stretched out gum around itself impossibly fast, into a complicated knot. She tossed it onto the plate still sitting in front of Clarence.

Clarence scrutinized it, started laughing, and said:

"I agree!"

ABOUT THE AUTHOR

M. Stern is an author of speculative fiction and weird horror whose work has appeared previously in *Startling Stories*, as well as in other magazines including *Weirdbook*, *Cosmic Horror Monthly*, and *Lovecraftiana: The Magazine of Eldritch Horror*, and in the themed horror anthologies *Funny As a Heart Attack* and *Strangely Funny VIII*. For the latest news on what weird, wild stuff he has going on, on this planet and beyond, visitmsternauthor.com and follow on Facebook atfacebook.com/msternauthor

ABOUT THE ARTIST

The incredible artwork for M. Stern's story is by none other than the masterful Vincent Di Fate. For more than four decades, Di Fate has been regarded as one of the world's leading artistic visionaries of the future. *People Magazine* said that he is "one of the top illustrators of science fiction... Di Fate is not all hard-edge and airbrush slickness. His works are always paintings—a bit of his brushwork shows—and they are all the better because of it." And *Omni Magazine* observed that "... moody and powerful, the paintings of Vincent Di Fate depict mechanical marvels and far frontiers of a future technocracy built on complicated machinery and human resourcefulness. Di Fate...is something of a grand old man in the highly specialized field of technological space art." We are privileged to have him for *Startling Stories*!

RISING FROM THE DEVIL'S PLANET

by **Adrian Cole**

Crippled, its spine cracked and all but pulling apart, the huge military assault ship (MAS) *Ramrod* hung in space, turning infinitely slowly, a gigantic beetle drained of energy. The Terran Moon hovered high above it, several thousand miles across the black gulf of space, watching like a solitary, diluted eye. Closer to the ship was the Portal. This perfectly circular artificial vent in space, with an apparently steel circumference, was thirty miles across. It pulsed like a living organism. Through it could be seen a gray haze, an opening into a realm of mist and confusion. *Ramrod*, recently ejected from the Portal, seemed to be drawn back, inch by space inch, to the massive circle, like flotsam being sucked into a whirling pool.

On *Ramrod's* bridge her captain, Dan Venner, glared out at the spangled night, swearing under his breath. "Some choice," he growled. "Either we get dragged back into that hell, or we abandon ship and take our chances with the lifeboats. Out here, we won't last. We'd simply be pulled back in as well. Only a matter of time."

"We've sent out another distress signal," said Croon, his first mate.

"There's nothing remotely close to us. You heard them on Earth Orbiter. Not a single ship docked. They're all out on tour. By the time anyone gets here, we'll be gone." He flicked a switch and contacted the engine room. "Give me something, Karl. Some glimmer of hope."

"I'm sorry, chief. The entire system is blown. Meltdown. We can launch a handful of lifeboats from the nose, but that's it."

Venner growled a fresh obscenity. He stared anew at the pulsing gate, its mocking ambiguity, the promise of more destruction to come. Why hadn't those things come through to finish this? Or did they know the bloody work was over?

"Sir, there's a message from comms,"

said Croon. "I'll patch them in."

Venner turned his attention to the line of lights on the communications panel. Somewhere down in the hub of the ship, his surviving men were still active. "Captain. We have an incoming message. It's an old frequency. Not registered."

Venner and Croon exchanged astonished glances. There would be no official presence in this sector of space. "Let's hear it," said Venner.

"Calling *Ramrod*. Are you receiving? Acknowledge."

Venner pressed various buttons, allowing him to transmit directly to the incoming caller. "This is Earth Communal MAS *Ramrod*. Captain Daniel Venner in command. Identify yourself, please."

"I gather you're in trouble, captain. What's the problem?"

"Identify yourself, please."

There was a pause. "We're prepared to be friendly, if that's what's bothering you. By the sound of your call, you need help."

Venner turned to Croon, his junior by several years, but a man who, like him, had a whole lot of experience out here in space, a hardened fighting man. "Who the hell are they?" said Venner, muting the channel.

"I'd say someone who doesn't operate under normal space law. Not registered. Trouble."

"Pirates?"

"Likely."

"Space punks!" Venner snorted. "The last damn thing we need."

"May be the only way out of this mess, Dan." Croon had been with his captain for a long time. He knew him for a direct, no-nonsense operator, a strictly by the book man. Croon was probably the only one in the fleet who could sometimes moderate him.

Venner nodded slowly. "Two years ago we were burning them out of the sky. Scattered them all to hell. They don't owe us any favours."

"Not many of them left, these days. It's a tough life."

"Yeah, my heart bleeds for the bastards—"

"Maybe they've had enough. Maybe they want to come in out of the space cold. If they get us out of this jam, perhaps we could negotiate a pardon for them." Croon knew how much his captain hated the renegades and just how far he'd gone in his efforts to wipe them out.

"Hell, you'd trust them, Mike?"

"Probably not, but what choice do we have?"

Venner swore again, but switched back to the open channel. "This is *Ramrod*." He gave his coordinates and waited.

"Thank you, Captain Venner. We'll be with you as soon as possible."

"There's on open Portal close to us," said Venner. "Steer well clear of it. That's absolutely imperative, you hear me? Come in from star-side. Is that clear?"

"Is the Portal damaged?"

"Possibly. I'll give you the details when you get here."

"On our way, captain." The line closed.

"Space punks," Venner murmured. "It would be."

Croon said nothing. This was not looking good.

* * * *

It took the incoming craft under a day, ship's time, to reach the vicinity of *Ramrod*. The unidentified craft was visible on *Ramrod's* surveillance screens, a surprisingly battered hulk, veteran probably of a score of skirmishes with the law, typical of the renegades who operated without licence in and beyond the trading lanes.

"What the hell kind of ship is that?" said Venner.

Croon grinned. "Something from a museum. Looks like space junk, which is a pretty good disguise. It'll have souped-up fire-power, though. I guess its engines won't be the originals. Wouldn't outrun us under normal circumstances, but faster than you'd expect."

The communication channel opened again, although there were deliberately no visuals transmitted.

"Ahoy, *Ramrod*. This is captain Kozakis. Permission to board you with two of my ship's officers. We're unarmed."

"And every gun on his ship trained on us," grunted Venner.

Croon nodded. "He's holding all the aces."

"Permission granted, captain." Venner almost spat the words.

Soon after Kozakis and his crewmen had entered *Ramrod*, they joined Venner and Croon on the command deck. The pirates—there was no question about what they were—wore a kind of uniform, surprisingly tidy, their manner slightly insouciant, their expressions cool, almost disinterested. Only their leader, a young man almost Croon's age, spoke.

"The visual damage to your ship is excessive," said Kozakis. "Would I be right in thinking you're crippled beyond repair?"

"We are," said Venner. He knew he couldn't disguise the truth.

Croon could feel the fury burning off his captain in waves, and watching Kozakis's calm face, guessed there was a mutual hatred brewing there, too.

"What happened?" said the pirate.

"That's classified information."

Kozakis looked up at the large screen dominating the bridge. It gave a perfect view of the Portal and its unfathomable haze.

"You came through that," said Kozakis.

Venner nodded, exchanging a brief glance with Croon.

Kozakis remained impassive. "You want me to evacuate your crew and get you back to Earth Orbiter, is that the plan?"

Venner studied the pirate's face. *I'm too old for heroics*, he thought. *I've had a good run. No chest full of medals, brushes with glory. Just years and years of good solid service. No hall of fame for me. The pirate has something—we should cut our losses and go home. Maybe.*

Kozakis's suspicions were easily read. "So what's on the other side? What smashed your ship up, captain?"

"I told you, that's classified."

Kozakis was about to take issue, when the face of the Portal on the screen shimmered, like the surface of a lake blown by a sudden gust of wind. The rippling effect increased, watched by the men on the bridge in silence, all of them tensed, held on the edge of panic. Something broke from the centre of the Portal, a long, green-black tendril as large as a spaceship, snaking out and writhing, steam pouring from it as though it had been immersed in liquid oxygen. Venner and the men with him felt *Ramrod* shudder, recognising the effects of her weaponry—what was left of it—being discharged uniformly. They watched searing beams of white light knife across the void, striking the huge tendril, exploding off its wriggling surface.

"You were expecting that!" Kozakis said as they steadied themselves in the aftershocks.

"I've had my weapons trained on the Portal since we left it," Venner said.

"Is that what you're running from? That thing wrecked you?"

Venner nodded. "There were three of us."

"*Three* military assault ships?" said Kozakis. He gaped at the monstrous, writhing tendril, relieved to see it withdrawing back into the Portal, where the grey mist closed in over it once more. It had left a cloud of shredded flesh behind it, burning and drifting into oblivion.

"The others are on the far side," said Venner. "For all I know, torn apart. There's been no communication for three days."

Kozakis shook his head. "What is it? And don't tell me it's classified, captain. If you want help, you're going to have to explain a few things. Mainly, why shouldn't I just take my ship and get the hell out of here?"

"You do that, Kozakis and it'll just be the beginning of the nightmare."

* * * *

Venner arranged food and they sat around a table. They could still look up at the Portal, now silent and grey once more, all of them half expecting it to burst into sudden, hideous life.

"We were on the other side. A new Quadrant to patrol and explore," said Venner. "That Portal is a recent one. It opens onto an area of space far beyond our own galaxy. There were a lot of objections to opening it so close to Earth, but Portal technology is very advanced and the Commanders knew best. I was sent through with two other vessels and we found a planet nearby that initially showed signs of life. Signs of life! Hah, that's only the half of it. The planet is teeming, but what's down there is nothing like anything we've ever come across before.

"Our initial surveys, from orbit, showed the surface was an equal mix of ocean and land, almost the whole of the land masses completely covered in biological growth of some kind, far too complex to analyse or even summarise quickly. One of my crew described it as a mad jungle, a nightmare of plant life gone berserk, although the vegetation is nothing like what you'd find on Earth, or even Earth-type planets. For one thing, it's vibrantly alive. It's constantly moving— *seething*. There was nowhere to land safely, other than maybe the polar caps, but we detected marine life there, too. So we made do with orbital surveys. My men call it the Devil's Planet.

"Whatever the hell is down there, it *knew* we were above it, I swear. Then the trouble began. We spotted the spores—if that's what they were—released from tendrils that must have reached a mile or more into the atmosphere. (The air is like any jungle air on Earth, same mix of elements.) The spores— or floating mushrooms as we called them, rose up in clouds—if you've ever seen jellyfish back in the Earth seas, that's what it was like. Didn't take much to figure they were heading directly for our orbit paths.

"Our leading ship, *Rigel*, was first to be hit. The mushroom-things, themselves the size of small airships, floated up to the assault ship and swarmed around it, closing with it and wrapping themselves round it. We watched *Rigel* blast away at them, to some effect, but the sheer numbers had it beat, like a virus. The lack of atmosphere made no difference to those things. We sent our second ship, *Kyros*, in to attack, and it scorched off a host of the mushroom-things, and managed to free *Rigel* so that all three of us pulled back, out of orbit.

"Something else was stirring down on the planet, some vast life form we couldn't monitor clearly. It was cloaked by an aerial host of the smaller creatures. Imagine the biggest hornet's nest you've ever seen, and then the queen, only she's bigger than any normal queen! We knew what was coming. That thing meant to tear us all apart. There was something else—weirdest damn thing. Like our *thoughts* were being invaded. Maybe these creatures had telepathic powers. Nothing you could put your finger on, but your worst nightmares were never as bad as this.

"All we could do was high-tail it back to the Portal—and shut it, sealing it. Whatever that place is, it has to be prevented from releasing its powers into our system."

Kozakis studied Venner's face. The military captain, clearly a grizzled, hard-bitten campaigner, was visibly shaken, the sweat beading at his temples. He wasn't making this up, and he didn't like describing this monstrous realm.

"We'd underestimated those things," Venner went on. "They crossed space faster than we could have expected. Like I said, they look like vegetables, but they're a damn site more than that. They caught up with us close to the Portal. We had no time to get into the formation required to begin the sealing process. Once it's completed, you just about have enough time to get back through the Portal before it closes and winks out of existence. There was a battle, the craziest battle you ever saw, as we used everything we had to hit those bastards. We blew them apart on all sides, but they kept on coming, until they brought up something bigger, like a battle-ship of their own—this huge creature?—God knows. It was like a biological aerial submarine, long and thin, but with flesh-like appendages, fins and a front end packed with long tendrils that snaked out and tore into the metal of both *Rigel* and *Kyros*.

"We were like three huge sharks being stripped alive by a giant squid. If that sounds insane—well, that's how it was. You saw that tentacle, or whatever it was, reaching through the Portal earlier. Well, it did for the other ships. If anyone's left alive on them, I'd be amazed. We were badly hurt—our spine is snapped. You've seen the shape we're in. At least we got through the Portal, back to Earth side."

Kozakis studied the Portal again. "What do you think those things intend? Have they gone back to the planet?"

Venner stared at the opening and the shifting greyness. "Who knows? What I do know is this—we have to close that Portal."

Kozakis scowled. "How do you intend to do that, captain?"

Venner studied the three pirates, but they gave little hint of any emotion. "What do you want out of this?"

Kozakis grinned. "Well, we've spent most of our lives ducking and diving out in the remoter spaceways. We don't have a lot to show for it. Most of it's tied up in that old space bucket of ours out there. Right now, though, that's all *you* have, captain. This ship of yours has had it. We'll take you and your survivors back to Earth Orbiter. In ex-change for that, we want to be settled down on Earth, with our own plot of land where we can see our families safe. No strings at-tached. Pardons, as it were."

Venner nodded slowly. "I could arrange that. But I need a bit more."

"Don't get any crazy ideas about my ship trying to extract some kind of revenge, cap-tain. If three military assault craft couldn't hold off those things beyond the Portal, my old tub sure as hell won't. We can make a swift exit, but that's about it."

"That's fine. I don't want your fire power. I need to seal the Portal. To do that I have to get *Ramrod* back through it and synchro-nise it with the two disabled ships. Once I've done that, I can initiate the shut-down of the Portal. You'll have time to exit before she closes."

"Provided those things don't snare us and rip us up."

"There's a risk, sure. But if we don't do this, and those things come through, espe-cially the big mother that was waking up planet-side, we'll be star dust. Earth Orbiter will be next, and after that, who knows? You want land on Mother Earth? If we get this wrong, there may not even be a piece of her left."

* * * *

"How many of your people did you lose?" said Kozakis, accompanying Venner and Croon on an abbreviated tour of *Ramrod*.

Venner's features became even grimmer. "Each MAS has a crew of one hundred and nine crewmen. I have nine left."

Kozakis sucked in his breath. "Hell, cap-tain, how have you kept this ship running?"

"I have men in key posts, just about. The explosions put paid to the bulk of the ship. You must have seen it as you came in."

"Yeah, it's a mess. You've lost whole sec-tions of it. If we try and attach lines and drag you, we'll pull the last of you apart. How are we supposed to take you through?"

"You get behind us and you push us in. It'll be the end of *Ramrod*, but the vital sec-tions housing the main control banks will be okay." Venner kept his voice level, but inside his guts were churning. He'd run this ship for four years. Now he was going to see it turned to scrap.

They'd reached a steel doorway and Venner tested its various locks and thick cross-bolts. "This is the end of the stern of the ship. Everything beyond this door is ka-put. If you push us, you'll concertina up the rest of the ship, but it'll give you enough purchase to get us through. This door will hold."

Kozakis was about to respond, when Croon stared up at a monitor. Its pictures were hazy, gradually focusing. "What the hell is that?"

Venner swore. "That can't be right—"

"People?" said Kozakis. "Survivors?"

Croon punched a keyboard under the monitor and sounds immediately crackled around them. Human voices, but stretched, discordant. In the monitor, there were dozens of bodies packed together, faces raised to the hidden camera. If they had been human once, they were no longer.

"They can't be alive!" said Croon.

Venner was punching keys now, adjusting the view, closing up on the faces. As he did so, the three men drew back in sudden horror. Each head that came into focus was obscenely adjusted, a huge blob, trailing a mass of tendrils that writhed and twisted like long strands of weed caught in an ocean current. There were no eyes, just globular orbs, misted and liquid, and the mouths gaped like those of huge fish, revealing several layers of spiky teeth. The air around these monsters was filled with spores, floating in clouds, reminiscent of jellyfish.

"They're like smaller versions of the mushrooms we saw rising from the planet!" said Croon. "And they've infected the crew. They're not dead—they're *changed*."

"No," said Venner. "They're dead." He watched as a number of the pressing bodies clawed at the camera with long, hideously distended arms, each arm thick with massed spores, like branches of trees riddled with mushrooms. Venner switched off the camera.

"Can they get out?" said Kozakis.

"Into space, but not to this part of the ship," said Venner. "Hell knows if those things can live out in the void. We can't take any chances. We have to destroy every last one of them."

Croon began to protest.

"We have no choice!" snarled Venner, for once his apparent calmness on the point of deserting him. "Any contact with those things will mean disaster. Kozakis—prepare your ship. Get us through the Portal. And when you come out, burn anything that hasn't gone through. Scrub your ship clean. If you don't—you can see what will happen."

Kozakis looked up at the blank monitor, as though he could still see the nightmare shapes. And worse—hear their obscene ululations.

* * * *

Back on his own bridge, Kozakis watched the curved monitor and the sweep of immediate space its view afforded. His helmsman was bringing the snub-nosed pirate craft around slowly into position behind the mangled carcass and sprawled debris that *Ramrod* had become, readying for the thrust that would begin the process of shunting the MAS through the Portal into the unknown beyond.

Krake, his deputy, stood at his shoulder. "What happens if we lose them?"

"Oh, we'll lose them, make no mistake. None of them are coming back." Kozakis slipped a thin canister from inside his jacket. "Venner was hell-bent on getting our help. He gave me this report for his people back at Earth Orbiter, explaining what's going on and our part in it. They'll have to honour his commitment. Pardons for all of us and land down on Earth."

"So if *Ramrod* and the last of them get wiped out, we'll still be home free."

"That's right, buddy."

"And what about Venner? Is it him?"

"Oh, yes. It's him. I was sure of it, but now I've met him, I know it. He didn't know me. I'm just another Space Punk."

* * * *

"Anything?" Venner asked Harmann, the crewman he'd left on the bridge to watch the Portal. Its frothing greyness hadn't changed.

"No, sir. It's been static."

Venner turned to Croon. "Okay, we'll go for it. We'll just have to pray that thing has retreated back to the planet, or at least moved away from the Portal far enough to allow us through." He picked up the transmitter handset. "Kozakis? This is Venner. Go ahead. And if you see anything come through, even a single spore, burn it. I've got my own cannons directed straight ahead."

"Good luck, captain," came the terse reply.

Venner and Harmann felt *Ramrod* grinding at the impact of the pirate craft as it eased into the MAS. A handful of scanners showed pieces of metal shorn away from the main body of the ship, neatly picked off by the pirate cannon. Venner gritted his teeth. Nothing must survive on this side. Anything from *Ramrod* had to be atomised, cleansed of potential infection.

The Portal loomed, its immensity dwarfing the two ships as they edged closer to the passage through it. Venner had given orders to the last of his gunners to let fly at anything that moved within. He knew it wouldn't be the other two craft. The grey mass thinned and *Ramrod* was in. As the mists of the gate parted, the view beyond was one of total chaos. The two ships, *Rigel* and *Kyros*, could be seen, adrift from each other. Both ships were nothing more than a conglomeration of metal, burned and partially melted, spars hanging loose, a halo of torn fragments circling each of them, miniature satellites. Between them and around them floated clouds of the mushroom spores, hanging in space like a great armada of ocean-dwelling jellyfish, trailing long tendrils. Many of these had snared sections of the smashed ships, pulling them slowly to smaller pieces.

Behind and looming over them, the planet watched like a malignant, baleful eye, its multi-hued surface lit up by its neighbouring sun. There was, as yet, no sign of the huge creature that had attempted to go through the Portal.

"Get us in somewhere between the two ships," Venner told Kozakis. "It's essential I can set the coordinates for closing the Portal. Once I'm in place and begin the shut-down,

you can pull out. You'll have enough time to escape if you step lively."

"Complying," said Kozakis.

The pirate ship doubled its efforts to move *Ramrod*, now squeezed up into a congealed, metal mass, only the nose section unscathed. Behind it the crushed main body—and more specifically, the things it housed—were pulped, with no chance of anything surviving the massive pressure. If Venner felt any last compassion for his former crew, his face betrayed no sign of it. He was focused entirely on the task in hand.

He had Kozakis bring *Ramrod* to a halt, midway between the two other ships.

"Before you leave us," he told Kozakis, "I need to get into those two ships."

"You're kidding, captain. That's a suicide mission. Those things out there will pick you off."

"I have to align the system and I have to do it from their control decks. I need you to cover me while I get a party across."

There was a long pause before Kozakis replied. "Okay, but I'm not jeopardizing my ship. If she's threatened, I'll pull her back through the Portal, whether you close it or not."

Venner wasn't about to argue. "Harmann, you keep *Ramrod* steady here. Get ready to switch in to the closing procedure. Croon, you bring two others and come with me. We need to board what's left of *Rigel* and *Kyros*."

Harmann stiffened, knowing the others were not coming back from the Portal if they ventured in again. They'd risk everything to close it, and if they did achieve it, they'd be shut in here. They'd last as long as the air they'd brought. Harmann also knew the idea of Venner somehow getting down on to that hellish planet, where he could breathe, wouldn't enter the equation.

* * * *

Kozakis watched as the tiny craft, sleek as a missile, emerged from the belly of *Ramrod* and speared across the void between the space wrecks. Immediately a cloud of floating fungi shifted towards the small vessel, attracted to it like moths to a flame. Kozakis brought his weapons to bear on them, and had his gunners pick them off as swiftly as they could, vaporising them but without damaging Venner's craft. It arced over one of the wrecks and slid down into its twisted spars, lost to sight.

Harmann's voice came across the intercom from *Ramrod*. He, in turn, was linked to Venner. "They've entered the remains of *Rigel*."

Beyond the three wrecked ships, around the deep green curve of the planet, another shape emerged, like a leviathan swimming through ocean deeps. Kozakis watched it with growing revulsion. Shaped like a huge submarine, it trailed a mass of tendrils that writhed and twisted, propelling the creature forward. Its front end pulsed with long, thick tentacles, each of them half the thickness of Kozakis's craft. This was the monster that had attempted to push through the Portal.

Krake swore. "We have to get out—now. Venner's got no chance of getting away."

Kozakis waited, the huge alien getting larger as it approached.

"If Venner closes the Portal, we'll be shut in here!" said Krake.

"Okay, move us out."

Krake had the steersman take the ship away from the crumpled remains of *Ramrod*. There was an immediate cry of protest from the intercom as Harmann realised what was happening, but Kozakis flicked the switch off. He turned his attention to the Portal. It was now a question of whether or not he could get his ship back through before the alien caught up with him. Fresh clouds of the smaller creatures drifted in space around him, but his cannons kept up the merciless, sweeping fire that blistered and burned them in waves.

* * * *

Venner nodded to Croon. "It's done. *Rigel* is linked in."

They'd found the bridge of the smashed

ship and mercifully enough of it remained workable. Not a single survivor was visible, all either atomised, or worse—transformed into those floating, bulb-headed things. Venner linked in to the closure process and they quickly worked their way back through the mass of space junk to where they'd left the smaller craft, boarding it and replenishing their oxygen tanks. The pilot took them out from *Rigel's* corpse and set a course for the last of the ships. The needle ship was set upon immediately by small clouds of the floating horrors, but a repulsor field charred anything that touched the outer shell of the craft, buying them enough time to get across to the last MAS.

Through the curved window over the flight deck, however, they could see what was surging across space towards them, the huge alien creature that could enfold them in its vast, waving tentacles. The needle ship accelerated, past the collapsed debris of *Ramrod*, which Venner now saw had been abandoned by Kozakis.

"Harmann!" he bawled into the intercom.

"They've cut us loose," was the reply. "They're making a break for the Portal."

Venner swore, but prepared to disembark again as the needle ship dipped down into the remains of *Kyros*, like a fly entering a cadaver. He and Croon went out and got among the broken parts of the ship. They ducked through a maze of crushed metal, barely wide enough to let them through, the only consolation being it prevented the mushroom creatures from drifting in with them. When they got to the bridge, they saw it was in tatters, but one main console was still working. Venner activated it and grunted with relief when he saw the programme he wanted flash up on the cracked screen.

A huge shadow passed above them, almost plunging them into darkness. Venner ignored it, setting the last co-ordinates for the closure of the Portal. He punched them in, activating the programme and signalled Croon to lead the way back out.

They made the needle ship just ahead of a

fresh wave of the mushroom creatures.

"Where's Kozakis's ship?" Venner snarled.

"Halfway to the Portal," said Harmann. "Shall I finalise closure?"

Venner had a clear view of events outside as the needle ship made for *Ramrod* and a final docking. He saw Kozakis's ship receding. Overhead, the huge creature was following.

"Are you going to delay long enough to let Kozakis through?" said Croon.

Venner knew that they'd all perish if the Portal shut them in. "I can't let that goddam thing through to Earth side," he snapped. "No matter what it costs."

"They're only Space Punks, Dan" said Croon. "We've exterminated enough of them in the past. And they were quick enough to abandon us. It's tough if they get locked in."

Or are they leading that thing away from us. Is that what Kozakis is doing? Venner thought. *Is he trying to save us, in some crazy way? Or is it his precious freight he wants to save?*

"Sir, shall I finalise closure?" Harmann sounded slightly desperate.

"Do it!" said Venner.

* * * *

Kozakis's attention switched from the Portal, directly ahead, to the growing mass of the huge aerial monster behind him. It was closing fast, preparing to snatch the ship and rip it to shreds the way it had torn up the others.

"The Portal!" said Krake. He pointed to its metal rim, which had begun to glow with a brilliant blue light. It was revolving, the space encompassed by it shimmering like the troubled surface of a huge lake.

"It's starting to close," said Kozakis. "Venner's initiated the process." He looked at the creature following them. "Turn every weapon we've got on that thing and fire at will!"

The ship rocked as its entire arsenal released beam after beam of white-hot energy

at the creature, striking its mass of tendrils, ripping off gouts of flesh. It barely slowed, surging forward, as if it knew the ship would escape.

Venner's voice came across the intercom. "Kozakis! You have to stop that thing from going through. Do you understand?"

"You want me to sacrifice my ship and its entire crew, Captain Venner? We mean nothing to you, do we? We're disposable, is that it? What's one more pirate ship to you, who've blasted any number of other pirate vessels into oblivion?"

Kozakis felt his ship shudder under the second wave of multiple blasts as his gunners sought to stall the huge creature. Its first tentacles reached out and were very close to the ship's rear, bathed in the heat and light of its fat exhausts.

"My job was to clean up the space highways," said Venner angrily.

"We're not vermin, Captain Venner. You treated us like rats in a drain. Whole families wiped out, no quarter given. *My* family."

"Look, Kozakis, forget the past! That thing pursuing you will be a threat to every family back home. You want a new home on Earth—earn it! If you prevent it from getting through, my crew will be stranded here. We know that, but it's a price we are prepared to pay. Is that the difference between us?"

"What about my cargo, Captain? You think I'll sacrifice what I have?"

That's it, thought Venner. *All that matters to those dam Space Punks is saving their cargo and the hope of a killing on the trade exchanges. The bastards would die before they let that go.*

"You didn't tell him what the cargo really is," Krake said to Kozakis. "Our families. Five hundred of our people—"

Kozakis stared silently at the Portal.

Krake gripped Kozakis's arm. "That bastard's got a hold." He was pointing at the screen above. It showed the rear end of the ship, where several long tendrils had snagged the hull.

"Keep firing!" said Kozakis. He lurched

around and studied another screen, which showed how close they were to the Portal.

"We could swerve," said Krake. "Use our evasion tactics and rip loose of that thing. We'd come around, away from the Portal. Make another try for it."

Kozakis watched the blue light blurring around the Portal's rim. Already it was beginning to close, like the slow blink of a titanic eye. "There's no time."

"It isn't dragging us back," said Krake, puzzled. "It's got us snarled up in its tendrils like a fly in a web. But it isn't pulling us back."

"It's wounded! It wants us to drag it through!"

"Three minutes," said the helmsman.

Kozakis snatched up the ship's internal intercom, his words relayed to every part of the ship. "Get everyone away from the ship's rear end—fast!" He knew most of his crew would be amidships, and with any luck everyone would already be well away from the engine rooms at the stern of the ship where the immense struggle with the creature was taking place.

Krake looked at him anxiously. "You're taking us through? You realise—"

"One minute." The helmsman's voice was like the pronouncement of a sentence.

Kozakis ignored him, watching the Portal as its whirling circle drew tighter. The ship nosed into it, like dipping into a wall of water. As the seconds ticked away, Krake stood back, certain that this was over. They were out of time and there was no way back.

Suddenly the ship shook as though it had been tossed into a boiling ocean, rocking from side to side, tumbling its crew to the decks. A deafening sound reverberated inside their skulls, as though something had screamed, the sound of an impossible storm. Numbed, temporarily deafened, they struggled to their feet. Again the ship shuddered, flung forward at an incalculable speed. Behind it the Portal slammed shut,

its light disappearing as though it had never been, the space where it had revolved healed over completely, uniform with the rest of the darkness around it.

* * * *

Venner and his own men watched events on their screen, realising that Kozakis was hell-bent on affecting an escape, regardless of what happened to the creature.

"They can't shake that thing off," said Croon. "And they won't stay here."

Venner smiled grimly. "They're not going to make it. It's too damn tight. There are only seconds—"

He gasped as the pirate ship entered the Portal. As it did so, the circle closed, like a gigantic steel trap. It caught the creature across its spine, slicing right through it like a knife through butter. Blood and ichor spewed out from the massive incision in a thick cloud. Drifting out of this, the back half of the creature turned end-over-end, like a crippled spaceship, more blood and guts leaking out of it and forming a slow spiral. The pirate ship had gone through, with the fatally eviscerated front half of the creature.

"They made it," said Croon. "They saved their precious cargo. It must have been some haul."

They saw the last points of light die out where the Portal had been.

Venner nodded, understanding. What cargo was more precious to the space punks than the loot they'd pillaged along the spaceways?

ABOUT THE AUTHOR

Adrian Cole has had some two dozen novels and numerous shorts published, including ebooks and audiobooks, for nearly fifty years, writing sf, fantasy and horror. *Nick Nightmare Investigates* won the British Fantasy Society Award for the Best Collection (2015).

SPEAKING WITH JOHN SHIRLEY
conducted by Darrell Schweitzer

John Shirley sent me two of his recent books, which I did not have time to read before doing this interview before the *Startling Stories* deadline. One is a novel, *Stormland* (Black Stone Publishing, 2021). It is a science fiction novel, set in the flooded, mostly abandoned wasteland that climate change has made out of the American South. Then there is *The Voice of the Burning House* (Jackanapes Press, 2021), a handsomely illustrated collection of his impressive weird poetry. At the same time, I have been enjoying his *A Sorcerer of Atlantis* (Hippocampus Press, 2021) a sword & sorcery novel which bears favorable comparison to the work of Fritz Leiber and other masters of the form.

But John Shirley hardly needs an introduction to long-time readers of science fiction. He made a significant impact in such early works as *City Come A-Walkin'* (1980) and the *A Song Called Youth* series (1985-88). He also stirred things up in the horror field, beginning with *Dracula in Love* (1979) and *Cellars* ((1982). He has published (to date) 84 books, including 10 story collections, one of which is significantly entitled *In Extremis: The Most Extreme Stories of John Shirley* (2011). He is widely ranging, versatile writer, who has also written everything from westerns to song lyrics to a non-fiction book about Gurdjieff.

* * * *

Q: Your origin story, please. I don't think you arrived in a rocket from Krypton as a child, but you have been around for a long while. I as a reader associate your first stories with the late New Wave period and I remember you as a controversial columnist in *Thrust*.

Shirley: I actually arrived in a rocket from Yuggoth.… Though I was born in Hous-ton Texas, we moved fairly often and eventually I spent most of my childhood and teen years in the Willamette Valley, in Oregon. I always felt vaguely alienated…I was rambunctious as a small child, varying between noisy and glum; I was creative, telling stories early on, spurred to fantasies easily. I would tell the other kids about "a dream I had" which I was mostly making up so I could transfix them with a wild narrative. It was an early form of being a writer…I felt a vivid connection to nature—gazing for hours into the otherworldly microcosm of a small creek, with its frog eggs and forests of water plants. I asked questions about life and death before other kids did….

After seeing Elvis materialize like some kind of Hindu god on Ed Sullivan, I was enchanted and tried to sing "just like Elvis" in my piping little boy's voice… Rock'n'roll, even that early, stimulated me viscerally—glandularly. I was late to become reasonably coordinated, so quickly became an object of bullying. I made up tragic stories about my childhood, stuff that hadn't happened, to keep other kids from attacking me…When I was in a softball game, in grade school, I dutifully waited with my glove in the outfield. Once a ball was struck right toward me but what I saw was a white sphere, spinning my way in slow motion. It seemed like a portent. I stared in at it in absorption till it fell at my feet—to everyone's exasperation. That is somehow emblematic of me….

My father died when I was ten, of meningitis. This knocked me further off center… When I was 12, in a Junior High in Salem, we had a school newspaper which I declared to be mere pablum and I came out with a mimeographed newspaper and passed it out to the other kids. It sniped at the school so naturally it got me in trouble. I wrote about the Vietnam war in it too, because I'd seen, in *Life Magazine*, photos of dead civilians, including babies, massacred by American troops at My Lai. That affected me deeply. Once I saw that, I no longer put any trust in authority at all.... I was also fascinated by imagery about psychedelic drugs—they seemed like magic to me. In childhood and Junior High I read books on the occult—I'm a skeptic now.... In a DC comic book I saw an advertisement for albums by *The Mothers of Invention*. Frank Zappa! It was a semi-psychedelic summoning of other "freaks" into Zappa's snarky, arty version of the counter culture. It gave me hope that I was not alone in the world. In high school I sometimes used mescaline—the very drug that inspired Aldous Huxley's *The Doors of Perception*. I came out with another underground newspaper, in photo offset, and I wrote for the Highschool Independent Paper Syndicate, "HIPS"...

I was an inveterate troublemaker, organizing anarchistic marches of people singing nonsense songs in the school hallways, publishing underground newspapers, acting out in class. Brazenly displaying my "public display of affection" with my girlfriend. Walking out of school when I felt like it. As I was a science-fiction fan (though also reading beat poets, and Poe, and Baudelaire and writers like Emerson and Thoreau—I was into Transcendentalism), the school decided that science-fiction was a bad influence and, for a long time after I left, I'm told, discouraged the reading of it.... As for *Thrust* magazine, I spavined my career by going off on Harlan Ellison in my column (which was called *Pointless Hostility,* so what does one expect) and he came down on me like a ton of bricks and told people not to work with me. He succeeded in getting some people down on me, but not others. I shouldn't have published that piece...Anyway years later we buried the hatchet and ended up friends and once more, as at the Clarion Workshop (see below) he was my supporter....

Q: Okay, so I don't trust my own aging memory (I am 6 months older than you) and looked it up. You have a story in CLARION III, ed. Robin Scott Wilson, 1973. So you achieved something I did not. I was rejected from CLARION IV (though I sold the story elsewhere). What was your Clarion experience like? Were you the sort of writer they wished to encourage?

Shirley: In a post-psychedelic haze, trying to get myself together for my mom's sake, I went to Portland State University for a time, sometimes seeming like a bit of a prodigy, other times really quite out of it, though I was no longer getting high. I suppose I put together about three years of college. I'm now a pretty well-educated autodidact—and my education continues.

Around 1973 I got into the Clarion Writer's Workshop, the six-week course at the University of Washington in Seattle, for those who don't know. We had a different writing teacher every week, people like Ursula Le Guin, Robert Silverberg, Harlan Ellison, Terry Carr, Frank Herbert (who confirmed he'd taken psychedelic mushrooms and they had some influence on *Dune*).... I was there with Art Cover and Gus Hasford (the guy who wrote the book *Full Metal Jacket* is based on) and Vonda McIntyre and Lisa Tuttle and others. They were patient with me...had to be because I was a handful, I think. Rather just too prone to wild behavior and attention-seeking and one day during Clarion I DID take LSD and I DID jump out of a tree sort *on* Harlan Ellison while on acid and this DID annoy him. But then he decided I had potential as a writer and he encouraged me and wrote a letter to the Clarion Anthology editor encouraging him to buy a story from me. So my first paid professional publication came from my messy but prolific attendance at this fabled workshop. More importantly, I was actually quite attentive to notes and editorial input and I did learn a hell of a lot. Clarion encouraged me, so I said to myself, "Never mind college, just start writing..." I got a day job as a typist and started selling stories and then paperback novels.

Q: When you started selling paperback novels in the late '70s, were you immediately able to make a living at it? I would guess that like most writers, you had by that point decided that your life's purpose – your vocation, so to speak – was writing, but there is also the practical need for survival. So how did you handle this?

Shirley: A living? More or less. It was possible in those days, because things were much cheaper. One could rent a nice house for a few hundred bucks. I found roommates to share the place. Money from writing came and went, feast and famine. There was a live-in girlfriend, too, a sequence of them, really, and these tolerant, kindly women actually had jobs. One was a stripper—*she* made money. Another had a straight job with the city. Sometimes I supported people, including my friends and girlfriends; sometimes the girls supported me till my next check came in. We were all sort of spontaneously communal, financially…But I also took work as a typist, when necessary. As a typist for The Oregonian newspaper I met guitarist and songwriter Dave Corboy, a legend in Pacific Northwest punk rock. He and I started a band he called Sado-Nation, with myself as "frontman".

Later when I moved to New York City— I got a job working in a PR agency. Eventually I was fired for writing novels at work. I was still prolific as a writer, sending out stories and novels, and just never giving up on selling it. Some of this stubbornness was the influence of Harlan, who lectured us at Clarion on trying to sell everything you write, by rewriting it for another outlet, if it's rejected; reusing ideas in new forms and so on, to just *survive* till you found traction as a writer.

Q: I remember that Harlan had an introduction to one of his books entitled something like "How Science Fiction Saved Me from a Life of Crime." Not that I am suggesting that was the choice for you, but were you able, through your writing to channel your natural rebelliousness into more socially acceptable channels?

Shirley: There is something to that. In those days I was something of an anarchist or anarcho-syndicalist, influenced by Le Guin's *The Dispossessed* and by Emma Gold-man (now I'm a pragmatic progressive, and a Democrat), so I was able to rationalize a radical attitude toward conventional property concepts, and this led to some low-grade cat burglary, especially when I was eighteen and nineteen. When I was a young freaky guy, before I went to PSU, me and my little gang of long-haired, stoned, cheerful miscreants broke into a movie theater after hours (easy to do in those days, the old theaters all had some kind of hatch on the roof if you could get to it) and stole giant bags of pre-made popcorn and hotdogs and candy bars and movie posters. Our small house in Salem was wallpapered with old movie posters. We also boosted some office equipment from other places, and sold it through classified ads. All this while other young people I knew were getting sensible jobs or getting into Reed College. And of course drugs were illegal. I sold some (nothing addictive) for a summer. Then there were little forays into, er, sex work, later.

Eventually I saw what real anarchy, at least on the street level, looked like—it looks like the neighborhood thugs using the power vacuum to take over. It looks like crack and heroin spreading without constraint, and women being forced by predators to walk the streets. It meant racists, without real Civil Rights enforcement, shoving people of color into ghettos and preventing them from getting good jobs and a good education. So I began to respect law and order and the concept of a reasonably progressive centralized government.

But still—how was I to live? My different drummer played *such* a different beat it was hard for me to hold a job long. I got kicked out of those marching bands. So I had to get there by doing the one thing I was good at: telling stories. Forming sentences, slinging narrative. Writing.

Q: You were kind of rabble-rousing and rebellious as a writer too. All those opinion columns which seemed (to me at least) to be deliberately provocative must have raised your profile in the field considerably. Of course there are some writers who quietly stay home and write, and never raise their voices, but there are others who are constantly involved in controversies. Was this something you just had to do, or was there (if I don't sound too cynical) an element of deliberate self-promotion to it? One does think about the example of Ellison again. He certainly made himself a very visible public figure, rather than just a byline on stories.

Shirley: *Deliberately* was something I didn't know how to do in those days. I did everything intuitively, by *feel*, impulsively—too impulsively! But unconsciously, sure I was being self-servingly provocative. Even besides the Ellison imbroglio, that sort of thing did my career more harm than good. But I remember one piece I wrote that was about the necessity of creating a new type of sf convention—a con that was more about the *literature* of science-fiction. I said it should refuse all cosplay and filking etc., it should eschew all emphasis on *Star Wars* or whatever movie, it should be a communing about the literature of the fantastic. This actually inspired something in the real world. They told me so! It inspired Readercon. And they eventually invited me to Readercon, and I went, because I had inspired the convention….

So I did something beneficial in one of those pieces. I have nothing against the old-style convention, or cosplay, but I thought we needed this alternative too. The only opinion piece I regret is the one where I went off on Harlan. The others, though they were risky to me, helped embolden other people to speak out (more sanely, I'm sure). Gadflies have their uses. They force people to look around and say, "Is this true?" They induce people to stop and ponder and wake up for moment.

Q: How do you feel about literary "movements," New Wave, splatterpunk, steampunk, cyberpunk, whatever? Other people certain tend to classify writers this way. Did you decide, consciously, that you wanted to be one of the cyberpunks, or was that just critics pointing at you?

Shirley: Such movements arise in other fields, for example painting. Art history discusses movements: e.g. renaissance painting, romanticism, symbolism, impression-

ism, pointillism, fauvism, expressionism, cubism, dada, surrealism, pop art, abstract expressionism—each seems inherently of value in itself. These movements are stages in an evolution in culture; they're humanity engaged in profound self-exploration. Why shouldn't genre writing have its corresponding movements? If the spectrum of the fantastic in writing didn't have its movements, it wouldn't be art. And at its best, sf and fantasy *et al.*—these are art forms! Even heroic fantasy, "sword and sorcery," is an art form in the hands of Fritz Leiber.

Movements, I suppose, become sub-genres. Some people set out to imitate them. "I am going to be a cyberpunk writer" they say. But people who originate the movement usually just find themselves doing it. It's "steam engine time" for a particular literary movement. Oh, Bruce Sterling had *fun* staking out cyberpunk, and we played the role a bit. But really it arose because it seemed to people like me and Bruce and William Gibson and Rudy Rucker and Pat Cadigan and Lew Shiner that it was the time to write the sf that was about the street's uses for technology. These movements provide needed *friction to the fiction*; they create friction with other forms, which again has a quality of "wake up and look around!" that everyone needs. They're a refreshment, and they add colors to the palette.

It felt natural for me to write what is called "cyberpunk." My newest sf novel *Stormland* is a fusion of cyberpunk and "climate fiction" and the futuristic detective story…. It arose naturally from my guesses about the near future and from issues I felt everyone needed to face and from the dramatic possibilities I perceived in all that. But I have been called "sui generis." I've said I'm like a pianist who can play blues, rock, classical, ragtime or jazz, each with some assurance. I can write creditably across genres. I've written in most genres—except Romance, with a capital R, *per se*. But there is usually a current of romance somewhere in my novels, whatever genre. Just now I'm writing a trilogy of westerns for Kensington/ Pinnacle. I was smitten by westerns as a kid, as well as fantasy and sf. There's a reason that there's a western hero sort of paradigm at work in much early science fiction. The lone hero come to a new planet to fight injustice, say. It's the story we males tell ourselves; it's male mythology.... Not that women can't write it as well; they do. Consider Leigh Brackett. She wrote it better than the male writers!

So some forms I'm especially drawn to. I like to create syntheses, and my trilogy of westerns is a synthesis of the traditional gun-fighter western with the historical novel. In my dreams it is a fusion of Louis L'Amour and Larry McMurtry.... The first book, *Axle Bust Creek*, will be out in September. It does involve a nineteenth century scientist—but it's not steampunk. This woman, somewhat more than the romantic interest, is a natu-ral philosopher and a suffragist. She and the gunfighter, a former Union Major with PTSD from the Civil War, fall in love and have ad-ventures.... So you see I go where my inspira-tion takes me.

Q: I am sure that if you had been a placid, conventional fellow, what you wrote would have been a lot different. So could we also say that all that angst and passion fueled your fiction? I see in your bibliography – which is more extensive than I realized it was – several obviously "commercial" projects, including men's adventure novels, game novelizations, books based on comic-book characters, but at the same time, aren't all your works infused with who you are?

Shirley: I remember a writer in *Rolling Stone*, reviewing the band Slayer, said "the band has an anger infused in it like the writ-ing of John Shirley." Sometimes I've been surprised, when people said much of my writ-ing seemed angry to them—because it was so much a part of me it didn't seem angry, it just seemed like "This is the world to me; everyone must feel this way." Some of this may arise from trauma—which I prefer not to get into here—but some of it, strangely, is from empathy. Because my "empathy filter" is broken. If I hear of an outrage, a travesty, some vile cruelty, some monstrous policy, I

seem to feel a deep empathy for the victims. I see them in my mind, too clearly for my own good. Maybe my trauma, my own PTSD, is all mixed up with my empathy....

Then again I'm also attracted to high energy, in its various forms—and I look for ways to evoke it. Perhaps that's why I was so taken by Harlan Ellison's writing as a young man. There was a period when, in raising money to buy a house and pay property tax, I had to write a number of novels "to order": a work-for-hire book based on a videogame or a movie franchise; a book I co-wrote with a rock star, Mark Tremonti (*A Dying Machine*), a book based on the TV show Grimm, and so on. Because I can handily write in vari-ous formats and genres, I was able to com-pose these works relatively smoothly, and yet I inevitably express my passionate, didactic side, or at least my high energy evocation, somewhere in the book. This is most obvious in *Bioshock: Rapture* (a best-selling book) and *Batman: Dead White*. I'm no longer writ-ing that sort of thing, having enough income now, although I did develop a techno thriller, somewhat to order, which will be out from Titan Books in March: *Suborbital Seven*. For that, however, I shall get royalties.

Q: A western? Why not? You've done ev-erything from *Dracula in Love* to Lovecraf-tian horror, and slipped very deftly into the sword & sorcery idiom with "Swords of At-lantis" in the John Shirley issue of WEIRD-BOOK (which I am reading now and enjoy-ing quite a bit), and of course you've done a lot of science fiction. So, how do you feel about genres generally? Are these classifica-tions restrictive, or are they more like literary forms, which you can take up and use the way a poet sets out to write a specific form, like a sonnet?

Shirley: Except for romance novels, which would annoy me to write, I am fine writing in most any genre. But what some-times happens, especially with short stories, is I have something I particularly want to say; an insight (I hope), or a strong idea about the nature of the world, and I write in the genre that's best suited to express that idea. Most of my short fiction, while it is written to be entertaining—to thrill, to horrify, to touch someone—well, it's also metaphorical. My story *"A Ticket to Heaven"* is an obvious example: the protagonist finds that heaven exists and there's a device that can take people there. But whatever pleasure they experience in Heaven is correspondingly taken out of the ordinary world, so chaos grows in the regular world when people take a shortcut to heaven. Now, this is a sort of Robert Sheckleyesque sf entertainment but it's also a pretty obvious social metaphor.

My novel *Demons* can be taken as a flat-out horror novel about a worldwide invasion of giant and quite *peculiar* demons—but it's also a metaphor having to do with our failure of stewardship of the natural world, and certain metaphysical ideas. I have a new novelette coming in The *Magazine of Fantasy and Science Fiction*, called "Sacrificial Drones," and I chose to tell the story with sf and cyberpunk imagery because that's what fitted the metaphor. Each genre does have its restrictions, but one can do meaningful writing in all of them. Consider what Larry McMurtry did with westerns—or consider the classic western *The Ox-Bow Incident*.... I also write song lyrics, for myself and for the Blue Oyster Cult and other bands, and I write weird-poetry style verse, in the shadow of Poe and Clark Ashton Smith, some of which appears in Joshi's journal *Spectral Realms*. Some of these have been collected in a book of rhyming poetry by Jackanapes Press, *The Voice of the Burning House.*

I sometimes get in an "imp of the perverse" mood and write stories which are designed to confront the reader's sense of reality—designed to really shake it up. These stories are surreal yet internally logical—albeit with twisted logic—and many of them appeared in a book called *Really, Really, Really, Really Weird Stories*. This story collection, divided into four parts, is unique: the first section is weird, the second is weirder, the third weirder yet, the fourth as weird as can be borne (or not borne as the case may be). A new edition of this book, re-edited with four new stories, is coming out from Jackanapes—and is available now as an eBook.

Q: Your story in this current issue of *Startling Stories*, for all the satire in it is aimed squarely at the present, could otherwise have been published in *Startling Stories* in the 1940s. It has that pulp feel, in a good sense. It moves swiftly. And your novella "Swords of Atlantis" (I've read the *Weirdbook* publication) also has all the same virtues, of vivid, rapid narrative and clearly defined characters. It occurs to me that if you'd been born a couple generations earlier, you'd have been a terrific pulp writer. Are you a fan of the old pulp fiction? Given that you've written men's adventure novels, you clearly have all the skills. Did you ever yearn to write, say, a Shadow or Doc Savage novel or something of that nature?

Shirley: I never read a The Shadow or a Doc Savage (enjoyed the Alec Baldwin *The Shadow* movie though), but as a boy I read a *lot* of Robert E Howard and Edgar Rice Burroughs and other writers of that era, sure—all in library reprint. (I'm not THAT old).... Later on, I found escape in Jack Vance's *Planet of Adventure* books and his Demon Princes novels. His Dying Earth fantasy is a great influence on me too. Leigh Brackett's Eric John Stark novels—which were originally in pulp mags—are a big influence, when I write adventure fiction, and Fritz Leiber's Lankhmar books, and Moorcock's Elric books. Also Arthur Conan Doyle's *The Lost World*.... But again, I can write in various forms fairly comfortably. *The Lost City of Los Angeles,* in this issue of *Startling Stories*, is not a parody of sf adventure pulp but it is something of a pastiche of it. It's a fusion of post-apocalyptic adventure with social satire. It retains a sense of humor but it's not making fun of the genre, not at all. (By the way, I think the movie *John Carter* is a *most* under-appreciated science-fiction adventure based on pulp novels... loved it...) Yes, years ago I wrote *The Specialist*, action novels under the name John Cutter—they are still in print, including a couple of new ones, *Firepower* and *Wildfire*. In *Firepower* the hero, Vince Bellator, takes on American neo-Nazis who are planning a big massacre in contemporary Washington D.C. He ends up having to kill more than a hundred neo-Nazis. "As far as I'm concerned, when it comes to Nazis, it's still World War II," he says. It was catharsis to write that....

Q: Could you give me some idea of what your writing methods are like?

Shirley: In a word, haphazard. And yet there's a general approach. I read the newspaper in the morning, online, and do my email correspondence, and maybe call my agent if I need to, and promise my wife to do some chores later, and then I make myself write, and it depends on a sort of ongoing writing momentum as to how much time I spend on it. You see, I'm *still writing* when I'm working in the garden or helping with housework, only it's going on in my mind. If my wife sees me scowling as I sweep the floor, it's not because I despise sweeping floors it's because—as she knows—that scowl means I'm thinking my way through a story. I'm thinking, "Will this work? What about that?" And often I'm visualizing a scene. I typically write in scenes almost as much as a scriptwriter—I suppose I'm a "scenarist" in a way—and I see them playing out in my mind. Now and then I'll stop whatever I'm doing and scribble down a note. Later I'll "upload" the scenes to a manuscript file, by typing them in. This will go on for days, with fits of considerable writing at my PC. If I'm feeling stymied, I'll use that time to go back and revise what I've written, which often brings me new ideas and momentum as well as improving the writing.

I "write on adrenaline"—Michael Moorcock told me that's what he did. I usually write at least six, sometimes as much as ten double spaced pages a day. But much revision is involved. Of course I do research, not all of it online but much of it, seeking out reputable sources for data. With the forthcoming technothriller *Suborbital 7* (which may be retitled), I consulted people I knew who had associations with aerospace. I read a couple rel-

evant books. I searched for pertinent articles in online journals and read them. Yes, I do a lot of research online, but it must be done with care because there is as much bad information as good on the internet...I often put on music, as I write, that seems to fit with the kind of fiction I'm engaged in, to help psyche me into right mood and to cultivate stylistic atmosphere...I have a strong work ethic and get very restless if I'm between projects. After a few days I MUST write again or I fall into a pit of discontent with myself....

Q: What are you working on now?

Shirley: What am I up to now? I am a recording artist too, and I have an album coming out with prog-rock legend Jerry King, my vocals and lyrics, called *Escape from Gravity.* (It's being offered by Jackanapes Press as part of a bundle with *Really Really Really Really Weird Stories*). We did two other albums as John Shirley & Jerry King: *Spaceship Landing in a Cemetery* and *Short Stories for Small Aliens.* The Blue Oyster Cult's first new studio album in 19 years came out, last year, using my lyrics on five songs. It has sold quite well—it's called *The Symbol Remains.* I wrote the words for the two singles off the album, and three other tracks, one of which is an amusing song that's also a kind of "startling story," it tells the tale of Florida Man, and the consequence of an Indian curse.... A song from the LP I *didn't* write that might interest *Startling Stories* readers is *The Alchemist* which is inspired by HP Lovecraft's first-published short story of the same name. It's a really enjoyable track, with a good video you can see on YouTube (the whole album is there in fact), that evokes the story quite well. The album is selling well.

After the western trilogy I plan to write a YA urban-fantasy novel based on a story Marc Laidlaw and I wrote... And—who knows? Possibilities are forever in ferment.

Q: Thanks, John.

✳

THROUGH TIME AND SPACE WITH FERDINAND FEGHOOT: *Alpha*

by Grendel Briarton, Jr.

Ferdinand Feghoot, long employed as an intergalactic troubleshooter, had been summoned to the Galaxy's Most Dangerous Animals Zoo on Pollux IV, where the literal-minded inhabitants had assembled the specimens from thousands of planets in the Galactic Federation. The head zookeeper immediately took him on a tour.

The zoo, which covered the planet's smallest continent, was truly impressive. Everywhere, Feghoot saw creatures he knew—and feared.

"Ten million exhibits," the zookeeper said heavily, "each a safety success—except one."

"Which one?" Feghoot said.

"The giant mouth-beast of Orion. It keeps eating our visitors. We need your help."

Feghoot raised his eyebrows. "I've never seen a giant mouth-beast. Are they large?"

"A hundred meters from teeth to tail," the zookeeper said. "Ours is the largest speimen in captivity and the crowning piece in our collection. You must see it at once!"

Immediately he jetted them to a monorail station in the mountains and summoned a private car. As they rode a trestle across a deep valley, they passed dozens of hovering signs that warned, "Do Not Feed the Giant Mouth!" and "Danger!" and "Off Limits to Hikers!"

"Aren't your signs sufficient?" Feghoot asked, remembering the literal-minded reputation of the inhabitants of Pollux IV. "Surely no one disobeys."

"They keep finding loopholes. The giant mouth attracts reckless youth. Look!"

Overhead, Feghoot spotted three jet-bikes ridden by teenagers. They flew fast toward the valley floor. When they were within fifty meters of the ground, what he had taken for a large pond suddenly lunged into the air, its giant blue mouth snapping. The bikers gunned their jets and roared toward safety—escaping the giant mouth-beast's equally giant teeth by centimeters. The creature settled to the ground, once again disguised as a pond.

"See?" cried the zookeeper. "They were lucky. Last week, it ate a dozen jet-bikers!"

"Leave it to me," Feghoot said grimly. This would require his greatest skill.

* * * *

The next afternoon, he met the head zookeeper and reported the giant mouth-beast problem as solved.

"So—so fast?" the zookeeper spluttered. "But—but *how?*"

"Easy," said Feghoot. And it had been, at least for the galaxy's most creative intergalactic troubleshooter. He flicked a button on his phone, which projected an image of the valley into the air between them. "I replaced your old hover-signs with a new one."

The zookeeper gawped.

The new sign read: "Trestle passers will be masticated to the fullest extent of the maw."

ABOUT THE AUTHOR

The character of Ferdinand Feghoot was created by Reginald Bretnor ("Grendel Briarton" is an anagram of his name) and appeared in more than 50 stories over the course of three decades. Following Mr. Bretnor's death, several authors—including David Gerrold—have been authorized by his estate to officially carry on the pun-filled tradition. This contribution is by John Betancourt, who has been a Feghoot fan since first encountering him in *Isaac Asimov's Science Fiction Magazine* in the late 1970s.

ABOUT THE ARTIST

Luis Alejandro Melo (who goes by Meloo0182 / Mr.M-Art online) is originally from Venezuela, was raised in France, and now resides in Colombia. Luis studied architecture in Caracas, Venezuela and took art courses in Calgary, Canada.

When asked for a bio, Luis wrote: "I love drawing mythological characters, fiction, and fantasy." Q.E.D.! See more of their work here:

www.behance.net/Meloo0182

HUA GU QUAN
(The Flower Drum Circle)
by Frances Lu-Pai Ippolito

The primary rule of the Hua Gu Quan was simple: you kept the flower if you held onto it while the Quan beat the shit out of you.

"Glad you're interested." Thirteen-year-old Todd took a break from cleaning his pile of smart tablet screens to pat Xiao-wu on the shoulder. The boys were both supposed to be cleaning, but Xiao-wu had gotten tired and stepped away from his stack. Tall and husky Todd loomed over the nine-year-old boy who rested on the iron garden bench in the outdoor courtyard of the International Florist Academy.

"The Quan wondered if you'd play. New kid and all." Todd turned his head and spat chewing gum onto a patch of artificial grass by his feet. The pink glob landed on mylar stalks, bending the synthetic grass and coating it with bubbled saliva.

Xiao-wu gathered his reading tablet to his chest and scooted to one side of the iron bench, making room for the much wider boy. Instinctively, he clutched his tablet tighter as the seat strained under Todd's weight and the bench legs wobbled. Todd held out his hand for Xiao-wu's tablet. When Xiao-wu gave it to him, Todd spat on it and rubbed an absorbent polymer pad into the glass, smearing the spit, rather than removing the handprint oils.

"Game's easy—ten of us sit in a circle while the Banger bangs on a drum in the middle. As long as he bangs, we pass the flower. One bang. One pass. Until…."

"Until?"

"Until the banging stops. Then whoever has the flower moves to the center. That person's gotta survive the same number of beats."

"Beats?"

"Like 20 bangs, 20 beats. The Quan takes turns."

Xiao-wu scowled. "You mean…you take turns hitting the flower holder?"

"We have to make sure."

"Of what?"

"That you've got what it takes."

"To?"

"To take care of the flower. If you drop it—if the flower touches the ground—we start over."

Xiao-wu stared at the older boy with the seafoam eyes and brawny shoulders. The tablet Todd still held looked like a slice of mirror in his thick hands. *It would hurt to be punched by you.*

Maybe there was another way to play? To make friends? "Why fight? Can't we just take turns with the flower."

Todd laughed. "Oh ho! You think this is fighting? None of us in the Quan had seen a plant or flower before that first time. I mean—" Todd tossed his chestnut hair that curled like orchid roots below his shoulders. "—I'd seen pictures of them on the learning pads. And once, Ms. Ning showed us a piece of *paper*. But, friend, have you ever seen a real flower? Touched one? Smelled one?"

Xiao-wu had seen plenty of flowers in his young life—glass blown, extruded thermoplastic from 3D printers, and polyester versions cut and sewn together with fishing line. In fact, flowers filled the school's nature garden next to the courtyard—silica peonies and styrofoam rose bushes lined up neatly like toy soldiers in the rubber mulch, and tiger tulips sat sideways in plastic whiskey barrels stuffed with silver tinsel.

When Xiao-wu first saw the tulips, they looked familiar, reminding him of similar ones he'd fashioned out of pipe cleaners and metal paper clips at his old public government school. Mama and Baba had put the ones he made in an antique wine bottle on the kitchen counter at their house. But the tulips weren't there anymore, moved out like him after his parents died.

"No, I haven't seen a real one," Xiao-wu answered.

"Great Burning!" Todd slapped his thighs. "Once we saw the flower—once we smelled it." He stopped to grab a fresh stick of gum out of his pocket. His hand shook as he unwrapped the foil and ran the pink strip along his nose, inhaling deep and closing his eyes. "We all wanted it." He popped the gum into his mouth.

Xiao-wu noticed he wasn't missing any teeth, not like him or the kids at his old school across town.

"A few kids died," Todd said, chewing with his mouth open.

"What?" Xiao-wu gasped, horrified.

"Well…maybe those twins went to the infirmary and were fine. I can't remember. They were new too." Todd scratched his chin and then burst out laughing. "Your face. You look so scared. I'm joking."

Xiao-wu swallowed. "But why do you have the flowers?"

Todd wagged a finger at Xiao-wu. "Well, it'd be ridiculous if a school for florists never had flowers! Haven't you ever thought about that?"

Xiao-wu hadn't considered that. Why would I? I'm only at this school because Mom and Baba died and I was good at twisting metal tulips.

Todd leaned closer and a rose fragrance wafted from his hair, tickling Xiao-wu's nose. The floral scent was concentrated and dense, stronger than the other synthetic versions Xiao-wu had experienced. It made him a little dizzy. In his shoes, he pushed his toes harder toward the ground and with one hand grabbed a bench handle to steady himself.

"What you really want to ask is how we get the flowers? Right?" Todd added in a quieter voice.

"I thought they were destroyed." Xiao-wu was too young to witness The Great Burning, but he'd read about the confiscation and burning of all plants and seeds from farms and gardens, the stripping of topsoil, and the burying of whatever fertile dirt remained under six feet of sterile alkaline ash.

"Plants are dangerous, poisonous." Xiao-wu repeated something he'd read.

"Pish-posh," Todd said lightly. "When you see a real flower, you'll realize how ridiculous that is."

"But…there was a reason…" Xiao-wu trailed off, trying to recall bits and pieces of books at his previous school. That school never let students near plants. He missed the way things were. He missed his parents.

"That's what they tell the *regular* people. The poor people. But the kids here, we get the real info 'cause our parents are in the know. My Mom is Sadako Ghazali so I know *everything*."

Xiao-wu stared down at his lap and at the frog buttons on his black tunic uniform. "Uh…. I don't know who that is."

"You? D-don't know?" Todd sputtered more spit. "My mom runs the Greenhouse. You do know what the Greenhouse is, right?"

That Xiao-wu did, sort of. The Greenhouse led the Great Burning to save the world. His brows knitted together. Saving the world from what exactly, he couldn't quite remember.

Todd took his silence as ignorance. "Bud, what school did you transfer from again? Didn't they teach you anything?"

Xiao-wu's mouth clamped shut. This private school was much nicer than the public school—better tablets, uniforms, and food. Orphaned, but talented in flower fabrication,

Xiao-wu learned what it was to be the "Noblesse Oblige" case—a poor kid recipient of room and board at an elite school of one percenters. He didn't want Todd to know any of this.

Luckily, Todd didn't care about Xiao-wu's answer. "*Diabolus in Animo* infected all the plants in the world. Like some sort of evolved defense against picking and eating. Made people funny. Hear things; do things. But it's not a problem anymore! I overheard my mom talking to her execs about exceptions and testing D.I.A. free and all that blah blah crap. Plus, my brother's been selling shit out of the lab for years as a side hustle. He's such a scammer. Ph.D Botanist moonlighting as a peddler. Anyway, I told him he had to give me a few or I'd tell Mom. He might be 99th percentile for IQ, but he still wets his pants like an old granny when Mom gets mad." Todd flipped his hair to the side and then looked satisfied with himself. "So you wanna play?" Todd asked. "Make some friends?"

Xiao-wu shifted on the hard bench, queasy and uncomfortable. He tugged at the high mandarin collar on his uniform. Sweat ringed underneath and the coarse raw silk chafed the scurvy rash on his throat. He didn't want to play, but the move to the private school had been abrupt and lonely. For the last month, he'd sat by himself on the bench with his reading tablet, watching a group of kids disappear every week into the shaded copse of PVC firs in the back corner of the playground.

"I know what you're thinking," Todd said when Xiao-wu's gaze darted from the artificial trees to the paved blacktop where several classmates played a game of basketball. Esperanza, Xiao-wu's classmate, played against all the other kids. Straight and lean like the bamboo trees Xiao-wu had seen in his botany reading app, she towered easily over the others as if they were shrubs, to score ball after ball through the metal hoop.

"You're thinking we're gonna get caught, right?" Todd continued.

Xiao-wu wasn't thinking that, but did when Todd said it.

"Truth is that an official-ish looking lady did come once. Flashed a Greenhouse badge. Asked questions. I thought I was going to get in so much trouble. Esperanza and the others took turns hiding that flower in our desks. And I sweet talked the lady the whole time. Told her how I'd make sure my mom knew about how hard her employees were working to keep us all safe. All that kind of stuff Mom always tells reporters. Anyway, she didn't stay very long, seemed happy that I was in charge. And, honestly, I don't think she even tried very hard to look."

Todd shrugged. "Maybe…after all these years since the Great Burning…maybe they don't care that much anymore. I never understood what the big deal was. You'll see soon," Todd insisted. "The flower we have tomorrow is special."

Curious, Xiao-wu asked, "How?"

Todd's voice hushed to a whisper and he cupped his mouth so that only Xiao-wu could hear. "It grants your wishes."

Xiao-wu scowled. Todd was nice enough, but Xiao-wu didn't like being made fun of.

"No, it's true!" Todd held up Xiao-wu's tablet. "I'll show you."

Xiao-wu stared as Todd swiped across the screen a few times and then flipped it around to show Xiao-wu.

Xiao-wu read through the highlighted text: Pu-gong-ying, Dandelion, Lion's Tooth—Legend has it that, if you blow all the seeds off a dandelion with a single breath, then your wish will come true.

Todd dropped the tablet in Xiao-wu's lap and then leaned his head back, puffed his cheeks, and blew out a pink bubble. It popped and went all over his face. "I wonder what I'd wish for," he said as he picked gum off strands of his hair.

Xiao-wu looked out at the basketball game and at the kids trying to steal the ball from Esperanza. He didn't need to wonder, he already knew.

#

Bang. Pass. Bang. Pass. *How many was that?* Xiao-wu had lost count in the Quan. He sat between Arjun and Fatima, knees grazing on both sides, as he watched Todd pass the yellow flower to Esperanza who passed it to Keiko and then Tamiqua. The other kids in the Quan looked familiar, but Xiao-wu didn't recall their names.

Jorge was the Banger. He stood in the center, wearing a gauzy white blindfold around his eyes so he couldn't cheat and see who had the flower while he drummed. In his hands, he twisted the bright red stick of a pellet drum. With a turn, the two strings attached to the drum head went flying and struck both faces with wooden pellets at the ends of the strings.

After another BANG, the flower came round again to Arjun who raised it into a beam of sunlight filtered through plastic tree branches. Xiao-wu couldn't see the dandelion's fleshy tap root, but he knew it was there from his research, probably folded up and encased in the spherical clump of dirt and clay, about the size of a tennis ball, that was held together by netted mesh. Several leaves grew from the base, creating a lush green skirt that collared the bottom of the stem.

Beside him, Xiao-wu noticed how Arjun avoided the saw-toothed leaves. Jagged like pointy teeth, the leaves were sharp and caught skin as Xiao-wu learned the first time Arjun passed the dandelion to him. It was an unexpected feature, not one that had been described in any of the dandelion entries on the botany app. Maybe another evolved defense like the D.I.A. had been.

Bang. Xiao-wu's heart skipped as Arjun gave him the flower. Todd was right. Real was different.

Xiao-wu cupped the root ball in his palm, careful to orient the flower properly. The green stem, a paler hue than the leaves, rose straight as a straw out of notched leaves to the crown of teardrop petals the color of egg yolk. It was heavier than he anticipated, even though he'd held it a few times already. He brought his other hand to support the root ball and lifted the flower to his face.

Xiao-wu's nose nuzzled the soft petals. He breathed deep, filling his chest. The scents of the old earth and ancient woods were new to him. Nothing he'd ever experienced. A strange exciting tingle filled his nostrils, spreading down his arms to his finger nails and from his chest to his legs and to the soles of his feet. It was warm and spiced; a delicious sweetened energy that buzzed and made Xiao-wu feel dizzy and sharp at the same time, and more alive than he had since his parents died.

He peeked over yellow petals at the other kids. They were all bigger than him, healthier, happier. It wasn't fair. He wanted; no, he needed this flower more than any of them. He'd take better care of it too. And when he won, he'd use its magic to wish his family back.

Bang.

Xiao-wu hesitated, reluctant to pass the dandelion. Fatima blinked at him with squinty maroon eyes. Her right hand reached out. Xiao-wu recoiled, knocking his knee against Arjun's.

"Ow!" Arjun yelped.

Fatima frowned. "My turn," she said.

"I know, I just—" Xiao-wu began.

Fatima frowned harder.

"Done," Jorge said, interrupting them. He tore off his blindfold and rubbed his eyes with his forearms. "Who has it?" he asked.

"He cheated!" Fatima jumped up. She stomped on the ground and dust rose into the air like glittering motes floating in the sun's rays. "He didn't pass it!" she shouted.

"Is that true?" Todd asked Xiao-wu.

Xiao-wu stood up and backed out of the Quan, clutching the flower to his chest. "Well…."

"Give it!" Fatima lunged toward Xiao-wu, who ducked under her long arms. "Not fair!" she yelled.

"Fatima," Todd said, holding up his hand. "We can settle this."

Todd got up and walked to Xiao-wu. "You want it that bad?"

Xiao-wu nodded and looked down at his feet. His grip on the root ball tightened, but the moist dirt calmed him. He lifted his gaze and stared directly into Todd's eyes. "More than anything," he replied quietly.

Fatima stomped her foot again.

"Double or nothing," Todd said without looking at Fatima.

Fatima hesitated. "Double?"

"Jorge, how many beats?" Todd asked.

Jorge counted on his fingers as if trying to remember. "Forty."

Todd turned back to Fatima and Xiao-wu. "Who's willing to take eighty?"

Fatima paled. "But HE broke the rules!"

"Fatima's right," Esperanza said, standing tall and towering. "The Quan must be fair."

"Ok, Fatima, what's fair?" Todd asked.

Fatima studied the yellow flower in Xiao-wu's hands. She bit her lower lip. "Umm, triple?"

Todd nodded. "One hundred twenty." He looked the small, skinny boy up and down. "No one's gone that high before."

Xiao-wu kept his gaze trained on the dandelion. The stem swayed and the yellow head moved back and forth like it was nodding at him, encouraging him to go ahead. He squared his shoulders. "I can," he answered.

Fatima sputtered, shocked he'd agreed to her bluff.

"Quan?" Todd asked the kids around him. They nodded.

"Fine, I'm first." Fatima tied back her mane of glossy red curls with a white nylon ribbon.

Todd moved out of her way.

"You ready?" Fatima asked. She was Todd's age, also thirteen and also tall with muscular arms and soccer legs. Xiao-wu kept his expression passive even though his heart was thundering in its carriage.

"Hold on." Xiao-wu walked into the center of the Quan and knelt onto the ground, sitting on his haunches. He hugged the flower close to his chest without pressing it too tight.

Fatima's brows knitted together as she stood looking down at him. There was uncertainty clouding her face, as if she hadn't expected him to give himself to her like this.

"It's ok." Xiao-wu smiled at her even though she was the one about to hurt him. I'll be fine, he thought. *Didn't the flower just promise me?*

"You ready?" Fatima asked again, rolling up her sleeves and fisting her hands.

Xiao-wu tucked his chin protectively over the flower's petals, breathed deep, and closed his eyes.

"Go ahead," he whispered.

ABOUT THE AUTHOR

Frances Lu-Pai Ippolito is a Chinese American writer based in Portland, Oregon. When she's not spending time with her family outdoors, she's crafting short stories in horror, sci-fi, fantasy, or whatever genre-bending she can get away with. Her work can be found in *Nailed Magazine*, *Red Penguin's Collections*, *Buckman Journal*, Flame Tree Press's *Asian Ghost Stories*, Strangehouse's *Chromophobia*, and *Death's Garden Revisited*. www.francesippolito.com.

ABOUT THE ARTISTS

We assigned this story to two different artists because we couln't decide between them for the project. We received very different (but both great) interpretations.

Somnath Chatterjee is a senior designer as well as art & animation director from India, with 25 years of industry experience (including more than 2,000 children's book illustrations and approximately 500 comic books). Since 2009, Som has been running the Dot.pixel studio. Info, visit: behance.net/somnathchatter5

Alexandr Chernushkin is a Russian immigrant currently living and working in Poland. His artwork is inspired by fantasy worlds and history of different ages. More info: artstation.com/alexandrchernushkin or behance.net/alexandchernus1

"YOU'RE SUNK!"

by Cynthia Ward

"Cut!" The director tilted his head up, scanning for the source of the propeller drone. "I can't believe how often airplane noise ruins our shots. We're at the South Pole, for Christ's sake."

"The Antarctic Treaty means 'no military bases,' not 'no planes,'" said the set production assistant, who was returning from the makeshift parking lot. "That's not the only problem, Chick."

Chick Cabane turned to the woman.

"We upload tonight's episode of *Alive!* in five hours, Mac, and we've just discovered a *mystery ruin* in the Antarctic ice. I don't care if there's a problem with a production cube."

"There's not a problem with the production cubes." Mac shoved a ring of motor vehicle keys in a loose sock and stuffed it in a pocket of her parka, then took off her sunglasses and faced the director. "There's a problem with the ruin."

Malachite MacReady was a tall, wiry woman who nearly vanished in her parka and boots. Her fur-lined hood was pushed back for frequent cellphone deployment. Apart from her gray-threaded black hair, the only visible parts of her body were the black eyes and brown skin above a mask with the *Alive!* logo: a shipwreck, encircled by a life-preserver bearing the motto "Sink or Swim."

"And just what is the problem with the ruin?" the director snapped.

"We don't know what's in it," Mac replied.

"Finding out will make *Alive!* the biggest TV show in history."

Chick Cabane communicated in superlatives, unwittingly informing everyone that this was his first prime-time gig. He'd worked on dozens of cable and streaming knockoffs of popular reality TV shows—ev-erything from yatch-flipping money-porn *Float Your Boat* to sleazy marriage-buster *Conjugation Station*. From its first season, *Alive!* had consistently topped the ratings of the venerable *Survivor*, but Chick Cabane clearly viewed the runaway hit as just another stepping-stone on the path to A-list feature film director.

Chick focused on the aircraft spoiling the extreme-wilderness ambiance.

"Take ten, everyone," he said. "That'll get the plane out of range. When we resume, the cast digs out the shack."

He returned his attention to Mac and removed his sunglasses, revealing pale skin like the negative of a raccoon's mask. The rest of his face was burned a bright red. Chick Cabane couldn't be bothered to wear a mask, scarf, or other face covering.

Most crew members followed Chick's lead. The cast followed their contract. Nicknamed "outcasts," cast members were obligated to reveal their faces, whatever the weather.

Chick's pale eyes almost disappeared in crow's feet as he squinted at Mac against the glare of sun, snow, and ice.

"Get over here," he rasped.

Mac approached the director, not hesitating when his laser-beam glare heated to ice-melt. Though a newcomer in the entertainment business, she'd spent twenty years in the U.S. Army, with multiple tours of duty in hot spots. As threats went, an angry director ranked several notches below a cranky wasp.

"Chick, seriously," she said quietly. "If there's no record of this place—"

"The ruined cabin's obviously part of some old explorer base, built and abandoned early in the twentieth century," Chick said with faux patience. "Looks like it burned. The men fled and never came back, and it was forgotten."

Mac studied him. Finally, she murmured, "You've never heard of the Big Magnet Project."

"I'm not familiar with every video on YouTube."

He started to turn away.

"It was a scientific expedition in the 1930s," Mac said softly. "My great-grandfather was the assistant commander."

Slowly, as if acting against his better judgment, Chick turned back to her. "An Antarctic expedition?"

"It was mostly wiped out," she said. "Because they found a spaceship buried in the ancient ice and—"

"And it held something—dare I say it? *Aliiiiiive!*" Chick's last word imitated the show's introductory voiceover, but he drew out the word in mockery. "Save the *Tommyknockers* crap for pitch sessions, gopher."

As Chick strode away, the script supervisor lowered his iPad and approached Mac, murmuring, "It does sound far-fetched."

"So's this show," Mac said. "A bunch of mactors running around Antarctica, playing survivalist in bikinis and G-strings. Sure, summer temperatures are a lot warmer than they used to be. But we've just moved base camp to the *South Pole*. It's dropped below freezing here, with no improvement in sight. People are going to die."

"That's why the outcasts signed a release longer than the Treaty of Versailles."

The script supervisor was a short, soft man with dead-black hair and the name Stuart Spivek. His mask bore the logo for the recent remake of *The Crow*. Removing Buddy Holly shades, he exposed dark eyes rimmed in kohl and crinkled with morbid humor.

"Only in Hollywood would they name a TV show after a book about stranded plane crash survivors who committed cannibalism."

"That's why I like you, Stu." Mac touched the back of his gloved hand. "You've heard of books."

"I never heard of any Big Magnet Project."

"I wish I'd made it up," Mac said.

"I believe you," Stu said. "But there's a big difference between a forgotten Antarctic expedition and an alien spacecraft."

"Oh, I know," she said. "But family lore says whatever my great-grandfather found, it scared a man who didn't scare easily. And he insisted no one go back to the South Pole, because what they found could infect any living thing, big or small, human or animal. My great-grandfather thought even a tiny fragment of the alien's flesh could infect someone."

"Infect?" Stu's eyebrows rose. "Like a disease, or maybe an implanted egg, like in the *Alien* movies?"

"Like demonic possession," Mac said. "Say the alien infected your best friend. He'd become an alien, too, but you wouldn't know it until it was too late."

"The new alien retains the infected person's appearance?"

"And all the infected person's thoughts, memories, and behaviors."

"Talk about the ultimate make-over," Stu said.

Mac didn't laugh. "You'd be totally convinced you were talking to your best bud, and the alien would use your ignorance to infect you. Then you'd both go looking for more creatures to infect. And no one would suspect what you were up to. Why would they?"

"The gift that keeps on giving."

"A threat to every creature on the planet," she said. "Infection was the space invader's means of reproduction, and reproduction its *raison d'être*."

"So why aren't we all aliens? Or—" Stu shuddered. "You're making me paranoid."

"Welcome to the club."

"If we were already aliens, we wouldn't even know it!"

"Are you telepathic?" Mac asked.

"What? That crap was debunked way

back in the twentieth century."

"I'm not telepathic, either," said Mac. "But the alien was."

"Well, that proves it, then," Stu said. "I feel much better now."

"We're not alien doppelgangers," Mac said. "The expedition survivors destroyed the alien, its spaceship, and everyone it infected."

"As far as you know," said Stu. "Is this why you told everyone to wear a mask before our ship got anywhere near Antarctica?"

Mac laughed grimly. "I said we ought to wear masks for the obvious reason—earth's already had three worldwide pandemics from diseases released by melting ice and permafrost, and we were heading straight for ground zero," she said. "If I'd added, 'There might be an alien down there, and its lingering cells will infect you with shape-shifting space madness,' do you think I'd be wearing anything now besides a straitjacket?"

"No," Stu said. "But few listened to your common-sense explanation."

"You did," Mac responded with a grin in her voice. "Which is why you're still getting some, lover."

He didn't laugh. "You don't believe your family story. Do you?"

"Believe an interstellar spaceship was buried in the ice since Antarctica first froze? *And* one of the passengers survived for millions of years, *and* it could read earthly minds and imitate earthly life? Obviously, that was a complete fantasy, generated by the trauma of multiple deaths during a long dark polar winter with no hope of escape," Mac said. "Or so I thought. But now, we've found the base—"

"I still don't see how it could be true. I mean, if the imitations fooled everyone, how did anyone detect them?"

"According to my great-grandfather—"

"Places." The shout came from the first assistant director, Cam Adebayo, a short, slight nonbinary in a brilliant red snow-suit.

Mac turned. She jerked in surprise. Then she said, "What the hell? Wait!"

"Now what?" said the first AD.

Mac said, "Chick's pomsky—"

"His designer dog?" said the AD.

Stu pointed at Chick's full-grown Pomeranian/Siberian husky mix, which weighed seven pounds and looked like a miniature wolf. "Whobert's dug something up."

Mac said, "A disembodied human hand."

"Dear God!" The AD raised their hands to their mouth and retched. "She's eating a *finger*!"

"We can't have the hand discovered by Whobert," Chick snapped. "Mac, get her away from that hand and rebury it in the ice. That's a perfect find for the outcasts!"

"Touching it is the last thing we should do," Mac said.

"We've heard enough from you, gopher," Chick told her. "Shut up and—"

Mac wheeled to face him, eyes narrowed. "You're not my handler. I don't take orders from you."

As Chick's red face went ice-white with rage, she turned her back on him.

"We need to quarantine Whobert and—"

* * * *

Whobert remained free. A security officer escorted Mac to the shipping container which served as her work-slash-living space and locked her inside.

Mac was alone. Security had taken her card key, walkie talkie, iPhone, and satellite phone. Some of her workstation software was operational, but full access to the local area network and any access to the internet were shut off. She didn't have a window, unless you counted the polycarbonate panel in her door. She couldn't unlock the door.

"Looks like I picked the wrong week to quit smoking."

She rarely smoked, and never while working, but she retrieved her electronic cigarette from the little ceramic plate on her nightstand, then withdrew several cartridges of THC oil from the drawer. She brought the items to her workstation and loaded one of the mini tanks in the pen. Bringing the mouthpiece to her lips, she inhaled, activating the heating coil. She began chain-puffing. When the flavor weakened, she replaced the tank. When the tanks were empty, she cleaned her pen, then connected it to a USB cord to recharge.

She was lapsing into a doze when she heard a knock. Rising from her ergonomic chair, she stretched, popping her spine. The arthritic ache had faded from her hips and knees. She loaded the vape with a full tank from the half-open drawer of her nightstand, then set the vape on its plate. Her movements were slow.

She crossed languidly to the insulated door on her stocking feet. Pulling back the blackout curtain of the little polycarbonate panel, she looked out. Clouds had covered the midnight sun, but she squinted her blood-shot eyes and made out the director's face, smiling at her.

She felt no surprise. Hers was an entry-level job, but she was a vital crew member. Everyone was vital. The shoot couldn't spare people for a sick day, never mind a disagreement with the director.

The crew and cast had undergone extensive medical testing, right down to sexually transmitted diseases, but everyone had still been quarantined for two weeks before shooting began. Since electronic and sat-phone communication could easily fail in an extreme location, all the live/work containers had an entry intercom. Mac pressed the button and addressed her visitor.

"The package uploaded in time." Her words were a statement. A question about finishing the episode would suggest she doubted Chick Cabane's greatness.

He grinned. "Another prime time knock-out."

"What's the upshot?"

"In tonight's episode," Chick intoned in mock voice-over, "Team Polar Bear found the cache of food, but Team Snow Lion found the hand." He developed a queasy look. "The hand's quite gruesome, really. Burned almost beyond recognition. But brilliant television, of course."

"Of course," Mac said. "What are we not telling the folks at home?"

"We've placed lights around the found building, so a 'sudden uptick in local temps' will melt the ice and expose the ruin. Maybe, the whole base!"

"An excellent idea," Mac said. "Who's out?"

"The outcasts told Blenden, 'You're sunk!'"

"He's been a schmuck, and not in an interesting way," Mac observed.

"He's in the 'hotel' now," Chick said.

A cast member was voted out of the show each week, but they had to stick around. You didn't return potentially talkative or vengeful insiders to the world before the season wrapped. Anyway, barring medevac, the budget prevented individual returns.

Mac and Chick studied one another's faces through the polycarbonate.

"Well," Chick said. "You might be in here a while."

I don't need a clock to know what time it is.

Hollywood had gotten more consistent in firing sexual predators. But Chick had smaller balls than a pigmy jerboa, and his occasional low-key creeping on female underlings went unnoticed by the higher-ups. Even some of his targets missed that he was coming on to them, including a few women who would happily screw a director in hopes of career advancement.

Mac gave Chick a slow smile. "You have a key to this joint?"

He grinned and raised a hand in a data-tip glove, card key pinched between thumb and forefinger. "I could spring you, you know. Under the right conditions."

"'Spring' me?" Mac's smile widened. "Why don't you come in and show me what that means."

Chick let himself into her open-plan container. Mac moved slowly as she closed the door and pulled the curtain over the pane. She locked the door (she could do that now). She braced herself, then turned.

Chick had shed his parka and boots and deposited his gloves and card key on her nightstand. His lanky body sprawled over the double bed she unofficially shared with Stu. Chick watched her intently.

"You sexy thing," she said as she approached the bed. "Vape a little cannabis first?"

Chick liked to chillax after a day of popping Adderall like Pez. His grin returned. Then he squinted, staring at her eyes. "Red as tail-lights. Somebody got a head start."

"Plenty left." Mac raised the vape, then paused, giving Chick a contemplative look. Slowly, she said, "I'm in the mood for some wet work."

He frowned in concentration. Then his mouth opened in astonishment and a trembling vulnerability. The rumors were true. He favored a very specific practice.

"Oh, Mac," he said finally. "You don't have to—"

She laughed. "Your blood."

"Please," Chick whispered tremulously.

"'Please, boss,'" she said. "What's the safe word?"

He laughed, low in the throat. "How about 'alien,' boss?"

"Shuck your shirt, grab iron, and don't let go until I tell you."

Chick sat up and peeled off his pocket tee, revealing a scrawny torso and alabaster flesh. No tattoos were visible, but a few faint, straight scars crisscrossed his front and back. Stretching out, he grabbed the cross-bars at the head and foot of the bed.

Taking the remote from her nightstand, Mac turned on the wallscreen, then activated the stored entertainment—a British reboot of *Babylon Berlin* so violent, one critic had labeled it *Babylon Bonnie and Clyde*. She hadn't gotten far into the new season—Stu found the show disturbing—but it helped Mac unwind after a 16-18 hour day.

She raised the volume. Her inner and outer walls sandwiched insulation, and her container stood at the edge of the camp, but the containers were close together. Her "evening" with Chick might get noisy.

She raised her pen and took several puffs, but didn't give Chick a hit, however much he begged. Then she pulled a straight razor out of her nightstand. As she unfolded the blade from the handle, Chick whimpered.

Theatrically, Mac polished the heavy blade on Stu's suede strap. Stu loved a close shave and adored lathering up old-school with soap and brush, and he kept his toiletries in her container. To avoid rust, he stored his razor with its strap in her bedside drawer. He'd taught her how to care for the blade, and she enjoyed the comforting weight of the "cut-throat razor" in her hand and the sight of the edge starting to shine. When she got back to civilization, she was getting her own open razor for shaving her pits and legs.

She smiled at Chick, and he spoke hoarsely. "You are *cruel*, boss."

"Want a hit?"

"Please—"

"Keep still," she said, "and I'll think about sharing."

He lay very still. She puffed, then returned her vape to the little plate with the image of the Tokyo Skytree, which she'd picked up during her three years in Japan. Despite the swampy subtropical summers, she'd enjoyed her duty posting at Torii Station.

When the edge shone like a mirror, she turned to Chick. His gaze jumped to the blade. He smiled as if Mac were presenting him with the Oscar.

She ran the edge of the blade very lightly across Chick's chest. A fine red line appeared, vivid against the milk-white skin. Chick bit his lower lip, but looked pleased when blood began to gather between his nearly nonexistent pecs.

Mac cleaned the blade and folded it into the scales, then dropped the razor in the breast pocket of her wave-patterned men's aloha shirt. Ignoring his pleading look, she raised her pen and enjoyed a toke. She showed the device to Chick.

"Your turn," she told him.

She lowered the pen slowly, the mouth-piece aimed at his lips. Then she abruptly brought the hot chamber close to the accumulating blood.

The blood flowed up his breast, fleeing the heat.

As Mac dropped the e-cig on his chest and reached in her drawer, the man altered. Red and white skin turned blue, as if blasted by a polar wind. Thick blue hairs poked from the base of the neck, like worms pushing from a corpse. Two pale eyes became the three red orbs of a hell-hound.

Face twisting with rage, the thing that had been Chick Cabane surged upright.

Mac whipped her hand from the drawer and fired her pistol three times, planting a bullet in each eye.

The thing reached for her with elongating fingers. Draining the Glock 17 of its remaining fourteen 9mm rounds clearly wouldn't improve the outcome, so Mac shoved the compact semi-automatic in her belt and her hand in the drawer. Her hand reappeared immediately, bearing the tool she'd relocated from the kitchenette.

The thing was about to seize her with its tentacle-fingers when she activated the tool. The thing sensed what she was aiming and reared back, its snarl exposing snake-like fangs.

Mac shoved her crème brûlée torch closer.

The eight-inch tool was intended for culinary use and jewelry making, so it hadn't been sieved out of the luggage she'd checked for her flight to Malvinas Argentinas Ushuaia International Airport and the ship to Antarctica (her Glock and ammo hadn't been removed because she kept her paperwork updated for international carry). With a full tank, the flame of the small butane torch would burn at 2372°F for up to sixty minutes. She'd made sure the tank was full.

It was difficult to destroy the thing. She set the bed on fire, and the thing set the bedroom nook on fire as it flopped on the floor and crawled away from her. The live/work space took flame with all the speed of substandard building materials.

The alien went still, but Mac didn't try to confirm if it was dead (did it even have lungs or a heart?). And she had barely enough time to seize card key and gloves and parka, step into her boots, and get out of the container alive.

Coughing smoke from her lungs, she locked the door. As she dropped the card in her breast pocket with Stu's razor, she wheeled around.

She stilled herself, ignoring the heat radiating painfully through the insulated door. Butt nestled in fresh snowfall, Whobert sat waiting for her master. She had a dense coat and was unconcerned with the flurry that had begun sometime after Mac closed the curtain. She met Mac's gaze with bright blue eyes and gave a playful bark.

I love dogs.

"Good dog," she said.

Dogs are the best.

As Whobert's tail wagged into overdrive, Mac pulled the semi-automatic from her belt and shot the dog in the right front leg.

The creature lurched but caught itself on the three intact legs. Its head reshaped, gaining a third blazing eye. Growling like a pit bull in a fighting ring, the thing lunged forward. The tentacles rising like blue vipers from its neck nearly reached Mac's ankle before she shattered the thing's three remaining legs with three more shots, then activated the torch.

When the thing finally collapsed in a burning heap, Mac risked a glance at her container. She couldn't see flames through the polycarbonate panel, but it was starting to melt, releasing smoke and British accents and the snap, crackle, and hiss of the fire. Smoke was also slipping around the door on all sides. Something else was sliding underneath the door—something amorphous and fleshy and covered by tiny flames.

The metal in her hands felt like ice. With numbing fingers, she applied her blue flame to the fleshy mass until it retreated under the door. Then, tucking the torch under her arm and returning the handgun to her belt, she drew on her gloves and surveyed her surroundings.

White flakes sifted gently from the lowering sky and danced gracefully among the shipping containers. She drew a deep breath. The cold air frosted her alveoli and set off another round of coughing, but she didn't care. It rarely snowed in Antarctica (which was a desert), and there was nothing as beautiful as falling snow.

Moving away from her container, she approached the motor transport. In the open, the wind strengthened, slipping into her open parka to slice through her cotton Hawaiian shirt and silk thermal undershirt like toilet paper. Her bare face ached. Her mother was Iñupiaq, and she'd grown up in Fairbanks, but her tours of duty had largely been in blistering climates, and upon retiring from the army she'd moved to L.A. The Arctic icecap had disappeared permanently over a decade ago. It was easy to forget temperatures could still drop as low as -144°F at the South Pole.

The snowfall was thickening as the wind raised the flakes of past flurries to mix with the new, but Mac could see the production cubes—trucks—and tractors and snowmobiles. Stepping carefully on the rippled blue sheet of ancient ice, Mac squinted against the snow-squall and counted the vehicles in the makeshift parking lot. Pot smoke was thick in her skull. She took her time, moving carefully and focusing on the numbers.

Finishing at the snowmobiles, she nearly forgot the total when Stu materialized from the snowfall.

"Let's go!" he shouted, extending a gloved hand.

Mac's heart pounded with relief. Stu believed her. He wanted to get the hell out of here.

She withdrew Stu's razor from her pocket.

He stopped in his tracks and spread his gloved hands in an appeasing gesture.

"You've got your gun," he said, staring at the grip near her belt-buckle. "Shoot me if you think I'm not me."

He wore his snow-suit, but was shaking as if he were naked in the polar cold. He stilled his trembling with visible effort. Above his mask, his bare eyes met her gaze steadily.

"I understand your paranoia," he said softly. "There's no way I'd trust me if I were you. I— Hell. Even *I* don't trust me. But I want to help you. How can we end this?"

"We need to rescue the people who haven't changed and get out of here," Mac said.

Stu grimaced. "And then what? Our ship isn't back again for weeks."

"We're not impossibly far from the Amundsen-Scott South Pole Station. I can inform an old army buddy there that we're incoming, if you have your satellite phone. Chick's still got mine."

"Of course." Stu fumbled in a cargo pocket for the bulky portable. "Any vehicles missing?"

"All present and accounted for."

"That's a relief." Stu kept his distance as he held out the satphone. "Wow, are your eyes red."

"I dipped into your stash."

Moving no closer, Mac pocketed the razor and reached to arm's length. She felt wobbly—shouldn't have gotten so stoned, maybe? But she got the satphone without touching his glove.

She moved quickly then, yanking her semi-auto from her belt and shooting Stu in the kneecap. As he fell, she blasted the other knee. Dropping her weapon, she plucked the torch from her pocket and set Stu on fire.

Abruptly, Mac faced a screaming, writhing thing. Its rubbery blue body flailed on the snow and lengthening blue hairs squirmed around an unhuman face. Wrath twisted like flames in the depths of three eyes.

Stu wouldn't have come here. Stu had no way to know where she'd gone. Despite her warning, someone—some *thing*—had fooled Stu fatally.

Alien cells must have infected Whobert before she noticed the dog had the hand. Then the canine ears overheard Mac's conversation with Stu and the alien intelligence understood it. Oh, God. Stu never had a chance.

Were those footsteps? The wind had dropped, but it could still hide or alter sounds. So could falling snow. She strained her ears—yes. Footsteps, approaching from every side.

No doubt the alien took pains to infect everyone else while she was incommunicado. Even with increasing numbers, it wouldn't have been a quick process—the total crew and cast numbered almost 350 people. But they were after her now. And, after weeks of pressure-cooker shooting on location, they knew her well.

But the space invader didn't have access only to the infected people's experiences, thoughts, and traits.

It had access to every movie, show, game, book, magazine, video, and website in their memories. It had absorbed centuries' worth of human entertainment, history, biology, sociology, and psychology—and mixed and blended them all with its otherworldly intellect and capabilities.

Mac didn't face merely a near-indestructible alien foe, bent implacably on replacing all life on earth.

It was a group mind of incalculable knowledge and insight.

That didn't mean it knew everything.

Mac activated Stu's satphone and punched in a number she'd never programmed into a phone or typed into a file or written down or shared with anyone. A number she'd been given when she last saw her handler, the woman who'd recruited her for the CIA when she'd retired from the U.S. Army Military Police Corps. The woman who had summoned her for face-to-face discussion of her upcoming undercover Antarctic operation.

Yes, Mac had a family story about her great-grandfather.

Yes, something had happened that had made him warn his family never to go south of the equator.

But Mac knew no more than that, until her handler told her.

There was an immediate click in her ear, and a voice: "Report."

She said, "Fire at the pole."

As she pocketed the satphone, the mob was sublimating from the snowfall. Tentacled blue things snarled at her with serpentine fangs and glared at her with live-coal eyes. Why pretend, when you've got the last uninfected person surrounded?

Instantly, she drew her Glock and fired, piercing a red eye and rousing a wrathful screech. But all the things flinched and began backing away. They ducked and weaved, hot eyes fixed on her as they melted into the swirling snow.

"Can't tell where I'm going to shoot next, can you?" Mac laughed. "Seems it's not so easy to read an earthling's thoughts when she's higher than the satellites."

She pivoted and fired, and an angry-bull bellow came through the snowfall.

"Bullets can't kill you, but you've been counting. You know how many rounds I have left, and you know a gunshot wound hurts almost as much as a kidney stone. And you've got a plan. Some of you will keep me corralled until I run out of rounds or hypothermia scrambles my wits, while the rest of you light out for the Antarctic bases."

She returned her Glock to her belt and straddled the nearest snowmobile.

"It's a cunning plan, but you forgot something: The set production assistant's duties include driving, and I was put in charge of the motor vehicle keys. And they're in the flaming wreck of my container. Most of them, anyway."

As angry cries came from every side, Mac reached in her parka pocket and withdrew the bulky sock. Since she didn't enjoy being jabbed by sharpish points, she bundled up the keys she carried. As a result, her keyring made no noise, and security didn't think to take her keys when they locked her up.

A voice came from the snow: "Nobody cares if you have the keys. We'll hotwire the vehicles."

The voice imitated Stu's perfectly. Mac shivered. The alien's mimicry wasn't bound to its original source.

"Hotwire? I'm screwed! Oh, wait." She pulled the razor partway out of her breast pocket. "I slashed every tire."

The sound of running feet rose as Mac started the Polaris Pro-X snow-machine and unpocketed her culinary torch.

The aliens burst from the snowfall around her.

They paused as Mac activated the torch flame. Tool extended in one hand, she sent her snowmobile plunging toward the things. The closest aliens leaped to either side.

Mac roared through the gap with a laugh.

One of the things sniffed at a strengthening smell in the air. The things looked at one another. They turned their backs on the speeding snow machine and stampeded in the opposite direction.

Mac's voice followed them. "You're sunk!"

The *Alive* crew had needed to truck in thousands of gallons of fuel for the shoot. They'd created a storage depot. Mac flung her flaming blowtorch into the lake she'd created by opening all the tanks.

The explosions shook the earth.

On a distant ridge, Mac halted her snowmobile. She watched base camp through the thinning snowfall and spoke into the satphone. As she described what she saw, the overcast sky began to drone. The approaching aircraft grew louder.

* * * *

The conflagration created by saturation firebombing was visible from McMurdo Station, Tierra del Fuego, and Tasmania.

The world mourned the Hollywood television crew and cast attacked by unknown terrorists, whose shocking act at the remotest spot on the planet had left a single survivor.

The last episode of *Alive!* was the most-watched show in television history.

⚛

Author's Note

Special thanks to David Bondalevitch, Melissa Hofmann, and especially Amy Wolf for information on television production.

ABOUT THE AUTHOR

Cynthia Ward has published stories in *Analog, Asimov's, Nightmare, Weirdbook, Weird Tales,* and elsewhere. She edited the anthologies *Lost Trails: Forgotten Tales of the Weird West,* volumes one and two. With Nisi Shawl, Cynthia co-created the groundbreaking Writing the Other writers' workshop and coauthored the diversity fiction-writing handbook, *Writing the Other: A Practical Approach,* which were honored with a Locus Special Award. Her latest pulp novella, *The Adventure of the Golden Woman: Blood-Thirsty Agent Book 4,* was recently released by Aqueduct Press. Cynthia lives in Los Angeles, where she is not working on a screenplay.

ABOUT THE ARTIST

Bob Eggleton is one of othe most acclaimed artists in the science fiction, fantasy, and horror fields. Especially famous for his illustrations of classic monsters (notable Godzilla—and many, many more), we knew at once he would be the perfect artist for this story. He's drawn the Things before, too, illustrating *Frozen Hell,* the recently discovered alternate novel-length version of John W. Campbell's classic story, "Who Goes There?" (where the Thing first appeared).

THOUGHTS THAT KILL

by John Russell Fearn and Ron Turner

INTRODUCTION
by Phil Harbottle

In the 1930s, there were very few outlets for science fiction short-story writing, the main one being the American pulp magazines. In one sense, this had a restricting effect, since the stories had to conform to certain pulp conventions, *i.e.* the need to contain plenty of action and to be very easy to read. The 'literary' side tended to suffer. But whatever its literary shortcomings, what was undeniable about the pulp period was that it acted as a hothouse for science fiction *ideas*, and many stories exhibited a real sense of wonder; there was an agreeable *frisson* experienced by both author and reader when they realized they were experiencing something new and innovative.

John Russell Fearn (1908-60) who in the 1930's was the *only* full-time writer of science fiction in the U.K, wrote many stories for the U.S. pulps, most notably for *Amazing, Astounding,* and *Startling Stories*, and pioneered many SF ideas and concepts. *Thoughts That Kill* (1939), with its curious ideas and sense of irony, was such a story, and it has long been a favourite of mine.

It has always struck me that this story in particular, along with several other Fearn stories, would transfer very successfully to the graphic medium... But how to bring this about?

In the 1980s I was fortunate enough to be put in contact with artist Ron Turner, through our mutual friend John Lawrence, a lifelong fan of Turner's work. John had managed to trace his reclusive idol, one of England's greatest innovators of visual science fiction images and archetypes in the early 1950s (which saw the first real flowering of SF comic strips in this country). Alongside the incomparable Frank Hampson's *Dan Dare*, Turner's pioneering work with *Space Ace* and *Rick Random* created an entire school of science fiction graphic art, giving it the 'designer look' we nowadays take for granted.

Thanks to John, it was my pleasure to be able to commission Ron Turner to adapt not only *Thoughts That Kill*, but several other Fearn short stories to the strip cartoon medium, along with those of two of my other favourite authors (E. C. Tubb and Sydney Bounds). With *Thoughts That Kill* especially, I think Ron Turner has succeeded admirably in capturing that elusive sense of wonder and excitement as this curious story unfolds.

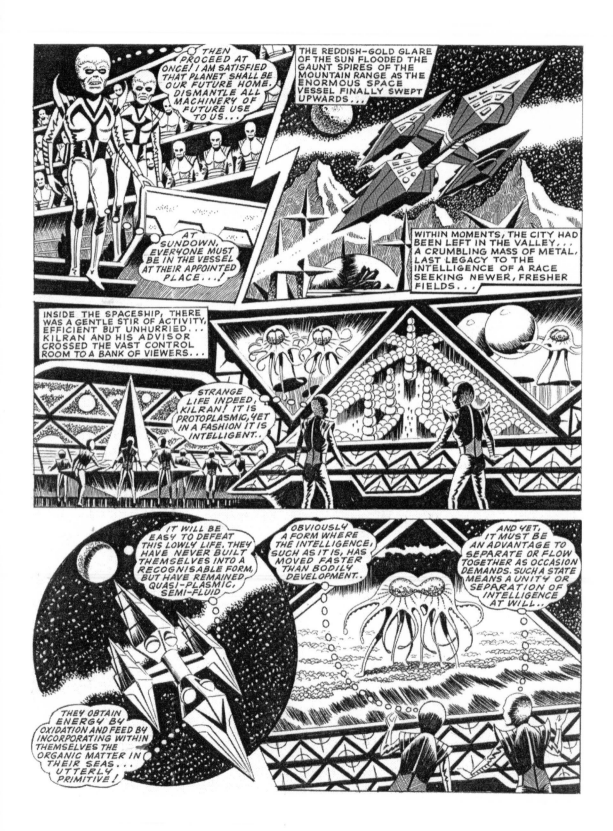

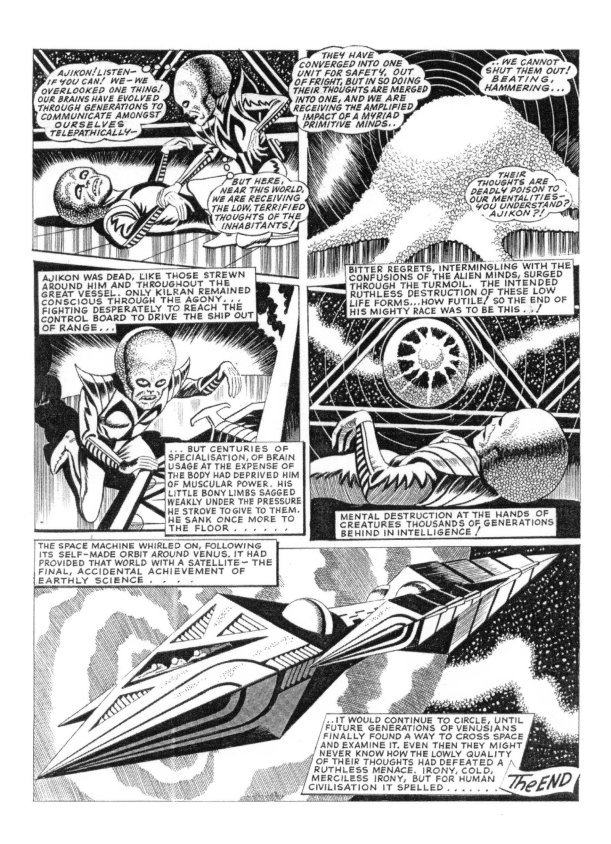

SHARPTOOTH

by Lorenzo Crescentini
(translated by Amanda Blee)

The illusion of harnessing life at the Genesis Research Centre lasted around forty seconds, then the transporter with the tyrannosaurus exploded. Shards of shatterproof glass rained down and the roars of the reptile filled Lab B, drowning out the screams of the people running towards the exit.

The beast tore up what remained of the Transportation Chamber and leapt onto the white linoleum floor, greedily eyeing up the tiny, two-legged mammals as they scattered all around. A moment later, he attacked, charging at those unlucky enough to be nearest the containment cell.

* * * *

"No, no, no, no, no..."

Kai was about to ask Boris what the problem was, when his gaze fell on the surveillance monitor and he turned pale.

For a few moments he could only stand and stare as sevens tons of dinosaur tore the containment cell apart and attacked the group of scientists and technicians who had been watching the Recall experiment. It was only when the creature turned towards the camera and roared once more, showing off two rows of sharp teeth, 30cm-long, that the Japanese regained control of himself: "The doors!" he screamed. "Boris, for God's sake, close those doors!"

Recovered from the shock, the Russian entered the emergency shutdown code. A siren screamed out and two airtight doors slowly began to descend, isolating the area, while screaming men and women crawled underneath them. Thirty seconds later, the metal doors came to a halt on the floor, sealing off Lab B and its voracious guest.

"Did they make it?" asked Kai, anxiously.

Together, they peered at the screen to see if anyone had been left behind when the doors had come down. By tacit agreement, no one mentioned the two pairs of legs lying on the pavement just outside the transporter.

Apart from the two victims torn apart by the Cretaceous fury of the predator, there was no one else in the room. Kai leaned back in his chair and let out a long sigh.

For a while no one spoke.

They sat watching the images on the screen. The reptile moved around the room, studying the environment. The pile of chairs which had been overturned in the rush to get out, looked like they'd been struck by a tornado, while in the opposite corner, behind the remains of the Chamber, a vending machine lay diagonally across the floor, looking like a large metal coffin.

"What do we do now?" asked Boris.

For the first time ever, Kai had no answers.

What had just happened was impossible. The Recall Chamber wasn't capable of transporting matter. It was unthinkable, contrary to every law of physics.

"But..." said Boris. "Weren't the Chambers supposed to show us *images* of dinosaurs?"

Any other time, Kai would have found his colleague's talent for stating the obvious at the least opportune moment unbearable, but he was too shocked. He said nothing and continued to watch the beast as it sniffed the steel walls.

It was true, of course. Those sophisticated instruments were based on their ability to trace a trail of tachyons and identify life forms in correspondence with a fossil discovery site, dated by radioactive isotopes, which were then projected into the Recall Chamber.

Energy, not matter. Energy, just energy.

Of course, the prehistoric beast in the main lab didn't seem to care much about this quantum anomaly. It seemed more and more irritated by the situation: it roared again, and, even filtered through the loud speakers of the control room, the noise froze Kai's blood.

"What are we going to do?" Boris asked again.

Kai had no idea. There was no protocol for an eventuality that was considered impossible. If they'd been in a film, they probably would have filtered nerve gas into the room from invisible pores or eliminated the problem by exploding a small nuclear weapon. But nobody in his right mind would have considered installing such countermeasures in an orbital station like the one they were on, where the greatest threat was a blackout caused by a power surge.

Kai's heart ached when he thought of all those people who had taken refuge in the research centre tunnels. He didn't even want to think about what might happen if the dinosaur got out of the lab. The only thing they could do, he thought, was hope the beast didn't try and escape.

With malevolent telepathy, the animal chose that moment to charge at the doors marked with a red letter "A". The impact was violent, and the repercussion sent the reptile staggering backwards. Cautiously, he moved in close again and began to study the thickness of the barrier he'd seen his prey disappear behind. Then he lowered his head and charged again.

They watched the scene from the control room.

"Will they hold?" asked Boris.

The Asian shook his head. "Those doors were designed to isolate chemical and radiation leaks. And radiation can't head butt! They'll give way."

All they could do was watch the beast stop, look around and charge again.

Kai wasn't sure if the T-Rex's eyesight was developed enough to notice the increasingly pronounced concave curvature in the steel doors, which were rapidly approaching breaking point.

He hoped not.

"We have to let Earth know," said the Russian.

"What for? It takes two days for a shuttle to get here from Cape Canaveral and those doors won't last another hour, if that."

Boris gulped. He knew that too, of course. But it was up to them to solve the problem, any way they could.

It was all down to them. Suddenly, Kai regretted ever boarding the space station.

* * * *

Kai and Boris didn't know it, but there was someone in an even more delicate situation than theirs.

Chevo had just raised his head over the side of the vending machine when Juan saw him and grabbed him by the collar of his overalls, pulling him back down.

He moved his lips in silence, miming a "You crazy?"

On the other side of the vending machine, the tyrannosaurus continued its battle with the laboratory doors, snorting and roaring raucously. Every now and then, it stopped and sniffed the air and the two men would held their breath, sure that this time the beast would sniff out the two tender morsels hidden in the corner.

Then it would go back to charging at the door and they could relax again, so to speak.

Juan figured that if they were still alive, it was thanks to the two scientists smeared on the opposite wall. The stench of their intestines filled the air and was enough to cover their own scent.

He cursed the scientists who worked there in all the languages he knew. They could have asked him to fix the drinks machine anytime, so why did they have to choose the exact moment a damn *dinosaur* was about to burst from the vortexes of time and land right in their lap?

When the beast had escaped from its prison—and a mighty swish of its tail had only just missed their heads and sent the vending machine flying—Juan had instinctively dived behind the machine. As he'd watched the stampede, he'd realised with horror that the enormous carnivore was halfway between the vending machine and the exit doors, which were already closing.

Juan had leaped to his feet, confident he'd be faster than the lumbering giant, but then he'd seen it lunge forward, clamping its jaws not once, but twice around the bodies of the two white-coated men who had delayed their escape by less than a second, tearing them apart.

As the monster threw back its metre-long head and swallowed its meal, Juan retreated behind the vending machine, face white, eyes closed, reciting all the prayers to the Virgin of Guadalupe that his mother had ever taught him, sure he'd be following the others on their journey to the beast's stomach.

Ten seconds later, when still nothing had happened, he opened his eyes. Next to him, Chavo was watching him with a mixture of fear and curiosity. In the sudden chaos, Juan had totally forgotten about his co-worker.

He'd looked at him in amazement, his mouth open, about to speak, when Chavo held a finger up to his lips, in an unmistakable gesture that meant, "Sssh, if that huge dinosaur hears us, he'll gobble us up!"

So, they stayed there. Silent and invisible behind the vending machine, while the doors came down, sealing off the area and leaving them alone with the monster.

Now, however, Chavo was getting restless and Juan couldn't blame him: his wife and young daughter, Carla, were behind the barrier that the T-Rex was trying to break down. The problem was, if they made even the slightest wrong move, it would mean a horrible death for them both. Whether he liked it or not, there was nothing he could do to help his family. Their only option was survival, hoping someone else took over.

It took all of Juan's self-control to remain calm and try and regulate his body's vital functions. So far, the dinosaur was unaware of their presence, but he was scared that if he sweated heavily, or even worse, if he shit himself with fear, the predator's sense of smell would lead it straight to them.

He wished he could make that clear to Chavo, but they couldn't afford the luxury of speaking out loud. All he could do was hold his hands out, palm down, as if to say, "Don't worry."

It was quite clear that Chavo wasn't just going to sit there. Juan thought of the dismembered bodies and tried to imagine what it would be like to be terrified the same thing could happen to your wife and child and shivered.

In the meantime, Chavo had moved around the shelter again, peeking out over the top.

A few seconds later, Juan couldn't resist it any longer and he too looked out.

The T-Rex must have been about 12-metres long from nose to tail. Its huge back legs, which ended in three-clawed fingers, were scaled columns, firmly planted on the floor. Altogether it wasn't much taller than four or five metres: despite what he'd always imagined, the T-Rex's position was decidedly horizontal, its raised tail in line with its head and body. Its small forelegs dangled downwards, with no apparent purpose other than to highlight the monstrous size of the rest of its body.

As he watched the creature, he was struck by a thought: maybe it knew they were there. Perhaps it was no longer hungry and had decided to save them for later, since they had no chance of escape.

He put his head in his hands. This was not the time to panic.

He threw one last look at the dinosaur and crouched down in the corner. Why him?

* * * *

"The antimatter!" Kai slapped the control panel so hard, it made the Russian jump before he stared at his co-worker questioningly.

The Asian's eyes glittered.

"What?" asked Boris.

"The antimatter experiments, the ones they keep in Lab C. If we could…get them near the T-Rex…you know what would happen, no?"

The Russian stared back, his expression eloquent.

Kai rubbed his hand over his face and wondered, not for the first time, how Boris had got a job there. He quickly tried to explain. "Antimatter annihilates matter and creates a void. They isolated particles of antimatter in C2. They're right there, suspended in xenoglass jars. The walls of the container create a magnetic field, otherwise the jars would disappear. OK?"

Boris nodded.

"If the dinosaur just happened to *trample* one of the samples and shatter its container…"

Boris' face lit up. "It would disappear!"

"Yeah," said Kai. "Exactly!"

He narrowed his eyes, concentrating on the images of the T-Rex trying to force its way through door A.

"We've got to get him away from that door," he murmured, "lure him over to the one that leads to C1. From there it leads to C2. Perhaps if we open door C, our friend will get curious…"

The Russian shook his head.

Kai looked at him, annoyed. "Why not?"

"The door to C1 is big enough for him to get through," replied Boris, "but the door to C2 is too small."

Kai punched his thigh in frustration. He was right. In his euphoria he'd forgotten that the door between the two astrophysics research labs was of 'human' dimensions'.

He flopped back in his chair. "We need someone to move the samples out of C1," he said, "so we can lure that bastard inside. But guess what? Three quarters of the crew are barricaded in the living quarters, with our friend trying to break in and eat them. Those who are left will be hiding out all over the station, and even if we knew where to find them, we've no way of contacting them. So?"

He left the "*So*" hanging lightly in the air, trying not to betray just how desperate they were for someone to come up with something.

Boris didn't answer. He was peering at something on the monitor.

For a moment Kai felt tempted to ask him if he was going to paint a picture of the dinosaur but held back. If he let his nerves get the better of him, they were finished. Everyone who worked at the research centre, that is. And what of them? If they called Earth for help, they'd have to wait two days, locked in the control room. Would they make it? And what could the reinforcements do to fight the beast? What if they couldn't…?

Boris's voice broke through his thoughts. "We can communicate with Lab B, no? With the loudspeakers, I mean."

Kai looked at him in amazement. "Yes. Why?"

The Russian indicated the monitor screen with his finger. Kai leaned in closer to get a better look.

At first, he thought Boris was pointing at the drinks machine that had been thrown to the ground in those first moments of terror. Then he saw the top of a human head.

"I might be wrong," said Boris. "But I think someone's in there."

* * * *

Juan raised his head, took a quick look around, then bobbed back down. The creature was too close. Too close to the door, too close to them, too close to the walls. Too close to everything.

He almost hoped it would break the doors down before realising they were there. He knew it wasn't a very noble thought, but he could imagine all too well what would happen when it finally sniffed them out. Those enormous, sharp teeth were something he wouldn't wish on his worst enemy.

"Calm down," he told himself. "Calm down. There's no reason why he should find you. If he could smell you, you'd already be soaking in his gastric juices. He doesn't know you're here and there's no reason for him to find out…"

"HEY, YOU, BEHIND THE VENDING MACHINE!"

The voice startled Juan and the urge to get up and run was almost irresistible. They had been discovered and it was only a matter of seconds before the T-Rex headed straight for them, its jaws wide open.

He made an enormous effort to ignore the primordial instinct to flee and sat there, in an ice cold sweat. Dinosaurs don't understand English, he thought, so whoever had spoken hadn't given them away. He heard an explosive roar and despite what his brain told him, raised himself up to take another look. The Tyrannosaurus seemed infuriated. He'd given up on the door and was now roaring at the two white speakers mounted high up on the wall, as they shouted, "YOU TWO, BEHIND THE VENDING MACHINE. CAN YOU HEAR ME?"

Perplexed, Juan and Chavo looked at each other. Juan was just wondering what to do when the voice continued: "WE KNOW YOU CAN'T ANSWER. WE'RE WATCHING YOU FROM THE CONTROL ROOM. WE NEED YOUR HELP, SO DO EXACTLY AS WE TELL YOU."

Juan looked at his co-worker again. Chavo shrugged.

* * * *

When Boris had explained his idea, Kai had found it unexpectedly brilliant.

He pressed the talk button. "In thirty seconds, we'll interrupt the Orbital Rotational System, and we'll be at zero gravity. We can't stay still for more than three minutes, or we risk losing our orbit and ending up drifting through space. So, we're going to open door C1 now and you have one hundred eighty seconds to get there…"

Juan's face turned pale as he listened to the voice coming from the speakers: "IF YOU LOOK, YOU'LL SEE A SERIES OF SMALL GROOVES CUT INTO THE WALLS. THESE ARE EMERGENCY GRIPS FOR INCASE WE LOSE GRAVITY. USE THEM TO REACH THE EXIT."

Juan looked at the wall and noticed what seemed like a series of fingerprints half way up, positioned around three metres apart, that stretched around the room. He'd never seen them before as they were white on white and had probably been designed with discretion in mind.

Chavo shook his head resolutely. Grips or no grips, they were crazy if they thought he was going to race a dinosaur to the door. No way. No way, Jose.

* * * *

"You think they'll do it?" asked Boris.

The Asian sighed. "They don't have much choice."

He pressed the button.

* * * *

Juan was thinking that he'd never seen a dinosaur float before. It was obviously a novelty for the beast, too, which was roaring and snapping its jaws in frustration. "Bastards" he muttered.

When gravity had been interrupted, he and Chavo had been careful not to make the slightest movement. They may not have been scientists, but even they knew it wouldn't take much to send them pirouetting around the room. The same couldn't be said for the dinosaur, which had been thrown into the air as it head-butted the doors.

The dinosaur continued its slow flight until it thudded against the ceiling: it roared again and began kicking its paws, which set it rotating on itself.

Juan turned to his co-worker. "What do we do now?" he whispered.

Chavo pointed and replied, "I don't know, but it's spotted us."

Juan followed the direction of Chavo's finger and felt his heart grow heavy. From his new position, the monster had a perfect view of them and every time it rotated to face them, its jaws snapped in their direction.

Juan gulped. It was highly unlikely that the beast would reach them in those conditions but, like the voice had said, they had three minutes and...

Chavo must have come to the same conclusion. "Let's get moving!" he said.

* * * *

The first leap was the most difficult. Juan was sure that, in some way, his weightlessness would betray him and send him straight into the animal's mouth. He moved slowly and, as soon as his feet left the floor, he began waving his arms like a madman, furiously reaching for the grips on the wall.

Three metres? It felt more like three kilometres. After what seemed like an eternity, his hands closed around the grips and Juan wasted no time in thanking the Holy Virgin of Guadalupe, patron saint of zero-gravity.

He turned and watched in horror as Chavo moved parallel to him and then flew past. In a flash, the fate he'd imagined for himself transferred itself to his colleague and Juan had a clear vision of the man being crushed between those enormous jaws. However, Chavo tightly clasped the next set of grips and motioned for him to hurry.

"Damn you!" he though, praying his next 'flight' would be a good one.

* * * *

They moved along the first wall without problems. Once he'd got into the rhythm, Juan told himself—apart from the roars of the predator—and once he'd somehow managed to stop spinning—it was almost fun.

He reached the corner and turned to make his way along the next wall and the fun suddenly ended. Lab B was L-shaped and the wall he was about to 'climb' ran along the inside of the shortest part. The dinosaur was right in front of them. This meant that if their leap was even slightly off—course, they'd end up right between the monster's jaws.

Chavo was the first to jump. Juan held his breath as he watched him cautiously make his way over to the next set of grips. He made it, clinging on tightly, leaving the path clear for Juan.

"OK," Juan thought, "It's OK. Don't pan-ic!"

He got into position, trying to shake off his nervousness. In front of him, the dinosaur looked delighted as it watched its prey slowly moving closer. As if to encourage them, it opened its jaws wide and kept them open, huge drops of saliva floating around the room.

Juan tried to ignore it, concentrating on his trajectory. He visualised his flight path and took off.

And missed

Chavo watched in wide-eyed horror as Juan reached towards the grips and overshot them by ten centimetres.

Juan had always thought that if he were to die like this—if it were possible to imagine dying like this—he would have screamed at the top of his lungs right till the end. But his throat was blocked, his body paralysed by pure, ice-cold terror. The dinosaur opened its mouth even further as it floated towards him. Just then, he felt a hand close around his ankle. He turned his head and saw that Chavo had leapt after him and caught him. Chavo's other hand grabbed onto the emergency grips, halting their flight. The dinosaur roared its disappointment and Juan whispered a faint "Thank you."

* * * *

Kai slumped back in his chair.

Thank God the big guy had managed to grab onto the other one and save their lives. Given the situation, he'd be happy if even one of them made it. The two repair men were now at the end of the corner wall. The last set of grips was right there, so they shouldn't have any problems moving over to the adjacent wall. Once they got around the corner, the dinosaur would be behind them and the doors would be right in front of them, just a jump away.

He allowed himself the luxury of relaxing for a few moments, then pressed the talk button again and announced, "Forty seconds left. We've opened the door. Once you're in there, you'll have to do something."

He watched the monitor as the two men

exchanged a glace. "It's vitally important," he continued, "that you find the antimatter containers in the next room and place one in the middle of C1."

He tried to remember just what they were like. "They look like jars. Big transparent jars. Make sure you don't drop them and that you put them right in the dinosaur's path. Is that clear?"

* * * *

"CLEAR?"

Chavo nodded, not really knowing where to look, then launched himself towards the door marked C1, now almost completely open. Juan followed him, happy to leave the prehistoric monster and his dashed expectations behind.

Juan had never thought that the simple act of leaving a room could bring such relief, yet, as soon as he set foot—not figuratively —in C1 he felt as though he'd just walked through the gates of Nirvana.

They quickly found the door into the next room and as they passed through it, they felt the air regain its usual consistency.

"Gravity's coming back," said Juan. "Hurry."

The glass jars were there on a table, together with other fragile objects. They waited until their feet touched the floor, then Chavo rushed forward and gathered up what they'd come for. They ran into C1 and watched what was happening in the adjoining room.

The dinosaur, once more with its feet on the ground, had picked up where he had left off and was once more trying to break down door A.

Chavo placed the container in front of the entrance and there was no need to wait for instructions from the loud speakers to know what to do. Juan put two fingers to his lips and let out a shrill whistle. Chavo covered his ears with his hands,

"Hey!" shouted Juan. "Hey, dinosaur! We're right here, *idiota*!"

He had no idea what was going to happen when the beast 'bumped' into the antimatter.

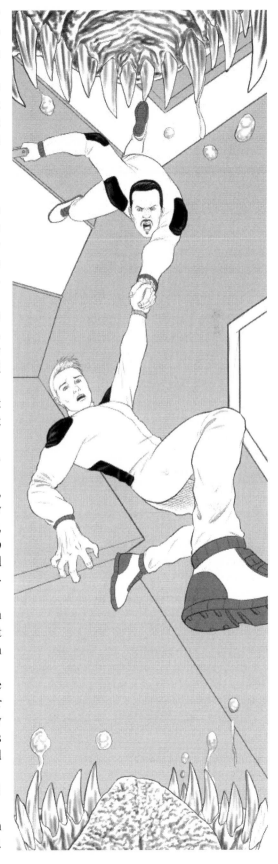

He was sure, however, that if it was something that could bring down a thousand-kilo monster, then they should make sure they were far enough away when it happened. His idea was to wait until the animal moved in their direction, then run as fast as they could, putting as many rooms as possible between them and C1.

"Hey, you! *Chico!*" he clapped his hands. "What's up? Lost your appetite? You turned *mariquita*? Come on, we're right here!"

He whistled again, shouted, and this time the dinosaur's enormous head turned in their direction. The T-Rex interrupted its work and stared at them…then went back to trying to destroy the door.

* * * *

"No!" Boris shouted, "It's not working. It's not moving!"

"I can see that!" replied Kai, his voice tense. He could see something else: the metal of the door had gone past breaking point and was starting to crumple. Door A was about to cave in.

Juan and Chavo were in the middle of the corridor, waving their arms, trying in vain to capture the reptile's attention. They continued like this until they heard the jarring sound of torn steel. Juan turned to his co-worker and saw that his face had gone white.

There was no need to ask what he was thinking: the only thing between his family and the monster's hunger was a sheet of metal. He saw him stagger, swallowing. Saw the beads of sweat gather around his bristly beard, then watched as he took two steps back and picked up the jar of antimatter,

As he turned towards him, Juan asked, "What are you…" then understood, his face also turning white.

"No!" he whispered, "No, Chavo, wait… you can't…"

Yes, I can," said the man. "I have to. I know you understand."

Juan opened his mouth to reply but realised he didn't know what to say. All he could do was nod.

Chavo put a hand on his shoulder. "Will

you tell them I love them?"

"Yes," said Juan, vaguely aware that he was crying. "Yes. Every day."

Chavo smiled. "*Gracias. Es un buen amigo.*"

Before Juan could say anything else, his friend was running towards the dinosaur.

"Hey," yelled Chavo. "*Soy aqui, mala bestia! Ehi!*"

When he got half way down the corridor, the dinosaur decided that its metal obstacle could wait a little longer, long enough to devour the little biped running towards it.

"*Maldito monstruo! Estùpido!*"

The reptile roared, making the walls tremble, then turned and charged.

Chavo ran on, the jar clasped tightly in his hands. When he was only a few metres away, the dinosaur lowered its head and opened its jaws.

Juan watched in silence from the doorway, Kai and Boris were glued to the monitor.

The dinosaur threw itself on its prey and roared in triumph.

"*Puerco maldido! Hijo de p…*"

A blinding light covered everything. Juan threw an arm up to protect his eyes, before the change in pressure threw him to the ground. A resounding roar bounced off the walls, making all the electric instruments in the control room whistle.

Kai and Boris yelled in pain at the piercing feedback from the short-circuited instruments.

When Juan opened his eyes, the room was empty.

❈

ABOUT THE AUTHOR

Italian author Lorenzo Crescentini was born in Forlì, and currently reside in Rome. His stories have been published in a number of collections and magazines including *Clarkesworld*, *Weirdbook*, *ARTPOST magazine*, *Future Visions*, and *Dream of Shadows* among others.

JUST LIKE YOU AND ME
by Stephen Persing

"**D**etective Patton, please wake up." said the voice, then repeated itself with only the slightest change of tone, a little extra urgency. By the third repetition I was awake, though still fuzzy-minded.

"I'm up," I said in a kind of raspy mumble. I tried to turn over, but my nightgown tangled around my legs and made any motion challenging. Besides, the bed was warm and I didn't want to get out of it.

"Good," said the voice, which I recognized as my boss's, a baritone, masculine voice: authority personified. He used this voice when he was strictly business. "Sorry to wake you, but I need you. Hollander Apartments, block B, unit 3-401. The data is on your phone now."

My phone lit up, and the screen appeared, hovering an inch or so above the handset with a photo and a column of data. My eyes were in focus by then, so I gave a quick look. An elderly man, short-cut hair salted with grey. Name: Dr. Francisco Morey y Pena. Address, but no other contact information. No living relatives. Long retired from a post in government—a classified position. Age: 121 years.

Then my eyes caught the time. "Chief," I said. "It's 4 a.m. What're you doing calling me?"

"Sorry," he said again, not convincingly this time either. "Been a bit of a busy night. A demonstration down in Center City got out of hand. Some labor dispute. I had to move most of the night shift to deal with that. You're the closest officer to hand."

"Lucky me," I said. I tried sitting up, with no ill effects. Perhaps last night's party hadn't been as wild as I recalled; I double-checked to make sure I was alone in the bed—I was. "I'll be on my way in a few minutes."

"Attagirl," the Chief said. I winced.

"Don't call me girl," I said.

"Sorry, Jeri," it said, this time with conviction. "You know what my programming is like."

I nodded, and reached over to the bed-side table. There are still occasional reports of people who do not like working with Artificial Intelligences or artificials—people grown in labs rather than in wombs—but, seriously, how could they avoid it? I suppose you could farm, with nothing but insensate robots assisting, but any job in the city or suburbs surrounded you with artificials. You just lived with them. They were your teachers, your neighbors, sometimes your lovers.

I put on my work clothes and donned my props—spectacles, ear trumpets, the latest technology for augmenting the senses, all supplied with names drawn from centuries-old counterparts. Except for the nasal augments; no one had ever figured out a good name for them. Armed with the eyes of a hawk, the nose of a bloodhound, and the ears of something that can hear very well (I don't know; I'm no naturalist) I felt ready to start out.

To be honest, they're not the latest technology either. Permanent augments were available, implanted in the brain or in various sense organs, but I am old-fashioned. Call me squeamish, but my body is mine, and I didn't want to let tech inside. The Chief had finally stopped trying to debate me on that, since the external augments worked well enough—or perhaps he just hated losing arguments. Also, there were legal precedents. I couldn't be coerced, and wouldn't be convinced. I want to be me.

A few moments later, my augments in place, and a breakfast muffin in hand, I

looked out the window, seeing the faintest blue in the sky beyond the lines of apartment blocks. Perhaps it was dawn, perhaps the city lights coloring the night. It didn't really matter which. The Hollander apartments were just out of sight, maybe ten minutes away. The window let in cool fresh air, not so cool I couldn't leave the window open overnight, but that's June for you. I strapped on my gun, turned on my ID badge, and went to work. No need to stop at the station, as everything everywhere is connected through the System—"the System is aware," as they say. I suppose it knew I stopped for coffee and hash browns along the way, making me officially late for work, unless it counted me as on duty the moment I got in my car... Who knows?

* * * *

The apartment was one of many in the block, a deep green door in a bland, slightly worn hallway, beige carpets not quite matching the beige walls. A uniformed officer, with the unwavering stolidity of an AI, was guarding the door.

"Detective," he said, nodding slightly.

"Officer," I replied. Chances are he didn't have a name, and a glance at his badge confirmed it. These grunts were barely more than robots. "Is it sealed?"

"No, ma'am," he said. "A neighbor went to check on him and found him as you will see. She's given a statement. Her story checks out."

"Coroner been by?"

He shook his head. "Orders. No one allowed in until you've seen everything."

That was odd. Usually forensics teams, medics, the usual crowd would be hard at work. I was about to ask that orders he meant when he thumbed the doorknob and it slid quietly open. It was an unusual move from the normally passive blues; with the public they could police openly, but with detectives they became little more than automata. I went in.

It was a small apartment, one bedroom, conservatively furnished, but with signs of elegance in the brocade fabrics and fine details in the furniture. Heavy drapes covered the windows, with lighter, sheer, but still opaque curtains behind them. I thought the walls were a fancy paint job, but a closer look revealed it to be wallpaper—who still makes that, much less puts it in such a basic apartment? The whole scene mixed rich and poor in a strange combination.

In the center of the room lay a body, amid the debris of a glass-topped coffee table. Glass? Anyone today would have had unbreakable plexi, or an adjustable poly that could be tuned to any color or pattern you wanted. The body was the man I had seen on my phone, medium height, slightly thick around the waist, dressed simply in a grey jumpsuit and teal sweater. He lay face down, blood staining the carpet from many lacerations to his face and neck. I scanned him with my phone, and watched the system read his condition.

"Classified," my phone said. "Examination not permitted. Coroner required."

"What? Since when is someone's medical condition classified?"

"Special orders," was the even more cryptic reply.

"Do we have to leave him here until the coroner comes?"

There was a pause of several seconds.

"Investigating detective's scans are sufficient," said the phone. "The body will be moved to the medical examiner's lab for further examination."

"All right," I said. "I'll look around. There are no obvious signs of entry or a struggle, except for the broken table. He could have had a heart attack and fallen on it."

"There was no entry," said the phone. "Sensors in the hallway and the building's facade would have detected it."

"So, open and shut, then," I said. "Hardly worth getting out of bed for."

I pinged the officer, and he peeked warily through the door, as though he smelled an ambush. I said, "The body can be moved. Tell the coroner he can examine it when it arrives. I want as few people as possible coming in here."

"Right away, detective," he said.

I walked to the door to the study. "I'll be in here. Ping me if anyone comes."

"I'll have to knock," said the officer. "There are no monitors in the study."

"None there either?" I said. "Guy sure loved his privacy."

I stepped into the study and felt a shiver run up my spine. Here was a room without cameras, sensors, or other electronic observers. Had I ever been in such a room before? I couldn't think of one. The silence was oppressive. The sole window was similarly draped, and, on inspection, did not open anyway. I went and looked through Morey's desk, which stood against the wall. His notepad was on, set to a daily journal that chronicled each days weather, hand written with a stylus. How quaint! I popped the drawers open. The side drawers held files, manila folders full of paper. Of course he wouldn't keep records electronically, yet he journaled that way. A digital photo album lay in the bottom drawer, its cover slightly rimed with dust.

The central drawer held pens, pencils, a stylus or two, erasers…usual office stuff, though some of it was old-fashioned. On an impulse I pulled the drawer out and peered into the desk: nothing. As I went to put the drawer back, my hand felt something on its underside. A small piece of paper was taped down. I carefully worked it loose.

"Alpha six. Gamma eleven. Beta one. Command override, authorization Aleph," it read and, seemingly added later at the bottom, "Imperator."

I put the paper in my pocket, and did not enter it into the inventory of evidence. I felt sure it had nothing to do with his death, and its implications tickled my imagination.

* * * *

"You've barely eaten anything," Lewis said. "What's on your mind?"

Lewis Yerxa and I are dating, if by "dating" you mean we have dinner together once a week (at most) ten months (at most) out of the year. The fires of passion never lit, but we settled into a very comfortable friendship, which could be used to deter other, less desirable, prospective partners. Could be used—but wasn't always used.

I frowned. "Just work."

It was his turn to frown, so he did. "You never tell me anything about work. Should I guess?"

"I can't tell you if you're correct or not."

"Nothing ventured, nothing to lose, then," he said, grinning a little. One thing I liked a lot about him: he never seemed to take offense. "You're investigating a mysterious murder, and aren't sure if it was Colonel Mustard in the library with the candlestick, or aliens."

"That's about right." I took a bite, and realized I really was hungry. I took another before answering him. "Killer robots can't be ruled out, either."

"I thought Asimov's laws prevented those?"

I nodded. "Alien killer robots might not be so benign. Besides, there have been attempts to circumvent the laws. Just none that have succeeded."

"That we know of."

I took another forkful, then put my fork down a little harder than intended. Lewis raised his eyebrows.

"It's not the case, it's the background. I could wrap this up in five minutes, except I can't figure out the background. Why is everything the way it is? The crime itself is simple; I'm just about convinced there was no crime. But I do have questions about the victim's lifestyle. He lived in the past, or there was something in the present he sought to avoid."

"And he's no longer able to tell you," he said. "So it is a murder, or a death of some kind."

"Brilliant deduction, Holmes," I said, sipping my wine. "It's just that he lived a very isolated way. In the middle of the city, he's a hermit. Was, I mean."

Lewis left me at my front door with a kiss on the cheek and a smile. As nice guys go, he's one of the better ones. That's why I hated myself a little for stepping inside, not even taking off my jacket, and calling Amina Orban.

"You busy?"

"Only if talking to you constitutes busy," she said. Her voice was like a song in my ear, her smile an invitation. I could almost smell her perfume—I could, too, if I owned a fancier phone.

"It's jazz night at Ciardelli's," I said. "Let's have a few drinks and watch the night pass."

Her smile widened. "Best offer I've had in days. See you there in ten."

I needed the drink, and her warm, enthusiastic company, which would likely continue back at my place until morning. But there was a thought, a question, that made me wish I hadn't called. She and Lewis were not so much different; in fact, I'm not sure they're different at all.

* * * *

Cameras are everywhere, but none of them look like cameras. In fact, nothing looks like a camera except antiques and movie props. Sometimes they're built into a phone, or an ID badge, or someplace less noticeable, like light fixtures, doors, and pieces of furniture. We are always being watched: "the System is aware" is the current catch-phrase. It can mean anything from "watch your language" to "let's show off." Paranoiacs and exhibitionists are not so different, when you're always spied on.

I couldn't get past the feeling I was being watched more closely than usual. Amina and I listened to jazz until late—a pianist with the touch of Bill Evans, though i suspect he might have been a robot programmed with the music. Still, it sounded spontaneous, and we smiled and clapped, and left a good tip for our server. But I couldn't shake the feeling. One problem with universal observation is that your fears have no focus; no way to catch the electronic eye. Hell, even the pia-

nist could have had a camera on him somewhere.

What was Dr. Morey afraid of? What was he doing that he wanted no observer, and who must he have been to get what he wanted?

* * * *

Amina shook a stray lock of hair back into place. "I tried seeing him for a few months, but we just didn't click. Opposites attract, they say, so I guess we were too much alike." She sighed. "That happens a lot when I try dating artificials."

"But you're artificial, too."

"Exactly. You understand the limitations of dating us."

I had to think about this for a moment. "So you go out with me because I'm natural."

"Not just that, but it's a big asset. You... you are natural, aren't you?"

Two nights later, at another restaurant, with another date, this one a colleague of sorts, Jenna Saturn—her patronym was her own choice; I don't know her birth name. She was a cop on the beat, who even wore her uniform to social occasions—and the way it fit her I could understand why.

"This isn't like you," she said. "Somehow, existential questions don't come up in ordinary police work."

"That's where you're wrong," I said. "We're always concerned with motive, desire, the twisting of priorities that leads to committing crime. A good policeman is a philosopher at heart, and part psychologist, too."

"And a parent, too?" Jenna added. She looked almost sly. "Have you ever wanted to be a parent?"

Her question caught me by surprise. Had I? It was a question I had answered to myself years ago, but hearing it asked by another brought thoughts and emotions rushing back. I sipped at my wine to fill the pause.

"I thought about it, but in my job..." I let the sentence trail off.

She nodded. "You're lucky, At least you

have the option."

"Why are artificials sterile?" I asked. "I don't think I've ever seen a definitive explanation."

"There isn't one, so far as I know," Jenna said. "Some stories say we have built-in sterility to keep us from outnumbering the naturals and taking over the world. Other say it's a flaw, and geneticists have been working for decades to try and get around it. All I know is, I'm not likely to have any."

"Adoption?" I said.

She grimaced. "I think it's legal, but it never happens. Only naturals can have babies, so only naturals can raise babies."

"Cloning," I said. "I know a woman who has a cloned daughter."

Jenna raised her eyebrows. "Hardly the same thing."

* * * *

Dr. Magarian, the chief coroner, was a woman today, as I prefer. Their male personae never seemed genuine, often with a touch of smarminess, the glad-handing faux joviality of a second-rate politician. As a woman they were more genuinely friendly, at times with some direct bluntness.

"So that's him," they said, looking cursorily over the corpse before shutting it in a drawer. "I've never met an Administrator before—if you can call this meeting."

"When will the autopsy be finished?" I said.

They frowned, and seemed to tense up. "There are special instructions to be handled. It could be a while."

"Special instructions?"

"Administrators could write their own rules," they said. "At least when it came to some aspects of their personal lives. One had herself cremated without an autopsy, another had this fancy mausoleum built in the middle of Spring Park."

"I know it," I said, "but I didn't realize there was an Administrator buried there."

They smiled. "There isn't. The whole thing is a monument, but no tomb. She was actually buried somewhere out in Kansas, with her family. Being in charge makes people crazy, I guess. Maybe that's why there are no human Admins anymore, just computers."

"I'm not sure how I feel about that," I said.

"I understand," they replied. "Being a computer myself, I'm wary of human decision making; I guess it's the opposite for you."

I smiled. "No offense."

They smiled back. "The System is aware."

* * * *

"If you were a man who wanted to hide from everything, how would you do it?"

Amina rolled over in my bed and raised her eyebrows. "First let's start by supposing I am a man…"

"You could be if you wanted to," I said.

"And get left at the front door like poor Lewis?" She wrapped one arm over me and kissed my shoulder. "When was the last time you invited him in?"

I smiled. "Jealous?"

She grinned. "I don't think so. Anyway, to the rest of your question. Hiding is difficult. Even the impulse seems to have been bred out of people."

"You can't breed out something like that. Certainly not in a few hundred years."

Amina had an animated tattoo of a butterfly on her right shoulder; I watched it flutter and turn from green to blue. Nice work, and expensive.

"If you really want privacy," Amina said slowly, thinking as she went, "you could move off-world. There are still wild, habitable places. The terraforming projects around Jupiter are opening up large parcels of open land."

I shook my head. "Too simplistic. Satellites can see you. I've heard there are spy systems buried into the ground in all the new colonies."

"Paranoia hasn't been bred out, that's for sure."

I sat up in bed, and she followed. "We've

become so comfortable being watched, it almost doesn't register. I've seen it in my work; time after time I've caught someone because they forgot to look for surveillance. What reason could there be for wanting to be unobserved?"

"Mental illness. An examination of the brain might show something."

"Only the coroner can examine him—and for some reason he won't. I checked. The body is in a stasis chamber awaiting autopsy. No exam has been scheduled. It's been days, and there aren't any other cases waiting."

"Don't these things have to be done quickly," she said. "Even stasis doesn't stop time completely."

I nodded. "And yet there he is, on ice, and nobody is doing anything about it. He's a void that things fall into—a black hole that keeps this case from moving forward.

* * * *

"I had a case," I said, looking Amina in the eye and toying with my food—most of my social interactions involve restaurants, as I don't know anyone who's a really good cook. "Aggravated assault. Suspect really put up a good chase, and left few clues. When I caught him, his manner threw me off. He was…indifferent. Not just a lack of remorse. He didn't care."

"Sociopath?" she suggested, a forkful of asparagus halfway to her mouth.

"Even sociopaths have feelings," I said. I sipped my wine. "I became convinced he was a robot, perhaps malfunctioning. No empathy, no ethics."

"And did you find out for sure?"

"No. The court wouldn't release the information. They said he served five years in prison, got out, then moved away, but I think they were lying. He's not in the database anymore; probably got disassembled and recycled. I still think about him, though."

"Why?"

"Because of all the people I've met," I said, "he was the most unnatural."

"He could be a hologram," Amina said. She poured a little more wine into my glass—so it was to be that sort of night. She caught my gaze and smiled.

"But I touched him," I said. "We had a fistfight before I handcuffed him."

"Tactile illusion," Amina said. "Supposedly, the best ones can leave bruises; the real person is so convinced of the other's reality they feel everything."

"I find that hard to believe. I know the Earth's population isn't what it once was—the Century of Plagues is horrible to read about—and holograms are useful to fill the stands at sporting events, but interacting with them? I'm not convinced."

"It's not so different from being a robot. The physical presence is made of photons rather than metals and plastics; the electrical field interacts with your nerve endings and affects what your brain thinks is happening." Amina sat back in her chair; the server removed her plate and brought our next course. "There are said to be five types of people: naturals, AIs, artificials, robots, and holograms. Can you tell me for certain which of your coworkers is which?"

I thought. Detective Hanh was starting to show a little grey in her hair, and made no bones about it; Officer Kelsey, who guarded the front door of the precinct station, had lost ten pounds due to a new diet. But was any of that real? All were designed or programmed or generated to age as naturals did; I had met Sergeant Takamoto's daughter, watched her grow into a lovely young woman, when I knew both she and her mother were artificials. The kid must have been grown in a lab.

I wondered if any of them ever thought about me that way.

"Wait," I said. "You said 'There are said to be five kinds of people…' Don't we know for sure?"

She shrugged. "If you believe conspiracy theorists, there isn't anyone; we're all data swirling around in a giant computer simulation. Or one person is dreaming all this. Me, I choose to believe some people are real," her smile reappeared, "such as you."

"That's the thing," I said. "What's true

and what isn't? This Morey investigation. Facts are being withheld; why not just lie? There's something different about this case, something that seems to be out of anyone's control."

"That's why you're here," Amina said. "To save the mystery. Life becomes mere data without it."

* * * *

Sundays were quiet, and had been for years. A resurgence in spirituality had driven a new Sabbath feeling; businesses closed, people went to church or synagogue or mosque or whatever, and weekends went from turbulent and crime-ridden to oases of calm. Of course, Mondays were a mess, as all the wildness was squeezed out of the weekend into the front and back ends of the week. Fortunately, few people had to work five-day weeks anymore. They could party on Thursday or Friday or Monday. I liked weekend duty: lots of downtime, few calls.

I had all the data from Dr. Morey's apartment on my phone, and scrolled through it as I drove or walked through the city center. The images spoke of a solitary life, not monastic, but of a man who had lived alone much of his life. The database held minor accounts of dalliances with women—a brief scandal involving an actress, a longtime companion who nevertheless lived in her own place—but other than that Dr. Morey seemed almost devoid of human appetites. I started to wonder if he was artificial.

As I was walking down Center Street, past the park and the playground, the sound of a racing motor hit my ears. I barely had time to turn around before a car raced past, careening down the street, striking a lamppost and caroming off to resume its headlong plunge down the road. My car was a block in the wrong direction. I called for backup and ran. The sound I was dreading, the crash of metal, hit me and rocked me backward. I almost fell, but staggered on to where the wreck sat, smoking.

The car was twisted through its center, its gull-wing doors sprung open, the win-

dows spiderwebbed with cracks. I motioned the gathering crowd aside, and looked at the figure sprawled out of the car, kept only by his seatbelt from drooping to the road. Hie eyes grew wide as he watched me, and I gave him a thorough examination before speaking. White shirt, probably faux-linen, chinos, unremarkable grey shoes. He had an ID badge with a state number on it. I scanned it quickly.

Perhaps I seem aloof, but I had started to feel a lack of urgency. The wreck was in no danger of catching fire; the batteries were sound, its electrical system was dark. I knew what he needed the moment I saw the clean, white upholstery inside the car. No blood, no viscera, nothing. This driver was hurt (his right leg was at an odd angle, almost jutting out the open door, then doubling back in itself) but he had not bled. Through a hole just below his right knee I saw a metallic sheen, barely catching the light. It was a robot.

"Mr. de Haan?" I said. "Can you tell me what happened?"

It looked up with wide eyes, and shook slightly. I muttered some reassurances.

"I…I think the engine malfunctioned," it said, its voice trembling."I tried to pull over, but the thing wouldn't shut down, leaving me racing down the middle of the road. Did I hit anyone?"

"Everyone's fine," I said. "Help is on its way. Is this your car?"

I already knew the answer, but it helps to keep them talking after an accident. Less chance of a freakout later.

It shook its head. "It's a public car. I don't feel very good."

"Not surprising," I said, nodding sympathetically, "considering the jolt you got. Your leg is broken, but the mechanics can fix that up in no time. Is there anyone I should contact?"

"I work on the subway," it said. "The R train. Someone should tell my boss I might not make it to work."

"I'll see to that," I said, about to stand up, but its hand shot out and gripped my shoulder.

"No, please," it said. "Don't leave me alone. I feel awful."

"I'll be sure the mechanic runs a complete diagnostic on you before you're cleared to go home," I said.

It sat up rigidly in the chair, bringing a protesting groan from the car's bent chassis, or was it from inside its body?

"Nothing looks right," it said. I can't seem to hear. Are you still there?"

I nodded, then said "Yes," as it seemed to look past me, without looking at anything.

I could hear the distant siren of the ambulance. A high-pitched chime rang from my phone, then repeated. I looked at the screen, which read, "Subject Inactive."

The robot was dead. Perhaps they'd be able to reboot it, or end up disassembling it. Death may not be permanent for robots, but it still feels like death to the rest of us. I stood by the wreck and watched as the ambulance drew to a stop.

"No hurry," I said.

* * * *

"Why haven't you examined Dr. Morey?"

"I don't have authorization," Dr. Magarian said (a man today, slightly overweight, strangely sweaty, short). Their voice was flat, emotionless.

"Who has that authority?"

There was a long moment. Magarian seemed to stare at the floor without their eyes moving down. They just…detached. I decided not to wait, but thought of the note in Morey's desk.

"Alpha six," I said. "Gamma eleven. Beta one. Command override, authorization Aleph."

I waited for some sort of response, but there was none.

"I order you to answer the question."

Dr. Magarian's head turned to me, their eyes unblinking. "Provision nine of the last will and testament of Dr. Francisco Morey y Pena specifies post-mortem exam by a natural physician. None is available."

"There are no natural-born coroners in

the precinct?"

"None."

"Some other kind of doctor could do in a pinch, I suppose."

"No natural doctors of any kind," they said. "The last natural physician, Dr. Jennifer Hamling, died twenty-four years, three months, seventeen days ago."

I had to take a moment and digest that. Most of my life my doctors had been artificials or AIs and I never knew it. I'd never even wondered.

"So override the provision," I said. "Take it to court."

"Not possible," Magarian said, their voice becoming more robotic, their movements freezing into mannequin stillness. "System Administrators agreed to the terms of the will and waived the right to challenge or appeal."

"Who were these administrators?"

"Mary Bates Lowndes, Ph.D., Curt Weisinger, Celeste White—"

I cut him off. "Were all these administrators naturals?"

"Yes," said Magarian. "The System was specially programmed to accept terms and conditions from Administrators without exception."

"And are any of these Administrators still alive?"

"No."

"Why would they agree to this?"

"They all incorporated the same terms and conditions into their wills. Dr. Morey, as the youngest of the Administrators, was expected to outlive the others, so his provisions were particularly carefully written, as it was feared there would be no one to interpret them on his death."

"And he was the last Administrator." A thought began to grow in my head, and I let it out. "Are there any naturals in System operations now?"

"No."

The thought grew worse. "How many naturals are there in the city right now?"

Magarian looked at me. "One. Detective

Jeri Patton."

"How many on Earth?"

"One."

"How many in the solar system?"

"One."

I turned and paced around the room once, twice, stopping in the third circuit to face Magarian again. "I'm the only human being?"

"In the eyes of the law," they said, "artificials count as human. In the sense you mean, yes, you are the last of homo sapiens."

I couldn't grasp this, so I changed perspective. "I've been investigating cases for six years. Arresting felons, murderers, white-collar criminals. Were any of them naturals?"

"No."

"All my colleagues, all my friends and schoolmates—they were all artificials, AIs, robots, holograms?"

"Two classmates were naturals, but one died along with his parents in the destruction of the trans-lunar shuttle twenty years ago. The other drowned in a boating accident five years ago; her parents predeceased her."

"Dr. Morey and I were the last people on Earth, and he didn't even know I was here. I didn't know he was here. We could have talked, we could have planned something."

"I believe Dr. Morey grew somewhat paranoid in his last years in the System," Magarian said. "It worsened after his retirement. Nothing pathological, just a growing distrust of non-human agency. He wanted to live unobserved by anyone."

"In a city full of people."

"Alone is not the same thing as isolated," Magarian said. "He wanted to be alone."

"And he very nearly was," I said.

"Since he never went out, he was unlikely to ever meet you. Your job did not have any connection to the life he led."

"My job," I said, in something close to a shout. "What is it for? Fake criminals preying on fake victims? Crimes without crime?"

"Oh, no," they said. "Artificials have free will, just as you do. Some of them turn to

crime, despite our best lessons against it."

"The robot whose car crashed on Sunday," I said, "was it programmed to do that? Something to distract me, perhaps?"

"The crash was a result of a computer failure in the car," Magarian said. "It was truly an accident."

I shook my head, hoping to dislodge some of the thoughts now racing through me. "Robot police could have done just as well. My…human fallibility has to be a problem."

Magarian's face softened—was that pity in his eyes? "The System was designed to continue civilization, perpetuate society in all aspects, good and bad. As the human population declined, artificial procreative methods were developed. AIs and holograms helped keep cities and towns populated as before. Crime has always been a part of human communities, so it was retained. That maintained the need for victims, plus police, courts, jails, attorneys, whole ranks of professions that would otherwise have been lost. Perfection is not a human state.

"Let me ask you," they said, a curious glint in their eyes. "Did you ever suspect that everyone around you was manufactured in one way or another?"

I had to take a breath before answering. "No. Some I know for certain, others I suspected, but many…no."

"I wish…" they said, then stopped for a moment. "Dr. Morey wanted to get away from…" Another stop. "…I believe his term was 'un-natural humanity' but his health prevented travel into space. With no isolated places left on Earth, he chose instead to isolate himself technologically, by disabling all System surveillance of his home, having his food and the necessities delivered, and barring the System from any remote examination of his person or his home. We didn't know he was dead until the sensors in the hallway outside his apartment detected blood."

"You were sniffing at his door," I said.

"Unintentionally. The entire hallway is

monitored for unusual odors."

"The neighbor who sent in the report was bogus."

"Yes."

"If it means anything," I said, "I think his death was of natural causes. A heart attack or stroke, perhaps. He fell and hit the table."

"A sound was detected that might support that theory," Magarian said, "but it was not sufficient to warrant an investigation."

"Where can I find more information?"

They told me.

* * * *

The office building was as grey as the moon, and about as sterile. A small wing of the many-branched Administration building, itself shuttered and long empty. A plain padlock held the gate shut outside the front door. I tried to pick it, but lost patience and blew the lock off with a single shot. That would attract attention, I knew, but my temper was not the best that day. My conversation with Magarian was sure to attract attention. The System was aware, but to what extent?

I ran through the corridors, raising a little dust in my wake—where were the maintenance robots? The lights were motion-sensitive, but some did not come on. Odd to see neglect in what was supposedly the seat of power. The offices were empty, stripped. Only a few telling details told of past habitation: a patch of wall where a picture had hung, now a slightly different color than the rest; a nameplate forgotten on an office door. A booklet—paper, stapled and everything— lay on the floor. I picked it up: instructions for a coffeemaker.

The room at the far end was a large cube, with single drawer was set in the wall opposite the door. I picked the lock on the drawer with my phone—there was a thumbprint scanner, but I knew mine would not suffice. A single tray of thin, translucent discs sat in the drawer—hologram discs. Each was labelled; I pulled the one marked "Morey" and tapped it with one finger. It glowed, and a man appeared in the center of the room, slightly translucent.

"Who are you?" Dr. Morey asked. I flashed my ID.

"I'm dead, aren't I," he said, but not as a question. "The only way you could bring me back like this is if I am dead."

"Yes, you are."

He nodded, and was lost in thought for a moment. "I can't decide whether to be outraged or delighted. I would never want to live like this, but I don't want to die again."

"Those are Dr. Morey's opinions," I said. "You're allowed to form your own."

"Free will?" he said, laughing. "That's an improvement from my day. Are holograms permanent? I don't think I want immortality."

"No. Well, many of the holograms we use today are just background people— 'extras' they used to call them in movies. They reappear many times in many places. If a hologram fills a specific spot—a certain job, a relationship with someone not a hologram—they appear to age and are shut off in a natural-looking manner. Dr. Morey, I'd like to ask you some questions about your previous life."

"Was I a suicide? I didn't leave a note? I intended to leave some sort of information, but I don't know what about."

My eyes widened, and I tapped my phone to access the System. Privacy was a polite fiction, but sometimes, as a formality, you draw attention to yourself deliberately. I scanned through the data on the hologram, which regarded me with curiosity. I opened the hologram's profile.

"This has been tampered with," I said, then addressed my phone. "Admin?"

"Yes, Detective?"

"Who last accessed this file?"

"This program was last modified by Dr. Francisco Morey y Pena, June 11—"

I cut it off. "Fine. I get it. Dr. Morey did his own cover-up. We won't get anything useful out of him."

The hologram looked abashed. "I did something wrong, didn't I?"

"No," I said, giving him a long look.

"Nothing illegal, anyway. As an Administrator, you had every right to alter files—you had given yourself that permission. It does mean that what I'm looking for isn't there."

"I am sorry," he said. "Or I'm pretending to be, anyway."

I felt sympathy, and wondered if I had ever felt that way toward a hologram before. Probably not. "Your death appears to have been an accident, or natural causes. I just wondered why you were living the way you were."

"Oh, well," he said, smiling slightly. "I know he—I—came to hate the world. The long fight against decay and corruption. I came to think that it would all end badly. Funny, now that I'm here I'm no longer so sure of that. Perhaps I have had a change of heart."

* * * *

"Hey, you a cop?"

I was heading back to my car when I turned to see a seedy, tired-looking young man in an armless tee shirt and breeches standing glumly beside me.

"Detective," I said.

"Somebody hacked my tats," he said, pulling his shirt aside to show a shifting array of tattoos across his chest, which kept forming and reforming into obscene shapes and rude phrases. One immediately made a personal comment about me, which I ignored.

"This the first time it's happened?"

He shook his head. "Last Christmas. I had to wear long sleeves all day lest my Gran see what it was saying about her."

I jerked my head toward the nearest police station. "Second floor, Tech department. Chances are it's the same hacker as last time. Got any friends mad at you?"

"You think a friend did this?" he said, bristling. Then, after a pause. "Nah, none of my friends have enough brains."

He turned and slouched off into the building. Nanotats could be reprogrammed to form whatever you wanted: tattoos that changed shape or color depending on mood,

time of year, some would respond to voice commands. They were not particularly secure, especially the older models. A string of obscenities began to march over his shoulder; he grimaced and vainly tugged his shirt over them.

I started to turn away, but gave one last look—did one of the tattoos change as he covered it, turning into the image of an eye, staring straight at me? And, at that final moment before his shirt fell into place, did it wink at me? The System is aware indeed!

* * * *

The coroner's office was brightly lit; day and night mean nothing to the dead. I knew Dr. Magarian would be on duty. As a robot, they had nowhere else to go. They showed no surprise to see me, despite the late hour.

"What will you do now?" they said, without any preamble, as though they read my mind. I sighed and ran my hands through my hair.

"Dr. Morey died of natural causes," I said.

"There will have to be an autopsy to confirm," they said. "Where will you find a qualified physician?"

"I guess I should start studying. If only a natural doctor can certify his death, I'm going to have to get a medical degree, and certification from the System. Can you still do that?"

"If you pass the exams, yes. The courses can be fed into your brain in the usual manner."

"So, I guess I'll get back to school. Keep his body in a stasis chamber; this could take a while. Oh -" I had a sudden inspiration. "I'm going to move into the penthouse suite at the Ritz. The department will pay the bill, if that's even necessary. Since I'm the last human being, I might as well live it up."

"Perhaps the last," Magarian said. "There are two manned deep-space probes due to return in about 150 years."

"I'll be dead by then," I said.

"About that...?"

I wasn't sure what he meant for a moment. I sat down on the edge of the examining table, feeling the cold metal under me.

"When Dr. Morey's case is closed, I will retire. I'm superfluous, and I'll be damned if I'm going to spend the rest of my life chasing pretend criminals. I'll lie around and read the great books, written by real people, and watch the great movies with real actors. Then, one day, I'll die. You have my full permission to watch over me, and investigate my eventual cause of death. But I wouldn't bother filing a report—who is there to read it?"

They nodded, but said nothing. I turned to go.

"Detective Patton," they said suddenly, as I was about to walk out, "I want you to know that I feel it a special honor to have worked with you. There seems to be no likelihood I will ever meet another natural. Perhaps this emotion is just programming, but..."

"I'm flattered anyway," I said. "Thank you."

I was flattered. After all, he was as real as anyone I knew. I walked out, through the glass-filled atrium (the receptionist said "Have a good day") and into the busy street. A mother and her little girl passed close by, the former trying to keep her kid in check— "Be sure to look both ways before crossing!" A ragged, dirty man sat by the corner of the building, a beat-up guitar in hand, and strummed a tune. I pointed my phone at him and dropped a buck into his account, and laughed. I tapped for a cab at the corner and one slowed out of traffic at once. A tall, thin man started to move toward it the same time I did.

"Do you mind if we share?" he said, smiling.

"Share," I said, as though I had never heard the word before. "There is only me here, isn't there?"

His quizzical smile made me laugh. We rode together, and I pretended to be charmed when he insisted on paying the fare.

❊

ABOUT THE AUTHOR

Stephen Persing (1963-?, Earth) is a carbon-based life form and writer of fiction and nonfiction. His work has appeared in *Daily Science Fiction*, *McSweeney's Internet Tendency*, *Cartoon Brew* (online), *Art in America magazine*, and something called *Startling Stories* (print). His hobby is writing about himself in the third person. His greatest regret is that his stories for *Startling* will never have Earle Bergey covers.

ABOUT THE ARTIST

There is no artist, *per se*, for this story. To the best of our knowledge, this is the first story in *any* print-based science fiction magazine to have been illustrated by an artificial intelligence—in this case, MidJourney AI, a Discord-based AI artist that we have been playing with recently. It takes text-based descriptions and creates artwork based on them. Knowing what commands to use, how to input them, and then adjusting the art output accordingly will undoubtedly become a necessary skill for digital artists in coming years. In this instance, your AI "command wrangler" was John Betancourt.

TEARS IN MY ALGABEER
by Eric Del Carlo

Emmie was nine kinds of pissed off when she finally stomped the brakes. Sprayed gravel sounded like hail. She flung open the door and said, "Get your ass *out!*"

I don't know what I'd been saying, not exactly. But I knew I was hollowed out with failure, and self-pity was clanging round all inside me. I must've been on a real tirade. I'd tried filling those inside-hollows with a bathtub's worth of algawhiskey, but that'd probably just given my tongue a sloppier and louder means to my frustration.

"Get out!" Emmie repeated. She belted it.

"Hey, c'mon—" Like a switch was thrown, I was reasonable, cajoling. The pickup's door still yawned wide next to me. Black tree darkness out there.

"I'm equipped with anti-theft, remember? Want me to burst your eardrums with ultrasonics? Or I could hit you with cyclobenzaprine darts, then do a doughnut and centrifugal-toss your sorry butt onto the road. Your goddamn choice, Nik!"

Emmie had given me plenty of lip before. She called me on my crap all the time. It was one of the reasons I loved her, even if it wasn't lovey-doveyness motivating me right now. I didn't want to get dumped drunk in the night far from home.

I sweet-talked. She didn't give, not a lonesome centimeter. And the hollowness in me finally started to fill up: with fear. Everything she was saying had a *last time* timbre to it, like the harshest chords in a breakup song, when that as much as the lyrics tell you these two are split for good.

"But, Emmie, baby, it's—" Christ, I was talking through tears now. Real ones? Crocodiles? Just slobby booze tears?

She said evenly, "Get out of me. I won't tell you again." And I knew like cold steel through my spleen what she really was saying to me. For the last time.

Stunned, scared, in a terrible drunk-sobered state, I reached behind the seats for my guitar. But it was in the only hock shop for a hundred twelve k'lometers, because I'd put it there, swearing I would never look at the damned thing ever again.

I got out on sea legs. Emmie took off in a gravelly uproar, yanking my heart out as she went. We'd been together a long, long time.

I'm Nik Ossett. There's only one reason you've heard of me.

* * * *

Algie was a whole different kettle of responses, judgments and calculations. I came in in the late morning, having finally flagged a ride after stumbling down the road for hours.

"I'm already drawing you a bath."

"Thanks, Algie." I felt like every rut and pothole and stone in that road.

I'd lit out of here last night with a full head of steam, outraged and hurt, and Algie had caught the opening bars of the self-pity song I'd sung for Emmie—and probably for every unlucky ear I could find in however many honkytonks and dives I'd gone to.

Algie was hunched at the work station, debugging harvesters four states away, probably. I was out of the line of sight, spared the embarrassment of shock-wide eyes at my ghoulish appearance. Was that a kindness? Or did Algie just not want to see?

My head ached like ice. I crawled into the bath, into fragrant steam and soapy restoration. I prayed for my memory to stay fuzzed. No need for details. I'd gone out telling everybody that Nik Ossett had failed again and how unfair that was and why wouldn't the universe let me win? just once? let me exercise the gift the impulse the fiery urge that'd been put into me? Why? Why? *Why?*

The tears came back. Clean honest mourning now. My beef with life was legit. My dreams had met reality, and reality had kicked my ass.

After I dunked my head to wash away the salt tracks, I got out of the tub and found fresh blue jeans, buttoned on a flannel and got some of the coffee that Algie had also prepared. Then I went outside, into one of the sheds on our property. This was how I was going to tell Algie. I pulled the tarp off, checked the battery, and fired up the trike.

I felt the presence behind me.

"The engine sounded wrong when you rolled up."

"Was Derek Ajam give me a lift in his old Minotaur."

"Figured, when it drove off."

"She meant it this time. Emmie."

"I'm sorry for you, Nik."

I heard the sincerity but still didn't turn around. I did have something I wanted to say, though. Finally just to *say* it. "I was always glad you weren't jealous, Algie."

"I could never be jealous of a truck, babe. Rural men and pickups—I get it. It's almost mythology."

Algie came from just outside Chicago. How we met is kind of adorable, but I'm not in the mood to tell it right now. I swung onto the three-wheeler. "I should make sure this still runs. I'll ride Willow Crick and back."

As Algie nodded and headed back inside, I goosed the throttle. It was weird, actually controlling the thing. I hadn't had to drive myself for a dang while. Maybe I'd get lucky and wipe out into a tree. But I couldn't even enjoy the gallows humor of that, because it made me think of Daddy. Great. Load on the sorrows, Nik my boy. We'll run 'em to the river, see if they float.

* * * *

If you've heard of me, it's because of Daddy. Boone Ossett was the real deal. I

watched him write his songs when I was a boy. He didn't bang them right out on a guitar; he had this miniature keyboard he kept in his back pocket, and sometimes when he was walking me through my chores or us just sitting around streaming stuff, he'd take out the 'board and start tapping notes. It didn't happen in a burst. He didn't get an excited look on his face, either. More like he was concentrating on a math problem he found interesting. The notes would turn to chords, and he'd begin saying, "There, *there*," when the sounds got righter and righter and lined up. Then he would drop vocals in—not words, just grunts, syllables. Finally he'd have a verse, and when he gave it a sort of backward twist he would get his bridge, and when that was done, he'd finally nod and smile a joyless smile and say, "Yep. Good enough."

Some of his most famous tunes happened just like that, in my presence. It seemed a bloodless way to make art, but I was a kid and impressionable, and when I began to pick at a guitar's strings, I tried it his way. But I couldn't do it. I *loved* Daddy's music. I loved music. Country, folk, Western, and every other label slapped on the genre. It rang in my soul. It brought a sweet ache to my heart.

But I couldn't just work out a song on my own the way Boone Ossett did, like I was solving an equation that had a perfectly logical outcome. I had to go tearing at my music, clawing it out of myself. I wanted to tell stories. I wanted to have the world acknowledge and appreciate what I did.

Daddy didn't take his fame for granted. He'd made an effort, and it'd paid off. But I also knew—because it's something I eventually figured out, from what I saw as a boy and a teen—that Daddy always thought he was getting away with something. That in his mind what he did didn't quite justify his outsize success. That people were, in a way, suckers for thinking that what he made was great art.

Whereas me…well, I'd been giving it

everything I had for years now, bleeding all over my music and laying it out on the altar. And all I had to show was washout.

* * * *

The trike needed a little work, so I worked on it. Algie had a car, a stolid little non-smart machine from a Puerto Rican plant, but I was obviously going to need to get around independently.

I let myself be seen around on the three-wheeler. I wasn't going to tell anyone Emmie had left me. It was too painful, too embarrassing, too everything that was rotten about it. Gossip could do the telling.

That night in bed I lay in a cage of arms, pressed back against comforting huskiness. Algie was about half again my mass, which was fine with me.

"I'm gonna need to figure what to do," I said.

The arms tensed, subtly.

"I'll have to take a job," I went on. Now I tensed, waiting for blowback.

"I'm making good pay."

"I know that—"

"So you don't have to work."

"My life, Algernon. I got to figure out what I'm gonna do with it." In as steady, non-self-pitying a voice as I could manage, I added, "My music is not going to happen."

Algie pulled me tight against him then. He cries different than I do, with, I'd say, more dignity. He does it less often. But he does cry. And this was something he thought worth crying over.

I was causing pain everywhere I went. But this was the way it had to be. A fresh start. I would act like a grown-up. Put away them childish things that killed me a little more every day.

* * * *

I spent another day getting my shit together, then rode into the collective. My chin was high, even if my confidence wasn't. On street corners more than one head turned. People had seen the trike already. Word had

got round. Probably everybody who knew me knew by now that Emmie had split.

I didn't gaze at the other self-drive smart trucks in the streets. Didn't look away, either. They were just wheeled machinery, I told myself, not fundamentally different from my trike or Algie's PR rig. A pickup with a brain and a personality still came out of a factory. That I hadn't been able to hold onto mine wasn't here and it wasn't there. My own frustration and depression had crapped things with Emmie. But I hadn't come to town to grieve in public.

Two days and two nights without alcohol. I felt painfully clear-eyed as I went into the collective's employment branch, a cheerless, non-threatening building at the center of things. There I was put into an office with a cheerless, non-threatening suit who was a fan of Daddy's music.

To his credit, he said as we both sat, "Sorry. Guess you hear that a lot. Too much of a lot, maybe."

"It's okay." I wanted to get down to business. "I'd like to work."

He nodded neutrally. His gaze flicked to text hovering in the air to his right. "You've got general skills."

I heard the silent *just*, as in "just general skills": which actually meant *You're just a warm body, without any aptitude for anything.*

I said, "I'll wash dishes. Work on an alga farm. Put me on a road gang." I wanted to squirm but didn't let myself.

"We'd need a time machine for two of those."

"The collective should give me a job if I want one." I stopped just short of demanding. My ego was too beaten down. I felt like a dumb kid, in a room with an adult who was trying to figure out how to gently tell me something I didn't want to hear.

The floating green text disappeared. "What about your music? You have a revenue stream there."

It was like saying a ditchful of water was Niagara Falls. Jaw clenched, I said, "The revenue is…negligible."

"In your field persistence is key."

"I've—persisted." The clench went all through my body now. It was an ugly combination of embarrassment and rage.

His manner remained as bland as ever. Maybe he didn't know how he was hot-footin' me; maybe he knew exactly. "I'd be lying if I said I hadn't listened to some of your work."

I knew why he'd done so. Because he liked Daddy's music. And because he'd wanted to see if some part of Boone Ossett's knack had gotten passed down to his offspring.

He added after too long a pause, "You have a very persuasive voice."

That I knew. My vocalizations were strong. I could go tenor to countertenor and hit high notes when I wanted. Daddy had kept it simpler. He breathed his words, in a way that disguised how uncomplicated his technique was.

"Thank you," I said, even though he was really telling me he didn't like my songs.

"I think you should continue to pursue your music."

"I'm done pursuing."

"Really? You may be on the cusp of success."

I closed my eyes. This was how it was done: you put a song up on LizzinUp and you hoped to draw ears and prayed for it and you sought the holy algorithm, and it's a piece of music you worked your fingers to bone on, and you get a few blips and blurps and that's it, because nobody really gives a rat's ass about your songs and, consequently, about *you*.

Daddy sang about gamblers and whores, hard luck men and worse luck women, outlaws, losers, heroes, all the archetypes. And he had songs about relationships crashing and burning. Marriages full of cheating, true loves gone to ash. Which was pretty funny, because he and Mama had maybe the most serene, unassuming, nonviolent marriage you could imagine.

I worked from his same list of topics.

He picked his tropes arbitrarily, as dispassionately as he first tapped out his melodies on that mini keyboard. He didn't much care what his tunes were about, so long as they went from start to finish and didn't stumble on the way. He'd said as much to me. He said as much.

When I opened my eyes, the collective's employment officer was staring at me, and his modest manner had slipped some.

"Mr. Ossett, I shift resources to where they're needed. If I put you to a make-work task, I'll be taking time away from you. Time you could be using to express yourself through music. And bettering that music. Perfecting it, even. Which means I—*I*"— here his eyes flared, and I understood the passion in him—"would be responsible for denying you to the world. That's above my pay scale."

We sat in silence a long moment.

I said, "You gave me your name, but sorry to say I've forgot it."

"Larrecq. Denver Larrecq."

I stood and put out my hand. He shook it with an even grip. "It's a pleasure to meet you, Mr. Larrecq."

"The pleasure was mine."

I went out of there feeling lightheaded, and with a spark in me, somewheres, trying to glow against all the self-pitying dark. Somebody believed in me. A stranger. Even if that belief was a little oblique: more along the lines of *I believe what you* could *be*.

I stood on the sidewalk on the main drag. The air had a little city taste to it, clean as the town was. I looked at traffic. Inevitably, a truck went by. A smart one. A sentient one. I could tell, because the good ol' boy in the front seat—nobody I knew—was laughing and jabbering, and no one was in there with him, no one but his best buddy, his automotive love, the mind and personality of his pickup. Algie had it right. There is a mystique to a country man and his truck, to the mud on its flanks, to the promise of open land and free skies and the ability to get anywhere.

Emmie's absence grabbed me hard. We'd been so good together.…

But when I went and climbed on my trike and fired it up, it was with a sense of purpose. I pulled evenly into daytime traffic, without a hitch.

* * * *

Mama doesn't care much for Algie. Says he has "Chicago manners." I suppose he does. I don't know what her real beef is, but she lives two counties over so I don't have to see them at the same time much.

Daddy, however, would've liked Algie. A lot. They would've been buddies. Daddy would have held his elbow in his big paw and whispered in Algie's ear, telling him embarrassing stories from my boyhood. And as Algie tried hopelessly not to laugh, Daddy would have winked at me, which would have been his way of saying *He's my son too.* I'm that sure they would've hit it off.

Daddy had a smart truck, and he got it the same way I got Emmie. He paid into the pool at the collective, a relatively small but not insignificant amount of money, and when a new vehicle was delivered to the county, he got to meet it. Interact with it. See if there was a connection.

There was. The truck took to him, and he had stars in his eyes for it. JN-7807. Jenny. He and Jenny were all over the dusty roads out here. They laughed and told each other stories. I rode with them, watched them. And I knew I'd want a truck when I became a man. Like I already knew I wanted to write and make songs.

A self-drive will get you home when you're drunk. Daddy wasn't drunk the night he got plowed into; the other guy was, at the wheel of an oversized hauler, with a front end like a giant steel jaw.

Daddy was still alive when the medics flew out there. But he only lived long enough to know that Jenny had died ahead of him. Her brain case was smashed, and she was silent, and Daddy's last incoherent words were to a paramedic who ignored them as she tried to restore vitals.

I tried eight times to write a song about it. Came at it eight different ways. Maybe folks—the ones who knew Boone had a kid that could pluck a guitar some—expected that song out of me. Maybe they waited. And got tired waiting.

A gal named Micaela Dèng with a voice like golden honey sang a song about Daddy's death. She did it from the point of view of a fan of his music, which was what she was. She hit the algorithm with it. She went big.

I could of course just cover Daddy's songs. It would be a straight road to some sort of success. But the words would be empty in my mouth, and the music would ring hollow. Some people would sense that. In a way it would be worse than my own failures, which were, at least, *mine.*

But now I had to try again. One more song. One more swing.

* * * *

I spent three and a half weeks with it. Dreaming it. Coaxing it. Angry at it. Stymied by it. I fell in love with it a note at a time. I've always been careful not to copy Daddy's chord progressions or any other telltale that'd make anybody think of Boone Ossett. Maybe Denver Larrecq, the first time he listened to something by me, was disappointed not to hear even a faint ghost of Daddy's picking.

I homed in on a subject. A river. The river the storyteller had gone to at the hot peak of a romance. I closed my eyes and saw white rushing water, breathed the clean wet scent, felt the spray and sweat. Lovemaking on a riverbank. Then, final verse, the return to the river, but it's been repurposed, most of it diverted, just a gurgle of a creek now. Yeah. Yeah. Cradle that imagery in a web of chords. C minor, devolving into C# minor. The hook? Where's the hook? You want those three notes that'll identify your song, make a listener pick it out of a wall of background sound. Daddy's wisdom there. The hook took a week all its own.

I had of course gotten my guitar out of hock. I snuck it in the house and for three days tried to hide what I was up to from Algie. He didn't say anything, but there's something warmer in his smile when I'm working on a song. He was smiling at me that way now.

Finally I went into the little home studio out back. It's not much. Daddy left behind a handsome estate, naturally, but I've got a passel of siblings and it got divvied down pretty good. I was the only child of Boone's who'd tried a hand at music. Once, I thought that made me special.

I conjured a backing band out of sound programs and instrument files. I put in, then took out some harmonica licks. Then I recorded them myself with a mouth organ. Took them out again. Put them back, liking how they added to the mournful memory ambience.

Mixed it. Remixed it. Re-remixed. Daddy had shown me some of this; the rest I'd learned on my own. But again I avoided any signature Boone Ossett atmosphere.

I loved the finished product. It felt like a complete song to me, worthy of listeners. I had told a story. I had satisfied the artistic urge forever burning inside me.

But making music wasn't the whole deal. You had to put your art out there, had to see how it was received—*if* it was received. The pure act of creation wasn't enough. I wasn't in this just to make myself happy. I needed to commune with the world through my music…or not at all.

* * * *

I used to keep Algie in on the songwriting process, from beginning to end. I'd talk about the crafting in endless detail. But the shame was too big now, and I couldn't look in the mirror and say, "I'm a singer-songwriter," much less make that claim to the love of my life.

So Algie got my music the same time and same way everybody else did: when I put it up on the LizzinUp site.

We lay in bed, in a quiet postcoital daze. I felt empty. Not bad, just vacant. Waiting. I'd uploaded my song an hour ago. Once, this had been an exciting moment, full of eagerness and anticipation. But the years had beaten the joy out of it, and now it wore a thin coat of dread and not much more.

And yet still—*still*—some stupid part of me expected a win. Success. The listening public downloading my tune, spreading it far and wide. Nik Ossett, with a hit on his hands, riding the algorithm's lightning.

"What did you think?" I asked in the stillness of the bedroom, countryside night outside the windows.

Algie stirred. The silence got thoughtful. I knew he knew what I was asking.

His voice was a little brittle when he answered. "Don't ask me that, babe, unless you want the truth."

I let it go. The truth would be too hard to hear. I closed my eyes. I had falling dreams most of the night.

* * * *

Nobody tells you when you lose. There're no bells. Lights don't flash. That's only for when you win, I guess.

My song floated on brief surface tension, on the attention of a handful of faceless listeners. Someone was curious, someone else on a whim. Someone maybe thought the name Ossett rang a bell.

Then the tune sank in the heartless rankings. And my heart was torn out. Again. *Again.*

Algie went about his business, at his work station at home. Farms were probably always going to be sabotaged, and debuggers were needed. They were crucial. He was awful good at what he did, too. Our household would never go under.

Me, on the other hand…

I broke seal on a bottle of algawhiskey. I was drunk by the time night settled in. There was no memory of me speaking directly to Algie, but I knew my jaw had been moving, muttery words said under my breath. Had to be the same old litany. The curses. The self-pitying. I damned Denver Larrecq. I damned my brothers and sisters, who'd put together effective ordinary lives for themselves. I damned Daddy for having talent and making me think—without ever saying it straight out to me—that I could do what he did. I damned Mama, because why not?

Suddenly I wanted to go out, hit some dives. I remembered Emmie was gone. The urge to go didn't leave. I would go wail in public, do the sackcloth and ashes bit. A grin cut my face, making my teeth hurt. I needed to punish myself for the shit dud failure I was.

Algie stood in my way when it was plain I meant to take the trike.

"You're too drunk to drive."

"No such thing."

"Take a sobe-tab. Or I'll drive you wherever you want to go."

"Don't want your company." I hate it when we fight, but my mouth belonged to somebody else, someone angry, ashamed and pushed past his limits.

"I could stop you." There were his Chicago manners.

I looked at his big frame. "You could have a time tryin'."

"I could call the sheriff."

"What I just said—only louder." There was a terrible, almost feral growl in my voice.

He followed me out half a minute later, as I was mounting the trike. I didn't have the 'whiskey bottle with its dregs with me anymore. He must have contrived to take it. Oh well. Plenty more booze out there, bars lit up in the inky night.

"At least take this coat," Algie said, and he somehow got my arms through the sleeves.

I wanted to say something nice to him. "You can tell me truth…'bout da song." It wasn't what I'd meant to say.

He studied my face with vast affectionate patience, but there was hurt in his eyes. It occurred to me in some distant corner of my algawhiskey-logged brain that if Emmie could leave me, so could Algernon.

He decided to tell me. "I thought your song was lovely. It touched me. I think you're a wonderful musician, Nik."

That death's-head grin came back as I hit the throttle. "Too bad only you think so!" The trike fishtailed going down the drive to the road, and that felt strangely good, like I was on top of something out of my control, that could throw me, hurt me.

I gunned out into the dark, heading for destiny.

* * * *

I gripped the trike's bars, and that kept me from sliding off on the turns I took too fast. Wind blew tears from the corners of my eyes. My teeth were bare, and my jaw ached.

The night was a screaming black.

I realized a couple k'loms out that I didn't want to go to a honkytonk after all. I didn't want to get off this trike. Riding it was better than booze. Something big was going to happen to me tonight. Maybe Micaela Dèng would sing a ballad about me. "Last Ride of Nobody, the Son of Somebody."

And my ears rang with the music. It wasn't all together, but I saw all its edges. I felt the structure. I could feel my fingers on the strings, making the hard luck tale come alive.

I let out a cry, a raw ugly yelp of pain to the trees the road cut through. No more songs. No more songs! Why had I tried again? Why had I let that pissant at the collective convince me?

Suddenly I knew where I wanted to go. The spot where Emmie had thrown me out. Yeah! What a great idea! If I could find—

The trike wasn't smart, but it of course had positioning, and by squinting one eye I followed a displayed route, almost wiping out a number of times on the way.

Now I was closing on it, everything coming to a crescendo. Last verse. Final lyrics. The strings rang under my fingertips….

MM-9349. Emmie. I loved you, girl.

Ahead was a tree, nearer the side of the road than any others. Thick trunk, stout branches. The kind of tough old tree that could stop anything.

I opened the throttle hot. I bore down. Nearly on top of the place where Emmie'd stomped the brakes and told me to get my ass *out*.

But suddenly I braked and struggled to wrestle the three-wheeler off the trajectory I had it on, back out into the middle of the blacktop of reprocessed plastic, scattered with gravel. I almost flipped it braking it, and when I got it stopped, I was a couple meters past the tree. And there I sat and I shook. And I shivered. And the grin was off my face and I hugged the coat Algie had put on me tight on myself, and felt in the pocket the sobe-tabs. I took one of the horrible chalky things and chewed it. A hundred seconds later the fumy alcohol was gone from my system. I was alone in the night, straddling the trike. I hadn't seen a single other vehicle the entire time out here.

I looked behind. Right there everything had ended with Emmie. I couldn't fault her. You can only hear a man whine for so long.

But as I stared, music came again into my head. The start of a melody. A simple progression. I began to utter sounds, and matched up vowels and heard the rhymes coming on, easy, loose. *Live oak* would go with *broke*, and I'd drop *-hearted* into the beginning of the next line, the way Daddy did it sometimes. It should've been awkward, but it wasn't. There wasn't even a live oak in sight, but the truth was still there, the truth of the tree. And the truth of the song. Emmie leaving me. That was what I needed to sing about. Not an imaginary scorned lover going to some river. Not any of the other things and people I'd sung about these past years. I wanted to tell stories, yes, but they had to be my stories.

I wasn't Boone. I couldn't put together a tune like I was working out of a kit. But I'd gotten some piece of Daddy's talent. And I had someone to play for. I had Algie.

I turned the trike around. I had half the song done in my head by the time I made it home.

* * * *

I'm Nik Ossett. If you've heard of me, it's maybe because of "Night Ellie Drove Away." Others have sung about their beloved pickups, but mine is maybe the definitive truck breakup song. The algorithm seems to think so.

But there's more songs coming. Daddy had a whole catalog. I hope I get to live longer than he did. My father was named Boone Ossett, and if you like what I do, I hope you'll check out his stuff.

* * * *

I saw Emmie, on the streets of the collective one day. She had a guy with a black beard and a jean jacket on her front seats, and he was talking and gesturing happily. I blew her a silent kiss and kept going the other way.

❀

ABOUT THE AUTHOR

Eric Del Carlo's short fiction has appeared Analog, Clarkesworld, Asimov's and many other publications over the years. He has co-authored novels with Robert Asprin, including the Wartorn series from Ace Books. He lives in his native California, where he has never written a country song. (Nor is he likely ever to do so.)

ABOUT THE ARTIST

Spanish artist Miky Ruis writes: "From a very young age I was attracted to drawing and painting. I soon realized that this is what my form of expression would be. I have a passion for all artistic disciplines, but after making several exhibitions in oil, watercolor, pencil, charcoal, I discovered digital art. That has allowed me to carry out a wide variety of projects within music, comics and illustration in general." retratoregalo.es/ Facebook: facebook.com/comicalacarta

THE LOST CITY OF LOS ANGELES

by John Shirley

I.

I didn't expect to wake up, not ever. I didn't *want* to wake up. The news was terrifying every day, and I was incurably ill

In 2048, when UCLA offered me the chance of taking part in their preservation experiment, I thought I'd hit a sort of jackpot when it came to ending my life. It was something like the old cryogenic plan, where they froze you and hoped to revive you once they'd found a cure for your fatal disease. Only it wasn't freezing; it was quantum stasis. Unlike cryogenics, it actually works.

The preservation tubes put you under, dreamlessly and painlessly. I figured eventually the power would fail, because of what was coming, and the tubes wouldn't last all that long on the plutonium charge and I'd probably die in my sleep. I never thought the tubes would survive what we were all sure would come.

I was partly right. The cascade of catastrophes came right on schedule. But it turned out the tubes were designed better than I'd thought. Some of them made it through.

When I woke, two people were standing beside my reclining tube. They had just activated the release mode. The way they were dressed made me think I'd awakened shortly after I'd gone under. Except for the peculiar headsets they wore, they were dressed in something approximating the casual clothing and whimsical wigs trendy at certain Los Angeles nightclubs in 2048. The long, quivering wigs were of the usual iridescent color-shifting fiber. The man wore an animated shirt, with images from 1960s psychedelic movies. The woman wore a clingsuit, with exposed breasts. While it was something you'd find in my time, it was strange to find it in this setting. The preservation staff usually wore white clinician apparel.

With a great effort, I sat up and tried to tell them that I wanted to be put under again, but then the woman touched an instrument to my arm, and I felt a rush of stimulants. I vomited the yellow gel that had been stored protectively in my stomach.

They helped me to a wheelchair and strapped me in. I was too weak to resist. They walked away and the wheelchair followed them to a recovery room. They were both rather tall, I noted. The woman seemed brawny; the man ganglier.

As we went, nausea surged over me and I threw up again on my lap.

The walls of the windowless recovery room were badly cracked; sections of ceiling had come down and some of the naked rock above the ceiling showed through. The entire facility was built within carved-out solid rock under Telegraph Peak, in the San Gabriel Mountains.

As they helped me onto the bed—which looked to be quite new—it adjusted with an eerie adaptability, as if it were a live thing cuddling me. Definitely not any sort of bed I was familiar with. A mechanism I couldn't see cleaned the vomit off me. I lay back, peering at the odd overhead light, a little saucer of pure glow near the ceiling. It was only later I learned that it was actually floating.

My nervous system was buzzing, and I felt a formless anxiety. My muscles ached and my head rang like a bell. I groaned. The

bed I was on said something I didn't understand. It sounded like gibberish.

But the woman, muttering something in the same unfathomable language, reached over and placed something soft and warm and clasping on my forehead. Instantly, most of the discomfort vanished. "Wish...I'd had that technology," I said. "When I was so sick..."

There were murmurs between them in the foreign language—a soft-edged language that sounded a little like English but wasn't; sounded like a little like Spanish but wasn't; sounded like Chinese but wasn't. The woman put a headset over my head, and adjusted it. Then she spoke to in her language—and words in more or less standard English were sent from her headset to mine. The headsets were translators.

"Ry-ann," she said, "welcome back. I am Marra George The Unexpected Sibling, and this is Krenny Josine A Time of Intensity." The translator was a woman's voice, not quite in sync with Marra's lips. "We are historio-medical anthro-ark researchers. You are Ry-ann Sutherland, yes?"

"It's pronounced Ryan," I said dreamily. "But yeah. You want my health number?"

"It is no longer applicable. Do you know what year this is?"

"You're wearing clothing from when I went to sleep, so...as odd as the sartorial choice is in these circs..."

"We wanted you to be at ease when you woke, so we used our fabricator to make clothing found in the media records of your time. You feel it is inept?"

"Close enough, that word, I guess. Or anyway—well, those are party clothes. Not clinician clothes."

"I see. Our research informed us that you were the owner of a Meenie Minie Mo club. That was all the information we could find about you. In our society we don't use clinician clothing. Our information on yours is... mottled."

"Mottled? Oh, *spotty*. And it's not Meenie Minie Mo it's *Mini Mono*. That's a music

form and a lifestyle. And—" I had put off asking this question, because having to ask it scared me: "When you say 'our society', which society do you mean?"

"I mean the Unisphere. Please believe me when I tell you—I know it is startling—but *sixteen thousand five hundred and seven years* have passed since your time. Now, while you digest that information, we will ask the bed to wash you, and we will provide a soothing nutrient drink for your refreshment. Your diseases have been cured, and little medicament will be required..."

The words *sixteen thousand five hundred and seven years* kept resonating through me. I must have become agitated, as additional "medicament" was needed, despite the discomfort modifier on my forehead, and they gave me a tranquilizer. They went out of the room as the bed cleaned me—using no liquid at all, and in a way that was startlingly intimate. The bed also made it clear that it was ready to receive my elimination, and it received it without spilling a drop. I sipped my tranquilizer *a la* nutrient and fairly soon I fell asleep.

When I woke I felt warm and fuzzy and not at all trapped though I was enfolded by the bed. I was feeling none of the perpetual fever, nor joint aches I'd had when the original staff had put me in the suspended animation tube. Krenny and Marra came in, now dressed in close-fitting dove-gray outfits, hers with a slight decolletage and a flash of musical notes across the front that appeared and disappeared as she moved about.

And that was the morning—at least I assumed it was morning—that they told me about the expedition to the Lost City of Los Angeles.

II.

Several weeks crawled by in the recovery center, while I did some working-out to improve the tone of my body, and the researchers did seemingly endless tests on me, and asked me at least two hundred questions. I asked questions of my own. Marra answered some of them them minimally.

But she and Krenny confirmed my worst fears. Everyone I'd known and loved was long dead—my mother, my brother Terry, my cousins and nephews and nieces, all gone. And their grandchildren and descendants— if they'd had any. Perhaps they hadn't any grandchildren...because the gloomiest scientific predictors of my time had been right on target.

Climate change, clearly driven by human activity, came to a head in 2050. Over the next two decades, extreme weather and relentless drought raced across globe, bringing permanent flooding in some areas, desertification in others. The Amazon basin, denuded of forest by miners and agribusiness, turned to sand dunes. Food crops were reduced, by 2080, to just twenty-seven per cent of what the overflowing human population needed. Diseases moved north from the tropics; peoples with no resistance succumbed. Gourmands of exotic animal-flesh ate the last few rare animals, learning nothing from the series of covid pandemics back in the 2020s, and more zoonotic pandemics swept in viral tidal waves over society. Wars were spawned over the scarcity of resources and it wasn't long before a Russian dictator in 2060 decided that his new missiles could annihilate the enemy launch sites before retaliation was possible so why not destroy Washington, Beijing, New York, Chicago, Fort Knox...But not all the Russian weapons reached their targets and the west coast was largely spared irradiation.

Yet nuclear winter came, and lasted long enough to strangle most attempts at preserving civilization. Los Angeles was starved, and shriveled by pestilence and heat and swamped by the rising seas and intermittent monsoons. . .

There were pockets of technocratic survivors—but war refused to be extinguished, it kept burning across the world, so that enormous swathes of historic information became ashes. The orbital electromagnetic pulse bombs erased the majority of digital records. Continuity with the past was curtailed—mottled and spotty.

Marra seemed reluctant to speak in detail about their own society. I learned that there are only about four hundred thousand members of the Unisphere, scattered about the former USA, in Canada, in the Pacific Islands and Africa. There are about three million more in the continent of Asia—another society entirely, but not terribly dissimilar. There are a hundred thousand people in South American and about ninety thousand Australians. The information was painful to swallow, difficult to bear. Most of the Earth's population had died. And now, reproduction was discouraged thanks to the historic consequences of runaway growth. Fear of war had repressed military aggression, but they were not without weapons.

Both major world societies were run by benignly competing Artificial Intelligences, given full administrative power by the technocrats. There was trade between some city-states, and between the Asians and the Unisphere. The AIs provided education, synthesized most of the food, and assigned work. It had taken the thousands of years to get to the point where they might be able to rebuild some of the old civilization—though without the old economic systems. Investigating ancient civilization provided information that could be applied to the building of the new one. Hence the mission they planned for me...

"What about animals—the ecosystem?" I asked.

"We saved some species of animals and insects, cloned others from DNA banks. Many species could not be restored. The Unisphere has worked for thousands of years to restore a healthy environment. The oceans, poisoned by agricultural chemicals and plastics and acidification, have been especially problematic. Now, conditions are... improved."

Hence, when the Unisphericals became aware of the UCLA suspended animation experiments, they started trying to revive people. There was only one other who'd survived. Each tube had a tiny supply of plutonium powering it, but most of the tubes were breached by Earth changes and EMP effects. The other who'd survived was Lottie Crenshaw…

"I'm afraid she didn't live long," Krenny said. "She was well treated, relatively free to move about, but this particular woman became terribly depressed and before we could treat her, she committed suicide. Before her passing, we enlisted her aid with your language."

I felt a bone-deep sadness, hearing that, for I'd known Lottie well. She had been a linguistics professor at UCLA; a brilliant woman, terrified by the deteriorating state of the world. I'd been a part time teacher at an annex of UCLA, and a part time journalist. When public schools and progressive universities were outlawed, I took over my Dad's mini mono nightclub, after he too committed suicide. White Nationalist vigilantes patrolled the streets. One had to have a place to hunker down at night. Suicide was its own pandemic about then.

The nightclub eminies dressed all in black, white and red, super minimal and stark—every day except Sunday, which was decreed party day, when they put on garish outfits like the ones Krenny and Marra wore when they'd awakened me. I never dressed like an eminie and I don't even like mini mono. But the club made money. And then, after a year of losing a lot of sleep running the place, a new virus came, 876 it was called, or just eight-sev, and I got very, very sick…

III.

"Ryan, are you ready to assist the expedition?" Krenny asked, as they woke me one morning. "Your strength has returned. We need you for topographical clues, and feature interpretations."

What could I say? They had revived me and restored me. Didn't I owe them something?

No sooner had I said "I guess so, " than the bed lifted me off of it and onto my feet, and the researchers handed me my new clothes.

I was hustled through long corridors outside to a dart-shaped flyer about the size of a four-seater Cessna, waiting on a stone pad. I was suddenly, startlingly, on a spur of Telegraph Peak. Fluffy cotton-white clouds floated through a cerulean sky. A hawk soared through the clean air. I could see thick greenery in the valley below. The breeze was rich with plant scents, and sometimes chilly.

"What time of year is it?" I asked.

"It is the Cycle of Reawakening," Kenny said, opening the door of the flyer with wave of his hand. "You would say 'almost summer.'"

The researchers ushered me to a seat behind the pilot. Marra sat down beside me.

Krenny got in the flyer beside the pilot. The pilot was roughly shaped like a human being but clearly artificial. Its movements were fluid. But its skin was the color of lead; in place of eyes it had a glassy grid, and it didn't breathe.

The flyer took off vertically, then darted southwest. I felt remarkably little inertia, despite these sudden motions. Anti-gravity at last? We flew out over what had been the Angeles National Forest and were soon over the shore of the Pacific. There, we headed south, flying over the rusted, pitted hulks of half-sunken cargo-container freighters, now become the basis of reefs. There was no sign of a moving ship; there were no sails. The coastal highway was gone; buried by landslides, and overgrown.

Krenny said, "We're approaching the area believed to contain the lost city of Los Angeles…"

We skimmed onward, inland, and I saw through the mists the Hollywood Hills and the Santa Monica Mountains rising beyond them. Their outlines were recognizable— but otherwise they were utterly changed.

IV.

The flyer silently reduced speed and altitude, coming to coast slowly over the water.

The region looked like a vast coastal swampland ringed by hills. It was wetland, its silver-green tendrils intermingling with the Pacific Ocean. But the swamp that was Los Angeles had bones; it had a skeleton. Much of the skeleton could only be seen from the air. Through the softly rippling translucent water, the outlines of street grids could be seen; the crumbled, mucky remnants of ancient buildings. The rusting hulks of cars and trucks.

Emotion rose up in me like an icy geyser and filled me with cold and despair and grief. I had been so angry at humanity, before I'd gone into the tube. The damage to the natural world, the bad decisions based on short-term thinking—the catastrophe. Once I'd angrily declared, "Humanity does not deserve this planet!"

Yet now, seeing a vast absence of the works of humanity, in a place where millions of human beings had lived, I ached inside. The people of my time had aspirations and family and love; many were artists, many were musicians. Many were people who wanted to do some good…

But someone had finally laughed at our civilization's house of cards—and the laughter had made a puff of air, and knocked the whole house down.

Then I saw the flocks of white cranes in the wetlands. Some were stalking their meals, others fluttering wings in mating dances. I saw pintails diving after food, and glittery fish surfacing to snatch at flying insects. I saw the green flash of dragonflies and an otter surfacing with a struggling crab in its mouth. Below the water's surface, schools of fish darted in and out of the rusting hulks of trucks and cars, and seaweed undulated. The sunlight danced on the waves above, as if glorying in all this life.

My heart rose. Where humanity is absent, the natural world flourishes.

"You people really were terribly destructive," Marra said. "But as you see, life has returned…"

We flew up to a ridge overlooking the wetlands. It was hard to clearly recognize landmarks, but I was fairly sure this ridge the giant Hollywood sign had once stood. It was replaced by a forest of eucalyptus trees; in a clearing overlooking what had been Hollywood, our flyer settled with scarcely a bump. "How is this flyer powered?" I asked. "I mean—it has no jets, no propellers…"

I was surprised when the android answered the question. Its voice came from a rubbery hole that passed for a mouth, lips moving to form words, probably so that human beings felt more comfortable. "This vessel's motile power employs hydrogen fusion to entrap and deploy gravitons, which are converted to anti-charge, creating degravitized pockets for acceleration and deceleration."

I decided to ask the android as few questions as possible.

We were soon standing in the clearing, up to our knees in fragrant grasses and California Poppies—and I was staring at several creatures in the branches of the nearest eucalyptus. Who were staring boldly back at me.

"Koalas!" I burst out. "They're not native to this continent!"

"We suppose their ancestors to have been released from a zoo," Marra said. "During the Upheavals, many zoos simply let their animals go to fend for themselves as best they might."

"Does that include tigers?" I asked, glancing nervously around.

"It does."

"Marra, look there!" said Krenny, pointing down at the wetlands. "Outriggers."

We walked over to the cliffside, followed by the android, and got a closer look at a procession of four outrigger canoes heading inland about a hundred yards below. In each canoe was a row of three paddlers, most wearing broad brimmed straw hats, all wearing colorful sarongs. Some had bared backs that were tanned, others had inherited dark skin. They seemed on average quite tall, and broad shouldered.

My pulse quickened. Here were a people likely descended from the sort of Angelinos I'd grown up around, lived with, and nearly died with...

I wanted badly to talk to them. "Do they speak English?"

Marra shook her head. "Not as you would recognize it. They speak a dialect with English and Spanish roots, and a considerable admixture of Mandarin Chinese, as well as some Filipino. As we captured two of them, on the first expedition, we are able to speak to them through our translators."

"What became of the two you captured?" I asked, afraid of the answer.

"One escaped, briefly, and was killed by our assistant, here. We dissected him. The other incorporated into the society reasonably well—for a time. However, she languished, refused to eat, and eventually perished."

"Why capture them?" I asked. "You could trade, build up a relationship..."

Marra and Krenny looked at one another, a little uncomfortable. Finally, Krenny said, "The Unispherical ordered us not to communicate with them except under the controlled conditions of the laboratory."

"The Unispherical—by which you mean the AI? What was its reason for this?"

"Conversation with extrinsic, non-AI-relational peoples has been known to create discontent and dissent. This is problematic for social harmony."

"And—what will become of *me*? Will I go to the laboratory too?"

"Until incorporation, yes."

Incorporation? "What does incorporation involve?"

"We are conditioned from infancy to incorporation. In your case—it would require the insertion of a command implant. It's quite painless and leaves you free to live your life, within Unispherical rules."

I nodded, just as if I was unconcerned... and I noticed that the android "assistant",

perhaps more of a babysitter for us three, had turned my way and seemed to be closely monitoring me for my response. "It'll feel good to be part of a healthy, thriving society again," I said. Hoping I sounded convincing.

The android was standing near the edge of the cliff. Now it turned to scan the indigenes in the canoes. I pretended to be concerned. "Should it stand so close to the edge? Suppose your friend there crumbles, and falls into the water?"

As if considering the matter, the android took one step back from the edge. Marra nodded. "It would be catastrophic for the assistant. There are some models that can operate sub-aquatically—but this one would never come back up again."

"So—what am I to do here, exactly?" I asked. "The place doesn't look much like it did when I was here. Not sure I'll be much of a guide."

"If you see anything you recognize, point it out."

"Where we are now was the location the giant letters of the Hollywood sign. It was a landmark. The name *Hollywood* in gigantic standing letters. These are the Hollywood Hills. Down there...I think I can see something sticking up out of the water that might be the remains of the famous movie theater with the hand and foot imprints of the stars pressed into concrete..."

"The stars?" Krenny frowned. "Your people believed the stars of space were gods who could come down to Earth and 'imprint' this concrete material?"

"Ah—no." I started to explain, then Marra interrupted with a touch of impatience. "We have a further, more urgent task for you. You will help us trap more of the local primitives for extraction to the laboratories. We will disguise you as one of their own kind, and use you as bait in a trap."

V.

I stood knee deep in sucking swamp mud, in the hot sun. It was an hour after the researchers announced their intention.

I was now dressed in a ragged tie-dye shirt and something printed-out that vaguely resembled tattered blue jeans. Is tie-dye and blue jeans really a thing still, a thousand or so years later?

Something slithered past my hip. I looked down, squinting against the glare on the water, and saw a large snake swimming past. It seemed disinterested in me.

A few yards to my right mangrove trees and swamp tupelos grew out over the muddy bank. Neither species was native to the Southern California I'd known. I wished I was in their shade.

Ahead, a channel opened out into a broad, glossy, sunlit estuary. Near the farther side of the estuary was a palm tree shaded island, much of it taken up by a village built on stilts. The outriggers were pulled up on the shore.

A small crowd of Angelinos seemed to be in dispute as they strode down to the water. They were carrying what were probably weapons. I waved my hands over my head to them and beckoned. They stared, there was more disputation, then two outriggers set out, three Angelinos in each one, and started toward me. Marra had assured me that the "indigenes" were capable of self defense but not inherently vicious. But suppose her research in the matter was faulty? Suppose they were cannibals?

As they approached, I saw carvings on wooden hulls of the canoes, one of them of stars forming the Big Dipper. At either side of the prows were carved large eyes with long eyelashes.

Something swam toward me from my left; something with scales and a long tail. Didn't seem to be a snake. An alligator?

Getting myself stuck here was supposed to be a tactic to get their sympathy and trust. I felt ridiculous. I tried pulling my feet from the mud but I had worked too successfully to appear like I was sinking... And I'd sunk. The only self-defense I'd been trained in was kick-boxing—my brother, centuries dead now and turned to dust, had trained people in it for a living. With my feet stuck in mud, my body half underwater, kicking at some predator wasn't an option.

I prepared to defend myself as it swam near me...and it passed me and clambered slowly up on the bank under the mangroves. It was an iguana. A *really* big one.

I was relieved—and then I saw the man at the prow of the nearest outrigger pointing a crossbow at me.

VI.

No one shot me with the crossbow. Instead, four men, leaning from the outriggers on either side, had to forcibly extract me from the mud. The outrigger pontoons kept the craft from upsetting as the Angelinos pulled me out like a tooth, while the others—and the blond woman at the prow of the second outrigger—watched the process and made comments about my strangeness and apparent stupidity. I was fascinated by the woman, with her intelligent green eyes and her strong, high-cheekboned features. Her hair was in dreadlocks, her teeth were intact and white, though some were imprinted with gold star-symbols. Like the others, she wore a tie-dyed sarong, but she alone wore a short cape of tiger fur over her shoulders. She seemed in her late thirties, like me. I found her very, *very* attractive.

The Angelinos all had fairly dark skin; some were Black, some were lighter skinned, but no one was pale. Their eyes were epicanthic; some were blue eyed, some green-eyed, some brown-eyed. The men had braided beards, with bits of wire and old rusted circuitry woven in. They all had a great many tattoos of somewhat primitive quality; of constellations, dollar signs, what appeared to be the Mercedes Benz symbol, and more cryptic imagery.

As they tugged at me, my translator headset fed me a jumble of their observations. "Stupidity" was repeated several times. "Getting himself stuck in mud like that," said the woman, as they pulled me into her boat. "Very stupid."

"Very intentional," I said, in a low voice, as I sat up in the outrigger. "Stupid as that too might seem."

I heard the translator projecting my words back in them, in their own language—or fairly close. Several of them were astonished, and made signs in the air. It looked like they were making pentagrams...I later found they were simply star-shapes. The Angelinos worship the stars—and astrology is integral to their belief system.

The woman in the tiger cape was not astonished by the translator. "I noticed the device," she said, translated. "The steelskulls wear them." I gathered that steelskulls was their term for the Unisphericals.

She pointed at me. "You! Are you a steelskull?"

"No, I am their prisoner. I still am—they're watching me."

"Why did you say getting stuck was intentional?" she asked, cocking her head to one side.

"I was forced to do it by their...I don't know if you have a word for robot or android. Mechanical man?"

She nodded. "I have seen them."

"He's damned strong and he's armed. I am supposed to be bait for you. I'm to lead a couple of you up to a place where they've set a trap—I'm supposed to say there is a fabulous treasure there. They told me that if I didn't lie to you, they'd remove large sections of my brain and make me some sort of mindless laborer. But I'll tell you nothing but the truth, I swear it. I don't want to help them trap anyone. And I don't want to be part of their society."

"You don't speak our language. Even the translator seems confused at times. What village are you from?"

I wasn't ready to tell her I was from the distant past. As in, *Technically I'm more than sixteen thousand years old*. I figured I'd tell her later, when she might trust me more and actually believe me. "My village—it's very...distant. It's called Ancient Place of the Angels. My name is Ryan."

"I am Calliope. I am the Mother Teacher of this tribe. You may call me Calli."

Mother Teacher—it sounded as if she were their leader. A matriarchal society, I thought. But I was to learn that it is a meritocracy—and Calli had the most merit.

"Two of our people were taken by the steelskulls six seasons ago," Calli said. "Have you seen the *taken* ones? Their names are Brad and Thalia."

"A man and woman…"

"Yes."

"I haven't seen them, but I heard what happened. The man was killed when he tried to escape. The woman…she refused to eat and got sick and…just gave up and died."

Calli covered her face with her hands and moaned. The other Angelinos groaned and hissed and glared angrily about, as if looking for the steelskulls.

When Calli looked back at me again, her hands fisted, her eyes streaming tears, she said, "Thalia—my sister! So, then…" She looked toward the Hollywood-sign ridge. "We will use a trap to set a trap. And the steelskulls will be punished!"

VII.

A tiger was padding along beside us. Just Calli and I and the tiger, following a dirt road up into the hills.

He was Calli's tiger, which she'd raised from kittenhood. A magnificent male Bengal tiger wearing a star-embossed collar of red leather, his every movement was imbued with a relaxed but powerful grace. His name was Fuego—the Spanish word for fire. Occasionally her language used recognizable Spanish words and phrases. Fuego adored Calli and was neutral toward me, though occasionally he seemed to give me a suspicious sidelong glance with his green-gold eyes. I was fairly confident Fuego wouldn't eat me unless she told him to. The tiger fur she wore had come from Fuego's mother. Calli had been forced to kill her, to save her people from its depredations—the mother tiger would swim out to the island and select one or two human delicacies from time to time. But in tracking the tiger, Calli found two kittens in the mother tiger's den. She adopted them both. One had died; Fuego lived.

Looking around at the terrain, I decided this had been the exclusive neighborhood Bel-Wood, in my day. No visible trace of the mansions remained. The road showed occasional patches of much-eroded asphalt, but there was no other hint of the wealth and privilege that had once reigned here.

"We are near the holdings of the Botoxians," Calli said. Her feet were shod in buckskin and she carried a handmade cross-bow, with arrows in a tiger-hide quiver on her back. She was intent on her journey, emanating a simple confidence. Oddly enough, she seemed to trust me. She'd decided to go on this mission without the others, saying, "This is my vengeance, alone. I will not risk them for this."

"What are these Botoxians like?" I asked.

"Difficult to describe. They live in an underground burrow, of metal and stone, and they have some of the old machines. Only one of them can be truly trusted—Angelina Sanchez. But the others are mad in their minds, and not to be relied on. That is why I brought Fuego with us. You will see the Botoxians soon."

I glanced at the sky, watching for the flyer, fearing that soon the Unisphericals would figure out I wasn't even remotely near where they'd told me to go. I peered through the woods, thinking I might see the android stalking us. I saw only a small herd of deer passing through, and the Koalas in the trees, gravely watching our tiger.

"I knew you were coming," Calli said, matter-of-factly.

"You did?"

"I saw you in a vision. I ate the sacred mushrooms, and saw you standing there in the mud. I thought, *Why is he so pale?* And then a wise old lizard spoke. She said you were no danger, and important to the future of our tribe."

"Yeah? A lizard said that? *That's* why

you trust me?"

"It is. Also, I like your face. It evidences curiosity and sadness and hope and it is pleasant to look upon. Even though its color is sickly."

"I was forced to be inside, out of the sun for a long, long time," I said. "But I tan rather well." I was very pleased indeed that she'd apparently decided there was a place for me in her tribe. I wanted to join Calli and her people. Anything but the Unisphere. And she made the tribe especially appealing to me.

We rounded the curve in the road and stopped in front of a barrier.

It was made of rusted steel, and it only blocked part of the road. We could easily have walked around it, except for the two muscular armed men on the other side. They wore billed caps made of some rudely tanned skin. Their lips had been cut off so they were constantly baring their teeth. They wore pieces of transparent black glass covering their eyes—wedged into the eye sockets. One was armed with something resembling a blunderbuss—a small hand-held cannon, apparently made out of an old pipe—and the other had a long, machete-like blade, crudely formed in some home smithy. They had squat, squinting faces, as if made of clay and someone had pressed down from the top of their heads. I suspected inbreeding. Both men wore shorts of crude ecru material, and deer hide boots, and were otherwise bare-skinned—but heavily tattooed. They were tattooed with what looked like the full images of security guard uniforms, rendering most of their bodies green and black. Both men had rough-edged metal ovals hanging from piercings the right nipple—I supposed these stood for badges.

"Sucks to be these guys," I muttered.

"I don't think that translated well, Ryan," Calli said. "These men are guardians of the Botoxian lair."

"Security guards," I said. "They seem insecure, looking at Fuego."

Fuego was in a crouch, staring at the

men, ears back, tail twitching. "They fear that if they try to kill him, he'll kill them anyway—which is true. He's too fast for them." She took a step closer to the gate. "Biggles, Scurmdrie—you must step aside and let us pass!"

"We cannot, Mother-Teacher— it is the Blood Walk today," rumbled one of the guards. "And this one—" He glared at me. "Is not known! He is…" Then the translation voice in my ear said, *"Untranslatable phrase. Philology unknown."*

"He is under my protection," declared Calli. "And he has the protection of Fuego!" She muttered an aside to the tiger and it reared up, placed its big paws on the barrier and snarled a warning.

The guard with the blunderbuss swung it impulsively toward the tiger and Calli. Instinctively I struck the barrel up with one hand the other grabbing the weapon's center. I felt it in my hand as it discharged into the air, a bucking vibration numbing my fingers, the roar of the blast making my ears ring as the guard twisted the weapon away—he was much stronger than I. There came a flash of golden-orange and black-stripes as Fuego leapt, a paw slapping the blunderbuss so it spun away—the guard knocked on his back in an instant with the roaring tiger atop him, dripping saliva on his terrified face.

Even as the tiger leapt, Calli vaulted the barrier, using her crossbow like a club to batter aside the other guard's machete. Her other hand, fisted, slammed into his belly, so the guard huffed and bent over double. I ran around the barrier and pried the weapon from his hand, tossed it into the brush.

"Deflecting the cannon was well done, Ryan," Calli said, as she grabbed the tiger's collar and tugged at him. Fuego grudgingly gave up his prey, not quite having feasted yet.

"Not going to let your mouser kill them?"

"Mouser?" She smiled. "I do not need a war with the Botoxians. We will let them go."

She spoke to the cowed guards, in a dialect my translator declared unknown. They scrambled away, and ran off into the brush. "Come along now, Ryan…"

After another thirty yards, the disappointed tiger still licking its chops as he loped beside us, we came upon what I took to be a cave entrance at the base of an outcropping of big rocks. Closer, I saw the heap of boulders was a tumble of ancient concrete pierced by twisted steel, and the cave was a metal-framed entrance to a bunker. A guard much like the others stood there—but this one fled at the sight of the tiger rushing toward him.

"Now we are free to find our way to the sorceress," said Calli. She spoke a few words of command to the tiger, who composed himself on his haunches to await us outside.

She led the way in, where the passage was lit by sconces of glowing crystals. The short passage took us to a broken elevator door, and beside it, a spiral staircase of metal-sheathed stone. Down we descended, a hundred steps at least, emerging at the bottom into an anteroom letting onto a cavernous space where torch flames lit a curious procession: the Blood Walk of the Botoxians.

Men and women in tattooed-on tuxes and gowns strolled down a long walkway of red-painted hide, with tatters of ancient cloth and bits of jewelry and metal on wires dangling from their crookedly bewigged foreheads. Attendants in rubbery black suits with S&M masked faces carried the torches. In a corner of the room conga drummers played a worldbeat rhythm. To one side were empty cargo-cult-like wooden constructions resembling limousines.

The women…Looking closer, I stared in horror…

The women's faces were stretched with wires, extended from gold bolts screwed into the bones of their jaws and cheeks and the corners of their foreheads, their skin like hides stretched out to dry, but smooth, *very* smooth and painted fleshy-pink. Their mouths were pulled into a permanent rictus of "smiling"; their teeth were bared, like the guards', and seemed coated in something glowingly white. From certain angles I could glimpse crusted-red subdermal tissue under the masks—masks, essentially, made of their own facial skin.

Their eyes were housed in gold-framed goggles festooned with peacock feathers. Their lips could scarcely move as they murmured and gave slight bows before costumed gawkers holding up small black painted rectangles of wood, with pieces of mirror glass pasted on...I realized the little rectangles were designed to represent smartphones. Shifting in the torchlight the mirror panels on the false phones glittered like camera lights flashing...

The walkway, I realized, represented a red carpet. They were slowly parading to a small stage where they took turns striking poses.

"That is the Blood Walk," Calli said. "It is human skin they walk on, covered in a mix of red paint and blood."

She led me around the edge of the room, and quickly through a side door. Down another passage she opened a rusted metal hatch, like something from an old submarine, and stepped through into a cluttered room formed of rusted metal walls...where we were met by a scuttling spider-shaped machine as big as a large dog, that came clattering across the floor...

It gnashed its chromium mandibles at us...

"Angelina!" my companion called. "It is Calliope!"

"Halt, Shelob!" came a woman's sharp voice. The machine spider stopped abruptly, and scuttled back to its mistress, who was stepping out from a side-room.

Angelina was a short, stocky woman, her handsome features making me think of an Aztec frieze. She had long black braided hair woven with bits of old copper wire and wore a sleeveless black suit. Her arms were tattooed with knotty Celtic symbols interwoven with astrological signs. She wore beaded moccasins on her feet. "Pleasurable seeing, bee-eff-ah Calliope!" said Angelina.

"Glad reunion, bee-eff-ah Angelina!" Calli returned, smiling broadly. She set her crossbow aside and the two women embraced. Then Angelina stepped back to look me over.

Her large deep-black eyes regarded me as if they were taking an X-Ray of my soul. I tried to smile but I was suddenly off-balance, nervous.

"This is the one you dreamt of," Angelina commented, using Calli's language.

"I believe so, Angelina."

"You really think he's suitable? He seems pallid and rather sickly."

"He had to spend a good deal of time underground, recently. And he is a man of action—he quite likely saved me from a pipe-cannon."

I looked back and forth between them, conscious that Calli was defending me after I'd made a poor first impression. "I'm right here in the room, you know," I said.

Calli chuckled. "Seer Angelina, High Sorceress of The Under, I present Ryan, the Most Peculiar."

"A good description of me, of late," I conceded, bowing to Angelina.

"Are the idiots still engaging in their Blood Walk heresy, Calliope?" Angelina asked.

"They are," said Calli, sighing. "You really should consider overthrowing them."

"They're constantly engaging in twit-twit battles, that always lead to violence," Angelina said, shrugging. "They will eliminate one another soon. I have foreseen it. Their tradition is beyond decadence; it rots with sheer antiquity."

"Vanity is persistent," Calli observed.

I was looking around in the glow of the sconced crystals, noting charts on the walls, that seemed astrological in nature, along with DaVinci-like sketches of arcane machinery. On a broad wooden table stood astrolabes; beside them were enigmatic metal and crystal contrivances, retorts and glass beakers, magnifying glasses on stands, and a microscope that seemed to have been cobbled together from many instruments. Ancient electrical circuitry, most of it blackened and gummy with the ages, was heaped in cabinet shelves. Then I looked back at the mechanical spider. Its eyes seemed to be camera lens, revolving over its mandibles as it watched me.

"Did you build that machine there?" I asked, nodding at the spider. "It looks new."

"I did not," Angelina said. She looked at Calli. "Can he be trusted?"

"He can," Calli said. "So my feelings tell me."

"I thought so," Angelina said. "But his appearance is off-putting. Have the steelskulls been toying with him?"

"Most perceptive," I said. "I only just escaped from them, with Calli's help. They did me no real harm—they didn't have a chance for the surgery."

Calli's voice was hoarse as she said, "Angelina—he's told me what happened to my sister and her mate. Correz was killed and Thalia starved herself to death in the custody of the Unisphere. Your remote-view was accurate."

Angelina nodded sadly. "I don't blame you for hoping I was wrong. You know—my periscope reports that the steelskulls are flying nearby…"

"I intend to exact my revenge on them," Calli said. "I hoped you might help me."

"So you found this spider thing *preserved* somewhere?" I asked, nodding toward the machine again.

"I did," said Angelina. "This complex was built more than sixteen thousand years ago, to preserve people from the advanced weapons of the ancients. One chamber of preservation was tightly sealed enough to survive all. It took me ten years to open it. A number of devices are there…"

"I was thinking of the Greeter," Calli said, smiling wickedly at Angelina.

"Yes—a good idea! But first, Ryan the Most Peculiar, I should tell you that my research has shown that the translator you're wearing is also a device that tracks your whereabouts. The Unispheric flyer is now hovering over the entrance to the complex, watching for you to emerge."

"They've been following, wondering where we're going," I guessed.

"Likely. We don't want them to come here. But there is a certain tunnel you may use, to lead them off…"

VIII.

Calli and I crouched in the brush under the eucalyptus trees, ten yards from the egress of the ancient tunnel. We were watching the clearing at the cliff-edge, where I had stepped out of the lander this morning. The flyer was gone, probably still hovering over the Botoxians, but the android was there. It was standing in the middle of the clearing— and it was looking our way.

We were well hidden, but I knew it had the tracking signal from my translator.

"I wish we had Fuego with us," I said. The tiger was still crouched outside the underground entrance. "Can you call him?"

"Not from here—and if the machine man is armed, it might kill him…"

I nodded. "I have an idea, Calli…If you could fire some of your crossbow bolts at the thing, and distract it, I'll plant the translator elsewhere. And you and I will have to find other ways to communicate."

"Very well. Act with the utmost caution, Ryan!" She reached out and squeezed my hand. "It wasn't only the dreams—the moon, the stars, the planets aligned, and informed me that my new mate would come. The dream warned me he would be strange…and so you are. But my feelings are clear. Do not throw your life away, Ryan. It has become precious to me…"

We scarcely knew each other and I don't believe in astrology, or prophetic dreams, but I wasn't going to argue with a good thing. The very best thing that had happened to me more than sixteen thousand years. "I'll be careful."

The android was coming toward us—and I dodged off to the right, removing the translator headset as I went. I sprinted through the brush, knowing the android would be turning to watch me. It would choose its moment and come after me.

Then I heard the twang and hiss of a crossbow and a *thunk* as the bolt struck the android. Running behind a tree bole, I paused to look—and saw that the android, though unhurt, was turning toward the source of the attack. Suppose this "cunning plan" of mine cost Calli her life?

It was even now moving toward her. I ran toward the brink of the cliff, to the edge of the clearing in a spot where it was hidden by manzanita and tree trunks. Another twang, hiss and *thunk*. I glanced over and saw the android closer to Calli. And the artificial man was faster than I'd hoped. I ran to the edge of the cliff, angling to get behind the android. I was about ten yards away from it. I crouched and hooked the headset on a bit of root sticking out under the edge of the cliff, then dodged back to the brush.

"Hey Pinocchio!" I yelled. "I'm over here!"

I flattened down in the underbrush, and saw that the android had stopped, was looking around—and I hoped to whatever god or goddess was in charge around here that Calli had gone to ground. She had stopped firing at it, and she was fast and wily—I was almost sure it wouldn't catch her. Almost…

"I said over here, Pinocchio, ya dumbbell!" I yelled, so loud it hurt my throat. Now the android turned and started my way—and then it changed directions, as I'd hoped, following the tracer in the translator headset.

It strode to the edge of the cliff—and looked down, puzzling for a moment. It knelt, picked up the headset, and stood, even as I got up and ran toward it. The android sensed me and turned. Its optical panel lit up. A flame-red beam hummed out from it—and burnt its way through the air, barely missing my neck as I jumped, in kick posture, just as my brother had taught me, and the flying kick-box move landed solidly: I struck the android with my right foot just above its

waist.

And over it went, falling backward off the cliff.

And over I tumbled over too, carried by momentum—

I fell, and figured I was going to hit a rock and die...

But I plunged into deep water. The impact after the long fall knocked the wind out of me. I felt brine intruding painfully into my lungs. But nearby, a little below, the android was sinking, its arms flailing. I'd extracted the critical information from Marra—the android was not a subaquatic model. It sank rapidly, even as I struggled to swim upward. It looked up at me, its optical grid flashed—then flickered, and went out. Grey fluid seeped from its thin mouth...

Darkness was closing around me, and my limbs went all rubbery, even as I looked down and watched the now-stiff android, falling face down into the seaweed...

Something slashed by me from above. Bubbles caught the light. I felt a tugging...

The darkness closed in—and then it burst apart as sunlight fell warm on my face, and water gushed from my heaving lungs. I coughed, over and over, with barely time to breathe. Something—someone—was pulling me toward the outrigger canoe skimming toward us...

Still coughing, I turned my head enough to see that Calli had an arm wrapped around me. With powerful strokes of her other arm and her legs, she was towing me to the canoe.

The Angelinos pulled me gasping into an outrigger. I lay on my back for a moment—and then the Unispherical flyer flew into my range of vision, and hovered. A window irised – and the muzzle of a weapon pointed out.

I pointed at the flyer—but Calli had already seen it and she shouted orders at the rowers. I didn't understand her orders now but the quickening of the rowing pace was translation enough.

Then a jet of energy spat down at us, hiss-ing into the water close by. The rowers cried out in fear and alarm and redoubled their efforts to get to shore. The flyer moved closer, the muzzle extruded. One of warriors fired a crossbow at the flyer but the bolt fell short.

I hope to God Angelina saw the flyer through her scope, I thought, as a jet of fire from above struck a rower—and instantly killed him.

But something else appeared in the sky and its presence let me know Angelina had been watching.

Lustrous in the late afternoon light, a cloud of metallic dots swarmed through the sky from the direction of the "under lair" of the Botoxians. The cloud stopped short of the flyer—and then formed into the words

WELCOME TO LOS ANGELES

in metallic micro-drone skywriting. It had been pre-programmed into the drone-control device Angelina had discovered. I remembered this effect from my own time. Based on the technology that had formed the interlocked circles of the Olympics symbol in the sky, at the 2018 games, skywriting using drones to form symbols and words had become a much-evolved technology, by 2048.

The sky words glimmered—keeping Marra and Krenny's attention on them—and they spouted electric energy, in a fireworks effect, while other drones formed outlines of palm trees, the L.A. Super Stadium, the faces of movie stars, VR influencers, and the mayor of Los Angeles at the time. All this was deployed for the delectation of tourists.

Then the words and images melted into a dense swarm which shot at the flyer, hovered over it—and whipped through the open window. The flyer rocked in place, and then twirled in the sky. I saw a red spray from the open window—blood.

The flyer suddenly rocketed off, at random—and crashed into the cliffside, where it exploded...

IX.

I spent several months learning the language of the Angelinos. It came fairly naturally, but the rituals of Marital Commitment were rigorous. I agreed to all of the rituals but one. I refused to be branded, with a hot iron, with a symbol confirming I was Calliope's mate. She sighed and said, "If you don't love me enough…"

"You're not after all so different from my ex," I said in English, as we sat on the woven front porch of her stilt house. In Calli's language, I said, "I just think the branding thing might be a bit on the primitive side." I shook my head. "Just not my style. Anyway, I don't want to brand *you*. I'd rather you got a nice tattoo with the interlocked stars symbol, like in the brand."

The smile she gave me then had the power of a stroke of lightning that never faded. "Yes, I shall tattoo you! But…the other rituals are necessary!"

So, I did the whole "walking on hot coals to her waiting arms" thing (it's not hard if you hurry).

I did the ritual killing of a crawling shark (alarmingly, certain sharks were genetically weaponized to develop legs, but they ate their creators and escaped).

I did the Marital Contortions Dance (very difficult, one's muscles require special training).

I did the ritual swallowing of a crystal to be read after it is excreted (don't ask).

I spent a day tanning the required picture of Calli's face onto my right thigh (she gave me a stencil that would form her face).

I did the ritual Rush Hour March down the ancient remains of a freeway (it's a six mile trudge in the sun).

Oh and I did the ritual gathering of flowers for my bride, in The Field of Numerous Scorpions (very tricky indeed)…

And then, after I delivered the flowers, came our mutual vows, as the villagers applauded. Following the vows, we went immediately into her house and consummated our nuptials, as Fuego guarded the door.

The next morning, I asked, "Was last night…fully satisfying?"

Calli tilted her head thoughtfully and said, "It wasn't bad. I will teach you, with great persistence, till you learn how to make it *fully* satisfying. Shall we begin, Ryan?"

"I think we'd better, my Calliope…"

⚛

ABOUT THE AUTHOR

John Shirley has authored numerous novels, including *Demons, Crawlers, Wetbones, Cellars, Bleak History, City Come A-Walkin', Eclipse, Bioshock: Rapture,* and *The Other End.* His story collections include *Black Butterflies,* which won the Bram Stoker Award. His newest story collection is *The Feverish Stars.* His new novel *Stormland* came out in 2021. His most recent novel is *A Sorcerer of Atlantis.* His first collection of poems, *The Voice of the Burning House* has recently been published by Jackanapes Press (rhyming poetry in the Weird Poetry manner). He is co-screenwriter of *The Crow* and wrote for *Star Trek: Deep Space Nine* and other shows.

ABOUT THE ARTIST

Igor Malahov writes: "I am a civil engineer, but since childhood, I have always been interested in arts as a hobby. I was born in Riga, Latvia, finished my secondary school in the United Kingdom and am doing my master studies in Finland."

THE COLOUR OF NOTHING
by Mike Chinn

A wild blast cut through plasteel a metre above Jem Strygeth's head. He ducked, swearing up a storm as fine shards dusted his unruly red hair. His Q'Alvin shield might be enough to deflect the blaster shot—but not the chunks of jagged plasteel shrapnel. He flipped open his sub-vox.

"Shenna!"

Her voice purred deep in his head. *"Almost done!"*

"So will I be if you don't skate it!"

"Don't get so chokka— Yodely!"

Jem risked a glance over his shoulder. Down the short corridor Shenna was on her knees, frantically keying the eyepad. She ducked lower, flicking bangs of purple hair away from her eyes, staring into the pad's securistrobe.

"Tell me we're in, Shenna!"

"Yodely!" She hopped lightly to her feet as the corridor's end wall faded away, dusting at her clingy white shieldsuit. "Such archy security. They deserve to be hacky-sacked."

"It's not just the doors—!" Jem saw the digithopter out of an eye's corner. He pivoted, striking with his longsword. The imager split in two, spinning away to bounce off a wall before lying dead on the floor. Several more blaster shots roared past him: splashing off a far wall, leaving it scored and molten.

"You want to warp it—the portal won't stay irised forever!" Shenna's voice sounded distant—Jem glanced back again. She was already through the portal. Jem snapped off a couple of wide-angle laser shots—maybe he could blind somebody—turned and raced for the gap. He leapt through—hitting the hard floor moments before the portal turned solid again.

"Thought you were in a hurry…?"

Jem got to his feet, holstering his laser but keeping longsword drawn. He patted at his dusty maroon shieldsuit with his free hand. Shenna was ahead, walking down a narrow aisle lined by faintly-lit alcoves.

"Look at the pretty glims," she crooned. "Just Q'Alvined and 'padded. You'd think they actually want it cloyed…"

"Skatey," Jem muttered. "They'll be through that port smartish."

"Not that squad of trucks: don't have the juice." Shenna ran a finger over an alcove. The pale blue light sparked. "'Sides, way I've jimmy-javved the 'pad, it'd take a voidie broadside to split it."

"Still feel better a couple of systems away from here." He followed her down the aisle, glancing left and right at the alcoves. Far as he could tell they were just opaquely-gleaming blanks. He had no idea how Shenna could ID any of them.

"Throttle," she called back over her shoulder. "Found your techie-toy!" She reached out a gloved right hand and spread her fingers over a pale, glowing oblong. White sparks scattered and danced, crawling up the sleeve of her shieldsuit. Shenna giggled. "Tickles…"

In her left hand a length of charyon wire—not much thicker than a strand of her purple hair—appeared. It waved and undulated, possessed of its own peculiar life. Shenna brought an end into contact with the sparking panel. The light went out, the panel gone—leaving just an opened alcove and its contents. Jem thought the whole procedure somewhat anti-climactic. There should be more lights, loud noises, seismic vibrations… Shenna always made it look too easy—but then she was the best gilt in the business.

She reached in and pulled out the alcove's only contents: a gleaming chunk of apparatus around the size of her head. It seemed to move, coiling and writhing, not a single component straight or true. Jem's eyes were unable to lock onto the tortured surface.

He sighed in relief. "Time to break. Warp it." As Shenna slipped their prize into a quantum satchel, Jem added: "How far to the other port?"

Shenna threw the satchel, with its now massless and volumeless contents, across a shoulder and grinned at him. Her pale red eyes sparkled. She pointed behind him, at the portal they'd just used.

Jem groaned. "Tell me you didn't..."

"Jimmy-javved." She laughed and skipped past him, dropping to her knees at the internal eyepad interface. Another flourish of her delicate hands over the 'pad, another securistrobe. The portal faded away—this time opening out on what Jem guessed was Fallorada landing field. His heart sank even as the gorge rose in his throat. He loathed using portals that had been bootlegged through voidspace.

"Warp up, hero," Shenna murmured. "Planetary grid's driving gigs through this. Only good for a few millis—then it'll be well novaed."

"You make a good point." Jem sheathed his sword, took a deep breath, closed his eyes, and ran for it. A moment later it felt like something had reached into his gut and torn it out. His legs turned to gel, hooked spikes slipped through his ears and into his brain, twisting slowly. He opened his eyes. He was lying on a strip of clipped green bucky-grass that was decorated by a pool of his own puke. Lucky he wasn't face-down in it.

He got to his feet, head swimming. It took him a moment to orientate himself, but they were definitely on Fallorada Field— their skiff waiting just a few metres away. To his left Shenna was jumping through a two-dimensional hole in the air. She landed delicately. A second later, the hole imploded with a meaty sucking noise. Ripples spread across the air like mirages.

Shenna readjusted her satchel. "Dramatic," she smirked.

Jem got another abrupt kick in the guts. This was a sensation he was used to: blaster impact on his shieldsuit. The yelling in colloquial Tenysh told him exactly where it had come from. A dozen of the local guard were racing across the bucky-grass, some waving blasters, others levelling halblasters and longswords. All were fully armoured.

"Time to break!"

They started to make for their skiff, but it didn't take Jem long to figure they weren't going to make it in time. He guessed the guards were using 'rators: they were racing across the field, dodging parked-up skiffs and jollyboats far too quick and easy. They'd get to the skiff seconds before Jem and Shenna. Only one choice.

Jem drew his laser, set on the widest spread, and fired. Two of the guard faltered, temporarily blinded by the attenuated light, the rest just came on faster. Jem dropped his pistol and unsheathed both long and short sword. At his side, Shenna lowered the quantum satchel to the ground and flipped her own blades from their pockets. They unfurled as she raised them: twin buzzblades with cavorium-edged teeth. The swords whined eagerly as they powered up.

"The sawbones is in," she purred, striking a dramatic pose. Jem shook his head. A second later, the first armoured figure raced into range.

Jem slashed across with short sword, a longsword downward stroke finished it. The guard collapsed to the grass, armour bleeding.

Shenna's buzzblades shrieked as she swept them at two more guards. There were four chunks left when she'd finished. The remaining nine men circled the pair, each trying to jab closer with sword or halblaster. All they did was get in each other's way. Undisciplined. Their gear was the best, but they squandered that advantage coming in too close or over-reaching. Shenna's buzzblades carved through cuirasses like they were webbing; Jem's traditional style with short sword blocked every lunge and clumsy riposte, leaving them open to his longsword. It was short, it was ugly. In minutes all twelve guards lay dead or mortally wounded on the bucky-grass.

Jem flicked blood off his swords and sheathed them. "In the skiff, skatey! Before they launch another posse."

Shenna powered down and shrank her buzzblades, pocketing them. She grabbed her satchel and ran for the tiny skiff, remotely lowering the gangway. Jem followed close behind. Shenna didn't wait for him to find a seat before punching the skiff's atmoshear. It leapt into the air, nose rising like it was sniffing its course. Jets bellowed. Jem almost lost his balance. He clung onto a seatback, watching through the nose holoports as the sky darkened from blue to purple to black. Ahead, growing rapidly clearer as Shenna swapped atmoshear for ion-ram, was *The Aiken Drummer*. Ramshackle, ancient, as much a danger to her crew as any enemy. Jem could kiss her.

He finally flopped into a chair, reaching into the quantum satchel still slung over Shenna's shoulder and removed their prize. He held the disturbing thing in two hands, trying to look at it full-on. His gaze constantly slid off. A gravolian modulator for the new-style voidie drive. And stiffing one had been easier than plucking frayberries.

"Chokka'ed if Anre'eq wasn't right," he smiled. "The Ekleiades *is* getting sloppy…"

* * * *

Lights flared on and the vast image of what remained of the planet Davolias faded. The Skopion Dome was left empty. Its high vaulted auditorium, looming over the countless tiers rising from the centre, would normally be stacked with the floating chairs and discs of Senate and Council. The vault's present two occupants stood gazing into space, each wrapped in their own thoughts.

One stood on the dome's floor. An old man—long hair greying to white, shoulders stooped, gaunt frame swamped by his official robes—well past four hundred years in age. That he'd reached such an age without taking a new body proclaimed him a follower of the old Orthodoxy—possibly a Drinwa or Gooraq. But his blue eyes were alight and mischievous, even as he bowed and dropped his gaze from the dwarfish figure standing above him on a hovering grav-disc.

Emperor Stenn XXVII continued to gaze at the empty spot where, moments before, he had watched the final moments of Davolias. A minor world, far off in a remote arm of the Voynich Nebula, its loss was unimportant. That it had been destroyed, however, was not. Who, and why? Especially who. And with projectile weapons—missiles, they had once called. Slipping past Q'Alvin shielding that would have held off a voidcutter's broadsides indefinitely.

Stenn allowed his grav-disc to drop, skimming it towards the old man in a graceful arc. He slowed it just before it reached the level of the other's head. "Neither Council or Senate must learn of this."

The old man bowed further. "Agreed, your grace."

"Then what do we know?"

The other kept his face downcast. "Very little, I regret, your grace. There has been no intelligence. No reports—"

"You mean the resources of the Imperium—not to mention the Ekleiades—somehow remained ignorant of all this?" Stenn barely controlled his anger. "That someone, somewhere, has built obsolete weapons without our knowledge? If, as seems likely, some form of Newtonian propulsion was used, they must have taken decades, or even centuries, to reach their target. How did we not notice? Or do these same someones also possess Bieg voidcutters from which to launch their little darts?" He allowed his disc to drop lower. His dwarfish body now stood at eye-level with the old man, if he'd only lift his eyes. "What is your name?"

The old man stooped even lower, exposing his neck to the emperor. "Carniz Jholenn, if it please your grace."

"It does not please us, Citizen Jholenn." Stenn enjoyed the terror radiating off the man cowering before him. "Is there anything else we should know?"

"Your grace...?"

"Is there anything other than the senseless destruction of Davolias by persons unknown and by weapons no one has built for thousands of years? Anything else the Empire's extremely expensive intelligence services have failed to uncover?"

Carniz Jholenn was trembling now, almost certainly imagining his death only moments away. "No voidcutters were used—no drive signatures or bio-signs. And no other vessel—of any design, ancient or modern—was detected. For all that can be ascertained, the projectiles simply materialised above Davolias before plunging to the surface."

Stenn floated his disc up and away from the old man, towards the dome's exit. "We thank you for your discretion, Citizen Jholenn," he called over a shoulder, almost an afterthought. "I will inform the Téokrat directly." *Although*, he added silently, *the devious bastard will almost certainly know already.*

His disc reached the dome's curving wall, a portal faded open. Outside, a squad of Stenn's personal guard—Feluq'ans to a man—snapped to attention, halblasters perfectly vertical, morrións and cuirasses glittering in the daylight. Several imagers and digithopters hovered in the warm air, their optics tracking every man. Stenn's disc rose a little at his command, so that his short body matched his guardsmen, head for head. The officer of the day stepped forward, dropping to one knee.

"Your command, your grace?"

Stenn allowed his disc to drift away from the Skopion Dome. At his back the portal opaqued. The emperor gestured for the guard to get to his feet, and glanced back towards the vanished doorway.

"There is a man back there—a Carniz Jholenn..."

The guard nodded. "I know of him, your grace."

"Good. We must visit with the Téokrat." They all genuflected, more for the benefit of the prying digithopters than from any true devotion. "Once we are gone, escort the good Citizen Jholenn to the nearest bodega. Buy him anything he wants. Express our gratitude. Be a friend." Stenn held the guard's gaze a moment, tilting his head by a fraction so small none of the imagers would catch it. *Then, at the earliest opportunity, kill him*, the motion said.

The officer bowed, understanding. "It shall be done, your grace," he said quietly.

Another man of discretion, thought Stenn. *How would the Ekleiades Galaktium survive without them?* "Of course it will," he added out loud. *And after, perhaps we'll have your head on a spike for daring to murder such a respected member of the government.*

* * * *

The blackness was almost complete. Just two pale ovals—almost white—broke the totally lightless abyss. Human faces, but for their inhuman pallor, they floated, disembodied, a metre apart. Dark eyes stared, thin lips pressed shut. The silence was as absolute as the darkness.

Abruptly, the oppressive blackness erupted into life: thousands of brilliant points of light sprang alive. Yellow, white, blue-white, red, orange, coppery-green—every shade of the spectrum. A starfield. The galaxy, filling the black void.

A moment after it appeared, the backdrop of bright lights began to move, drifting at a leisurely pace. The white faces, their black-clad bodies now revealed in occasional silhouette against the clustered lights, seemed to flow through the cosmos.

The drifting slowed, ceased altogether. Now the black figures floated against a cloud of tumbling particles, some no bigger than dust-motes, others ragged chunks bigger than a mountain. All glittered in the light of a distant blue-white star.

One of the faces spoke: gaunt lips barely parting, voice a harsh whisper. "Davolias."

"Yes." The second voice was equally hoarse. "The star is Tertius Pentane."

Silence returned for a moment. The surrounding starfield moved again, zeroing in on the blue-white sun.

A disk of light spread at the figures' feet. It drifted up to waist height. A black hand rested across it. "All is ready?"

"Yes."

Fingers performed a complex dance across the bright disk and withdrew. The disk sank, dimmed and shrank. The figures turned slightly: now facing the image of Tertius Pentane. They waited.

Nothing changed. The star blazed brilliantly, solar flares arced across its surface, azure convection currents swirled majestically across the surface.

Then the star began to brighten. The convection currents grew more agitated, paling to almost white. Streaks of brilliant gold swirled across the photosphere. Solar flares multiplied; grew vaster.

Tertius Pentane receded a little so the observers could see more. Even so, it seemed to swell up to meet them, growing darker and more violent with every second. Millions of kilometres distant—the remains of Davolias a shroud of dust between star and observers—and still the star dominated the image. Bloated, scarred, soon to erupt.

It did so abruptly, flaring to a blinding glare that overwhelmed the light of every other star.

Once the nova faded, there was nothing to be seen of Tertius Pentane, other than skeins of cooling star-matter sprayed across the void. Even the remains of Davolias had gone, consumed by its sun's final agonies. A sphere of space, billions of kilometres across, had been scoured clean. Planets, moons, any nearby ships caught in an un-precedented storm…

The starfield winked out. Once again the only visible occupants of the blackness were two white faces. The thin lips of one moved at last, drawn into a ghastly smile.

"We are ready."

* * * *

Stenn slowed his disc as they reached the Téokrat's portal. There was little to distinguish this stretch of palatial wall from any other. There were no iconic images, no guards, no overt weapons. All a keen observer might notice was an increased number of digithopters, snoopers, imagers and sniffers. More than any other sector of the palace. And Stenn knew well just how many assault blasters, incinerators, buzzbows and pikes were hidden in those plain walls. The Téokrat could easily hold off a concentrated assault for over three hours. That was all it had taken to destroy every last besieger during the Stealth Riots five years earlier.

The emperor reached inside his robes and pulled out his hailer. Rubbing a thin finger over the device's gold and topaz surface, he felt rather than heard the sub-oral gonging that announced his presence to Mygré Keddyth: his Supreme Holiness, the Téokrat.

The portal didn't open immediately. Stenn was left waiting a full ten minutes before a section of wall—four times the height of a man, and three times the width—faded, revealing the gloom beyond. He dismissed his Feluq'an guard with a careless wave. They would be of no use to him inside. The Stealth rioters, torn apart and half-melted, had been blessed in a way. If they had made it into the Téokrat's chamber, there were the Begeen. They would not have been so merciful.

Stenn hovered forward, raising his disc so that his head almost grazed the portal's lofty peak. Be damned if he was going to skulk inside.

The gloom was relieved by the hundreds of two metre high blazing light pillars dotting the floor, hanging in floating chandeliers, or burning in sconces on holographic walls, flying buttresses and gothic arches. There were huge windows depicting scenes of glory from the Ekleiades' millennia of history. It was all show: a grand parade. Mygré's personal recreation of how a spiritual leader's palace should look. If there was any solid architecture beyond the grandiose holograms, it was little more than flickering highlights and hints.

Stenn risked a smile, wondering if the Téokrat recognised how apt a simile it all was for his endless rule? As with the Skopion Dome, there were no imagers or sniffers allowed within the Presence, but there were other ways to pry and observe.

The galaxy of light pillars left behind, Stenn drifted towards the last avenue: leading to the Presence Himself. Lining it were ranked a thousand figures all in white, their robes a riot of grotesque patterns and figures, many of which twitched in the dancing light. Tall, conical white hoods covered their heads. In each hood were two black slits from which no eye ever glistened. They bore no weapons that Stenn could see, but he knew they could kill in more ways than it was possible to imagine. The Begeen: Mygré's personal guard. Young virgin girls, always a thousand, never more nor less. At the emperor's approach, every face turned in his direction. As he drifted past, the cowls slowly followed. It was like riding a wave of distrust and paranoia.

Stenn floated his disc above the cowls, keeping his short body just a few centimetres higher than the empty black eye-slits. He glanced at them as he passed, wondering—as he did every time—which one was Kith. Were any of them Kith? Was his lovely sister still living, or had she fallen in defence of her master?

His formal announcement rocked Stenn from his thoughts. A disembodied voice, inhuman in its perfection, echoed deep and loud throughout the Téokrat's chambers.

THE EMPEROR STENN LYMATÉN, TWENTY-SEVENTH OF THAT NAME, LORD OF THE NINE-HUNDREDTH DYNASTY, DEFENDER OF THE FAITH, RULER OF THE NINE BILLION SYSTEMS.

Ahead something shifted. In perfect synchronisation the ranks of Begeen bowed from the waist, the combined rustling of their white robes almost as loud as the announcement. Stenn dropped to one knee, lowering his head, though not so low he could not see. No one but a fool ever took his eyes off an enemy.

The Téokrat appeared out of the carefully-engineered gloom. A barely-seen figure enthroned on a vast white chair that sprawled in baroque splendour. It shone too bright for Stenn to look at directly, its outlines hard to discern. But it rose up in a vast peak which echoed the Begeen's robes. The dark shape hidden in that blaze could have been human; it could have been anything. As short as Stenn, or a giant, no one living knew for sure. Mygré Keddyth had been on the Téokrat's throne longer than the Ninth Empire had existed. It was impossible to know how many times he'd renewed his body, or in what way. Stenn knew Mygré better than most men—only the Begeen knew him better—and he barely knew him at all.

MY LORD EMPEROR. Like the announcement, the voice came from everywhere and nowhere, filtered and processed into something synthetic. TO WHAT DO WE OWE THIS PLEASURE?

Stenn raised his head fully—though he never looked towards the throne. "Your Holiness must be aware of the fate of Davolias…"

WE ARE. AN ENTIRE WORLD DESTROYED, REDUCED TO DUST. There was a pause. AND WE HAD BELIEVED ONLY OURSELVES CAPABLE OF SUCH PUISSANCE…

Stenn smiled. "As did we all, Holiness." The emperor paused himself. Let the ancient bastard read into that what he likes. "I regret that, so far, the Imperium has no suspects."

WE ARE SURE. The vast throne moved closer. Thin arcs of light spun off it, flashing into the darkness beyond. The Téokrat's seat was a small sun, blazing in the lightless void of his own chambers. *ARE YOU AWARE THAT TERTIUS PENTANE HAS ALSO BEEN DESTROYED?*

"Davolias's sun?" Stenn frowned. He had no reason to doubt the intelligence, but still marvelled at how quickly the Téokrat had learned it. "By what means?"

BY THE SAME MEANS THAT THE PLANET WAS OBLITERATED. OR SO WE ARE LED TO BELIEVE.

Stenn thought quickly. "Forgive me, Holiness, Whilst the destruction of a planet may be rare, it is not unprecedented. But an entire star—?"

WE FURTHER UNDERSTAND THAT SUCH AN ACT IS NOT DIFFICULT. THOUGH IN THE PAST WE HAVE HAD CAUSE TO CHASTISE VARIOUS SYSTEMS, WE HAVE BEEN MERCIFUL...

You just send a fleet of voidcutters to slice their planets into asteroids. Stenn kept his expression neutral. Not even the Téokrat could read minds. *But are you saying you could have destroyed their suns, too? Interesting.* "His Holiness's mercy is proclaimed throughout the empire..."

There was silence again for several moments. Eventually, the Téokrat spoke again. *STENN, YOU HAVE HEARD OF THE SALGA ASHTOREEN...?*

The emperor found himself smiling again. "Not since I was a child, Holiness."

THEN YOU DO NOT BELIEVE IN THEM?

"Believe, Holiness? No more than any other of the bugbears used to discipline me and Kith. Behave, or the Salga Ashtoreen will come tonight and slice you into ribbons." He wished he hadn't mentioned his sister.

WE HAVE REASON TO THINK THEY EXIST AFTER ALL.

"Holiness?" This was unexpected. Perhaps senility was catching up with the ancient bastard after all.

THE SALGA ASHTOREEN IS MORE

THAN A CHILDREN'S BOGEYMAN. THEY ARE REAL—AND THEY POSE A GENU-INE THREAT TO BOTH EMPIRE AND EKLEIADES GALAKTIUM.

Stenn thought carefully. If Mygré's ancient and desiccated brain wasn't collapsing into gibbering madness...? "You believe they are responsible for the destruction of both Davolias and Tertius Pentane?"

THE ENTIRE SYSTEM, STENN. TER-TIUS PENTANE WAS FORCED INTO A SUPERNOVA—IN MOMENTS. EVERY PLANET IN THE SYSTEM WAS SWAL-LOWED. A 'CUTTER PATROL HEADING FOR GALLIFORNUS NARROWLY AVOID-ED THE SAME FATE...

"Did the patrol detect any other vessels?"

NOTHING. OTHER THAN REGULAR TRAFFIC, SPACE WAS SHIP-FREE FOR PARSECS. The throne retreated a little. Stenn couldn't be sure, but it seemed to him the smudge in the centre of the blaze was twitching. With agitation? *DO YOU APPRE-CIATE WHAT THIS MEANS, MY LORD EMPEROR?*

Stenn did, all too well. "The Salga Ash-toreen was supposed to be an organisation of assassins. Fanatical, skilled beyond a superhuman level, relentless. If they are more than the monsters of childhood, and they are somehow connected to the destruction of the Tertius Pentane system..."

AND IF THEY HAVE RE-EMERGED FROM WHEREVER THEY HAVE HIDDEN FOR THE PAST MILLENNIA...

The Téokrat didn't finish. He didn't need to. If the Salga Ashtoreen was real, and they possessed weapons powerful enough to send even young stars supernova... "The empire is in tangible danger, Holiness."

FIND THEM, STENN, PURSUE THEM. BEFORE THEY CAN ECLIPSE US; BE-FORE THEY CAN DESTROY US. WE WILL NOT PRESIDE OVER THE LOSS OF THE NINTH EMPIRE. THE EKLEIADES GAL-AKTIUM WILL PREVAIL! THE EKLEIA-DES WILL TRIUMPH! IN THE NAME OF

THE IMPERIUM; IN THE NAME OF THE TÉOKRAT!

The deep, atonal voice rose higher until it drowned its own echoes. The only other sound was a swelling chant, slowly matching the Téokrat's speech. Stenn rotated his disc. The ranks of Begeen were raising their arms in salute, calling on their master. A mantra that drummed in Stenn's ears.

But as he watched the display of fanatical devotion, all Stenn thought was, *Kith? Where are you? Can I save you? Is it too late...?*

* * * *

Jem was barely out of the skiff when Anre'eq's voice sub-voxed in his head.

"Hold on tight, you two—we need to break orbit, skatey-like!"

A moment later the floor under Jem's feet tilted at an alarming angle. He half-fell, half-dived for a bulkhead, activating a holo-port. A metre-square section of internal hull turned into a view outside *The Aiken Drum-mer.* At first, all he could see was Tenysha, glowing like a pearl-blue globe in space. Tracking the field brought two distant blips into focus. Ships: probably monitors.

"Not a time to say better late than never...!"

Tenysha's distant surface quivered gently, blurring, and seemed to draw back. As Anre'eq accelerated the *Drummer's* stardrive, the creaky old corvette broke out of orbit, leaping into free space with all the sprightliness her ageing hull could summon.

"Bosey!" Jem flinched as Shenna laughed right in his ear. "We sure got the break on those trucking rumblers!"

Jem waved the holo off and stood away from the bulkhead. The ship was stable now Anre'eq had quit with the fancy manoeuvres. "Just hope they don't have gravolian upgrades, Shen, else they'll pass us like we're in reverse in a couple of millis."

She slapped his shoulder. "Told you, cap, Tenysha's archy. Security's in eclipse, local fleet real coalnoil." She laughed again.

"Couldn't catch an empty third-stager."

"If you say so. C'mon—Ani will want to play with that new toy you cloyed."

Up on the control deck, Anre'eq was slumped comfortably in the pilot's chair, watching stars doppler by on an untidy array of holoports. He actually had his boots resting on a side console, lost in a black shield-suit that looked two sizes too large for his tall, lanky frame. He was barely touching the stick with a forefinger.

"Comfortable?" Jem dropped into the seat beside him.

Anre'eq glanced carelessly in his direction, grinned, and went back to half-eyeing the holos. "Good trip?"

"Productive. Locals not too friendly, but we got you a souvenir. Shen?"

She squeezed between them, holding up the gravolian modulator with the flourish of a hanky illusionist.

Anre'eq's dark eyes widened in delight. "Bosey!" He took the squirming, eye-watering thing from her, stroking it like a favourite pet. "As I said?"

Jem nodded. "Authority real slack: no guards on the arsenal; no buzzbows, polasers on the port. Nothing. You'd think they want their tech cloyed."

"Seen it a hundred times."

"*You've* seen it?"

"You know what I mean." Anre'eq sat up in his seat, gazing almost lovingly at the modulator. Jem didn't know how he could bear to keep his eyes on it. "Provinces always get novaed. Central government becomes so consumed with its own private games it forgets what's going on outside. That's when it all starts to fall apart."

"Let's hope." Jem nodded at the modulator. "You going to install that thing or have its baby?"

Anre'eq smiled at him. "Let me enjoy the milli, boss. Not every day I get a chance to admire the latest Bieg tech—"

The deck shuddered. From somewhere Jem heard a deep, almost sub-vox clanging. On Anre'eq's holoports, the images of two Tenyshan monitors sheared by, port and starboard.

Jem lurched from his seat, firing an angry glance at Shenna. "Local ships just coalnoil, are they?"

Shenna shrugged, coming lightly to her feet. "Might be they've uppied a couple."

"I know which couple. Ani—!"

The skinny engineer raised an eyebrow.

"Try not to let 'em draw a bead on us."

"Boss!"

"And Shenna—find out just what in hell they're firing!"

Jem made for a seat to the right of Anre'eq as Shenna hopped into one directly opposite. He gestured a couple of holos into life, sweeping them individually onto the two monitors. They were old ships, sure enough—even older than the *Drummer*—but they'd been refitted pretty recently by the look of them. Their exoskeletons had been careened clean of the scars of battle and interstellar debris. They bristled with new probe limbs, sniffers and imagers. A dazzling violet trace sparkled back from their engine compartments. Maybe they weren't voidcutters, but they still stank of recent Bieg tech. Even if they weren't upgraded with gravolian drives, they still had pretty big fires in their gnarled abdomens.

The monitor to port spat a dirty white cloud from one of its spiracles. A moment later, the *Drummer* shuddered with impact.

"Cannon!" Shenna called. "Either steam or superheated roborium."

"How quaint," muttered Anre'eq.

"Doesn't matter." Jem sparked a row of ignitors in careful sequence. "Only takes one ball to rupture a plate." But that did mean they'd have to fire reaction bursts on the opposite side of the hull with each volley, to cancel recoil.

At his gesture, the *Drummer* fired off a salvo of heat-seeking tunnellers. Next time the monitors let fly, the tunnellers would zero in on the spiracles venting anti-recoil jets—give the ships something to think about.

The monitors sprayed another broadside. Anre'eq dropped the *Drummer* right under the assault. Jem imagined he could actually hear the shots hurtling by overhead. Checking his holoports, Jem was just in time to see the cascade of plasma discharges along the far flanks of the Tenyshan ships: the tunnelers, drilling down the hot anti-recoil spiracles and detonating deep inside the monitors' carapaces. Both ships peeled away, their cannon temporarily silenced.

Jem fell back against his chair support. "Wish we'd had time to fit that gravolian manifold," he sighed. "Put some cosmos between the *Drummer* and those bandogs."

Anre'eq turned to face him. "I think there's a way, cap—if I'm right 'bout how a gravolian drive works…"

"Which is?"

"Don't understand the tech so much, but—" he held up the stolen manifold as though it helped, "—way I understand it, the new 'cutters aren't driven through voids so much as the void's dragged over *them*."

Jem frowned. "You lost me."

Anre'eq sighed. "Somehow they compress space, without dropping into hyper or sub. If a 'cutter's leaving Eklesia Prime bound for…Goraxia, say. Instead of flipping in co-ords and punching it, the gravolian matrix somehow finds Goraxia and…squeezes the space between the two worlds. It actually bends and twists the continuum."

"Chokk!" muttered Jem, getting it, although he still didn't see how it helped. The manifold wasn't installed into the *Drummer's* drive, and they wouldn't have time to fit it before those Tenyshan rumblers careened their spiracles and came after them again. "But we ain't uppied yet!"

Anre'eq laughed. "Doesn't matter. We don't need to high-tail for Tytaroth with those rumblers sniffing our dungbie all the way, just shorten the space between *them*!"

For a moment Jem wondered if he understood what he was hearing. Then he began to laugh himself. "How?"

Anre'eq glanced back at the purple-haired girl. "Shen? You ready?"

She flourished a white hand across her panel. It peeled back like a blossoming flower, exposing the twisted, glimmering anatomy of the ship's circuitry. "Yodely, my amp-tramp."

Anre'eq stood, cradling the manifold like an ugly baby. "Wanna take the con, cap?" Before Jem could reply, he was up and gone.

Jem slipped into the vacated seat, angling the holoports aft. The foundering monitors were dwindling astern. He ramped up the *Drummer's* drive, putting as much space between them as he could. Giving Shenna and Anre'eq time.

At her station, they were head to head in conversation. Techy-talk: a private language far removed from galingua, making as much sense to Jem as colloquial Tenysh. But he was happy to let them carry on. Ever since they'd joined *The Aiken Drummer* both had meshed tighter than a drive shield. Bent over the gravolian manifold they were oddly-matched end-pieces: purple-haired Shenna in a snug white shieldsuit clinging happily to every curve, dark-haired Anre'eq in his own ill-fitting black get-up. A perfect couple. It was hardly surprising when they'd coupled, become shipmates. It was so obvious. Shen had shared Jem's cot more than once, it was how they'd met, after all—in an ordinary back at the Korfulan Ranges, shortly after he'd cloyed a whole arsenal of buzzbies and she was on the run from Cannith bounty-scalpers. They'd fled the Ranges, leaving one bandog dead, the other shorter by a leg, and never looked back.

Their coupling had been a brief thing, soon snuffed, and in the end Anre'eq was obviously more her speed. He'd been part of the *Drummer's* crew longer than Shenna, even though Jem knew far less about him. Reserved, quiet, pretty solitary even when they were back in the dives of Tytaroth. But he'd saved Jem's dungbie more than once, even if as a swordsman he made a great amp-tramp.

Shen's delighted squeal announced

they'd finished whatever it was they were doing. Jem glanced at his holos: the monitors were nothing more than glints against the starfield, still showing no signs of renewing their pursuit.

Anre'eq flopped into the seat next to Jem. His long, gnarled fingers tapped the central console. "The manifold's paralleled with the *Drummer's* deflector keel. If the monitors catch us again, just flip this—" he ran a fingertip along a glowing red line "—and the drive output will do the rest." He stood, moved across the cabin and sat himself at the ranks of holoports Jem had recently vacated.

"Oh, and cap—" he added like an afterthought "—be edgy you're not between them when you flip…"

"Keep it in mind." Another glance at the aft holos. The monitors still hadn't moved. Maybe they'd been lucky. Maybe the tunnellers had done more damage than he'd—

"Chokk!"

The thought was premature. Two sleek, carapaced shapes abruptly loomed against the void, sliding along rails of dopplering stars. Several puffs of dirty vapour announced a salvo from bow-cannon. Jem dropped his gaze to the central console, and the red line that was pulsing faster as the pursuing monitors closed it.

"Smartly, cap," Anre'eq murmured. Jem fancied he caught the tension in the man's voice.

Jem lowered a forefinger, brushing the red line—now flashing wildly—and flicked it. The line turned green, expanded, and extinguished. Jem looked up at the aft imagers. The pursuing monitors were gaining at alarming speed. Their images filled the holos.

Abruptly, the gap between both monitors fuzzed, turned a milky violet, and went black. Jem had just enough time to realise he couldn't see a single dopplering star in the space between the ships before they lurched together, clashing broadsides. The impact crushed both into a single, splintered whole, before their stardrives erupted, briefly igniting their atmospheres and scattering both ships across the void. The wreckage instantly decelerated, dropping out of 'cutter speed, and vanished off Jem's holos.

Shenna was clapping with excitement; Anre'eq smiling quietly. Jem just stared at his holos, now showing nothing but a streaming starfield, and wondered at the odd sensation in his gut. It felt like fear, but that couldn't be right.

* * * *

At the heart of his throne room, Mygré Keddyth thought deeply on past events. The Téokrat was uncharacteristically uneasy. Events were happening quickly. Since he had assumed the mantle of the Ekleiades Galaktium he had never known such a headlong rush. History had always been calm, ordered, easily managed. The inertia of the trillions who inhabited the Imperium made it so. Even the collapse of the Anèmarq Dynasty—the eight hundred and ninety-ninth since the Ekleiades Galaktium and Empire had been established—had taken centuries. There had been no descent into barbarism, no terminal decadence. Just the replacement of the old guard with a new one. Emperor Stenn XXVII's grandfather, Klyff, had brought the rein of Clan Anèmarq to an end with a single sword-stroke, heralding the dynasty of Clan Lymatén. The Téokrat had always assumed that eventually, inevitably, Clan Lymatén would succumb in the same way. The nine hundred and first dynasty would be born and he, as Téokrat, would maintain ultimate power. Perhaps he had been wrong to assume.

Multiple holo images from digithopters and imagers hovering throughout the palace formed a cupola around him. At a thought, they changed and zoomed, constantly informing Mygré of the state of his loyal courtiers. Beyond—forming a larger, outer dome—were holos from elsewhere on Eklesia Prime. Further still an even greater hemisphere of images from across the Imperium. The Téokrat sat at the centre of a vast web of intelligence. There were few places his boundless fleet of probes and sniffers couldn't pry. And even there secrets rarely stayed secret.

Mygré focused on one holo—showing the emperor in urgent conference with his personal Feluq'an guard. Stenn looked anxious, as well he might. He had been given a near-impossible task: to seek out and destroy the Salga Ashtoreen. To find the unfindable. The emperor could hardly refuse the duty, to do so would be to end the Lymatén dynasty prematurely. But to fail would be no better. And Stenn was unlikely to succeed—not where the Téokrat's own limitless resources had failed. Or could a man strive higher than a god?

Mygré's ancient features stretched into a cold, arid smile. He was aware of Stenn's personal ambitions. His desire for the Téokracy, his personal hatred for Mygré Keddyth, his consuming determination to find his sister Kith and restore her to his side. The man was transparent. Before the Téokrat had recruited Kith into the ranks of his Begeen, Stenn had been tall, wildly handsome. Since that day his every resurrection had been as a hermaphrodite dwarf. Each body identical to the last, with death awaiting any lazarite engineer who varied from the pattern by so much as a freckle. Did he honestly believe Mygré couldn't see why?

Mygré shuffled the holos. He summoned one showing images from several hours earlier: the theft of a gravolian modulator from the arsenal on Tenysha. It showed the swarthy, red-haired features of a Jemorl Strygeth: a romantic, a low-level freebooter operating out in the Qax quadrant. A little man, of little ambition, other than being a thorn in the side of the Imperium. Mygré watched the theft, switching from holo to holo to keep track, culminating in the final moments—viewed from on board a Tenyshan monitor—before that local ship was destroyed. He felt a twinge of admiration. This Jemorl Strygeth was resourceful. Good.

Dismissing the holo back to its out-er sphere, the Téokrat sank back into his thoughts.

One of the holos in the closest orbit abruptly expanded, swallowing all those around it, until it dominated the hemisphere directly in front of Mygré. The Téokrat frowned. He hadn't summoned this.

The holo remained uniformly dark. Mygré shifted uneasily: he had seen this utter blackness once before. It wasn't the black of unlighted shadows or his audience chamber, nor the black of the interstellar void. It was something altogether more terrible: the blackness of an event horizon. The colour of nothing.

A white smudge appeared in the centre of the portal, growing sharper as it increased in size. Eventually it filled the whole holo: a white face—as absolute as its background.

Pale, thin lips quivered. *"Mygré Keddyth, presently Téokrat of the Ekleiades Galaktium."* The voice was as ghastly as the face, the voice of something that should have been long dead.

"I am Téokrat."

The face smiled with no humour. *"At present..."*

"And you?"

"I am no one, your Holiness. I do not exist. I am but the humble servant of others. The blade in another's hand."

"You give yourself too little credit, I think."

The ghastly smile widened, exposing more of the void behind it. *"Without the will of others I would not be, Holiness. I act not for myself, but only at another's behest."*

"So you claim the Salga Ashtoreen do nothing but what is asked of them?"

"You know this to be true. For millennia we have awaited our charge, but none has come. We were nothing but fanciful tales, legends from forgotten times, a joke. We were unwanted."

"Yet now you return, destroying systems to announce your reawakening. Is this at the behest of another?"

"I stand by my claim, Holiness."

"Then who?"

The white face laughed: it was the echo of a lifeless galaxy. *"I am not present to play games, Holiness. I am here to announce the start of our campaign. A campaign requested by...another."*

"And what is the purpose of this campaign?"

"I said I am not here to play games, Mygré Keddyth. Nor answer questions to which you already know the answer. Only to confirm: it has begun."

The Salga Ashtoreen's white face fragmented, vanishing among the myriad other holo images.

Mygré touched cold, dead fingers to his withered lips. *Yes*, he agreed, *it has begun.*

* * * *

Deftly, Jem piloted *The Aiken Drummer* past the tumbling mountain of rock. The first indication that Tytaroth was nearing: a jumble of fragments ranging from planetoids to dust, spreading in an unstable sphere across light minutes of space. Hunks of rock of every size, orbiting, pulling or pushing their neighbours. Unpredictable, impossible to chart. The remnants of some vast planet which had exploded in the unrecorded past. In defiance of all logic neither drifting away nor re-coalescing, remaining scattered, forever in motion. Only the desperate or insanely confident ever tried to navigate Tytaroth; both stood an excellent chance of dying. Jem had always thought himself a mixture of the two. So far it had kept him alive.

"Just entering the Reefs," he commented.

Close by, Anre'eq nodded, offhand. As ever, the lanky man seemed indifferent to the unique danger Tytaroth presented. "Just bimble it, boss."

"One day some chunk of rock is going to shear right through the *Drummer's* hull, and we'll be well fried," grumbled Jem. "Hope I'll have time to say I told you so."

"Yodely!" grinned Shenna. "And one day I'll be bandog of bandogs."

"Why the hell would you want to be emperor?" Anre'eq laughed at her remark.

Shenna shrugged. "Best cloy job there is, my amp-tramp. All them coffers!" She wiggled upturned fingers as though running them through imaginary loot.

"Never realised you were so sentimental." Jem twitched the helm a fraction as an asteroid hove into view, cutting across the *Drummer's* bow. His holoports were also showing three masses, each large enough for them to be exerting significant gravitational pull on the others, directly in the ship's path. He changed course, giving the three erratic, mutually orbiting bodies a wide berth. Tytaroth was a dream to the kind of pilot who preferred seat of pants to auto control. Headache-inducing, though.

Weaving through the increasingly dense debris field, putting his old ship through stresses she should really have retired from, Jem brought them closer to Tytaroth's crowded centre. The homeworld for just about all the galaxy's best starpads: Aurora. A pretty name for a bleak, hostile planetoid too deep inside Tytaroth's rocky cloud for starlight and not enough gravity to hold onto a breathable atmosphere. Luckily, stolen Bieg technology made up for most of its shortcomings. The rest everyone put up with.

"Home sweet home," Jem announced. "That gravolian modulator all ready?"

Anre'eq raised the odd, disturbing piece of equipment up, perching it between narrow fingers. "For whatever you have in mind, cap." He slipped it into Shenna's quantum satchel.

"You know what I have in mind." Jem was only half listening as he concentrated on spiralling the *Drummer* in towards Aurora's surface while not hitting any of the chunks of ice and rock circling in uneasy orbits. Only ageing Bieg tech stopped any of it plunging down onto the planetoid when their eccentric orbits were disturbed. At least all the security optigrators and 'ruptors hidden among the drifting debris had sense enough to get out of the ship's way.

"We know fine you're loco, cap." Shenna made a disparaging noise. "So when you gonna disseminate?"

"Pretty soon." His attention was split by the up-rushing landing port and orbiting fragments sailing erratically by. "At *Jenny's Teacup*."

He was aware of the two exchanging glances.

"You netting?" asked Shenna.

"Big announcement." Jem throttled back the *Drummer's* atmoshear and engaged landing hovers. "I want everyone in on it."

Anre'eq pulled a face. "Including Borich Fydar and Magen Idwardes?"

"Everyone. Even those dungbies."

Shenna and Anre'eq shared another look.

"Just be in the *Teacup* by the end of Two-Dog." The *Drummer* settled on her landing struts, complaining no more than usual. Jem leaned back in his seat. He gave his crew his best smile. "More the merrier, after all."

* * * *

Stenn sat in his central apartments, lost in thought. His lavish rooms, attached to the Skopion Dome, were bright and airy—so different from the darkness the Téokrat seemed to prefer. Artworks selected from a million worlds hung or stood in spots chosen to show them at their best. High up on the pastel walls was a row of screens, imitating the windows of ancient times. They looked out on landscapes of superlative beauty from the most exquisite worlds in the Imperium. Some showed scenes of Clan Lymatén's homeworld, Xentharius Hekra, light centuries away: its golden forests and blue crystal deserts. Today, he was in no mood to appreciate them.

Several of his wives and husbands were gathered close by, playing softly on traditional Xentharian *luuks* and singing a folk tune he should recognise. Each one had been redesigned to Stenn's specific criteria by the same lazarite engineers who had constructed Stenn's own bodies for centuries. Identi-cal, so only their individual robes identified them. He was in no mood to appreciate either them or their music.

The Téokrat's orders were a multi-bladed knife that the emperor was all too aware of. If he failed, it gave the ancient slug the perfect excuse to call for his removal. And although failure was unthinkable, it was more than likely. The Salga Ashtoreen had all the substance of a nightmare. How did one track a bad dream?

Stenn wriggled in his shapeseat, mental discomfort translating itself into a restless body. As emperor he was well acquainted with the patience required to lay plans and allow them to bud and flower, but the task given him by the Téokrat had a threat of urgency that was hard to ignore. Deliberate, of course. If he rushed he was far more likely to make an error. A fatal one.

Yet he would not be pushed.

With a gesture he raised a blank between him and his harem. He could no longer listen to them—and he did not want them to hear. Another wriggle of his fingers, and a holo of his private secretary, Pallin Jenz, materialised in the room. The image was so perfect, the man could actually have been standing before his emperor.

Jenz bowed, masking any surprise at his abrupt summons. *"Your grace?"* Although Jenz looked no more than a beardless boy, Stenn knew the man had been his grandfather Klyff's own closest advisor. For that reason alone, Jenz was one of the few people Stenn trusted.

"I don't suppose you have found out more than we already knew?" Stenn was reluctant to name the Salga Ashtoreen—even over a channel as secure as his own. Extreme caution was its own reward.

"Hints, fables, stories. The subject of our investigations has been a part of common myth for so long, it is all but impossible to differentiate any truth."

"All but?"

Jenz smiled. *"Idle chatter, your grace. Ramblings by drunken tramp freighter crew-*

men or starpads under interrogation. Inconsequential in themselves, yet consistent enough to suggest there is a kernel of truth."

Stenn leaned forward, his shapeseat flowing to support his back. "Can these… consistencies be traced?"

"In time, your grace—"

"We do not have that luxury, Jenz."

The young-looking man bowed again. *"I am aware, and have taken what steps I can to expedite matters."*

Stenn grunted, remembering how even all the intelligencers of the Ekleiades itself had been unaware of Davolias' destruction until it had happened. No idle chatter there. "Expand your search, Jenz. Use every asset we have. Probe the darkest, most remote corners of the empire."

"It will be expensive, your grace."

Not as personally expensive as having my head removed by a buzzblade at the Téokrat's convenience, thought Stenn. "Do it, Pallin."

"As your grace commands." Before Stenn could dismiss the holo, Jenz raised a delicate finger. *"There is one more thing…"*

The emperor was irritated by the interruption. "Yes?"

"During my researches, it has come to my attention that we are not the only persons taking a similar interest."

Stenn sank back into his chair, irritation giving way to intrigue. "How placed?"

"In the most august quarters."

So the Téokrat was also using his resources to find the Salga Ashtoreen. That was of no surprise. "Recently?"

"Not at all, your grace. My understanding is it all began at least a decade ago. Perhaps two."

Interesting. "Thank you, Pallin. Keep looking. Rake the galaxy dry if you have to. If they're out there, they can be found."

"As your grace commands." Jenz bowed a final time as Stenn gestured the holo out of existence.

So that devious bastard had already been searching for a mythical caste of assassins well before they had allegedly destroyed a planet, and then a star. What had he found? What had he been planning? Had his search provoked them? And if he had found them, why charge Stenn with the same task?

Or, as Stenn was coming to believe, had the Téokrat grown so old and senile that his mind and power were finally slipping? Had he reached out for the Salga Ashtoreen in a senile attempt to bolster his position, and failed to locate them? Did that suggest the destruction of Davolias and Tertius Pentane were, in fact, at the hands of the Téokrat, and not some imaginary assassins. That Mygré Keddyth now had Stenn chasing shadows so that he might remove the emperor when he obviously failed to find them.

Had be become so inept?

Stenn removed the blank. His wives and husbands glanced his way, resuming their music. The emperor allowed himself to relax, once again able to enjoy his harem.

* * * *

Jem made his way down to the subworld hidden below Aurora's uninviting surface. It was always lively down there. The planetoid had no natural periods of light or dark, so it was always night. An evening in full, permanent swing. The streets, burrowed into the ancient rock and lined with bars, apartments, restaurants, sutlers, cafés, lit by garish signs and actinic decorations that seared the eye, were always busy. People bought and people sold. Anything the mind could conceive—as long as that mind also had a poke full of creds. The shouts and screams of countless souls determined to enjoy themselves were a constant echo, drowning out the low thrum of oxygen processors and circulators, and the insect whine of gravitators. The only things more numerous than humans were digithopters and sniffers, flitting endlessly along the dazzling streets. Distrust was at a premium. Only to be expected in a world populated by starpads, gilts, cloys—and maybe even a spy or two from the empire or Ekleiades Galaktium. One of Emperor Stenn's own intelligencers had been caught a year earlier. He was probably still out in Tytaroth somewhere, his frozen body spinning aimlessly among the rock and dust. Along with the dungbies who'd unwittingly brought him in.

Jenny's Teacup was the largest eating establishment and cat house in Aurora, built in a circle around a deep shaft that may once have been natural, but was now lined by tier upon tier of balconies. The Galleries: rooms to let by the hour, or the artificial day if your creds stretched that far. So close to the main landing stage the *Teacup* had both a guaranteed customer base and the best cuisine. The choicest foods, cloyed from unlucky transports on their way to galactic hotspots; the finest grog, sourced in similar ways. And bed partners to cater to every taste and persuasion. Nothing was off limits. So long as the creds kept coming, it was possible to eat like the Téokrat in the *Teacup*. Maybe better, if the rumours about the half-immortal old ascetic were true. Certainly screw better than him.

Jem found himself a table and dropped into the formless lump next to it. Instantly the shapeseat came to life, forming itself into an ideal chair for his height and weight. Jem looked around.

The place was noisy. Lights flashed in time to a thudding beat, a tune he couldn't quite make out above the babble. Even though the air was refreshed constantly it was still thick with the odours of roast meat, sweat and spilled grog. It was good to be back.

A digithopter buzzed past, pausing just long enough to ID him before zipping away. Moments later a servitor drifted to his table, slow and unthreatening, a circle of tell-tales flickering around its circumference.

"Greetings, Jemorl Strygeth. Your credit is fully topped. What do you require?"

He stared at the unassuming, floating ball, thinking. "What's best in house today?"

"We have torran steaks, fresh from Glaupius. Or on special—"

"The steaks sound bosey." Jem never touched the so-called specials—he could never be sure what was in them, aside from leftovers given a fancy name. "I'll take two, medium rare, with everything on the side."

"Excellent choice. And to drink?"

"Surprise me. Oh—and a *hooja*, loaded with the finest gjangam weed."

The servitor slipped quietly away. Jem settled back in his shapeseat. It readjusted.

"Well now, Red Jem. I heard your rumbler had just docked…"

He glanced to his left. Standing on the edge of his vision was a tall woman in a pale blue shieldsuit. He'd been unaware of her up to that point. She stepped around so he could see her better, though he'd recognised her instantly. That waist-length chestnut hair was a giveaway, the shieldsuit matching her angry eyes—along with the two battered blasters slung from her waist. Her right hand was resting negligently on the grip of one barking iron, as though she was considering drawing it.

"Hoy, Mags. Long time."

Magen Idwardes stared hard at him for long millis before dragging a shapeseat across and dropping into it. "What's the action, Jem?"

He tried to look innocent. "Is there any?"

"You and that shiftless duo have been away for standards. Blether is you've been to Tenysha."

"You don't want to believe everything you hear—"

"If you've been out to Tenysha, you've cloyed something. Something mighty big, since you're sitting here ordering the best in the house."

A hole at the centre of the table irised open, and a tall, frosty stein of something frothy rose up, accompanied by a metre high *hooja*, already lit, the minty fragrance of gjangam drifting from it. Jem slid both towards him and took a careful sip from the stein, all the while watching Mags. It was ale of some description, icy cold. His mouth went numb pretty skatey—either from the cold or the level of alcohol.

"I'll tell you the same as I told Shenna and Anre'eq. The end of Two-Dog, and I'll spill."

At the mention of Shenna's name, Magen's eyes grew volcanic.

"Jealousy doesn't look good on you, Mags."

She actually got as far as half-drawing her right barker before an alarm shrilled. A couple of digithopters hove up to the table. *"Magen Idwardes—sheath your weapon!"*

"Better do as it says, Mags. I'd hate to see you novaed before I get a chance to eat."

It was an uncomfortable bunch of millis before she rammed the blaster back into its holster and relaxed into her shapeseat. The digithopters retreated, still watchful.

"The end of Two-Dog?"

"Ay. Let Fydar know, too. Tell him to keep it to himself so I can be sure the whole of Aurora hears in time."

Magen stood slowly, hands still resting on her barking irons. "It better be big, Jem."

"Oh, the biggest." He raised the *hooja's* vent pipe to his lips and took a lungful. It numbed him like the ale had numbed his lips.

There was a warning chime as most of his tabletop opened. Plates of steak, greens, and vegetables—some of which he actually recognised—presented themselves. Jem pulled it all closer, enjoying the rich odour. He cut a slice off one steak and tasted it. After so many standards eating recycled stuff from the *Drummer's* galley, it was almost too much. He sighed, even finding a smile for the woman glaring down at him. "Later, Mags."

Jem gave his meal all his attention. He wasn't aware at what point Mags walked away, but when he put his head back to drain the stein she was no longer there. He placed the empty mug in the table's centre and enjoyed the last morsels of steak as the drink was replenished.

Anre'eq and Shenna appeared at his table

as he pushed the scraped-clean plates aside and settled back to enjoy the *hooja*. Anre'eq was looking at the streaks of sauce—all that remained on the plates—with an expression of regret.

Shenna waved a hand in front of her face, her features puckered in disgust. "Air's still bellfin."

"That's just the gjangam," smiled Anre'eq.

Jem pointed at the shapeseat Magen had left behind, and another by an empty table. "Moor yourselves. What you drinking?"

They both glanced at his half-drained stein. Jem raised a hand, but a servitor was already hovering close by.

"What may I bring you, Jemorl Strygeth?"

"Two more of these for my gallant crew." He realised he was already part sheeted. The grog was somewhat stronger than the *Drummer's* galley normally brewed up. "And whatever they'd like to eat."

Shenna grinned and sat. "I'll tuck up whatever my brave capitano had. But duo it."

The servitor bobbed. *"Of course, Shenna Maak. And for Anre'eq Pol?"*

Anre'eq was glancing around the *Teacup's* busy interior. "Nothing for me, thanks. I have an— Ah!" Something—or someone—across the room caught his attention. "Later, cap. I'll be finished in time for your big declaration." With a wink he angled his gaunt frame into the shifting crowd. His baggy shieldsuit disappeared in a milli.

"Whoever they are, they must be good for him to miss a free drink," said Jem. As though conjured by his words, two fresh steins rose onto the tabletop.

Shenna took a handle in each hand. "Bosey! Gizzit grog—the best." She raised the first drink and pretty well drained it in one go. "Not too bellfin. Could be a milli more fridged, though." She grinned again and started on the second.

Jem shook his head. "Chokka'ed if I know where you put it."

When the food arrived, Shenna shoved

it on board as fast as she had the ale, washing it down with two additional steins. Jem paced himself. If he sunk grog at the same rate as Shen, he'd not be able to speak when the time came. Maybe not even stand.

Two-Dog ticked towards its end. Jem followed time's progress by the virtual chrono floating up close to the ceiling. Its digits were easy enough to read, even in the *Teacup's* bright interior. No matter where you stood or sat—at the bar, down in the Galleries—it was always facing you. Some fancy Bieg tech he couldn't figure.

Eventually, the time came. Jem stood, summoning a servitor.

"Clear the table. And I need to speak to the whole establishment."

The servitor's tell-tales spun around its circumference at a lightning rate. *"Such an order will leave you with few creds, Jemorl Strygeth."*

"Acknowledged. Do it."

"The establishment is yours." The servitor bobbed away as the table swallowed the dirty plates and steins. Shenna snatched her still half-full one away before it disappeared.

Jem stepped up onto the table, drew his longsword and raised it high. *"CITIZEN STARPADS—I ASK FOR YOUR ATTENTION!"* His voice overrode the voices, the music. It boomed up from the depths of the Galleries, echoing off the sides. Everyone in sight turned to look at him—in interest, irritation, or simple confusion. Over by one of the *Teacup's* entrances, Jem spotted Magen alongside Borich Fydar—Mags still in her shieldsuit, Fydar in some outrageous, rainbow-striped getup that made him look like a giant Tryvian melon. A broad, drooping hat obscured his face.

"YOU'VE ALL HEARD THE BETHER, I GUESS. AND FOR ONCE, IT'S MORE OR LESS TRUE. THE AIKIN DRUMMER *HAS BEEN TO TENYSHA, AND WE BROUGHT BACK A LITTLE SOMETHING!"* He bent towards Shenna and whispered. "The quantum satchel…" She handed it over and he held it up, sheathing his sword.

"IN THIS DITTY BAG IS OUR FUTURE, CITIZENS. A TASTY SOMETHING THE EMPIRE WOULD MUCH RATHER IT KEPT TO ITSELF."

"You're sheeted, Red!" Mags called across the room.

Jem grinned at her. *"MAYBE, CITIZEN IDWARDES—BUT I DON'T LIE."* With a flourish he dug the gravolian modulator out of the satchel, careful not to look at it directly, or drop it. *"ANYONE WANT TO GUESS WHAT THIS IS...?"*

All eyes gazed on the strange thing in his hands. Most shied away almost immediately, blinking.

"Your bellfin underkecks?" That was Fydar. Jem recognised the harsh, almost-whisper.

"THIS, MY FRIENDS, IS A GRAVOLIAN MODULATOR. THE LATEST MODDED GEWGAW FROM BIEG. IT MAKES EVERY OTHER DRIVE—WHATEVER PUSHES OUR SORRY FLEET OF TRUCKS AND RUMBLERS—ARCHY."

There was a rustle throughout the room. A kind of sigh. Mostly of disbelief, Jem guessed.

"I'M SERIOUS, CITIZENS. THIS CRAZY LITTLE SCRAP OF BOOTY WILL UPPY YOUR SHIPS BEYOND MEASURE. YOU'LL SKATE AS SMARTLY AS ANY OF THE EMPEROR'S LATEST VOIDCUTTERS."

"Bullyrag!" rasped Fydar.

Jem walked across the floor towards the other starpad, juggling the modulator between his hands. The crowd made way, most looking at him rather than the wriggling thing he was carrying.

"DON'T BELIEVE ME? BOSEY—" Jem tossed the modulator suddenly. Fydar, unprepared, caught it awkwardly. His drooping hat slipped aside, revealing his face. *"—FIT IT TO YOUR OWN TRUCK. SEE HOW SHE PERFORMS..."*

Fydar's expression was even more hate-filled than Mag's had been. His ruined face—half-melted where a blast from Jem's blaster had cut through his malfunctioning Q'Alvin shield long ago—stared back at Jem. If he believed the digithopters would be too slow, just once, he'd have drawn a weapon and cut Jem down right then.

"And have my ship torn apart the moment I engage it? You'd like that…"

Jem shrugged and snatched the modulator away, offering it to Magen. *"CITIZEN IDWARDES, THEN? SHE MORE SPORTY? NO?"* He turned his back on both, addressing the crowd once more. *"ANY OF YOU HAVE THE RODS? GIVE IT A RUN. SAIL TO THE GALAXY'S RIM AND BACK IN STANDARDS—MAYBE EVEN LESS—"*

"So what's the deal, Jem?" Mags asked his back. "Say I believe that gewgaw is what you claim. What good is it?"

He didn't face her, keeping his full attention on the rest of the *Teacup's* crowd. *"WE BUILD OUR OWN, OBVIOUSLY. WE HAVE ENOUGH AMP-TRAMPS TO BACK-TECH THIS ONE. ANI OVER THERE—"* he nodded at the tall black figure who'd just pushed through the crowd. Anre'eq gave a jaunty wave and bowed. *"—ALREADY USED IT TO FRY TWO TENYSHAN MONITORS. DON'T ASK ME HOW—I JUST FLY."*

There was a sporadic chuckle at that. From pilots, no doubt.

"THIS—" he held up the modulator again. *"—THIS GEWGAW CAN JUICE OUR SHIPS. WE NO LONGER HAVE TO HIT COALNOIL GIGS ON THE EDGE OF THE EMPIRE. HAVE TO DODGE SHIPS THAT OUTGUN AND OUTSPEED US. HIDE OUT IN TYTAROTH BECAUSE IT'S THE ONE PLACE BIG VOIDIES ARE VULNERABLE..."*

"And then what?" sniggered Fydar. "We lay siege to Eklesia Prime?"

Jem lowered the modulator. *"WE WON'T NEED TO, CITIZEN. NOT ONCE WE'VE DESTROYED THE EMPIRE'S VOIDCUTTER BREEDING GROUNDS AT CRIOCH."*

* * * *

The Téokrat stirred. There was an in-coming transmission, cutting through void-space. Mygré recognised the signature. He activated his response mode.

"Speak."

"Holiness." The image before him was of a tall, plain white trapezoid. Cautiously anonymous. *"Matters are about to take a serious turn."*

"Indeed?"

"The pirate Jemorl Strygeth has managed to outfit a small fleet of raider ships with freshly-hatched, retrofitted gravolian modulators, as you suspected. He plans to lead them in a raid on Crioch."

"Is the emperor aware?"

"Not as yet, holiness."

The Téokrat smiled thinly. "Perhaps, in the interests of the empire, he should find out."

"As you command, holiness."

Mygré raised his hands in a blessing—although the anonymous messenger would not be able to see it. "The Ekleiades Galaktium thanks you." He killed the link, still smiling.

* * * *

The Aiken Drummer hung in space. Immediately astern were Magen Idwardes' sloop *The Nacreous Fire* and Borich Fydar's hulking xebec, *The Anaphei Rex*. Beyond them were ten more starpad ships, all rigged with the bootlegged gravolian drives ret-roed by Anre'eq and a bunch of other amp-tramps. Jem still didn't understand half of their techie-talk, but he'd caught the gist: the original modulator they'd stiffed was easy to clone. Too easy, if anything. The strange device had been eager to reproduce, once they'd figured which part to stimulate. Its re-productive organs, essentially. Like so much Bieg tech, the modulator was, to all intents and purposes, alive. It relished the idea of offspring. Asked nicely, it laid eggs. Probably how the Bieg techies planned to create enough to fit the Galaktium's entire voidie fleet in the shortest time possible.

That the voidies themselves were living

organisms, seeded and grown in the breeding grounds at Crioch, probably didn't hurt. An egg could be grafted into a ship's immature drive system, growing naturally into it once it hatched. Become a functioning part.

Anre'eq and his crew didn't have that luxury. The starpad's ships were inorganic: the interface between ship and modulator was far from natural. The techies had killed dozens of hatched modulators before figuring out how to link them safely. And when a modulator died, it didn't go alone. The surface of Aurora had acquired plenty more craters in the standards since Anre'eq's experiments had started.

Jem glanced at his holos, muttering to himself. The gravolian drives on all eight ships had cut out abruptly, dropping them into non-compressed space-time, nowhere near their destination, and light centuries from Tytaroth. All the holos showed were alert signatures, and nothing else.

"Lightships. You're sure?"

"No doubt, cap," said Anre'eq.

"So what are they out here for? What's beyond?" Something pretty big for the modulators to shut down in self-preservation.

Shenna glanced up from the holo she'd been examining for millis. "Anti-light nullity," she said, stroking a length of purple hair out of her eyes. "It's an Aphie." She grinned at Jem, enjoying the moment.

"An Aphotism," he groaned. "We can't pass through that!"

Anre'eq ran his fingers across his console. "We can't go round, either. We have no idea how wide it is, and the co-ordinates we stiffed are relative to Eklesia Prime. We've recalculated relative to Tytaroth, but steering who knows how many light years off course might nova the calculations." He turned to look at Jem. "Gravolian drives are pretty absolute, cap. You tell them where you want to go, they compress space-time and get you there, shortest route possible. If you're going to divert, you need to know exactly where you're diverting to." He pointed at the holos. "We're far away from the Qax quadrant and

our normal raiding grounds, cap. Out here be dragons."

Jem didn't like Anre'eq's turn of phrase. He'd heard wild rumours about what existed inside Aphotisms. Apart from vast areas of space where the laws of physics no longer operated, there were entities which somehow survived; perhaps living off the chaotic energy generated by the light/anti-light reaction.

"Can we just use the gravolian drive to warp straight through?"

"The drive bootlegs normal space, cap. The insides of an Aphotism is far from normal. The fact the modulators shut themselves down before entering tells us everything. They don't want to die, either."

Jem groaned. "You're saying we have no choice but to sail through, using plain old ion-rams to do it."

Magen Idwardes sub-voxed in Jem's ear. *"What's the delay?"*

"Anti-light nullity."

"Which you didn't know about..."

"No one knows about them, Mags. That's why we're bimbling."

Borich Fydar joined in. *"Go round!"*

"If you're so keen, maybe you should take the lead, Fydar."

The other starpad didn't reply.

Jem glanced at his crew. They stared back; both knew the risks.

"We can't go back," said Jem. "Not now." His pride wouldn't let him, for one thing.

"Yodely," murmured Shenna. "Warp it, bossie-boy."

Anre'eq gave a thin smile. "Sanity's overrated, I say."

Jem took a deep, ragged breath. "Set course: directly between the nearest lightships. Skatey-like."

"They'll try to dissuade us," said Anre'eq, directing the navcom.

"Tell them to go fry themselves."

The Aiken Drummer began to edge towards the lightships: pale, towering needles hanging against ultimate blackness. Telltales flashed up and down their skeletal frames, further demarking them.

At first the lightships seemed unaware of the small fleet approaching them, then a blinding light flared from the centre of each: wide lasers playing against the hulls of all eight ships.

TO ALL APPROACHING VESSELS: IT IS YOUR BEST INTERESTS TO TURN BACK INSTANTLY. THERE WILL BE NO OTHER WARNING.

The deep, inhuman voice spoke dated galingua with a provincial accent, but its meaning was pretty clear.

"What they going to do?" muttered Jem. "Kill us to stop us getting killed?"

THERE IS WORSE THAN DEATH intoned the voice.

"Listening in, is it?" Jem glanced at Anre'eq.

"Archy sub-vox. Laser transmission medium. Very early Bieg tech. Maybe even pre-Bieg."

"Fine." Jem raised his voice. "Listen, you ancient trucks! We mean to beat through. Don't try to belay us!"

IT IS NOT OUR INTENTION TO PREVENT YOUR FOLLY, JEMORL STRYGETH. ONLY TO WARN YOU.

Jem was less than happy that the carking rumbler had figured out his name. What else could it hackysack through those lasers? "Anre'eq, prime the bow-chasers."

"Cap, if they're not going to stop us—"

"I want to make a point."

Anre'eq shrugged. "Bow-chasers primed."

Jem powered up the *Drummer* and steered towards the nearest lightship. "Target it dead centre and fire."

Anre'eq's fingers danced across the panel. Jem felt the shudder as the ship's forward disruptors fired. In his holoports, the nearest lightship cracked open, drifting sedately apart. The top and bottom sections slowly moved out of vision.

Jem swallowed and took a deep breath. "Here we go..."

In his holos, the second lightship sud-

denly erupted—destroyed by something much more powerful than a disruptor. He heard Fydar sub-voxing a hoarse cheer.

"What was that for?"

"Eh? I thought we were target-practising..."

The Anaphei Rex was fitted with the biggest plasma cannon in Tytaroth, and Fydar enjoyed using them. No point getting weejie about it.

"Save it for whatever's in the nullity."

Fydar didn't reply, but Jem caught the faintest grumble.

The Aphotism dominated all his holos. A complete lack of...anything. Even in the most remote region of the galaxy there was always something; a few, distant stars pinpricked against the black. The nullity was a total absence. No distant stars, no faint skeins of cosmic dust lit from within. Even if there were any suns within sensor range, the anti-light properties would cancel the visible light out. Photons negated in bursts of Toksvig radiation which would itself be almost immediately absorbed.

Jem angled his holos to stern. Behind him, one by one, the starpad ships winked out of sight. He ramped up the *Drummer's* sniffers to maximum, but they detected nothing. Just a hint of Toksvig radiation here and there which never lasted long enough to pinpoint. Until they re-emerged into normal space, all eight ships were on their own. Adrift in an all-encompassing sea of nothing.

Jem raised the *Drummer's* ion drive to max. Creaks and pops along the ageing corvette's hull were the only indication their speed had increased. The engines were silent. Any glowing plasma leaking from the drive's badly-serviced baffle plates was instantly negated. For all Jem could tell, they might just as well be hanging in absolute darkness.

He tried not to show his jitters, but he was clearly no good at it. Shenna stood behind him, massaging his shoulders gently; Anre'eq shot him a smile and a wink. They may have been trying to buck him up, but it felt more like they were giving away their own inner nerves.

"We'll be bosey," he said, to no one in particular.

"Sure we will," said Shenna. He could hear the wide grin. "Be outta this dungbie no-glim pretty skatey." She patted his head for emphasis.

"Be over 'fore you know it," said Anre'eq. "Painless, like."

Jem glanced his crewman's way. Somehow he didn't sound like his old self.

Fydar stood in the irised doorway, his face tight with anger and loss. Jem leapt up—although Mags tried to stop him.

"It's not—!" she started.

"Be fried if it's not!" Fydar's hand grabbed for his blaster. Jem rolled across the bed, scrabbling through his clothes. He snatched up his own barker, firing at his old comrade, knowing the blast should ping off Fydar's shieldsuit, just throwing the man backwards. Giving Jem time to warp ou—

"—okay, cap?"

"Huh?" Jem blinked, looking down at his empty hands. What the hell was that? He shook his head. "Nothing, I—"

"Flashback?" said Shenna. "Hokey dreamy bits?"

Jem turned to look up at her, for a moment expecting Mags to be standing there. He nodded silently.

"Aphie stuff," she said, red eyes peering at him closely. "Old thoughts—bad ones, as normal. Sometimes all wrong, too. Reality hackysacked. Different modes. Or new ones uppied by the trapcase." She tapped her forehead.

Nullities might be hotspots where the cosmos bled into other spacial dimensions? Maybe even creating its own realities? *Bosey*, Jem thought. "You could have warned me."

She grinned. "I have, bossie-boy. Fairly warned."

Jem looked back at his black holos, hoping this particular anti-light nullity was stretched wide but thin, and they'd break through in no time. If time meant anything here. A moment later the darkness shredded. Through it blazed a cluster of stars so dense it rivalled the lasercomms off the destroyed lightships. Jem sighed and fell back against his chair.

"That was smooth and skatey…"

"What was?" Anre'eq said.

Jem glanced his way, about to point out the obvious. The gangling man was coming apart just like the nullity had—his black shieldsuit fraying into tatters, wriggling like so many dark snakes, then reforming in bizarre ways.

"'Smatter?" asked the boiling shape. Several voices came from it, all Anre'eq's—more or less. The shape spun apart like smoke, filling the ship's cabin. Jem blinked. When he opened his eyes, there were countless Anre'eqs crammed into the limited space. All the same. All different.

"CAP?" The single word sounded like it had been yelled by the entire population of a planet. "WHERE AAAAAAAAAAAAAAAARE—?"

"—you?" Anre'eq was staring around the cabin, his thin face puzzled. His eyes focused on Jem and he smiled. "Well, that was pretty drifty. You completely eclipsed for a milli."

"While you…" Jem shook his head. "… Doesn't matter."

He looked back at his holos. Unsurprisingly, the blazing starfield had gone, replaced once more by total blackness. A moment later, the cabin blinked out, leaving Jem floating in the dark. Panicked, he snatched for breath, but somehow there was air in the Aphotism. Which was drifty as hell.

Fydar walked in on Jem and Mags. Jem shot at him. Fydar's shieldsuit failed…

Fydar walked in on Jem and Mags. Jem shot at him. Fydar ducked and fired back at Jem's unshielded, naked body…

Fydar walked in on Jem and Mags. Mags fired both of her barkers. Fydar disintegrated into burning motes…

Fydar walked in on Jem and Mags. Mags leapt to his side, throwing her arms round his neck and bussing him hard. They both aimed their weapons at Jem…

Fydar walked in on Jem and Mags. Mags grabbed Jem's face and held it still as red hot eyes stared into him. "Don't chokk it, bossie-boy."

A pyramid bigger than Aurora pinned him to the nothingness under its pale base. Hard red lights burned near its peak.

"Jimmy-javved!"

Voidcutters tumbled onto the pyramid's surface, exploding harmlessly. Stars spun as the galaxy shrank about them. It formed a rotating wheel under Jem's pinned body, slowly grinding him to ash against a vast construct which now filled the universe.

Giants that could be midgets marched endlessly across Jem's body, each footstep an agonising electric jolt along his nerves. Someone was bounding down one of the colossal pyramid's faces. Mags—or was it Shenna, or someone he'd never seen before. She raised a blaster that looked more massive than a planetary system, aiming down at Jem.

"I win."

She pressed the firing button—and flew apart in a burst of white-hot meteors. Jem couldn't duck the deadly shower.

He tried to jerk aside, yelling.

Anre'eq and Shenna were holding him down against the drive console, each pinning a shoulder. Behind them the Drummer's main cabin loomed: familiar, grimy, half the tell-tales only working periodically.

"Is this real?" Jem gasped.

Shenna pulled a face. "Massive as you, bossie-boy!"

"You were blethering," Anre'eq said quietly.

Shenna nodded. "Yodely. Named me a bellfin bandog!"

"Did one of you hit me?" Jem muttered, feeling a throb along the left of his face.

"Just a dode. Name me a bellfin bandog and you're lucky I only stoke you once!"

"You were steering the Drummer all

over," said Anre'eq. "Like to drive us into one of the other ships in the dark. We had to stop you."

Jem's tongue probed at his teeth. He tasted blood. "I'd likely do the same," he admitted, reluctantly. He looked at the hands holding him down. "Can I get up now?"

Shenna looked doubtful. After a moment, Anre'eq stepped away. Reluctantly, Shenna did the same.

Jem shrugged his red shieldsuit back into place and cast an eye over the holos. The darkness didn't seem to have changed. "Any word from the others?"

Anre'eq shook his head. "Voxcomms just as fried as light. We'll know nothing until we break."

Which means the Drummer *could be the only ship left*, thought Jem. Specially if their pilots all caught a dose of whatever happened to him. He wondered if Fydar and Mags were enjoying reruns and what-ifs of their mutual past. Not likely to improve their moods if they were.

Something bloomed across the port holos. A smudge of light or paleness against the nullity. Were they finally coming free?

The smudge resolved itself gradually. Not a thinning in the Aphotism—a shape. A vast, pulsing, opalescent bell, trailing pink and purple streamers along which ran waves of acid light.

Another crazy image.

"You wanna steer off that beastie?" murmured Shenna.

"You see it too?" said Jem.

"Yodely! Massive trucker. What's to not?"

"But it's visible. It's giving off light. How can it?"

Anre'eq shoved his face right up to one holo, as though that helped. "Must be something native to the Aphotism, or adapted to it…" He glanced down at the console. "Getting sporadic readings of Toksvig radiation. It must absorb the particles, or be made up from them…"

"You're making no sense," said Jem.

"Nothing here makes sense," muttered Anre'eq. "But there's a colossal…*something* out there that's visible under anti-light and squirts out enough TR for our sniffers to actually pick it up."

"You make it sound dangerous."

"How careless of me."

Jem was already steering the *Drummer* clear of the huge, flickering thing. Instantly, another appeared in the forward holos. Jem adjusted course, only to find a third in their way. A rapid scan of all the holoports showed the *Drummer* was surrounded—fore and aft, top and bottom. The Aphotism had become a sea choked with pulsing, drifting giants.

"Arm all weapons!" snapped Jem.

Shenna chuckled and made for the gunnery station.

"What you thinking of throwing at them?" asked Anre'eq. "Tunnellers'll be no good. We don't have plasma cannons to match Fydar's xebec. Lasers are obviously out—"

"Jimmy-jav the tunnellers," interrupted Jem. "They're heat-seekers. Instead of thermal radiation, get them to search for Toksvig."

Anre'eq chuckled. "Maybe… Shen!"

"There before you, ampy Ani!" Jem could hear her chatting in techie as she instructed the tunneller 'ware to rewrite itself. "All done!"

"Then fire!"

Jem heard the distant, hollow sound of a tunneller salvo firing. Nothing to see on any port, of course, but he looked anyway. The colossal bell-shaped things were getting closer. Something about the *Drummer* was attracting them.

The nearest one abruptly collapsed, half folding in on itself. Its trailing fronds lashed in a slow motion frenzy. To its side, another one of the things imploded. There was a breach in their ranks. Jem figured the *Drummer* could just squeeze through.

"All ahead—and fire another salvo. Keep 'em occupied."

The ship closed on the two damaged

whatever they were. They expanded in Jem's holos, vast bell shapes part deflated. One tried to reach out with its nest of writhing fronds, but another tunneller must have found it, and it burst apart in a slow, almost gentle cascade. The *Drummer* made it past. There were no more of the things in front.

A milli later a starfield filled the holoports. Three lightships—even more ancient than the ones of the Aphotism's far side—drifted close by, unresponsive. The *Drummer* was clear.

Jem brought the corvette to a halt, heaving-to until the rest of the small fleet emerged from the Aphotism. Fydar was the first to appear, *The Anaphei Rex* scarred and torn. Then seven more. *The Nacreous Fire* wasn't one of them. The crews of two ships were howling over their voxcomms: the cries of damned souls, minds shattered. One crew was screaming, the other laughing hysterically. One ship blew up millis after emerging into normal space. The other sailed on, the breathless laughter dying as it drifted out of vox range.

"What happened to Mags?" Jem sub-voxed.

"How in hell would I know!" Fydar snapped back, his hoarse voice shaking. *"It's blacker than your soul in there. She—she was on my flank going in."*

"We wait," said Jem.

"Cap—" Anre'eq began."

"We wait, Ani."

"For how long?" Fydar sounded like he wanted to be furious, but had lost the will, somewhere.

"We wait!"

They waited. The antiquated lightships kicked themselves into life and asked the ships' purpose. *The Anaphei Rex* broadsided one and the remaining two went silent again.

They waited some more. Half a starpad ship slipped out of the nullity, tumbling gently, shedding pieces of itself as it passed. It wasn't *The Nacreous Fire*.

Eventually, they gave up waiting.

* * * *

The darkness was split by a thin line: lancing up to a height of two metres before expanding into a blinding oblong, burning with a light from no normal spectrum. A tall figure stepped through, ducking slightly, and the blazing portal collapsed in upon itself. The figure paused a moment, orientating itself.

Only part of a face showed, and that was a ghastly white, even in the muted illumination of the Téokrat's chamber. The rest was covered in a tight material that had no colour of its own. It reflected its surroundings perfectly: shadow on shadow, highlight on highlight. The visible portion of white face almost seemed to float, disembodied in the dark. There was nothing about the figure to indicate whether it was male or female.

It began to move forward, stepping with an inhuman grace and silence. It knew its arrival had triggered many silent alarms—it was not possible to bypass the palace's many security devices entirely. Besides, it had no desire to be hidden.

The self-important holograms were passed without comment. It recognised that any ultimate authority which found it necessary to proclaim itself so loudly was more than insecure, that authority enforced and fragile. The ranks of Begeen, which the figure saw to either side of the path it must take, were a testament to that.

It smiled at such a hollow display. The Téokrat thought himself safe behind his massed, fanatical army, cocooned within his sealed pocket universe. Such delusions were only possible in a galaxy that had forgotten the Salga Ashtoreen.

The closest rank of Begeen were already alerted to the intruder's presence. They turned slowly, white robes rustling in the silence. The tall figure recognised the subtle, all but invisible tension in the robed bodies as they readied themselves to kill. It was unimpressed by their old, proud boast: *a million ways to kill*. It knew a million and one.

The first Begeen advanced. They approached the figure with the same care and silence it had entered the palace. It did not wait to see which of their many fabled martial arts they would employ. With an economic movement it folded a close-range evaporator from a quantum pocket in its stealthsuit and activated it. There was an almost animal howl, the evaporator flared, and the Begeen vanguard boiled out of existence.

The figure tossed the depleted evaporator aside and moved on.

A second rank of Begeen broke from the mass. These moved swiftly, buoyed on 'rators—they would not make the mistake of their sisters.

The intruder stretched skeletal lips into a smile. The Imperium and Ekleiades had relied for too long on Bieg technology; they had become dependent on it. In the centuries during which the Salga Ashtoreen had passed into myth they had explored to the very galactic rim and beyond. Had the Téokrat and his minions learned nothing from Davolias and Tertius Pentane? The Salga Ashtoreen possessed technology far beyond that imagined by the decadent Bieg, and their lazarite subsidiaries.

The intruder ran an all but invisible hand along their chest. Instantly their motions accelerated a hundredfold. The 'rator-enhanced Begeen seemed almost to be standing still. The intruder slipped two compact buzzblades from more quantum pockets and hefted them. Speeding through the unprepared Begeen, it left them dismembered and worse.

The second wave of defenders destroyed, the intruder decelerated itself to normal speed. It spoke, voice oddly-pitched. "Mygré Keddyth—face me, alone, and I will spare your women."

There was a deep chuckle, emanating from the shadows beyond the poised Begeen.

ONE AGAINST A THOUSAND? I THINK NOT...

The intruder indulged itself with a glance back at the remains of the Begeen second wave. "A little less than a thousand now, I think."

IT IS OF NO IMPORTANCE. YOU CANNOT KILL THEM ALL.

"Indeed?" The intruder shut off its buzzblades, all the better to be heard. "The Salga Ashtoreen has been charged with the destruction of both the Imperium and Ekleiades Galaktium. They take no commission lightly and never fail."

THEN PREPARE TO EXPERIENCE DISAPPOINTMENT FOR THE FIRST TIME.

The intruder's thin smile widened. "You speak like a character from some ancient drama, your Holiness."

THE PREROGATIVE OF ONE WHO HAS RULED THE GALAXY FOR CENTURIES, AND WILL DO SO FOR CENTURIES MORE.

The tall figure shrugged. "I believe you have your own disappointment to anticipate." It reactivated the buzzblades as more Begeen abruptly charged. Speeding up its stealthsuit, the intruder carved a path through the defenders. Rank after rank died, all of their skills and techniques useless against one they could see only as a blur, the buzzblades a high, insect whine. Yet with each passing moment the acceleration took its toll. Muscles ached, then throbbed, then screamed at the abuse. The intruder's entire body burned with effort.

It fought its way to within a hundred metres of the Téokrat's gaudy throne. Begeen littered its trail. Those who still lived, barely more than fifty, hung back. The tall figure knew why.

AND NOW? came the Téokrat's disembodied voice.

The intruder sucked in a breath. "Now you will try to destroy me with your own weapons, Holiness."

INDEED.

Disruptor beams erupted from below the Téokrat's towering throne. Its hands moving even faster than before, the intruder activated its stealthsuit's shields. The disruptors splashed harmlessly off, the air shimmering and glowing.

A fusillade of buzzbolts spat out. The intruder spun its buzzblades, cutting the shrieking flechettes out of the air. Even so, a dozen or so managed to get past the accelerated defences, slipping easily through the force shield. Two slashed its left arm, and it dropped a blade, hand suddenly numb. The rest struck deep into the abdomen. The intruder gasped at the extra pain load, almost falling to one knee, its movements once more normal speed.

The remaining Begeen stirred.

NO! roared the Téokrat. *THIS IS MINE!*

The intruder pulled itself slowly upright, dragging the still active buzzbolts from its body. It was still smiling. Pale, watery blood dripped through the torn suit.

"The Salga Ashtoreen never left," it said. "True, we explored the universe, venturing farther than anyone in the Imperium has ever dared, but we went inward as well. Deep within the Ekleiades. We went nowhere—because we are everywhere."

STIRRING LAST WORDS—WOULD YOU CARE FOR ME TO RECORD THEM? The Téokrat sounded smug. *YOU HAVE STILL FAILED. I LIVE. THE EKLEIADES SURVIVES.* There was the faintest of hums, coming from all across the shadowed chamber. Weapons of every description, powering up, aimed at the intruder.

The tall figure drew itself upright. "On the contrary, your Holiness, it is not I who have failed. My mission was never meant to see me alive at its conclusion."

Its right hand moved across its stealth-suit, moving unnaturally fast—even without the acceleration field—ignoring the close to paralysing agony. Fingers performed a complex pattern, touching shoulders, abdomen, chest. Another whine—this one louder and more localised—drowned out the Téokrat's weapons.

The intruder's suit detonated.

* * * *

Disruptor fire sprayed across the *Drummer's* Q'Alvin shields. Photons, excited by the interplay of shield and assault beam, flared. An alarm howled.

"What's our status?" Jem yelled above the dim.

"Take a guess!" Anre'eq shouted back.

A skimmer tumbled past the *Drummer's* bow, filling Jem's holos for a milli. It was trying to bring its cannon to bear. A moment later the *Drummer's* bow-chasers opened fire, distracting the small ship's crew long enough for Shenna to launch harpoon grenades, wide spread. The three metre shafts slipped through the skimmer's light shielding and detonated upon contact with the hull. The ship yawed, losing way as its drive momentarily failed. Shenna launched another volley. This time the grenades impacted on the skimmer's starboard nacelles. It tumbled, disabled.

Jem steered the *Drummer* past the adrift ship. It was no longer a threat. Fydar seemed to think different.

Astern of the *Drummer, The Anaphei Rex* fired a broadside. The skimmer's Q'Alvin shielding flared under the impact. Fydar fired again. This time the *Rex's* plasma cannon pierced the damaged shielding. The skimmer flew apart, its internal atmosphere briefly igniting.

Jem clenched his teeth but said nothing. Ever since Mags hadn't come out of the nullity, Fydar had been looking for someone to suffer. Better it was some poor imperial lugs than Jem himself.

There was a deafening howl across all voxcomm channels. A starpad ship had gone down, destroyed by one of the ships forming Crioch's outer defences. That was the second since the present engagement had started. Jem's assault fleet was down to five ships. If he didn't think turning about and warping it would be just as fatal, Jem would do it in a milli.

He angled his holos aft. As predicted, *The Anaphei Rex* was coming about, making for the second skimmer, bow cannon firing continually. If he didn't ration himself, Fydar would be out of juice before they reached their target. He'd be no use to Jem then.

"Belay that!" Jem voxed. "Save it for when we sight Crioch!"

The *Rex* continued to fire. The skimmer sparked and faltered. It came apart like an impacted asteroid.

"What was that?" Fydar voxed back. *"Didn't hear above the blaster fire."*

Jem broke contact. The man was a loose cannon. He'd either save them all in some insane manoeuvre, or sink the lot of them.

"Something downing you, bossie-boy?" called Shenna. She was watching him from her station across the cabin, concern in her red eyes.

"Beginning to recognise what a gigging deal this is," he said quietly.

"Beginning?" Anre'eq laughed. "From the moment you cloyed that data on Crioch, you've been wanting to be all hero-like and save the galaxy. Late now to start fretting."

Jem laughed back, though it was subdued. "Hero? I just wanna cause havoc and kick the empire up the dungbie!"

"Then whatya waiting for!" cried Shenna. "Letsie go kick!"

Jem took a breath and re-opened the voxcomms. "Reform on me. Standard drive from now on. Next stop, Crioch."

* * * *

Pallin Jenz's far too young face interrupted the Emperor's dreams. Stenn grumbled awake and turned over to face the holo, the neural interface of which had disturbed his meagre rest.

"I hope this means you know the exact co-ordinates of the Salga Ashtoreen…!"

"My apologies, your grace, but no—"

"Then it better be good."

Jenz's expression remained neutral, masking whatever fear he may have been feeling. *"There is a freebooter, Highness, by the name of Jemorl Strygeth…"*

"So?"

"A petty character, normally too incon- *sequential to even be considered a nuisance, but he has recently made himself a little more…annoying."*

"Circle around the courtly language, Pallin…"

"A short while ago he, and one other, successfully stole a gravolian modulator from a Tenyshan armoury."

Stenn sat upright. "How?"

"It would appear security in that sector has grown haphazard over the past years, your grace. Criminally so. Plus, it is believed he had inside information."

"Why am I only now hearing of this?"

"The news was supressed."

"By Tenyshan authorities?" Some local magistrate trying to save their skins. Well, too late for that.

Jenz shook his head. *"Much higher up, your grace."*

The Téokrat? That ancient pool of pus knew but didn't think it worth mentioning? What was he hiding? "What else?" Jenz wouldn't have dared disturb the emperor's sleep just to pass on old data.

"This same Strygeth has managed to equip a small fleet of freebooters with upgraded gravolian drives and is even now heading for Crioch."

"Crioch? How?" The exact co-ordinates for the breeding grounds were known only to the emperor and Téokrat. Even the few humans required to oversee the automated hydroponic sheds and seeding grounds were mind-wiped, with no idea as to where in the galaxy they were.

"That is unknown, your grace. But again—"

"—Someone must have betrayed that information." Stenn knew it wasn't him. Which left…

The emperor rolled out of bed, summoning a grav-disc. "Assemble a fleet of 'cutters, Jenz. With the latest upgrades. My explicit authority, if anyone asks."

"Immediately, your grace." There was the briefest of pauses. *"Should I inform His Holiness?"*

"No." The devious bastard will know soon enough, Stenn thought. If he wants to stop me then, he can try explaining it to the whole Ekleiades. "Have the ships' commanders ready to warp out immediately."

Jenz inclined his head. *"As you command."*

Stenn stepped his tiny frame up onto the grav-disc. Hovering dressers were already removing his sleeping clothes and replacing them with a fleet admiral's robes. "Keep this absolutely quiet, Jenz. No one must know—is that clear?"

This time Jenz actually bowed. *"Absolutely, your grace."* The holo vanished.

It was a direct disobeyal of the Téokrat's orders—Stenn was no closer to uncovering the Salga Ashtoreen, and warping to the farthest edge of the Ekleiades did not seem likely to bring him any closer. Yet Stenn could not but help thinking all of the events of the past standards—Davolias, Tertius Pentane, the theft of a modulator, and now a frankly unbelievable assault on the voidcutter breeding grounds—were somehow connected. And sitting in the centre of that web of events had to be the Téokrat. All Stenn had to do was expose Mygré Keddyth's role, and he could likely depose the devious fossil with the Imperium's blessing.

Stenn allowed himself a smile as he floated from his apartment, immediately flanked by a dozen loyal Feluq'ans.

* * * *

Jem cycled the holoports through another three-sixty scan. There was still nothing in range.

"Shen?" he asked. Again.

"Same as last, bossie-boy. Space clear as a careened hull."

"So where are they?" Jem gnawed at a knuckle. The lines of defence cutters should be getting thicker—not disappearing altogether.

"Maybe they're falling back to defend Crioch," said Anre'eq, running his own, equally futile, sensor probes.

"Cos we're such a terrifying flight of trucks," muttered Jem.

Off the *Drummer's* port beam, *The Anaphei Rex* was edging forward, ion rams at full rev. Fydar wanted to be down by the planet's surface, burning something to the ground. Anything. If Fydar didn't get his fix soon, Jem figured it'd be *The Aiken Drummer* on the receiving end.

"How far to Crioch?"

"Still no sniff," Shenna answered. "Couple of light mins, I'm figuring. Should be in range soonest, anyways."

Anre'eq slid a finger over his console. "Lot of background rads. Someone deploying a blanking shield alongside Q'Alvins? Signature looks off."

Jem had had enough of the universe making itself invisible. Didn't seem polite.

Shenna swore. "The chokkin' cuch is that?"

"What?" Jem checked all his vids. He saw nothing.

"Peak in the ultras. Check it!" She clone-flicked her display onto one of Jem's holos. Ahead a large portion of space was abruptly off the scale in the ultraviolet range.

Anre'eq stared at his own cloned display. "Q'Alvin shield busted, I figure. Planet-sized one." He played his hands across his console. "Yodely. Shield fried. Surface generators no-vaed."

Jem blinked at what he was seeing. It took a lot to shatter a planetary Q'Alvin shield. More than just a fleet of voidies. And Shenna's shared data showed nothing so mega.

"Heat 'em up," he sub-voxed his remaining ships. "Someone's done us the big of taking down the shields."

"Bosey!" yelled Fydar. *"Saves us the bother!"*

"Until we know why, assume they're not friendly."

"Like I ever!"

The *Rex* surged forward, the xebec finding extra thrust from somewhere. The ship slipped into full assault mode, cannon bristling.

"Cap?"

Jem shook his head. "Let him go, Ani. He wants to draw fire, that's his business."

Anre'eq stared at him briefly, but said nothing.

A few millis more saw Crioch appear on all sensor and holo channels. It was a huge, plain ball of mud hanging against the thin starfield. Nothing to identify it as the source of the Imperium's biggest warships. Jem expected nothing less. Tiny motes of light sparkled around it, winking randomly.

"Cannon fire?"

Anre'eq nodded. "Big league. Voidie strength—though I'm reading nothing like them in the vicinity. Small defence ships—like the skimmers we encountered back there. That's all."

"All?" Shenna cloned her display again. There was something close by Crioch's mass. Something big enough to be a moon—except it was pumping out rads like a fresh new star.

"What the cuch is that?" muttered Jem.

Shenna continued to shuffle through her holos, muttering breathlessly. As the Drummer plunged closer to Crioch most of Jem's attention was taken up by the object hanging close by, like some kind of grotesque portent.

It was so ornate it could reasonably be described as shapeless. Columns, towers, spines and twisting lengths of clear material covered the thing. If a planet had been torn apart and its parts reassembled in the most arbitrary manner imaginable, then buried under countless projections, it would have been no less bizarre. There were no obvious engine nacelles or thruster vents, no hint as to what moved it. It stood out against space and Crioch's muddy ball like a pale, random spray. It was ugly—yet at the same time possessed of a compelling beauty. And it was huge, more massive than half a dozen squadrons of voidies. Almost half the diameter of Crioch, it hung over the planet; so close Jem was surprised both bodies weren't interact-

ing in some way. Lights flickered around it—sparks and pallid beams that twinkled. That explained the absence of skimmers—they were all engaged with this monstrous thing, their weapons flickering uselessly against its mass. Jem couldn't tell if it was fighting back. Maybe it didn't need to, or the defending skimmers were beneath its notice.

It looked like something that could stand off from a world, while single-handedly carving it up.

Jem rotated the Drummer's engines into reverse, heaving to before they got too close to the colossus. Fydar paid no attention: The Anaphei Rex steered straight past, followed by the three remaining starpad ships.

"Always knew you were marked yeller!" came Fydar's voice.

"Belay it!" Jem voxed. "We come for the planet, not trading shots with...whatevers."

Fydar's answer was a short, hoarse laugh before he cut off sub-vox. All four ships curved towards Crioch, giving the huge unknown craft a wide berth.

Jem gave the Drummer's engines a brief pulse, steering his ship in an elliptical course that would take her around Crioch without attracting the massive construction's attention. He hoped.

"What is that?" he repeated.

Shenna laughed, even as she flipped one holo past another. She seemed to be looking for something. "Ever seen its like, Ani?"

The man remained silent.

Jem frowned, turning. There was something wrong about Shenna. The way she spoke, the way she moved—both were different, somehow. There was a calmness about her he'd never scanned before. An aloofness.

"Shen—?"

She stepped back from her displays, thoughtful. Her actions were measured, economic—almost predatory, Jem thought. So different to the jittery, half-crazed gilt he knew.

She gestured at one of Jem's holoports and reduced the magnification to minimum.

The vast construction they were passing still overfilled it. "That is a Salga Ashtoreen kinship, yes?"

"Is it?" said Anre'eq, sounding disinterested.

"A what?" asked Jem.

She turned her attention on Jem. "Do you remember where you cloyed that fid—?" She smiled, apologetically. "I'm sorry, too long in character. The data on Crioch's co-ordinates, Jem Strygeth—do you recall where you got them?" Her hands were resting idly on her white shieldsuit, right about where she stowed her buzzblades.

"You know fine well," he said, baffled by the question. And the threat implied by her stance. "On the body of a bandog after we stiffed all that Bieg loot on the Korfulan Ranges."

"You'd just signed on to replace Vinsha," added Anre'eq in a quiet voice. "After she'd been shivved by some lug in an alley. Remember?"

"The only ones who know the co-ordinates of the breeding grounds are Emperor Stenn and the Téokrat," said Shenna. "Did the body look like either the emperor or his Holiness?"

"His Holiness, now?" Anre'eq smiled lazily. "Interesting."

Shenna stared at him, her eyes cold. Then her attention returned to Jen and she smiled: contemptuous, mocking. "Well?"

"Shen, what are you saying?" Jem was starting to lose patience with whatever game she was playing.

Anre'eq laughed. "She means the co-ordinates were planted, cap. I think we've been played."

Fydar's cracked voice burst over the voxcomm. *"Strygeth, you lying caching dungbie! Where are the chokka'ed seeding grounds?"*

Jem turned to look at a display of the planet below them, glad to ignore his crew. "Right in front of your eyes, Fydar! Open them for once!"

"There's nothing here, cucher! Just

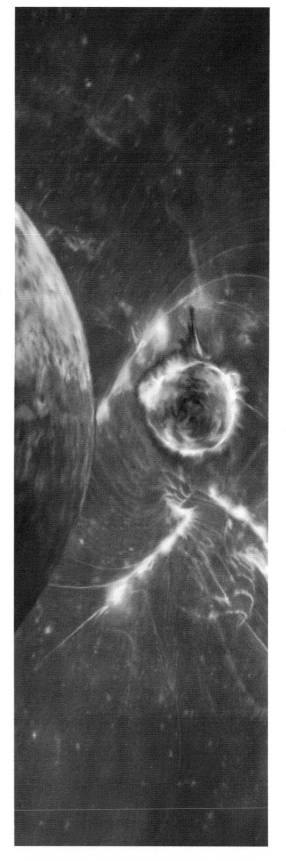

rocks and that dungbie taking up half the sky!"

Anre'eq joined in. "Are you sure?"

"I'm not blind, you wormed-up amp-tramp! This chokka'ed ball is just scorched rocks and crashed skimmers. It's dead. What's the game, huh—?"

Anre'eq's temper exploded. He never lost it. "That devious half worm!" he spat. "We really have been played." He turned on Shenna. "Has he been ahead of us at every move?"

She smiled lazily—although Jem was sure she'd looked pretty baffled a milli before. "Always."

"Get back up here, Fydar!" Jem sub-voxed. "No profit down there. We're all fried!"

Anre'eq was shaking his head. "No time, I'm afraid." He pointed at the various holos. The huge ship was no longer registering on any of them.

Jem ran his hands over the console, knowing it would do no good. "Where did it go?"

"Back where it emerged from. And if you want to be still breathing in a few millis, might I suggest we warp it, mega skatey!"

There were several objects registering on the sniffers: small, fast moving. Making straight for Crioch. "Fydar! Shift your dung-bie!"

Shenna pounced on the drive controls. She slammed the *Drummer's* ion ram into full reverse, finger poised over the gravolian activators. "Wonder if these things work blind…?" she murmured.

Jem took one look at her face, then back to the Crioch holos. "Fydar! Warp it! Everyone!"

He was aware of Anre'eq shaking his head.

"Borich!"

Crioch erupted in a violent flash. A shockwave of debris rippled out towards the *Drummer*, overtaking her. Before Shenna could engage the gravolian drive, the ship was tossed like a flag in a storm.

* * * *

Mygré Keddyth sat in his sanctum, shaken. The Salga Ashtoreen were far more resourceful than he had imagined. For an assassin to simply enter the throne room undetected—taking advantage of the lack of digithopters and snoopers. Besting most of the Begeen warriors and—far too easily—make its way to within metres of the Téokrat's throne. Keddyth had gravely miscalculated. He was sobered to think the only thing that had saved him was the pocket universe around which the high throne was constructed. A bubble of alternate reality within which he had resided for centuries. It would take more than a simple explosion to rend the barriers between one cosmos and another. Even one of the magnitude the assassin had unleased.

Keddyth looked out at the devastation. There was little remaining of his throne room. The holographic splendour once adorning the hall was gone, leaving only darkness. No more than twenty-two Begeen survived, miraculously, many seriously injured. Of those, the Téokrat estimated six would not live for much longer. The walking bomb—of a type Keddyth did not recognise, something unique to the Salga Ashtoreen, no doubt—had been thorough. That the Salga Ashtoreen had underestimated the Téokrat's resources as much as he had underestimated theirs was of small comfort.

He ran through the holo displays still surrounding him, all still working, still spying on the galaxy beyond. What had happened within the Téokrat's halls remained unknown to the Ekleiades at large. It would remain so. He could rebuild and recruit. Once his throne room was as resplendent as it had been the first task of his replenished Begeen would be to silence the builders, and remove from their own ranks those who had failed to reach the excellence required. Life would go on.

Several displays attracted his attention, covering the raid on Crioch and Stenn's initiative. He allowed himself a thin smile. That much at least was as Keddyth had anticipated. The freebooter, Strygeth, still lived, but he was of little consequence. He had played his part; no doubt soon to perish under the guns of the emperor's voidcutters.

He prioritised his displays to the systems immediately around Eklesia Prime. If he had reasoned correctly, there would soon be something unusual to be detected. For a moment he considered putting the planetary defence 'cutters on alert. He had already made a dangerous underestimation, another would most likely be fatal. He dismissed the idea, instead sending a simple sub-vox message.

* * * *

Jem dragged himself back into his seat. The cabin throbbed with numberless, deafening alarms. That he was still in shape to hear them was a little encouraging.

Shenna was bent over the console, fingers running over the various contacts. She didn't look particularly concerned, but there was a tenseness in the way she stood, an impatience in the movement of her fingers as she ran through holo after holo. She seemed to be looking for something. Jem guessed she couldn't find it.

Anre'eq was slumped in his seat, out cold, it looked. Jem wondered if it was a result of the blast wave—or Shenna had stoked him.

The cacophony abruptly ceased. Jem was grateful. He groaned and Shenna glanced his way, although she didn't look concerned.

"Problem?"

"What do you think?" He angled all of his ports into a three-sixty, trying to orientate himself on the *Drummer's* position. Chunks of glowing rock were still tumbling past, which mean Crioch was—had been— over— "Chokk!"

A squadron of voidies floated roughly where the planet had hung. They were big and sleek, clearly not long harvested. Energy to their drives and Q'Alvin shields pulsed along veins crossing their pristine shells. Spiracles punctuated every surface—firing nodes and plasma vents. Antennae grew like gnarled limbs along the medial line, sprouting bipectinate sensory fronds. Ancillary gunnery pedipalps were arrayed across the shells, at this magnification looking like sleek hairs. Living, breathing organisms. Bred to transverse space, supply food and air for their crew, a single ship carried more weaponry than all the trucks ever to have moored at Aurora combined. And if these were equipped with gravolian drives, they could cross the galaxy in standards.

Jem zoomed in on one vessel. Proudly displayed across a large vertical sensory node was the sigil of Clan Lymatén. Emperor Stenn's own ships. Jem wondered if the poisonous little runt was actually on board one of voidies. Come to rescue the breeding grounds. Too late.

"How long have they been there?"

Shenna stared at the magnified holo. "Warped in millis after Crioch was obliterated."

"Hope he enjoyed the show."

"Likely he came to stop us."

"Us?" Jem shook his head. "How?"

"There's a Salga Ashtoreen kinship forming a reception committee the milli we arrive, the emperor's own fleet warps in too—just a little late. How are your feelings on coincidences, Jem?"

"You know fine well. And what in hell's come over you, Shen? Something wear off, or just now kick in?"

There was a pained chuckle from Anre'eq. He eased himself into a sitting position, wriggling his shoulders as though they'd stiffened up. "Something like the latter, I'd guess." He rubbed at his neck. "Slick move. Never knew you could move that fast."

Shenna just smiled back: a cold, confident quirk of her lips. So unlike the jittery gilt Jem knew.

"I said earlier you've been played, cap." Anre'eq came to his feet. His hands flickered across his baggy shieldsuit, fingers pressing seemingly random points on his torso. The ill-fitting suit began to move, tightening, the wrinkles smoothing out, spreading across Anre'eq's rangy body like a dark second skin. He looked more like a man-shaped hole, an absence, his body absorbing every photon striking it, reflecting nothing. "And I regret to say I was one of those who played you."

Shenna had tensed, the cold smile vanishing into a wary alertness. "So. You are Salga Ashtoreen, then."

"And you are one of the emperor's Begeen virgin warriors. Although a little less virginal now, perhaps." He winked at Jem. "I suppose I should have guessed."

"We both should," said Shenna.

"Yes." Anre'eq sighed. "We're good at what we do, aren't we?"

Jem's head was spinning. "Shenna— you've been one the Téokrat's killers all along? And you—" he nodded towards Anre'eq "—I have no idea what you are…"

"A hired assassin," said Shenna.

Anre'eq shrugged. "Oh, I am so much more than that, Shen—or whatever your name really is. And save the moral outrage. There is little to choose between us, ultimately."

Shenna drew her buzzblades. They whined to life. In the confined cabin the noise was close to deafening.

Jem wasn't sure what happened next. Anre'eq seemed to flicker, and Shenna was abruptly on her knees, both of her buzzblades in Anre'eq's hands. The woman's red eyes glared up with undisguised hatred. Anre'eq shut the screaming weapons down. A moment later they were unrecognisable crumples in his hands.

"A colleague of mine will have recently taken down most of your sisterhood," he commented, voice calm. "Don't imagine you pose any kind of threat to me."

The holoports drifting around the cabin abruptly flickered. For a moment they went blank, then the enraged features of Emperor Stenn filled each one. The high, studded collar and golden epaulets of a Fleet Admiral were just visible below his head.

"In the name of the Emperor and the Ekleiades Galaktium, identify yourself."

"That tiny little wart certainly picks his moments!" Jem muttered. He straightened, brushing down his shieldsuit and facing one of the holos. "Captain Jemorl Strygeth, your Imperial Highness, of the free corvette *Aiken Drummer*. Red Jem to my friends—among whom I most certainly do not count you. I'd introduce you to the rest of my crew, but they're both presently…otherwise engaged."

He risked a glance behind him. Shenna was still on the floor, Anre'eq applying a couple of fingers to her neck. Whatever he was doing, it seemed to be holding her in a kind of paralysis.

One of the holoports swooped around Jem, facing the two on the floor. Anre'eq glanced up and gave the emperor an easy smile. "Anre'eq Pol, your emperorship. Please forgive Shenna Maak—she's just received news about some close friends which has left her somewhat stunned." His grin widened, showing white teeth. "Heartbroken, in fact."

Shenna twitched, clearly trying to fight her paralysis.

Stenn frowned. He seemed to be staring at Shenna. Certainly spending more time looking at her than he had the two men.

The vidiport drifted back, joining the others in a crude semicircle about the cabin. *"You will surrender yourself to my fleet and face charges relating to the destruction of Crioch. You must realise than any attempt to flee will only incur your instant destruction."*

Jem rested a hand on his longsword hilt. He realised how absurd he probably looked—and sounded—but bluff was pretty much all they had left. "We thank you for the complement, your Highness—but even you must realise that this wee ambling tug could hardly destroy so much as a small moon. Never mind a whole world—"

"Crioch is gone, you are present. That

is all I need to realise, freebooter. Stand by to receive boarders."

"And the Salga Ashtoreen kinship you so narrowly avoided…?" said Anre'eq, not quite making it an accusation.

Stenn's face twitched into a thin smile—although Jem was pretty sure there'd been the briefest tic of alarm before the emperor had regained control of his expression. *"You would lay the blame for this atrocity at the feet of a myth?"*

"Ay," said Jem. "One berthed aboard a truck that could eat your biggest voidie for breakfast. We escaped that easily enough—think how smartly we'll warp past your pack of rumblers."

"You are playing for time. Time you do not have."

"I really think the Téokrat should be informed," said Anre'eq. Shenna was starting to move. Jem saw Anre'eq jab down sharply. She spasmed, falling still again. "If, of course he doesn't already know."

The emperor stared at all three starpads. Jem was pretty sure he saw indecision in the man's eyes. He hadn't expected that.

"You have until all of my fleet's cannon come to bear. Surrender or die—it is all the same to me." His face vanished from the holos, replaced by images of voidcutters, space and various marching readouts.

"I think he means it," said Jem, already powering up the *Drummer's* gravolian drive. "You think we can outwarp a voidie blast?"

"Now's the time to find out."

Anre'eq came to his feet. Instantly Shenna lashed out, not as paralysed as she'd seemed. Anre'eq stumbled, caught off-guard. As Shenna stood, Jem drew his sword but she blurred forward. Seeming to just caress his wrist. The agony was all-consuming. Jem dropped his sword and doubled up, clutching his right hand. Through teary eyes he saw her snatch up his longsword, moving far too fast. 'Rators?

Shenna buckled, struck from behind by something Jem didn't see. She hit the floor, just stopping short of smashing her face

against it. Anre'eq blinked into sight, standing over her.

"Get us out of here, cap!"

Jem limped to the console, blinking away tears of pain. With his left hand he ran fingers over the engine controls, watching both Anre'eq and Shenna, unwilling to turn his back on either.

Shenna spun onto her back, her feet lashing out. Anre'eq dodged easily, moving just a fraction faster than her. She came to her feet with rapid grace, facing Anre'eq, Jem's sword raised. She lunged, and the longsword shattered against a dark blur.

Shenna turned and ran, moving with a speed she'd previously not shown. Overrunning her 'rators, most likely. She blurred to the cabin exits, vanishing in a moment.

Jem powered up the *Drummer's* drive. The gravolian modulator kicked in, and the voidie fleet vanished off all the holoports in a blink. He leaned against the console, nursing a throbbing hand.

"Where did she go?"

Anre'eq nodded towards a flickering tell-tale. "She launched one of the skiffs, somehow."

"Before the drive fired up?" Even moving as fast as she was, he didn't think she'd be to launch the small ship that quickly.

The other shrugged. "If not, both her and the skiff are spread across light years." He touched his hip with a gloved hand, momentarily distracted. "And she's cloyed an adjunct matrix, to boot. She *is* good."

* * * *

On board his flagship, *The Xentharius Ascendant*, Stenn raged silently as he watched the freebooter ship vanish. He should have ordered their destruction without warning—but who could imagine such scum being able to master a gravolian drive so quickly. And now they were gone—halfway across the galaxy, in any direction. Unless they'd had a course prepared and already laid in, it would have been little more than a blind jump.

The emperor tried to comfort himself with the thought they may have driven straight into the heart of a distant star.

"Imperial Highness!" One of the crew augments manning the flagship's control Pit looked up to where Stenn hovered. "There's a small vessel approaching. A lifeboat or similar, by its mass."

Stenn sank down into the high-sided hemisphere of holoports, tell tales and data screens. The only light came from the countless images and readouts, and even though the Pit measured many metres in diameter the emperor always felt hemmed in. He preferred the much more airy space of the Skopion Dome.

"Where away?"

A complex network of fine tendrils sprouted from the console, growing up and into the augment's shaved head. The tendrils swarmed and twitched constantly, crawling across the augment's scalp as they accessed whichever part of their brain was needed at any given moment. The augment ran a hand over a dark image. It expanded. Sharp points of light—distant stars—resolved into focus. One dot was clearly moving.

"From the last location of the freebooter corvette, Highness."

"Making for the fleet?"

"Yes, Highness."

Stenn pursed his lips. "Life signs?"

"Just one that we can detect."

A lifeboat? That was highly unlikely. The corvette had sustained no damage that the fleet could detect. A decoy, then? If so, an obvious one. Or was it some form of explosive device? Rigged to detonate once it was within optimum range of the fleet, or inside any voidcutter whose commander was naïve enough to take it on board.

"Just one life sign?"

The augment nodded, their nest of tendrils rippling.

"And no other readings?"

"Highness?"

"An atmoshear drive about to implode? Kraitbombs? Ion-ram bootlegged into a primitive nuclear device? Anything to suggest it isn't just an escape pod or similar."

The augment rechecked their readings. "Nothing, Highness. All telemetry indicates it's just a small ship with a single occupant. No offensive capabilities. Its drive has barely enough megas to power even the shortest interplanetary—" The operator broke off. The nest of tendrils on their head shifted and wriggled, as though a tiny animal was crawling between them. "They have begun to broadcast a signal, Highness."

Stenn half-smiled. "Some obsolete Imperial code, I suppose."

"No, Highness." The augment winced as the tendrils across their head swirled in agitation. "It is employing one of the Téokrat's personal codes. An old one, true, but still valid."

Stenn thought carefully. Pirates were rarely so subtle—or guileful. Besides, no one outside the Téokrat's closest circle would have access to His Holiness's personal codes. "Very well. Instruct Captain Torgelli to take it on board *The Balba Corfax*. Once he has secured ship and occupant, I will pinnace across to interrogate the prisoner."

"Yes, Highness."

Stenn rode his grav-disc up and out of the dimly-lit control pit and into the ship's wide circulatory system. He rode the disc along the tortuous, endlessly forking corridors, glowglobes marking every two metres. Numerous digithopters and sniffers drifted by, paying him little attention. His digital signature was continually broadcast for any floating snooper to pick up. The occasional passing human snapped to attention. They needed no prompting: the emperor's image was common currency throughout the Ekleiades Galaktium.

His disk drifted down a tributary. At the corridor's abrupt end was a single door, guarded by two Feluq'ans. They saluted at their Emperor's approach, bringing halblasters to their shoulders with matchless precision. The door irised open.

The room beyond was simply furnished.

Even the most prestigious voidcutter had no room for ostentation. The only concession to Stenn's exalted position was the presence of two husbands: Feunn and Yallas. They were dressed in robes of the finest Hedilorran silk, two dazzling blossoms in an otherwise dull chamber. They came quickly to their feet. A holo blinked off, too slow. Stenn could see they had been following the incident with the freebooter corvette. He wondered if a divorce wasn't in order: he hadn't married them so they could look over his shoulder. He snapped his fingers at Feunn.

"Get me a drink—quickly! And you—" he turned his attention on Yallas "—find that disruptor carbine I was presented with by the Mayorines of Thassalorkin Gen." Both husbands bobbed and hurried to obey. "If I'm going to have to kill whoever's on that small ship—someone quoting Téokratic private codes—I need something appropriately gaudy to do it with."

Both Yallas and Feunn returned together. Feunn handed over a large bowl containing a pinkish-yellow liquid. Yallas carried a polished silver object that was so ridiculously ornate it was all but impossible to tell it was a weapon. The firing button in particular was exceedingly well hidden. Stenn had sometimes wondered if the damned thing was meant to be fired at all.

He snatched it up and hung it from his belt, next to his ceremonial dagger. He took the drink from Feunn a little more carefully, taking a deep pull at it. Potent. Mostly alcohol. Feunn knew him so well.

"Imperial Highness. Captain Torgelli presents his complements and says the prisoner is ready for you."

Stenn took another drink from the bowl before handing it back to Feunn. "Good. Is my pinnace ready?"

"Of course, Highness."

"Then I am on my way." He left his quarters, passing between the Feluq'ans as they again came to attention. He had gone little more than a metre when a thought struck him. He drifted his grav-disc back to the guards.

"My quarters require a category one decontamination. See to it."

"Category one, Highness?" said the guard to Stenn's left.

He hung eye to eye with the man. "Was I unclear, lieutenant?"

"No, Highness—!"

"Then seal this door and commence decontamination immediately."

The lieutenant bowed. Possibly so he did not have to meet his Emperor's gaze. "At once, Highness."

Stenn nodded and turned his grav-disc. He drifted back to the circulatory system's main arteries, wondering how soon would be appropriate before he added two new husbands to his harem.

The Emperor's pinnace was docked in a well-protected vacuole in the depths of *The Xentharius Ascendant*. A vaguely insectoid shape, it squatted on six multi-jointed limbs. Like the voidcutters it possessed a rudimentary sentience. Stenn could almost imagine it watching his approach, anticipating its flight into free space.

He slipped on board, quickly settling into a large shapeseat as the access hatch irised shut. The smooth walls glowed with the pinnace's own generated phosphorescence.

"On your command, Imperial Highness," came a voice—the pilot's. Stenn had often entertained the conceit that, should they ever breed enough intelligence into the pinnace strain for them to fly unaided, the voice would be much more strident.

"Proceed," he acknowledged.

The vessel launched without so much as a nudge. The holoport covering most of the forward bulkhead showed the vacuole dilating, sweeping by as they slipped into space. Voidcutters littered the darkness, their smooth shells dark against the barely starlit background. The images swooped and tumbled as the pinnace orientated itself upon one particular ship: *The Balba Corfax*. The voidcutter grew rapidly larger, an opening dilating in its port flank to accept the Emperor's transport.

There was a phalanx of guards lined up outside the pinnace's hatch. Not one a Feluq'an. Stenn barely acknowledged them as he floated past, over two metres above the floor. Captain Torgelli was present to greet the Emperor: a tall, fussy man with white hair and beard, his uniform clearly self-designed.

"This way, Imperial Highness."

The guard falling in behind, Torgelli led Stenn along *The Balba Corfax's* circulatory system, the Emperor chafing at the man's pedestrian slowness. If he had just sub-voxed the location of whatever cell the prisoner was locked in, Stenn could have floated there in moments.

Eventually they reached a short branch, at the end of which was a heavily-locked door and two more guards. Stenn drifted forward. Torgelli, with an uncharacteristic speed, intercepted him.

"If you intend on interrogating the prisoner, my marines are at your disposal."

Stenn made a show of looking back at the uniformed men, all standing smartly to attention. "Is that cell nulled?"

"If she has any form of tech on her person, it will be useless."

"And there are digithopters and sniffers inside?"

"Null-field shielded—as are the holo observer cams."

"Then a squad of your men cluttering the cell will only complicate matters. I can handle a lone freebooter, captain. Kindly stand aside."

Reluctantly, Torgelli backed away. Stenn floated towards the door. At a gesture from one of the guards, it irised open. Stenn drifted inside.

A woman was immobilised on a plain metal chair. It looked uncomfortable. Good. She was the one Stenn had seen on board the freebooter ship, he realised. White shieldsuit, purple hair and red eyes. Faked, he guessed. The simplest augments.

He sent an interrogation query to a snooper which was hovering just above her head. It returned a negative. No digital signature, no discernible subdural ID. Her face logged two hundred million close matches, but none close enough to identify her. The snooper could not link her to a single individual in the Galaktium's database. It seemed quite put out by that.

Stenn floated closer. "Who are you?"

She stared at him. He had no idea red eyes could be so cold. "My name is Shenna Maak."

"I doubt that. You have no ID signature—which is impossible. Your face is not on record—also impossible."

Her answering smile was savage. "Perhaps I know a rogue lazarite surgeon."

Stenn considered the possibility. It was conceivable, but linked with her lack of subdural ID, unlikely. Sculpting new features would be a simple matter, but not even the most skilled lazarite could detach cerebral overmapping without killing the subject. Or at least leaving them severely brain-damaged. And the snooper's assessment of her mental facility was of one well above average.

"I repeat the question."

She tried to tug at her bonds—reinforced stellium alloy backed up by a contrall loop system which fed into her shieldsuit circuitry, turning the whole thing quite rigid. "You pride yourself on your intelligence, Highness. Ask yourself, how do I know his Holiness's private codes? Who gave them to me?"

The snooper fed back a few details it had gleaned about the name Shenna Maak. "It would appear you are a remarkable thief and picker of locks," said Stenn. "Is it possible you stole them?"

She laughed. "His Holiness was right about you, emperor—you are a little man, in all respects. How could I—remarkable as I am—steal what exists only within the Téokrat's mind?"

Stenn bit back on his rising anger. She

was trying to goad him; he would not oblige.

"Further," she continued, "ally the colour of my shieldsuit to my obscure knowledge. Perhaps I should add that I will be free of this chair in—" she paused, browed furrowed "—thirteen seconds."

The Emperor's grav-disc drifted back a metre, driven by his brief uncertainty. "Impossible."

"Why not? I am already that, according to your—" she cast a dismissive glance towards the snooper "—data."

A moment later she stood, carelessly. The stellium manacles had unbonded, falling away from her wrists, waist and ankles. Her white shieldsuit moved as gracefully as she.

Stenn fell back further, drifting towards the doorway.

The woman lashed out. The snooper flew across the cell, shattering against the wall. She raised her left arm and ran her right forefinger down it from wrist to elbow. The digithopters hovering just of reach dropped to the floor. A quick glance told Stenn that the array of holo cams mounted close to the ceiling were equally lifeless.

"There," she smiled, "another impossibility. Your null-field is itself nulled and we are cut off from the rest of this ship. That door, by the way, is also locked and sealed by my shieldsuit's own neurofield."

"You're Salga Ashtoreen!" murmured Stenn.

The woman snorted. "I've all but told you, but you still seem incapable of seeing the answer to your question. Who else, small emperor, would carry contrall loop disablers as a matter of routine—suitably disguised of course—as well as any number of sonic keys, hasptrips and neuropicks." At a touch a flat earphone unfolded across the right side of her head. She seemed to be listening to something. Whatever it was, from her increasingly rigid expression and thinning lips, Stenn did not imagine it was something she wanted to hear.

"I am, as you said, and in the quaint jargon of my erstwhile starpad comrades, an excellent gilt." Despite her expression her tone remained light, taunting. "And what made me so is Bieg tech. *Imperial* tech."

It came to Stenn. Perhaps it was her face, half hidden under a white semi-cowl. It was obvious. He should have seen it. "You're Begeen."

"Congratulations, Imperial Highness."

"But—on board that freebooter ship. Why?"

"To ensure that simpleminded captain not only found the co-ordinates to Crioch, but that he went looking for it." She sat back down in the chair. No longer manacled, she did not look so uncomfortable. In fact, Stenn thought, she appeared to be enjoying herself. Making fun of him.

Well, let the bitch have her moment. That shieldsuit might have every square nanometre crammed with Bieg tech, but ultimately she was but one person. Begeen, yes, but one alone.

"Letting that fool have such delicate information has resulted in the empire losing its voidcutter breeding grounds…!" Another charge to lay at the feet of the senile Téokrat.

She laughed again. "You have been emperor too long, your grace. Subtlety is beyond you. Do you honestly think Crioch was the breeding grounds?"

"I share that knowledge with the Téokrat—!"

"His Holiness shares that knowledge with no one." The earphone semi-cowl rolled back. She looked at him with her full face again. Her expression looked more murderous that ever. "Unlike his personal codes." She tapped her forehead.

Stenn was silent.

"The Salga Ashtoreen have returned, as you know. In fact I believe his Holiness charged you with tracking them down." She looked at him, then the cell surrounding them. "How is that going, by the way?"

Stenn bit back his response.

She shrugged. "No matter. His Holiness conceived a plan that was elegant in its simplicity. It's certain the Salga Ashtoreen would eventually wish to destroy our void-cutter production capabilities, so why not let them? Allow a braggard freebooter to learn where the breeding grounds are—he will almost certainly want to make his name by attacking them. And also announce it to his lowlife comrades in the grandest possible way. The Salga Ashtoreen will have spies infiltrating all aspects of the Galaktium—there is one on that freebooter ship, for example—and they would report to their masters immediately. I have no doubt the one aboard *The Aiken Drummer* passed on the exact co-ordinates the moment they were laid into the ship's navcom. Of course, the very fact that you acted as you did the moment you learned of Strygeth's delusional plan only added an extra layer of credibility to the scenario." She smiled up at Stenn, baring too many teeth. "I suspect there is at least one Salga Ashtoreen informant on your own staff, your grace."

The Emperor remained silent, admiring the strategy even while despising it.

"A kinship was despatched, reaching Crioch moments before what remained of Strygeth's tiny armada." She looked thoughtful. "I think we were lucky. That Aphotism could not be predicted, of course. We may all have died there."

Stenn drew in a gentle breath. "It would not have mattered. The plan was in motion and you had played your part. Whether or not you made it to Crioch, the Salga Ashtoreen would have believed what they needed to believe, and destroyed the planet."

The woman bowed her head. "Quite so. We are none of us indispensable." Her tone had grown harsh, matching her expression.

"And what did His Holiness anticipate would follow?" asked Stenn.

"An invasion of Ekleiades Prime. There has already been an attack on the Téokrat, with most of my sisters killed by a lone assassin—"

"Salga Ashtoreen?" Stenn felt a little pang of satisfaction from the news. "Then

his Holiness underestimated them, too."

"Not at all—such an attack was inevitable. And inevitably fruitless. His Holiness is unharmed. He anticipated such an event, as well as the imminent invasion by kinships. A fleet, perhaps, to make a point."

Stenn thought of the destruction of both Davolias and Tertius Pentane. "They don't need to send a fleet. The destruction of Ekleiades Prime—the entire star system—can be accomplished remotely."

The woman stood. "Then we need to return home immediately."

"Agreed. Although if they employ whatever weaponry they used on Tertius Pentane, every voidcutter in the fleet would be helpless."

The Begeen came closer to Stenn's gravdisc, staring up at him with eyes that held no mercy. "Then you'd best pray they are in the mood for taking prisoners…"

* * * *

The gravolian drive shut down. *The Aiken Drummer* coasted through space punctuated by drifting hunks of rock of all sizes. Jem cycled through all of the holoports.

"We're back at Tytaroth!"

Anre'eq looked up from the console and frowned at the nearest holo as though he'd never seen it before. "So we are."

Jem flopped down into the seat next to Anre'eq and stared at him, hard. "If we could just warp back from Crioch without encountering that Aphotism, we could have gone the same way!"

Anre'eq gazed up, his eyes focused on nothing. "Yes. I suppose that's possible."

Jem grabbed the other's shoulder. Anre'eq didn't seem to move, Jem just found himself stretched across the console, staring up at the ceiling. His whole body tingled.

"You're worse than Shenna!" he mumbled past a numb tongue.

"Better, actually." Anre'eq came out of his seat and walked towards the cabin's side. A flotilla of holos followed him. "At least I won't try to kill you, just because I can." He cycled through the holos. A frown began to etch his face.

"I suppose I should be grateful." Jem stood, carefully. Centimetre by centimetre, the tingle left his body. "So why won't you kill me?"

"It's not my job." Anre'eq was combining the holos, creating a larger, higher resolution image of the rock-strewn exterior. He spread his arms, zooming in, panning. "When the Salga Ashtoreen has a task to finish, as many of us as are necessary are given smaller parts to play. We do our jobs—nothing more, nothing less."

Jem watched him shuffling through the views of Tytaroth, clearly looking for something. "So what are you doing now?"

"Improvising. It's my life as well, remember." He took his attention away from the holos for a moment and stared at Jem. "I can't find Aurora."

Jem glanced at the console. "You've jumped us right up to Aurora's position."

"Yes."

"Straight through all the uncharted rocks with unpredictable orbits."

"Uh-huh."

"Which you said couldn't be done..."

"You're missing the point, cap." Anre'eq flicked one holo out of the combined image and cast it towards Jem. "We're here, but Aurora isn't."

Jem checked the console readings again, then stared hard at the holo floating half a metre from his nose. Anre'eq was right: Aurora should have been filling the image. It wasn't. Instead there seemed to be—

"Are those voidies?"

Anre'eq nodded. "Three. Shenna must have transmitted Aurora's co-ordinates, along with an optimal course through Tytaroth."

"She betrayed us...!"

"She was never *us*. And in case you've forgotten, neither am I."

Jem ignored him. Betrayal was hardly rare among starpads, but it was always a punishable offense—if it could be proved.

Trust was a hard currency to come by; once it was spent it could never be fully saved again.

Anre'eq swore. "They've scanned us!"

The *Drummer* shook. The voidcutters were already firing. Polasers, most likely.

"Get that gravolian drive heated up again!" snapped Jem. "We need to warp out here skatey!"

"Ah," said Anre'eq softly. He was looking at a holo which covered the *Drummer's* stern. While they were talking, a fourth voidie had slipped in behind them, firing nodes already glowing with excreted radiation.

* * * *

Even though it was an incursion the Téokrat had been expecting, its very nature was more than a little shocking.

Around him, his throne room was being rebuilt. Its grandeur replaced. As a variety of top engineers and artisans—the best to be recruited from the Galaktium's myriad worlds—rewove the towering holo displays and replaced more solid decorations, the last of the Begeen stood in a cluster around the outward manifestation of Mygré's pocket universe. It was little more than a comforting illusion—his physical presence was far removed from Eklesia Prime, after all—but he allowed them the comfort of believing they were guarding him.

Within his dimensional bubble, Mygré ran assessment after assessment. Endlessly rechecking the state of the empire and Ekleiades, running statistical projections of a myriad probabilities, collating data from every sniffer, digithopter and shipborne sensor spread across the galaxy. Even so, when the Salga Ashtoreen came, he was unprepared for the sheer scale of it.

It was as though the Eklesia system had suddenly acquired another planet. Arriving with an abruptness far in excess of even a gravolian drive, a huge mass was hanging in space where previously there had been nothing. No long range monitors had detected its passing—no matter how fleeting. No gravi-

metric analysers had sensed even the minutest of perturbations the transit of such a mass might have caused.

The Téokrat wondered if the planet-sized vessel didn't in fact employ some form of trans-dimensional drive. Transitioning in and out of normal space in a way similar to his own pocket universe throne, but scaled up by many factors of ten. The power required would be…unimaginable.

Alarms began to wail across Eklesia Prime. The Begeen snapped to full alertness. Everyone involved in repairing the throne room looked about uncertainly. Invasion alarms had not been heard in generations. It was unprecedented.

All of the Téokrat's holos filled with a familiar, disembodied white face.

"Mygré Keddyth. We are here to honour our contract."

The Téokrat looked at the world beyond his pocket universe. No one in the throne room had reacted to that cold voice. The Begeen stood poised, awaiting battle; the engineers and artisans beginning to flee—although where they thought might be safe was a puzzle.

"Indeed?"

The face twitched in a humourless smile. *"You continue to play games, Holiness?"*

"I never play."

"That is debatable." The voice paused a moment. When it came again there was an air of ritual about it, as though its words were a requirement. *"We have been charged with destroying the Ekleiades Galaktium. This will come as no surprise to you."*

"I surmised—"

"No, Holiness. You requested it. It may have been passed through a galaxy-wide network of feeders and sniffer protocols in some childish attempt to disguise the request's origins, but it was simplicity itself to trace them. And it is no more difficult to understand your reasons, Holiness—they are such simple ones, after all. Games, Téokrat. Foolish ones. And now we are here to end them."

Mygré leaned back, trying to look relaxed. He had thought his messaging network unassailable. "Your ship is of an impressive size, I grant you. But your assassin was unable to take me down—"

"A single combatant, who dispatched nearly all of your overvalued Begeen—even though that was not their primary target."

The Téokrat smiled. "And he failed in that, too."

"You flatter yourself, Holiness. You were not the target, but rather the co-ordinates and access points of your private little dimension."

Mygré's smile faltered.

"The detonation which destroyed our operative also contained a shielded cloud of nanoprobes. Unseen and undetected, they have been relaying data to this kinship..."

The Téokrat reached forward, ancient fingers brushing the command feeds.

"A category one decontamination of the throne room will do you no good, Holiness. We already have all the data we need." The white face deformed into a hideous smile. *"It will, however, save us the trouble of killing the few remaining Begeen warriors presently standing guard. It's of little consequence, but if you wish to do us that one small favour..."*

"Every voidcutter in the fleet is presently making for Eklesia Prime! A squadron alone can destroy an entire world—!"

"While we can obliterate stars with no more effort than you take to swat a bug. We are doing you the honour of meeting with you face to face—"

"You hide in darkness—!"

"While you try to hide beyond space." The white face began to fade. *"We have come to carry out your request, Mygré Keddyth. We are Salga Ashtoreen, and we never fail..."*

The Téokrat was alone in his bubble. His various holos reported on the imminent arrival of hundreds of voidcutters, as well as the launch of the smaller planetary defence frigates. The Salga Ashtoreen vessel—the kinship—was drifting towards Eklesia Prime at speed. Even so, the vessel was so massive, at such a distance it seemed to be barely moving.

He zoomed in, appreciating the kinship's size for the first time, its random construction. It was hard to say what, of all the spires and warped constructions rising from its surface, were weapons ports. Or if any were. It was a vessel designed by a mad child, so different from a sleek voidcutter.

The first of the defence frigates rose into view. Not one managed so much as a single shot before a dazzling arc rose from the kinship's surface, running pole to pole, circumnavigating its globe. The arc cut through every frigate, sweeping them from space, reducing them to dust in an instant.

Mygré tensed. So many ships lost, so quickly. He had factored at least eighty-six percent fatalities among the defence forces from the moment of opening exchanges of fire, but nothing on this scale.

A second wave of frigates met a similar fate. The third and final wave managed to keep clear of the destructive arc, peppering the kinship's skin with several broadsides. Then surface weaponry opened up—supercharged polasers or disruptors, or something unique to the Salga Ashtoreen, Mygré could not be sure—and the last of the frigates was destroyed.

Voidcutters swarmed into the Eklesia system, dropping out of gravolian-folded space. They deployed out of range of the cutting arc, surrounding the kinship in a practised, three hundred and sixty degree manoeuvre. Pedipalps began a systematic barrage of disruptor fire, backed up by clusters of tumbling kraitbombs. The kinship returned fire. Space was alive with the flare of weapons discharge. Spent energy flared across the voidcutter's Q'Alvin shielding; kraitbombs detonated kilometres above the kinship's surface.

The Téokrat indulged in a faint sense of relief. The Salga Ashtoreen's mighty weaponry was, after all, not superior to a voidcutter's arsenal.

A faint glow began to pulse deep within the kinship's towering constructions. It spread across the surface, running between spires and jutting, twisted towers. Within seconds the kinship looked like it was encased in a burning network of veins. The planet sized vessel ceased firing.

The Téokrat held his breath.

The burning network erupted from the surface, filling space with a twisting web which spun and wriggled. The first voidcutters it touched flared bright as Q'Alvin shielding attempted to absorb the energy. The burning web continued to spread, wrapping itself around the voidcutter's shells. They became enmeshed, burning brighter and brighter as their shielding compensated.

Abruptly, the flaring shields winked out. The web engulfed each ship, wrapping itself tightly. Like a hot wire through ice, the web sliced every voidcutter into pieces. After a moment or two, their gravolian drives erupted, scattering the web and what remained of the 'cutters across space.

Across the kinship's surface, another burning network began to form.

* * * *

The Aiken Drummer shuddered again. The ship's Q'Alvin shielding took most of the impact, but it had never been one hundred percent. Recent events had left it even more unreliable.

"Can't you warp us out of here?" Jem demanded. "Persuade that bootlegged modulator to send us up or down?"

"Unfortunately, gravolian units are vector drives," said Anre'eq, clutching at the console. One of the voidies sailing up from the position of destroyed Aurora had let fly with a volley from its bow-chasers. "They compress space-time only in one dimension."

"Stow the techie-talk!"

Anre'eq gave him an exasperated look. "We can only go forwards or backwards. And those voidcutters are in the way."

"Bosey!" The ship vibrated from another impact. Jem didn't need to look at the holos to tell him the voidies were getting closer. "Another couple of shots like that and the shielding'll fold."

Anre'eq looked far too composed. "Agreed."

"Then think of something. You're the amp-tramp. Use some of that Salga whatever juice to get us out of here."

"You overestimate my capabilities, I think. There's—" Anre'eq tipped his head, expression quizzical. "Then again…"

"What?"

"The voidcutters are leaving." He pointed at the clustered holos.

Jem turned to look. The three voidies which had been bearing down on the *Drummer* had gone. The fourth ship across their bows was turning, changing course. A moment later it too vanished as its gravolian drive opened up.

Jem blinked. "We more fearsome that I thought?"

Anre'eq shrugged. "Who cares." He slipped a tangle of ultra-thin filaments from the wrist of his black suit. They unwound, wriggling like pharon snakes, and fed themselves into the console. A milli later a babble of voices filled the cabin, readouts marched rapidly across several holos. Jem couldn't make sense of the overlaid blether, but he kenned the readouts just fine.

"Eklesia Prime's under attack!"

"A single kinship," said Anre'eq. "The same one which destroyed Crioch, in my expert opinion." He grinned savagely. "The Téokrat has his wish."

"A stand-up fight with your people?"

"To sweep the old Galaktium away. To reinvigorate it by cutting it down and encouraging fresh growth. He couldn't do it openly—even Mygré Keddyth can't command that kind of suicidal loyalty—and surreptitiously would be too complex and take too long. Téokrats don't live forever, and Keddyth's getting on in centuries." As he spoke he flitted between consoles and displays, hands moving with a speed and dexterity Jem had never seen before. "He wanted it done swiftly. As painlessly as possible. And so he anonymously contacted the Salga Ashtoreen—or so he thought. Paid for us to destroy the Galaktium so that he might rebuild, in his own image no doubt."

"I always thought he was a devious old bastard."

"And, like all despots, not half as clever as he thinks he is. He'll get his wish—the Ekleiades Galaktium will be destroyed—but he will fall along with it."

"You're pretty confident."

Anre'eq looked up and smiled. "The Salga Ashtoreen has never failed any of its commissions, cap. It never will. We learned ultimate patience a long time ago. Eventually, we succeed." He dropped back into his seat, hands resting on the console.

"So where are we going? Hiding out somewhere until there's no one left standing?"

"Not at all, Captain Strygeth. You wanted to make history? We're going to Eklesia Prime."

Anre'eq fired up the ship's gravolian drive.

* * * *

The Téokrat had never felt so helpless. He sat, surrounded by his dimensional bubble, watching as one by one his prized voidcutters were destroyed by the vast kinship.

He took a tiny measure of comfort in the knowledge that the conflict was not entirely one-sided. Several Imperial ships had managed to impact kraitbombs on the kinship's surface—hammering away with disruptors until whatever shielding the Salga Ashtoreen vessel deployed cracked enough to let a few bombs through. The kinship was burning in three places, towers crumbling as the kraitbombs' corrosive, incendiary innards slowly dissolved their materials, creating fuel and oxygen for the spreading fires. But it was not enough. The kinship would have battle scars, but no serious wounds.

He summoned the planetary defensive collective at a gesture. There were no more cutters left, but a full complement of surface to ship skimmers—armed with multiple antimatter warheads—was ready to launch. Keddyth didn't think they would trouble the kinship unduly, meant as they were for assaults on vessels similar to voidcutters in mass and armament. They would prove a distraction, however.

He launched every skimmer.

Eklesia Prime was surrounded by a network of guidable pulse satellites, all poised in orbit. He ordered each of those to join the assault, once again not confident that their high-energy EM pulse cannon would do more than inconvenience the kinship.

But all the Téokrat needed to do was survive the Salga Ashtoreen assault. The planet's surface could be reduced to rubble, its inhabitants decimated. As long as Keddyth lived, he could raise the world back from its ashes. Be proclaimed the saviour of a New Galaktium—while its stunted emperor chased pirates at the other end of the galaxy.

First, however, he needed to obliterate the kinship, before it created more damage than was convenient.

The long-range alarm beeped. More ships had entered the Ekleiades system. Voidcutters, by their signature. Keddyth scanned, finding the new ships quickly.

It was Stenn's personal fleet. The emperor had returned from his futile chase a little more expeditiously than anticipated.

Keddyth frowned. No matter, Stenn's voidcutters would no doubt prove to be as ineffective as all the others. Perhaps the emperor would do his Téokrat the immense favour of getting himself killed. He could be a hero of the Battle of Eklesia Prime. A symbol for the people. A martyr to the cause.

The first of the skimmers had reached the kinship. Their multiple warheads deployed, firing laboriously collected dots of antimatter in a wide spread at the kinship's surface. As Keddyth had anticipated they impacted on the vessel's unknown shielding. There was a dazzling surge, the kinship momentarily eclipsed by an actinic flare.

The Téokrat dared to hope. Had the skimmers taken out the shielding after all. The combined might of all the voidcutters still attacking the Salga Ashtoreen fired broadside after broadside. Every shot impacted the towering structures and surface.

Keddyth exulted—falling silent almost instantly. The voidcutter's disruptor cannon were no longer getting through. He saw the broadsides striking fresh shielding—even though it rippled under the impact. The kinship had regenerated its shields, although they did not appear to be as robust as the originals.

The pulse satellites were rapidly nearing the kinship. What damage could they inflict?

Outside Keddyth's dimensional bubble his Begeen had become restive. He glanced up from his displays. There was movement in the darkness at the throne room's furthest reaches. The workers?

A group of black-clad figures coalesced from the shadows. Salga Ashtoreen. Twenty or more of them.

The last of the Begeen moved into position.

* * * *

The Xentharius Ascendant listed to port as another blast struck the ship broadside. Stenn struggled to maintain his balance. He'd grounded his grav-disc on one of the highest tiers of the voidcutter's control pit. Even so he almost toppled.

"What are they firing at us?" he demanded. Several augments, far below him, tilted their heads as though listening. Their cranial threads twitched.

"Unknown, Highness," came a voice from the wall nearest the emperor. *"It is a weapon of a type and magnitude so far uncatalogued."*

"They all are!" snapped Stenn. "What about their shielding?"

"Sensors indicate the replacement shielding is only ninety-two percent as effective as the original. However, that is still three hundred and four percent more efficient than Q'Alvin shields."

"Then what do we have that will penetrate?"

There was the briefest of pauses. *"Nothing, Imperial Highness."*

"Not entirely true."

Stenn turned, not surprised to see the Begeen—Shenna Maak—standing beside him. It would be pointless to ask how she'd escaped from her cell, or made her way to the control centre so easily. "Meaning?"

She slit open her shieldsuit and reached far inside. A quantum pocket, Stenn guessed. She could have an arsenal stowed away in there. How had it not been detected?

He shook his head. *Because she's Begeen.* As bad as the Salga Ashtoreen, with their secrets and surprises.

Shenna held up a compact black item. It looked shapeless, jutting with jagged edges and sharp, needle like protuberances.

"And what is that?"

"Salga Ashtoreen tech. I lifted it off…a shipmate of mine."

Stenn stared at the thing. It seemed to absorb every photon in the control centre, reflecting nothing. A black hole. "And what does it do?"

She juggled with the object, one-handed. "As far as I am able to tell, it's a 'rator of some sort, or an amplifier. Far beyond Bieg tech. I believe Salga Ashtoreen link themselves and their ships to such devices—although the size varies, depending on requirements. This is for personal use." She smiled, distantly. "The Saga Ashtoreen are just men after all, your grace. With all their old vices and faults. Easily distracted."

Stenn grunted. "If you say so, but how will that device help us?" It occurred to him he was becoming repetitive.

"As I said, it's an amplifier of some kind." She gestured down at the pit with the dull black thing. "May I?"

Stenn nodded, knowing the Begeen

would likely do as she pleased anyway.

She climbed down among the ranked augments, glancing at each station as she passed. The voidcutter shuddered and lurched periodically as it was impacted by the kinship's barrages. She never faltered once, her balance almost preternatural. Eventually she reached a station that met her requirements. Whatever they were.

She crouched beside an augment, who regarded her with little curiosity, placing the black object on the flickering console before her.

Stenn's finger found the firing button of his over-elaborate disruptor carbine and rested on it. He slipped the ridiculous weapon off his belt.

Shenna was fiddling with the Salga Ashtoreen tech. Stenn wondered if she actually had the faintest idea how to activate it.

She came to her feet abruptly, stepping back. The small black object was outlined by a faint blue radiance. It looked larger. Shenna climbed up another tier, never taking her eyes off the glowing shape. Stenn raised his disruptor.

The black object spat out two wriggling masses of fine threads across the console, all outlined by the blue radiance, all totally black. The threads grew, wrapping themselves around the augments on either side. In seconds they had swamped the augments, ripping free the nest of connections in each one's skull and replacing them. More threads grew from the augments' heads, swarming around the tier's circumference, absorbing one augment after another. The whole tier became a writhing connection of glowing black threads, disappearing beneath them.

Shenna climbed back to Stenn's side. "What did you do?" he asked.

She shrugged. "I did nothing. That device was even more alive than a gravolian modulator. It wanted to spread, to…multiply."

Stenn looked at her face. Her eyes were shining, there was an almost childish smile tugging at her mouth. It reminded him so much of Kith. Suddenly angry, he pointed his ornate disruptor up at her. "If you've somehow—"

"That tier is fire control centre, I believe."

It didn't surprise him that she was familiar with a voidcutter's divisional layout. "Your point?"

"In the words of an old friend, I think it's been jimmy-javved…"

The circle of squirming threads was solidifying. Forming a torus of…something. Stenn could not describe what he was looking at: the growing shapes, the peculiar lights. Most Bieg tech had varying levels of sentience, some even the co-opted matrix of actual organic life, but if this was life it was like nothing found on a single Galaktium world. The emperor had no words: they didn't exist.

The entire tier was now a solid, pulsing unit. A network of strange light ran along and through it. It hummed. It moaned. A not entirely unpleasant smell wafted up the sides of the Pit.

XENTHARIUS ASCENDANT WILL COMMENCE FIRING.

The voice came from nowhere, filling the command centre. A moment later, Stenn heard the distant, metallic thrum of cannon being fired. With each discharge the glowing alien tier pulsed all the brighter. Abruptly it expanded, surging upward in a liquid flow. The tier above was engulfed, every augment swallowed without a sound.

The pulsing grew brighter still. To Stenn's ears, the distant sound of cannon fire was louder, more insistent.

Shenna's smile was wider than ever. "Ah—Salga tech against Salga tech. Delicious."

* * * *

As his Begeen engaged with the approaching Salga Ashtoreen warriors, Keddyth's attention was momentarily distracted by something on his holos. A voidcutter, one of Stenn's—his flagship, by its signature—was directing fire at the kinship. Cannon fire like nothing the Téokrat had ever seen. It blazed in the most unholy manner, colours Keddyth's brain barely registered. The whole ship was encased in a dark glow which seemed to intensify with every salvo. Broadsides which were having distinct effects on the Salga Ashtoreen leviathan.

It appeared to be listing, hanging in space, wallowing like a small planet nudged from orbit. It answered every shot from *The Xentharius Ascendant* with its own strange weapons, inflicting damage, yet so far failing to destroy the voidcutter as easily as it had the others.

Stenn was winning, perhaps.

Keddyth was quietly impressed—the emperor had finally managed to surprise him. A small part of his ancient mind took note, wondering if Stenn was now too dangerous to continue living. If he survived this battle, of course.

Something splashed against his dimensional bubble's outer shields. Blood. One of his Begeen had just met their end in the most violent way. It focused the Téokrat's attention on the now.

The ranks of black Salga Ashtoreen were advancing, unhindered. The last of the Begeen were all dead. Keddyth was unsurprised, after what a single assassin had done, but it was a bitter acknowledgement. The finest warriors in the whole Galaktium swept aside like the rawest of recruits.

The Salga Ashtoreen were almost at his outer shields. With economic gestures, the Téokrat cut all of his dimensional bubble's links with the universe containing Eklesia Prime. Even his holos. For now he was blind. He must wait out the battle, isolated, and pray.

Although it was true he had underestimated the Salga Ashtoreen, it appeared they had all underestimated Emperor Stenn. The man might yet save them all, and reinstate the Téokrat's initial plan, albeit unwittingly. Keddyth would have to think of a fitting reward.

In ultimate darkness, he waited.

* * * *

Anre'eq slid *The Aiken Drummer* through the Eklesia system like a minnow among fighting giants. The holos were clotted with images of drifting wreckage, dead vessels, the vast kinship and one last functional voidie blasting the cuch out of each other. By Jem's reckoning, both ships would be little more than scorched spare parts pretty soon. And if that kinship lost whatever was driving it and started to drift...

"Let's hope it falls into Eklesia's sun before causing any more damage," he murmured.

Anre'eq glanced his way. "You say something, cap?"

Jem shook his head. "And can we stop pretending you're not in charge, Anni?" He sighed a deep breath. "I've never been in charge, have I? Not from the milli you and Shenna signed on."

The other spread his hands. "It's complicated."

The *Drummer* took a wide berth of the two ships locked in combat. Neither seemed aware of the small corvette, but sailing too close to either would likely be fatal.

"And when we get to Eklesia Prime?" asked Jem, watching the kinship and voidie drift away astern, both burning, even as the Galaktium's centre of government grew in the forward holos. Grey and ugly, every square kilometre buried under plasteel and silicite, protected by the most powerful Q'Alvin shields Bieg could manufacture.

"Add to the mayhem." Anre'eq cocked his head. "A Salga Ashtoreen paraforce has secured the Téokrat's throne room. Mygré Keddyth has barricaded himself in his pocket universe." He smiled. "Seems to think he's safe in there."

Jem thought carefully. Ever since he'd cloyed Crioch's co-ordinates he'd dreamed of dealing the Galaktium a mortal blow. This Salga Ashtoreen might have beaten him to the voidie breeding grounds, and already be setting fire to the Téokrat's underkecks, but that didn't mean Jem Strygeth couldn't be around at the moment the empire died. It'd be something to boast about in his last years.

"Bosey! But I'll need a new longsword."

* * * *

Multiple alarms deafened Stenn. On the holos the huge kinship was faltering in its attack. Whatever the device installed by Shenna had done, it had upgraded *The Xentharius Ascendant's* weaponry to a point where the emperor believed his flagship could single-handedly obliterate an entire star system.

At the expense of the control centre, admittedly.

The entire Pit was now enveloped in the glowing alien construct. Every augment was a part of it, each console, tell-tale and readout. It was linked to the ship. It was the ship. The great sentient voidcutter now had a brain. A mind of its own. The thought both terrified and exhilarated the emperor. *The Xentharius Ascendant* was an unstoppable, undying weapon. With such a fleet he could own the galaxy, displace the Téokrat and his army.

As long as the ships followed his commands.

"Finish the Salga Ashtoreen ship," he ordered, talking to the air, wondering what the response would be.

AT THIS PRESENT RATE OF ATTRITION THE KINSHIP WILL FAIL IN ONE HUNDRED AND THIRTY-TWO POINT FOUR SECONDS. FULL DESTRUCTION IS ASSURED IN A FURTHER ELEVEN POINT EIGHT SECONDS. The voice was calm, inhuman, filling the voidcutter with echoing certainty. *WE WILL CONTINUE THE ASSAULT UNTIL THE KINSHIP IS DESTROYED.*

Stenn felt a surge of relief. The ship was still under his command.

DO YOU ALSO REQUIRE THE DESTRUCTION OF THE RENEGADE CORVETTE WHICH PASSED US BY TEN POINT FIVE SECONDS AGO?

The emperor glanced at Shenna. She shrugged. "Strygeth, most likely. Somehow."

Stenn nodded. If it was the freebooter, he could be dealt with later. "Ignore. Finish the kinship, then proceed to Eklesia Prime."

AS YOU COMMAND.

The construct rose further, overlapping the deck where Stenn and Shenna stood. They retreated a metre.

"Do you think it will fill the whole ship?" said Stenn.

The woman shrugged again. "If it does, I imagine we're of less use to it than augments. But perhaps retiring to your pinnace might be a wise move. We can watch the downing of the kinship from there."

Stenn agreed. He elevated his grav-disc and led Shenna back into the ship's circulatory system, heading for the pinnace vacuole.

The vibration of cannon fire and impact followed them all the way. *The Xentharius Ascendant* barely quivered, and Stenn wondered if the alien Salga Ashtoreen tech hadn't done something to the Q'Alvin shielding as well.

Feluq'an guards snapped to attention as they passed through the vacuole's entrance. The pinnace's pilot saw them coming, and saluted smartly, although she seemed surprised.

"Can I be of assistance, your grace?"

Stenn shook his head. "Just let us on board and be ready to lift off on my order."

The pilot bowed. The pinnace's hatch irised wide and Stenn drifted inside. Shenna followed.

He activated the holos, telling them to show a wide-angle view of space beyond the voidcutter. An image of the kinship filled half of the pinnace's passenger cabin.

It was burning. Fires raged across its surface: clearly the vessel was massive enough to have its own atmosphere. Half of the curling, towering structures had crumbled. Its shielding was fading, if it hadn't already collapsed entirely. It still continued its assault, however. Lasers stabbed from hidden projectors. Solid projectiles catapulted up from what looked like enormous rail guns—an attempt to batter through the Q'Alvin shields. Stenn's flagship shuddered, but withstood the assault: its shell was designed to resist anything up to a planetoid strike. Although too many impacts on the same spot would likely crack it.

Stenn watched in fascination as *The Xentharius Ascendant's* upgraded weaponry hit the vast ship again and again. Each time debris flew kilometres into space. One by one the rail guns vanished and laser projectors died. The kinship fell silent.

Seconds later a crack appeared in its surface. Matter from deep within sprayed out, filling space with a whirling cloud of debris. Tremors rocked the vessel. Towers that had so far withstood the assault fell. More cracks spread across the vessel. Parts fell inward, others spun off into the void.

The kinship flew apart.

The expanding sphere of debris swept the flagship up in its wake. The pinnace's interior shook as the voidcutter was flung like a bug in a storm. Stenn grabbed at a chair back and held tightly, his grav-disc compensating for some of the violent pitching. The holos blinked out. Only the internal phosphorescence remained, showing the Begeen woman stretched out on the cabin floor.

After a moment's thought, Stenn drew his disruptor and gave her the full stun charge. That should keep her quiet long enough.

As the ship stabilised and systems settled, he sub-voxed the armoury, on the remote chance they might have what he had in mind.

* * * *

Mygré Keddyth hung suspended in nothingness. Time meant nothing, as did space. Although the pocket universe existed merely to contain himself it was, practically, infinite. There was no beginning and no end. Only a void which, his senses told him—since they had nothing with which they could compare it—was an ultimate black. In truth it had no colour at all. There was no light to create colour. Even the Téokrat was invisible to himself.

Over the centuries he had learned a terrible patience, mapping plans which were measured out over decades. That patience served him well now. He was content to wait out whatever was happening beyond, certain of his security—despite what that Salga Ashtoreen spokesman had claimed. The engineering which had created his dimensional bubble had been a fluke, discovered many lifetimes back by loyal Bieg researchers who were working on prototype stardrives. Such was their carefully directed loyalty they had informed their Téokrat, and no other. Once they had designed and built his pocket cosmos, Keddyth had rewarded them with a swift and painless death. With them died all outside knowledge of Keddyth's bubble universe—and all of its trans-dimensional interfaces.

The Téokrat reached inside his loose clothing, feeling with gnarled fingers for the quantum pocket stowed within the folds. Fingertips that had lost much of their sensitivity decades ago fumbled out the angled shape hidden inside the pocket. An equilateral pyramid of a base and three sides. Normally each face would gleam with a different colour—blue, yellow, red and black. In this realm of no colour, nothing was visible. No matter, each face had a raised character directly in the centre, large enough for even Keddyth's numb fingers to detect. One for Eklesia Prime, two more for the other interfaces, and the fourth—the black one— He kept his fingers well clear. It was to be hoped it would never come to that.

A faint glow appeared before him. Had one of the extra interfaces activated? Had he pressed too hard by accident?

The glow intensified, taking form. Enlarging.

A white, skeletal face floated in the colourless void. Something like a smile tweaked the gaunt lips.

"Welcome, Holiness." The shadowed eyes looked down to where Keddyth held the pyramidal shape, if the Téokrat could but see it. *"If you are entertaining some notion of opening your interface on Bevathik Trajj, I regret to inform you that world and its star system are no longer in existence."*

"You're lying."

"You know we can do it. Push a star to nova in mere standards.

"I would have known—"

"The destruction coincided with the arrival of our kinship in the Eklesia system. I imagine you were distracted."

Keddyth twisted the shape, feeling for the other raised character.

"The same is also true of Quaddron Sais." The skeletal smile widened into an ugly grin. *"Neither of your boltholes exists. Save for Eklesia Prime, you no longer have anywhere to go, Holiness. And don't imagine that fourth trigger will do you any good. The nanobots infesting the Throne Room have already severed all contact with this pocket dimension. You may return only at our whim, and imploding your tiny universe like a petulant child is impossible."*

An unfamiliar emotion tugged at Keddyth's attempt at clear thought. At first he didn't recognise it, so long he had been in control of himself and the Galaktium. His options were gone. He had been outmanoeuvred. His ancient brain took refuge in the most basic reactions: fight or flight. Except he could do neither. He began to panic, hands fumbling with the useless pyramidal object as though it was a child's comforter.

Faint, misty shapes appeared in the void beyond the mocking white features. Gradually they sharpened, coming closer, filling the Téokrat's vision.

"Come back to us, Mygré Keddyth. Your destiny awaits."

The colourless void splintered, flying apart. The Téokrat found himself once more looking out across his throne room. A throne room that was filled with unaccustomed light and air. He was slumped in his towering throne, weighted down by unaccustomed gravity. The light of the distant Eklesia star lanced through the skeletal remnants of the roof. Beyond, Keddyth saw the Skopion Dome—cracked and smoking—and a city. Its towers and arching pathways dazzled eyes that had grown used to dimness. Everything looked deserted.

Gathered around the Téokrat's interface—now just a dusty clear silcanium sphere—were several Salga Ashtoreen troops. Their pale faces stared at him as though he was some kind of prize exhibit in a collection.

One of the troops raised a black hand and placed it, palm down, on the sphere. The silcanium shattered, pulverized, scattering like grains of sand across the dusty throne room floor and bodies of the last Begeen.

"Welcome, your Holiness," smiled the Salga Ashtoreen. Keddyth recognised the voice.

* * * *

The Begeen woman recovered quickly. Stenn had just enough time to secure her before her red eyes fluttered and she swept herself into a sitting position. The emperor quickly floated out of range.

She tugged at her wrists, secured behind her, expression vaguely amused. It turned to puzzlement. Stenn allowed himself a relaxed laugh.

"Ancient metal restraints. I think your freebooters colleagues might refer to them as bilboes—" He laughed again. "I have no doubt you will find some way out of them eventually—you are a master lockpick, after all—but there's nothing for Bieg or stolen Salga Ashtoreen tech to manipulate. Just a mechanical lock."

She struggled a moment longer before relaxing. Pragmatic. Stenn admired that. Her eyes promised the emperor payback, though. He admired that, too. It was an attitude they clearly had in common.

"We will be making our assault on Eklesia Prime shortly," he continued.

"Assault?"

He shrugged. "Expeditionary landing. Relief convoy. Call it what you will. The reality is that Salga Ashtoreen have taken the capitol. Your sisters are certainly all dead. So, in all probability, is the Téokrat. Intelligence reports are, as you might imagine, sporadic and unreliable. However, the Salga Ashtoreen ship is gone. They can no longer depend on reinforcements."

"And you intend to remove whatever ground force the Salga Ashtoreen have left behind with the crew of a single voidcutter."

"Feluq'ans. The greatest warriors in the Galaktium." He caught her look. "Perhaps. I have always wanted to match my finest against the Begeen, to establish once and for all which was the best. Now, alas…"

"If the Begeen fell before the Salga Ashtoreen—"

Stenn floated closer, smiling at her angry expression. "The Begeen were too dependent on personal martial skills and weaponry. The Salga Ashtoreen clearly have better toys. Naturally, *The Xentharius Ascendant* will bombard sectors of the capitol with her upgraded weapons—my thanks for that—before my troops land. That will most certainly thin the opposition." *And make sure of the Téokrat, if the bastard is still alive*, he added silently.

"Your ambition is showing, your grace."

"Don't be too dismissive. Once I have established myself as total and unquestioned ruler of the Galaktium I might recreate the Begeen. Or something similar. Shock troops. You might be good at that—" An alarm sounded. "Ah, planetfall. Make yourself comfortable, Shenna Maak. I don't imagine the flight down will be uneventful."

He floated higher.

"Are the troop carriers ready?"

"Fully manned, your grace."

"Then launch. *The Xentharius Ascendant* to provide cover fire, concentrating on the capitol. Full saturation fire in the square kilometre around the Skopion Dome and throne room." *Let them out-race that.* "My pinnace will follow immediately."

"As you command, your grace."

Stenn smiled down at the Begeen woman. "I would offer to strap you in safely—but I don't entirely trust you won't somehow spring a little surprise." He raised his ornate disruptor and fired at point blank range. "Just a little tranquilliser shot this time. Enjoy the ride."

* * * *

The Aiken Drummer's spare skiff made a bumpy landing just under three kilometres from the Skopion Dome. Jem stepped out smartly, new longsword in one hand, blaster in the other. The area was deserted. All around towers reared for the clear sky, transit ramps arced and dipped like fine traceries. It was unnervingly quiet.

Jem glanced down at the ramps crisscrossing far below where the skiff had come down. Nothing. No people. No trans-hovers. No grav-discs. Not so much as a digithopter.

"They all dead?" he asked as Anre'eq joined him.

The Salga Ashtoreen agent pulled a small crystal cube from his suit and panned around. "They've all fled. Once the kinship started peppering the place with sonic grenades, I'm guessing." He put the crystal away. "Seems like the good people of Eklesia Prime aren't used to being on the receiving end."

"Always the way." Jem sheathed his weapons. "Throne room's this way."

Anre'eq pointed over Jem's shoulder. "That way, actually."

They made their way along the transit ramp. As they drew closer to the Skopion Dome—its damaged hemisphere visible through a gap in the towering architecture around them—there was more evidence of a fight. The ramp was split in many places, chunks of plasteel missing along its edges. Some of the towering constructions were partly toppled, sheared through as though a huge blade had sliced down from the sky. Rubble grew more prevalent, piling up in dusty layers. They began to find bodies, both in uniform and civilian clothing. None of them were Salga Ashtoreen.

"You're an efficient bunch of dungbies," Jem commented.

"Keddyth wanted the Galaktium brought down," commented Anre'eq. He was consulting another small device. It threw off twisting pale green beams in every direction, raking the immediate area as though searching. The device seemed to be muttering to itself in a small peeved voice. "And we aim to please."

The device began to wail, all of its light beams focusing on the sky. Anre'eq glanced up before grabbing Jem by the shoulder. "Quick!"

He dragged them through the shattered entrance to a building which rose into the sky as a series of pale orange fluted columns of varying heights. Inside the floors and walls, constructed from a polished roseate stone, were covered in a fine patina of dust.

Anre'eq handed Jem a hand-sized, star-shaped object. It pulsed faintly, pale light radiating out along its eight arms. "Put this on."

Jem placed it against his shieldsuit. Instantly it attached itself, the arms wriggling into the suit's nano-weave. He felt his suit throb like it had just been impacted by a high energy, cross-spectrum disruptor blast. "What is it?"

"Shield augmenter. It'll amp up your suit enough to take what's coming."

Jem didn't like the sound of that. "And what's coming?"

"Saturation downfire. At a guess, the emperor's about to join the fun."

There was a sudden flash that left Jem's eyes dancing with afterimages. The dust coating every surface glowed white-hot for a milli, leaving the stone veneer blackened. Jem felt as though the building had fallen on him.

Anre'eq gave him an apologetic smile. "Didn't say it wouldn't hurt." He started to leave.

"We're going out in that?"

"Why not? It won't kill you."

Jem flinched as another half-blinding flash brought tears to his eyes. This time it only felt as though he'd been dropped a hundred metres or so. Around him the once polished stonework charred.

"Maybe not at first…" Reluctantly he followed Anre'eq out onto the transit ramp. Ahead, the Skopion Dome was glowing with latent energy, the cracks in its surface half-molten.

"Stenn continues to underestimate who he's dealing with," said Anre'eq.

"You mean any Salga Ashtoreen on the surface won't be any more phased by his assault than us."

"Naturally."

Jem sighed. "You do realise you're just going to wipe everybody out in a tit-for-tat firefight."

"Let's hope it doesn't come to that." Anre'eq started down a rubble-strewn ramp that curved towards the smoking dome, and whatever remained of the throne room beyond it.

* * * *

As the emperor's pinnace drifted away from his flagship, Stenn spun the holoports' outside view. *The Xentharius Ascendant* was a hulking shape against the starscape, every pedipalp trained on Eklesia Prime, firing nodes glowing as the voidcutter rained down a continuous curtain of fire. Plasma vents exhausted luminous gas.

Amidships, just where the control centre would be, the exterior shell was marked by a slatey, almost metallic sheen. Stenn recognised it: the Salga Ashtoreen matrix was spreading further, either absorbing more of the ship and its crew to fuel itself, or incorporating the 'cutter's part-organic body as it created something…new. A mutated species where organic and inorganic life was even less easily defined.

He wondered what the ultimate product would be. And how it might best be exploited.

The view blurred. The pinnace was entering the upper atmosphere. Stenn rotated the view back to the planet's surface, watching as the capitol swooped up to meet them. Twenty landers, crammed with Feluq'ans, led him down.

* * * *

What remained of the throne room was a lot more empty than Jem expected. The walls and ceiling had collapsed, leaving the floor littered with bodies, debris and dust, yet there was little sign of anything else. Aside from a tall, angular dais containing some sort of shattered globe in a corner, it looked more like a deserted warehouse than the majestic centre of the galaxy. Jem had expected more grandeur. Certainly more booty. He felt vaguely disappointed.

The dais was surrounded by a crowd of figures dressed similarly to Anre'eq. Something inside the broken sphere was holding all of their attention.

Jem felt the impact of another aerial bombardment. It was like having an invisible roof dropped on his shoulders. He glanced around. The Skopion Dome was glowing, drooping inward like thick lava. Parts of it sparked and smoked.

"How come this whole area isn't vaped?"

Anre'eq shrugged. "Most likely they've cloaked the throne room with a field version of the augmenter you're wearing. It'll hold off the assault for standards."

"And what if whoever's attacking uses tunnellers, or kraitbombs?"

"How fast can you run?" Anre'eq stepped onto the debris-strewn floor. Jem drew his sword and followed, although he doubted it would be much use against these Salga Ashtoreen killers. He'd seen Anre'eq in action.

There was the briefest sensation of trying to walk against a hurricane, gone in a milli, then the air was choked with dust, the stink of burnt plasteel, the sweet smell of ozone. Jem coughed.

The figures around the dais looked up. Anre'eq raised both hands and made a complex salute. They all responded. Several of them looked towards Jem, their pallid faces briefly questioning. Then they turned away, as if he was of no importance.

Jem walked towards the dais, curious about what they were all looking at. No one stopped him. After their first glance, none of those almost white faces so much as acknowledged his presence.

Squatting in the centre of the shattered globe, like a newly-hatched bird in its shell, was a grey wrinkled thing. At first Jem couldn't make out what he was looking at—then a watery, colourless eye blinked, swivelling towards him.

It was vaguely humanoid, with a recognisable bald head and stunted arms, on the end of which were hooked fingers that looked too heavy to move. Its skin was gnarled and desiccated, like an ancient tree Jem had once seen somewhere, the last of its kind. A slit opened just below the eye, and a thin tongue slipped out, licking at shrivelled lips. A laboured breathing rattled deep inside its shrunken chest. It smelled disgusting.

"So this is the feared Téokrat." Anre'eq was standing across from Jem, peering down into the globe.

"This?" Jem took another look, trying to reconcile the myth of Mygré Keddyth with the pathetic thing before him.

"I suspect our dimension doesn't agree with him." Anre'eq reached out a gloved finger and poked the grey flesh. "I'm amazed he survived the transition from his own private one. I don't imagine my colleagues were particularly gentle."

None of the other Salga Ashtoreen paid any attention to Anre'eq's disrespect, or indeed anything aside from the wrinkled shape cupped in the ruins of its silcanium shell.

"So what are they doing now?"

Anre'eq looked up at the circle of pale faces. "Waiting, I think."

"For what?"

From close by came the strengthening

wail of atmoshear motors. Jem looked up. Descending around the collapsed throne room were Galaktium troop carriers—ugly saucer shapes supported by dozens of articulated limbs. Once the carriers were down, armed troops rapidly disembarked and deployed around the ruined building, forming a cordon. Then a final vessel landed, within the throne room itself, passing awkwardly through whatever form of shielding the Salga Ashtoreen had erected, and landing on its insect legs.

The black figures around the dais turned to face the newcomer, spreading out in a single line across the rubble.

From the last vessel two figures emerged: a dwarfed male raised up by a grav-disc, and a purple-haired woman in a white shieldsuit.

"Obviously, the last performers in our little play," said Anre'eq.

* * * *

Stenn was disappointed to see the throne room wasn't burning like the Skopion Dome. Even more so that the Téokrat was clearly still alive. No matter, he could enjoy that privilege himself.

At a sub-voxed order his Feluq'ans marched forward, halblasters lowered, closing the circle. Without waiting for the Salga Ashtoreen paraforce to react, the Feluq'ans fired their weapons. The dusty air lit up. Fire seemed to sear across the ruined landscape, splashing off the Salga Ashtoreen.

There was another by the Téokrat's destroyed throne, Stenn noticed. The pirate—Strygeth. He threw himself flat as the halblasters fired, allowing the blazing energies to pass over him. Even so he should have been seared, caught in the backwash. Somehow he wasn't. No matter, the emperor would deal with him afterwards. Presently, the Salga Ashtoreen were his main concern.

The figures in black didn't move at first—simply standing in the halblaster fire as though it were nothing more than rainwater. If they were making a point it was lost on the Feluq'ans, who continued to close in,

firing in a constant stream.

Stenn also noticed a lone Salga Ashtoreen, standing close to the Téokrat's ruined throne. He had made no effort to join his comrades. Was he guarding the Téokrat, for some reason?

"Leave him to me."

The Begeen woman—Shenna Maak—had stepped forward. She had obviously seen the lone man in black too. Was he her erstwhile shipmate?

"Your restraints—" Stenn's voice trailed off as he saw thin charyon wire filaments coiling around the metal bracelets. The wire cut through as though the bracelets were little more than stiff cloth and retreated back into her shieldsuit. So, she could have freed herself at any time. The woman was too resourceful. Too dangerous.

He fingered his disruptor. Perhaps when this battle was done, and her back was turned...

She made towards the single Salga Ashtoreen, circumnavigating the ruined throne room, all the while watching the small battle at its centre.

The Salga Ashtoreen troops abruptly moved. Once the Feluq'ans were within three metres the black figures blurred into motion. Little more than faint smudges against the dusty background, the Salga Ashtoreen seized weapons from baffled Feluq'ans' hands, hurled the men the length of the empty ruin. The black figures moved so quickly, generated so much momentum, that living Feluq'an bodies were torn and dismembered like bugs in a child's hand. Their halblasters were snapped like straws.

Stenn drew his disruptor, blasting away at the dark streaks, but it was impossible to hit them. He widened the dispersion angle, knowing he was certain to hit his own men, and fired again. If his shots impacted on any Salga Ashtoreen, it failed to slow them. He did kill at least three Feluq'ans, however.

His prized Feluq'an guard was rapidly reduced to nothing. Only two Salga Ashtoreen were down, and neither seemed seriously hurt. Stenn backed away, his grav-disc scraping against tall pillars of debris. The squad of black figures stood together in the centre of the desolated throne room, pale faces staring out. Stenn readied himself for the rush.

A blinding crack split the air, peeling back to reveal a glimpse of something dark, radiating a silky sheen and fireflies of dazzling light. As one, the Salga Ashtoreen marched through it.

The split sealed itself. The throne room was deserted, apart from the dead and five living. Only the last Begeen and a remaining Salga Ashtoreen moved—fighting in a start-stop, on-off blur that confused Stenn's eyes.

He raised his disruptor, keeping his finger on the firing button until all the charge cells were dead.

* * * *

The Téokrat slumped in his broken shell, interface disabled, the few remaining holos sputtering as their power faded. He had few resources available, even if he could summon the strength to move.

He had lived too long in his own bespoke dimension. Now the laws of the primary universe weighed heavy on his aged body. He felt every moment of his centuries' long life.

He had been raised a devout Gooraq. Lazarite surgery was considered an abomination. Keddyth thought he had found a way to circumvent those ancient, inescapable prejudices: enjoy limitless age without subjecting himself to the whims of lazarite doctrine. But ultimately the universe—the primary one—had the last say.

He sucked in a shallow, painful breath.

Beyond the shards of his sphere, the throne room was a chaos of fallen plasteel over which small, personal battles were being fought. The emperor's Feluq'ans against an unbeatable Salga Ashtoreen force; the last of his Begeen against a lone man in black. There was also a figure in a dirty red shield-suit huddled on the floor—the freebooter, Jemorl Strygeth, of course, completely out

of his depth—and beyond, trying to hover above the destruction, was Stenn—no less outmanoeuvred.

Keddyth attempted to move one of his wrinkled arms, reach for the erratically blinking console, tantalisingly out of reach. After a few seconds he gave up. His muscles were too wasted for the gravity of Eklesia Prime.

He felt his lips quirk in a feeble smile. Was that, he wondered, some kind of joke?

The last of the Feluq'ans fell. The Salga Ashtoreen grouped and marched through the gap they ripped through space-time, leaving just the one engaged with the Begeen.

Keddyth was curious. Why? Why desert when you are in the ascendant? Both Téokrat and emperor no more than a moment's grasp away. They could squash both without a thought.

And why leave one behind?

Keddyth would have laughed, if he'd had the breath and strength. But of course. In a moment of clarity he had nothing but admiration for the Salga Ashtoreen.

He tried once more to lay a gnarled hand on the console.

* * * *

Jem came to his feet, wondering how he was still alive. The energies raging through the throne room had been like the heart of a sun. It was a wonder none of them was incinerated.

Anre'eq and Shenna were still battling. Fighting hand to hand, Salga Ashtoreen against Bieg tech—although Jem had a sneaking suspicion Shenna had uppied her own gear with whatever she'd cloyed off Anre'eq. They were too closely matched. He couldn't best her as easily as he had aboard the *Drummer.* Unless she'd been faking. Jem didn't know what to believe any more.

It was like a dance, choreographed by a killer. They twisted about each other, spun, flipped. Blows were deflected, vectored or simply taken. All the while accelerating or slowing apparently at whim, each trying to catch the other off guard. Just once.

Jem turned to look at the Téokrat, collapsed in his ruined universe. Both eyes were open now. Jem didn't like what he saw in them: the wrinkled monstrosity looked far too happy.

There was the howl of a disruptor. A sigh. Distracted, Jem looked back and saw both Shenna and Anre'eq slumped on the floor. The emperor drifting closer, an ugly, over ornate weapon in his small hands. He'd shot them both, at close range, with a full charge. Their shieldsuits would have taken most of the force, but obsessed with their private fight, suits already battered by the range of close-hand weaponry they constantly unleashed, the sudden extra impact had likely caused a momentary overload and stunned them.

It wouldn't last long.

The emperor knew it. He swooped closer to the Téokrat, giving Jem a brief, dismissive look. His grav-disc drifted higher until his short body was hovering directly above Keddyth. He levelled the ugly disruptor.

"One thing before I kill you—Holiness. What happened to Kith?"

From the broken sphere hissed a faint, struggling wheeze. Jem realised the Téokrat was laughing. Sort of.

A movement caught his eye. Shenna was getting to her feet, unsteadily.

"What. Makes. You. Think. Any. Thing. Has?" gasped Keddyth.

Stenn floated a little lower. His feet were parallel with the top of Keddyth's shattered silcanium sphere. "All your Begeen are gone! Did she die then, or years ago!"

"Not. All."

Behind Stenn, Shenna raised a hand; his grav-disc stalled. He toppled, catching the rim of the shattered sphere before smashing into a chunk of sharp-edged plasteel. Jem thought he was dead, but after a milli or two the small man rolled to his feet. His uniform was torn and filthy. Blood ran freely from a head wound.

He raised his disruptor again. "Tell me!"

Shenna stooped. Charyon wire slipped out of her suit, coiling around the emperor's neck. It tightened a pinch. Pinpricks of blood stood out.

"Hello brother," she whispered in his ear. There was a wide grin on her bruised face. Her red eyes were insane. "I'm sorry I haven't kept in touch. Things to see, people to do. I'm sure you understand."

Stenn's lips moved, but Jem didn't hear any words.

The Téokrat was laughing again.

Shenna tugged on the charyon wire garrot. Stenn's eyes bulged. Shenna snatched the emperor's dress dagger from his belt and plunged it into his back, up to the hilt. Stenn's lips moved again—but all that passed through them was blood.

She held the emperor off the floor for several millis, the wire cutting deep, almost severing his head. Eventually she tossed the small body aside.

Jem lunged forward, pointing his longsword down at the grinning, wheezing Téokrat. Shenna dusted herself off, the charyon wire retreating. She looked at Jem, and where his sword pricked the Téokrat's wrinkled hide.

"Be my guest," she said, offhand.

Keddyth's laboured amusement stilled. "Your. Con. Di. Tion. Ing—"

"—works fine when all you have to do is stand around this black hole, intimidating anyone who wants to talk to you and continually tell you what a god you are." She glanced back at Anre'eq. He was coming to his feet, just as battered as she was. "Somewhere amid all the intrigue, close run-ins with death—and the occasional theft—"

For a moment Jem saw the old Shenna— or the Shenna he knew.

"In between all that, your conditioning faded. Or was superseded." She glanced down at the grey sunken heap. "I'd suggest looking into that—but I suspect there'd be no point." Her red eyes met Jem's. "You asked if I'd want to be emperor, once." She held up both hands, as though weighing booty. "Well, here's your answer."

"Shen—"

"Kith. Kith of Clan Lymatén. Now Emperor Kith the First, I think."

Anre'eq walked by her, cautiously, and stood next to Jem. "You weren't fighting to win…"

"You and bossie-boy here? Just not to lose. And I did win, ultimately."

"And us?" asked Jem.

She gave them both frank looks. "You may go. I have no particular argument with you. I'm sorry—*we* have none. Must get used to that. And as for *that*—" She nodded towards the Téokrat.

"The. Sal. Ga. Ash. Tor. Een…"

"Are gone. Back to wherever they came from, I—we—hope. All they achieved is—" the white half-cowl flipped briefly across her face "—a voidcutter which is now entirely overwritten by their own matrix. An amalgam with Bieg tech. Retreated now, of course, along with their ground assault force."

Jem realised the bombardments had ceased. He hadn't noticed when it happened.

Shenna/Kith held up her right hand. It crawled with dark, metallically-gleaming motes. They formed and reformed into shapes so quickly, Jem couldn't be sure what he was seeing.

"While we have also combined their matrix with our own tech. On a smaller scale—for now."

"The. Sal. Ga. Ash. Tor. *Een…*"

She glanced down at the Téokrat. Jem thought the ugly cucher looked agitated, his mismatched limbs twitching. Without thinking, he thrust his sword through the thick, wrinkled hide. Barely any blood flowed, and what there was looked watery, anaemic.

"If nothing else, at least I can say I got to kill a Téokrat," he muttered.

The new, self-proclaimed emperor was smiling. She looked so like the old Shenna. "Thank you, captain. For that small service we give you both an extra standard to disappear." She walked to an overturned plasteel pillar and stepped onto it. "Just be certain our paths don't cross again. We may not be in a giving vein again."

Anre'eq leaned close to Jem. "I think that's our cue, cap…"

* * * *

Back on *The Aiken Drummer*, Jem sat morosely at his console. The corvette was far away from the Eklesia system, her gravolian drive flinging them light years across the galaxy.

"Cheer up, cap," said Anre'eq, tweaking his controls.

"What's to be cheery about? We've lost Aurora, and all the starpads. Mags. Shenna—even if she wasn't Shenna. Crioch's gone—but it wasn't what we thought." He sat upright. "We have no one, and nowhere to go." He stared at Anre'eq, a thought coming to him. "Which begs the question, why are you still here? Shouldn't you be off with your Salga-mates somewhere?"

"Hmmm?" Anre'eq peeled off his gloves, laying them meticulously across his console. They spread, grew opaque, and dissolved into the panel's surface. "I have one purpose, Jem—to follow you to the voidcutter breeding grounds and pass on their co-ordinates."

"Perhaps you didn't notice, but Crioch didn't contain the breeding grounds. We don't know where they are…"

Anre'eq smiled. "The Téokrat did. He was the *only* one who did."

"And now he's dead."

Anre'eq patted the part of the console where the gloves had melded. Dancing patterns of figures sprang onto a holo.

"Would you like to know where they really are?"

* * * *

Magen Idwardes looked all around her. There was nothing to see. She was surrounded by a black void. Or was it white? She had no words for whatever colour it was—if it was a colour. Just nothing.

A face appeared before her: skeletal, bony white. It was vast and minute at the same time, up close while an infinite distance away.

She always wondered what death looked like.

YOU ARE NOT DEAD, MAGEN ID-WARDES."

"Then what—? Where am I?"

IN THE NULLITY. THE VOID YOU CALLED AN APHOTISM.

She remembered: going in, all the things she'd seen—Jem, Fydar, the hallucinations… "I'm seeing things."

NOT THIS TIME. The ghastly face smiled. It didn't improve its looks. *WE ARE THE SALGA ASHTOREEN. WE EXIST BEYOND SPACE AND TIME AS YOU UNDERSTAND IT. AN APHOTISM IS ONE WAY BY WHICH WE ACCESS YOUR UNIVERSE.*

Mags tried to think. "I'm in another universe?"

YOU WERE LED INTO THE APHOTISM. WE NEED YOU, MAGEN ID-WARDES.

She laughed at that. "Things that live in another universe need me?"

WE ACCEPTED A COMMISSION, TO BRING DOWN THE GALAKTIUM AND EMPIRE.

"And have you?"

WE HAVE BEGUN. WE NEVER FAIL.

"So why do you need me?

I THINK YOU WOULD LIKE TO BRING DOWN AN EMPIRE, MAGEN ID-WARDES.

She thought about Jem, and his crazy, grandiose plans. To destroy the breeding grounds, to hit the Galaktium where it would hurt. To make a name for himself. She'd gone along with him years ago, inspired by his idealism, his passion. Later it just became a habit for both of them, something a starpad would do. But now?

"How can I help?"

The pale face seemed to nod, smiling again, fading back into the colour of nothing.

⚛

ABOUT THE AUTHOR

Mike Chinn lives in Birmingham UK with his wife Caroline and their guinea pigs. He is the author of almost ninety published short stories (with a few on the way), two novels, two Damian Paladin books (the first of which was short-listed for the British Fantasy Award in 1999) and two volumes of collected weird fiction. Once upon a time he scripted fourteen issues of the digest sized comic book *Starblazer*, published by the Scottish newspaper and magazine giant DC Thomson, the first of which were pure space opera. "The Colour of Nothing" is a natural progression from those rip-roaring days.

ABOUT THE ARTIST

Jyothish M. Dharan illustrated "The Color of Nothing."

Made in the USA
Middletown, DE
24 September 2022

11159635R00118